The Choice

The Choice

Jean de Sponde, Kingmaker

FLORENCE BYHAM WEINBERG

Maywood House
San Antonio, Texas
2021

The Choice, Jean de Sponde, Kingmaker

This is a work of fiction. All concepts, characters and events portrayed in this book are used fictitiously and any resemblance to real people or events is purely coincidental.

Maywood House
an imprint of F M Weinberg Co
331 Royal Oaks Drive
San Antonio, TX 78209
www.florenceweinberg.com

First Edition: December 2021

ISBN 979-8-9850251-9-4

Cover and Book design by Tamian Wood, BeyondDesignBooks.com
Printed in the United States of America

Table of Contents

Chronology

1517 – Martin Luther nails his ninety-five theses to the door of the cathedral of Wittenberg.

1541 – Jean Calvin organizes a theocratic republic in Geneva.

1553 – Birth of Henri de Bourbon, who will become King of Navarre, ultimately Henri IV of France.

1555 – Evangelical ministry from Geneva begins in France.

1557 – Birth of Jean de Sponde in Béarn.

1560 – Conspiracy of Amboise against King François II de Valois; death of the king in December. His younger brother, Charles IX, accedes to the throne.

1562 – French Wars of Religion break out after massacre of Protestants at Wassy.

1564 – Death of Jean Calvin; Théodore de Bèze succeeds him as head of Calvinist Church.

1568 – Birth of Henri de Sponde

1571 – Jean de Sponde begins his studies at Lescar.

1572 – Henri de Navarre marries Margaret de Valois on 18 August. St. Bartholomew's Day Massacre begins 24 August.

1574 – Death of King Charles IX in May; his younger brother, Henri III, accedes to the throne.

1576 – The Holy League (*La Sainte Ligue*) is formed, headed by Henri, Duc de Guise, and his brother Charles de Guise, Cardinal de Lorraine.

1576-77, ca. – Jean de Sponde studies at the University of Toulouse.

1580-83 – Jean de Sponde studies at the University of Basel; engages in the study and practice of alchemy.

1583 – J. de Sponde publishes his translation of Aristotle's *Organon* with commentaries; five months later, a translation of Homer with commentary. He leaves Basel for Geneva, afterwards Béarn.

1584 – J. de Sponde taken into service of King Henri de Navarre. The death of the Duc d'Alençon(de Valois) makes the Huguenot Henri de Navarre direct heir to the throne of France. Treaty of Joinville signed between the League and representatives of Philip II of Spain.

1585 – Treaty of Nemours signed between King Henri III de Valois and the League revoking all privileges and protection for Huguenots. Pope Sixtus V excommunicates Henri de Navarre, barring him from inheriting the French crown. J. de Sponde is sent to Germany and Switzerland to recruit troops for Henri de Navarre to fight the League.

1586 – Sponde travels in Italy; meets Jacques Davy du Perron, Bishop d'Evreux.

1587 – Henri de Navarre wins the Battle of Coutras against the Royal French and League forces. Sponde marries Anne Legrand.

1588 – The Prince de Condé assassinated in Rochefort, his wife accused. Assassination attempt on the life of Henri de Navarre. The Seize (a subdivision of the League) usurps supreme power in Paris. King Henri III exiled to Chartres. The Guise brothers convoke the Estates-General at Blois. December 1588: Henri III assassinates both Guise brothers, Henri and Charles, Cardinal de Lorraine.

1589 – Catherine de Médici dies. Sponde's first son Jacques is born. King Henri III assassinated by a monk, Jacques Clément, placing Henri de Navarre in direct line of succession to the throne of France. Sponde accepts an appointment by King Henri de Navarre to a post in La Rochelle (Lieutenant-général of the Sénéchaussée). Henri sends Sponde as spy into Paris; he is caught and jailed.

1590 – Sponde is released from the Bastille, returns to La Rochelle and his family, joins Henri de Navarre's campaign against the League in Normandy, fights in the Battle of Ivry. Navarre besieges Paris (May-September); siege is broken by Spanish troops.

1591 – Sponde discharges his duties in La Rochelle; publishes Hesiod's **Works and Days.** Second son Jehan baptized 23

September. In Paris, Spanish ambassador Bernardino de Mendoza seeks noble French husband for Philip II's daughter, so that Philip can annex France as Spanish possession.

1592 – Henri de Navarre besieges Rouen in Normandy. Spanish general Duque de Parma breaks the siege.

1593 – Estates-General meets in Suresnes; Sponde sent as messenger to the meeting by King Henri de Navarre. Sponde imprisoned in Orléans. Henri de Navarre converts to Catholicism in July; holds ceremony of abjuration in Saint-Denis. Sponde converts in September and is repudiated by the king; Sponde's daughter Catherine is born.

1594 – Henri de Navarre crowned King Henri IV of France in February. Henri IV occupies Paris in March. Sponde retires to Pyrenees in April to write refutation of Théodore de Bèze's ***Traité des marques de l'Eglise***. Sponde's father murdered by Leaguers in August. Sponde falls ill and moves family to Bordeaux.

1595 – Death of Sponde. Henri IV receives absolution from Pope Clement VIII.

1598 – Death of King Philip II of Spain

1610 – Assassination of King Henri IV of France by Ravaillac.

Prologue

I am Henri, Jean de Sponde's younger half-brother. For many years, I have intended to do something about publishing his work, but only now in my retirement have I found the leisure to edit the memoir and send it to a publisher. In the box his wife Anne gave me, the one that contained Jean's manuscript, I found two additional packets of papers bound with colored ribbon: a red one for a sheaf of musings by Diane d'Andoins known as Corisande, who had been a mistress of King Henri IV and who maintained friendly though tenuous contact with my brother after her affair with the king was ended.

The other sheaf, bound in lavender ribbon, consists of journal entries and letters by Cardinal Jacques Davy du Perron—who was Bishop d'Evreux at the time he wrote this material. His packet is prefaced by his letter sent to Jean in my brother's mountain retreat, a response to Jean's information that he was writing a memoir of his life and times. In the letter, Du Perron urges Jean to use his own "jottings" as he sees fit, since they explain certain happenings in both their lives. I have incorporated them into my brother's narrative—as he himself had intended to do—where they clarify some of the complexities of the history and religious controversy of the century just past.

I believe this memoir to be of great importance, to vindicate my brother and to inform future generations of the indispensable role Jean played in convincing his king to convert to Roman Catholicism to quality to inherit the throne of France. Thanks to Jean,

France enjoyed peace under the reign of one of the best, most just and equitable of kings.

I preface the memoir with this letter, which Jean wrote to me shortly before his death, since it serves to introduce him to his potential readers. I am ashamed to say I did not heed my brother's plea that I come to see him at once, probably because I could not believe he was so near his end.

2 February 1595

My dear brother,

Since I last wrote three weeks ago, I feel that my physical condition has deteriorated drastically. I wish you could tear yourself away and come for a visit, so I could have the consolation of seeing you before it is too late.

My own concerns have not changed; they have merely become more urgent. I've driven myself unrelentingly to finish the theological treatise I'm writing. The importance of this work goes beyond refuting the ideas of any one individual, for I haven't the slightest doubt that my writing is of great moment for the future of Christendom—all of it—as it has been and still is tested and persecuted by these cursed wars, this never-ending Catholic-Huguenot conflagration. These hellish fires have dominated my life, from my fifth year to this moment, just as they have plagued all of yours. For me, time began in 1557; the Wars of Religion in France broke out in 1562, six years before you were born.

My dear brother, please do not think I exaggerate. I deeply believe I must do what I can to save the next century from the cruel legacy of this sixteenth century, a confusing era of Luther, Calvin, of the Council of Trent, the Reformation and the Counter-Reformation—from the legacy of savage war.

I do set this most serious work aside from time to time when fatigue and frustration overcome me to concentrate instead on my memoir. I only began it a few months ago, while still on the mountain in our father's lodge. I had obtained some documents—notes from private journals and such—entrusted to me by Corisande, who made me promise to write about my life. My friend, Bishop Jacques Davy du Perron, gave me still other documents, and I now place both collections together with the manuscript.

I feel a pressing need to compose this memoir to make clear to my children, to you, and to my future readers how I lived and thought, and why I am writing from such a strongly Catholic point of view. My story, as I look back over my life, is one of constant movement, personal conflict—both mental and physical—and adventure, love and war.

People should know something about us. For example, that our parents were Calvinists, newly converted and fervently devoted to the Reformed Church. You know what excellent, hard-working, Christian parents ours were, taking good care of all seven of us children, and giving us the opportunity to attend the best schools available at that time in Béarn, our corner of southwestern France. Thanks to them, both of us were able to study seriously, you to become a Calvinist pastor, and I to become a humanist: a scholar of Hebrew, Greek, and Roman Antiquity.

As you know, and as I'm proud to repeat, my books show that I eked out a moderate success: books on Homer, Aristotle, and Hesiod, and I'm working on a translation of Seneca—did I tell you that, Henri? And, of course, you know that early in my adult life I had the privilege of practicing the Great Work, alchemy, although service to my king took me far away from that arcane effort. You and Anne are the two people closest to me and best acquainted with my most intimate pastime: my poetry. It has kept me sane during times of greatest stress, affording me a means of expressing my deepest desires and bleakest fears.

As for public life, I served King Henri IV as a scholar and a knight when he was still merely King of Navarre, and I also acted as a magistrate and jurist. I fought beside him in battle, helped save his life, spied for him, would have died for him, and nearly did. My proudest success was not in public service but in winning my adored Anne, my red-haired beauty, marrying her, and having the good fortune to father three children with her, children who are with me yet, as is she, my most faithful friend and companion.

I realize I have rehearsed things in this letter that you know very well but writing it all down worked like an inventory of my life to convince me that this memoir is worth completing. I think I do have good material—at least for family use, and perhaps for others as well.

My dear brother, I suspect these writings will surprise even you with some secrets of my inner struggle that you had only guessed at, and I hope you and any other future reader will follow my lonely path with compassion. I pray that your own road will be less burdened with the agony of self-doubt, guilt, and spiritual toil. The greatest adventure I relate in these pages is that of spiritual awakening and transformation.

Do try to make time to come to Bordeaux soon, for my sake if you love me, and, of course, Anne and the boys would greatly enjoy seeing you as always.

Your loving brother in Christ,

Jean

Chapter I

Alchemy, the Divine Work

The heat in this underground chamber has become oppressive, and I begin to gasp, laboring to breathe. I pull out my handkerchief and mop my brow with trembling hands. I'm not sure whether I pant from anxiety or from lack of breathable air. But though I suspect it is uncomfortable and perhaps dangerous to be here, I'm far from being here against my will. Even before I left Béarn, far away on the slopes of the Pyrenees in southwestern France, I was training for this moment. All over Europe, scholars, both Calvinist and Catholic, practice the Divine Science. It is certainly studied and pursued by scholars of both persuasions. We adepts understand there is nothing in our Work that contradicts the revealed truths of Christianity.

The transformations we bring about are divinely revealed methods that imitate, in very short time-periods, the changes taking place over eons in nature. I learned still more and honed my skills at the University of Toulouse. Here in this Swiss city, Basel on the Rhine, much Great Work is being done. Tonight especially. My master, Théodore Zwinger, cannot be here with me on this night of nights, but he has entrusted me with this mark-weight of silver to transform into gold. I am working alone, using the alchemical treatise, the *Book of Abraham,* as my guide. Herr Zwinger has not seen the book and expressed his skepticism about its accuracy regarding the final steps. Now, with all things in readiness, I shall put the book and myself to the test.

Last week, Herr Zwinger and I completed many preparations. We purified the *prima materia,* the mercury, freeing it from the four elements, earth, air, fire, and water, or rather from the qualities that represent the elements: the earthy, the liquid, then starving the mercury for air in a thick glass alembic. All these operations were completed by application of the fourth element: fire, transforming the quicksilver into a pure white powder. Tonight, using information Abraham supplies, I further reworked our mercury to take the form of a red powder, using purified sulfur combined with arsenic to obtain that result.

I am right now measuring a tiny quantity of the product of our combined operations. I am convinced that this powder embodies the essence of what traditionally has been called the Stone of the Philosophers.

My measurements are complete. When the furnace has heated enough, I will continue the transformation. This room inspires concentration and meditation upon the Great Work. Although I am below ground here, there is no oppressive sense of the dungeon, for the ceiling is high and vaulted, and the many candles and lamps swinging from chains in the ceiling provide abundant light—even though their flames seem to be burning low. They, too, are hungry for more air.

The room, entirely of stone, including its ceiling, walls, and floor, is long and narrow, with waist-high cabinets on either side, their shelves containing the precious substances we need for the Work: salt, sulfur, and mercury, stacks of herbs, phials of various mineral salts, ingots of lead, brass, and copper, and the many other substances needed for purifications and combinations. Also on those shelves are the containers and tools for our operations: mortars and pestles, brass jars, bowls, platters, and plates, spoons and funnels, measuring and weighing apparatus, pottery vessels of various shapes and sizes, and crystal clear glass retorts, their round bellies glittering in the light, and with long, sometimes twisted spouts, in which substances are distilled or decomposed by heat. There are black iron rings on three legs sitting on the cabinets, some holding empty retorts waiting to serve as well as those containing mysterious liquids such as the various "waters," the *aquae fortes* in which one should never, never wash. I mean those waters otherwise known as nitric and hydrochloric acids.

I stand facing the large, black, egg-shaped furnace, the Athanor, representing the World Egg, at the end of the room. It is roaring as it consumes the fuel I have fed into it, producing the Philosophical Fire necessary for the final transformations of the Work. A door opens on the side of the furnace to admit the fuel for the sacred fire, a door pierced by a small window to enable the alchemist to monitor the fire and keep up a steady heat. The top surface of the furnace, somewhat flattened, supports the crucible—the Philosophic Vase, the Aludel—which, once my operation is complete, and when the sacred substance, the Stone of the Philosophers, has been incorporated—will contain the purest gold.

Once again, I marvel at my privilege—that I have been allowed to work alone in these hallowed precincts. But I must hasten now. The temperature is surely approaching its maximum. I must melt the silver before the heat grows so great that I cannot approach. I must not allow the silver to vaporize. Once it melts, I will add my mercury of the philosophers, the spoonful of the Philosopher's Stone, and watch the transformation take place. This is the last step in the process Master Zwinger and I began weeks ago. What a pity he cannot be here to witness the final triumph—or to prove the invalidity of Abraham's Book!

I step across quickly behind the Athanor to open the flue to the outside air. This I must do so any vapor will escape from the room, for mere human flesh cannot withstand its breath. I now take up the silver ingot from the side cabinet and approach the Athanor, my excitement and fear mounting. Any miscalculation or misstep and the Aludel—the sacred vessel in which the transformation takes place—could shatter and I could be terribly burned, even permanently disfigured. I must not inhale any of the vapors, not even the slightest, or I will die either at once, falling against the nearly red-hot Athanor, or slowly, forever unable to breathe God's air normally. And, of course, I must not slip, must not miscalculate, must carry out the operations to the letter, or the miraculous transformation will not take place. I pause to recite the ritual prayer, dating from the time of Hermes Trismegistus—the prayer that must precede the final operation, the creation of gold from baser metal.

The silver is in its crucible now, and I back away from the furnace, yet remain close enough to watch it melt. Yes, it begins... yes, the silver ingot has become a shapeless lump floating in a blackish-silver sea. Of course—black. The first color of the sacred process. From the dragon, the black dragon of the *prima materia,* will come the white lion of transformation, ending in the red lion, the gold of purity.

As I watch, I see that the silver is now liquefied entirely. I approach again holding the brass bowl of purified mercury, the philosophical mercury, the Stone of the Philosophers. I shake the red powder into the blackish liquid mass. I hold my breath as I stir, quickly but steadily, not splashing. Then I back away, eyes stinging. A great cloud of white vapor rises from the mixture, and I thank God it is sucked up greedily by the flue.

I trust it will disperse itself in the atmosphere and no passerby will be sickened by it. With it go the last impurities of the silver in the form of the white cloud rising to the Moon, the inferior female principle of silver. If Abraham is to be trusted, what will remain in the Aludel will be the refined principle of gold: the superior, worthier, male Sun-principle.

I am instructed to wait, allowing no impure air to enter the laboratory, until the mixture ceases to steam and until the heat from the furnace burns down somewhat. And I wait, sweat pouring from my body, my eyes still smarting, tears mingling with the sweat on my face. At last, the final wisps of vapor vanish up the flue, and I dare approach once more. The material in the crucible, the Aludel, is reduced drastically in quantity—down to about two crowns in weight, I think, but is of a warm yellow color. I decant it into a mold and carry it to a metal counter to cool. I kneel, weeping in joy at this victory and praying fervently in thanksgiving. I have transformed silver into gold!

After my prayers, I stand up again, fighting an atrocious headache that crept upon me unaware. At last I dare open the door to the stairs, and as I do, I notice that the candles and the lamps, whose flames had diminished to a mere series of points, suddenly flame up again. I open my mouth, sucking in the air and filling my lungs again and again with its coolness. The headache seems to diminish a bit, the stinging eyes also begin to smart less.

I sit on the stairs, relaxing and cooling my sweating body against the cold stone, waiting for the gold to harden. I will take it with me to my rooms, without removing it from the mold. It will need the rest of the night to cool. Better to take it and keep it safe than leave it in the laboratory where it might mysteriously disappear before I can present to Herr Zwinger the proof that I have made gold purer than the finest gold of India.

After a time, my heart, which had been racing with excitement, slows to a normal rhythm, but my exaltation remains. I begin to put the laboratory to rights. The fire in the Athanor has burned down to embers, and I can safely close the flue and allow it to burn out unsupervised. I shake the ashes under the embers into a tray, which I carry up the stairs and out the back entrance. Stepping out into the cold and starry night, I breathe in its purity, meanwhile carefully emptying the ashes in the alleyway along the wall of the building.

Back in the laboratory, I take up the essence of mercury that remains and place it in Herr Zwinger's cabinet, where I lock it in. The Aludel is clean and ready for the next operation—perhaps by Herr Eusebius Bischoff, my master's friend and mine. Now, I wrap the mold and its golden contents in layers of felt, take it up in my gloved hands, and hasten home to my dark little rooms. Tomorrow, I will visit Herr Zwinger, bringing him this proof that I, unworthy as I am, have succeeded in taking the final step of the Great Work.

I narrated that scene in the present tense because it is and will be eternally present to me. As I look back upon those times from the vantage point of my life today, I now see clearly that my night of triumph was a turning point. It was a divine lesson in quite another science than that of alchemy. At that moment, I was not conscious of any connection between the Great Work and any other realm of thought or activity. But in my heart a connection was made that would bear fruit much later. For I had seen that even mere mortal devices could transmute one substance into another of infinitely greater worth.

Herr Zwinger did not take me and my accomplishment as seriously the next day as I had hoped. He complimented me highly, accepted the gold, remarking that it certainly looked and felt like the real thing, but "time would tell." I had no idea what that meant. He also pointed out that two crowns-weight of gold would not quite buy one mark of silver—not to mention paying for the other precious substances we had used to bring about my final result.

Friends of mine back in Béarn had told me that the Swiss are notoriously tight-fisted—and I was seeing their warning borne out. I waited a few days, and then asked Master Zwinger for more money to pursue the Great Work, to no avail. He referred me to his colleague and my patron, Herr Bischoff—and he even let me take the little golden ingot to him to show what I had been able to do. But Bischoff also remained skeptical, and in the end, neither man offered to subsidize me. Consequently, my progress in the Work had to be suspended for the time. I did not foresee that the hiatus would be permanent. If I had foreseen that, I would have fought harder to prevent the loss of contact with the Divine Science.

It is no wonder that my masters took me lightly, for after all, I was still a young man of twenty-six, and though they both agreed that I was a competent scholar of Greek, Latin, and Hebrew, I was too young to carry much weight with seasoned humanists. My outward appearance, I suspect, was unimpressive as well. A true practitioner of the Great Work should be a man of middle age at the very least, white of beard and shaggy of eyebrow, stooped by years of labor dedicated to the discovery of the True Stone, scarred with the evidence of dangerous experiments that had failed.

I remember myself as thin and scholarly, of medium stature—about five feet six inches—with a long, rather narrow face and a long straight nose to match. My eyebrows are rather heavy and dark although well arched, nearly meeting over my nose, giving me a brooding look that often fits my mood. My eyes are gray with black rings around the irises, and I have a generous smile revealing good teeth that belies the sometimes-gloomy eyebrows. Back then, all that was topped by a shock of nearly black, straight hair that has gone gray in the last few months. I was never robust, always prone to catch any illness that came along. The trial I had just inflicted on my lungs foretold future vulnerability to colds and worse.

I had been fortunate in being born to a family much in favor with the royal house of Navarre. My father, Iñigo de Sponde, was Secretary to Jeanne d'Albret, Queen of Navarre, who afterward appointed him Councilor and *Maître des requêtes*—an office with duties ranging from Royal Counsellor to Royal Auditor. I remember him as a calm and deliberate man, a logical and penetrating mind, pious and fervent in his adopted Calvinist religion.

His first wife, my mother, Catherine d'Ohix, bore him four children: three boys, of which I am one, and a girl. Mother died in childbirth with the fifth child. Father married again when I was only four years old, choosing Salvata, daughter of Martín de Hosta of Pamplona, herself a fervent Calvinist. She bore him three more children, among them my most beloved half-brother Henri, more than a brother to me.

I began studies at home quite early, so by the age of six I already knew Latin well, not to mention French and Spanish. I entered the strict Calvinist school of Lescar at fourteen with a scholarship from Queen Jeanne d'Albret. By that time, I had begun the serious study of Greek, and had added Italian and German to my modern languages. The schoolmasters at Lescar were thorough and very competent, and I particularly remember Master Claude Legrange who taught me Greek with such flair that I was able to translate and annotate all of Homer by 1577, when I was twenty.

Master Jacques Trouillard taught me philosophy, but unfortunately, he was very much taken with the ideas of Pierre de la Ramée, otherwise known as Petrus Ramus, and he badly neglected Aristotle. Ramus was a professor at the Collège Royal and a convert to Calvinism, among those murdered in the Saint Bartholomew's Day massacre. He had developed an anti-Aristotelian logic and a view of the world that reduced everything to binary pairs. Any subject would be divided into two parts, each again subdivided in half, then again divided—and so on. This "method" could be applied to external reality as well as to mental constructs.

I realize that Master Trouillard's choice was a matter of doctrinal preference: Aristotle is, after all, at the foundation of scholasticism and the theology of St. Thomas Aquinas. But the Philosopher is also an excellent source of discipline for young minds, arming them for debate, enabling them to distinguish truth from false-hood—and thus to refute heresies. Although I would later trans-late Aristotle's *Organon*, I have never felt that I have caught up with the limitations I suffered thanks to Master Trouillard's prejudices.

Queen Jeanne died in 1572 and I became a protégé of King Henri de Navarre, who was godfather to me and to my half-broth-er Henri. Thanks to the king, I was able to complete my studies at Lescar and later to continue them at the University of Toulouse and in Basel.

I remember one incident that happened during my school days, around 1575. Brother Henri, eleven years younger than I, had been sent to a school begun by Queen Jeanne in a former Domini-can monastery. He was only seven years old at the time. I had rid-den from Lescar with books in my saddlebag that I had used at his age, and that I knew he would enjoy.

It was a gloomy day in November, with low-hanging clouds already drizzling a chill rain. I was depressed by the intermittent wind that penetrated my damp woolen cloak, by the dour silence of nature around me where no bird or beast was visible, by the rutted and muddy road I followed, where my horse slipped and stumbled, and by the leafless trees along the roadside. They were stunted and deformed by peasants who had cut their branches for firewood so often that now the clustered stumps atop their trunks resembled deformed heads sprouting a few straggling hairs.

As I neared my brother's school at Orthez, I heard high-pitched shouts and screams. The boys had been allowed half an hour to have their lunch, and instead of eating it quietly, they had chosen to play tag or some such game, I thought. As I turned into the unkempt road leading to the school's entrance, a skeletal hand suddenly thrust itself through a ragged shrub by the wayside and plucked at my ankle. My horse shied and tried to bolt as a figure stepped out of the shrub. A half-naked skull, bits of skin and a wispy fringe of hair still clinging to its cranium, grinned up at me, staring with vacant eye-sockets. "God save me!" I gasped, as I gripped the horse with my legs and turned us both to face the apparition.

My brother could not contain himself any longer, but burst out in a fit of childish giggling, removing the skull and the cape, revealing his pink-cheeked and very mischievous face, dirty and smeared with mud. "Admit it, Jean, you really thought a demon had hold of you, didn't you?"

"Henri, you scamp! You surely did scare me! But where did you get that skull? That hand and arm? What in heaven's name have you been doing?" I dismounted and came close to examine the musty-smelling trophies he was holding out to me.

He spoke as if talking of a game of dice. "Oh, they're from the graves. We're just playing with the bones in the graves."

I stared, aghast. "The graves? Whose? How do you dare play with the bones of the dead?"

"It's the cemetery here behind the ruined church. It's all right. Come and see!" He thrust a malodorous hand in mine and led me as I, in turn, led the horse. We crossed an acre of brambles and tall weed stalks and came upon the boys' playground. I took it all in with a glance. The monastery's chapel had been burned to the ground, its walls collapsing into heaps of rubble. Behind it, the cemetery had been desecrated, the graves opened. This atrocity had taken place at least a year earlier, I could tell, since grass and weeds were already sprouting on the mounds of earth next to the opened graves.

But the boys, ever curious, had discovered the bodies still lying inside the open tombs, and my brother Henri's companions were busy collecting ribs from skeletons, breaking them free of the spines and carrying an armload into the ruined church to throw them at the pillars. It was a variant on the game of horseshoes. Whoever landed the most bones nearest the pillar without touching it won the game. All the boys were muddy and stinking of long dead flesh.

"Come with me, Henri." I scowled and turned towards the former cloister and refectory, now the school of Orthez. "Hold my horse for a moment," I ordered him, and I entered to find the Rector, Guillaume de Montgéron. He was a short, broad man dressed almost entirely in black, who approached me limping badly and leaning on a cane. I had met him before in our home, and knew my father respected him. I therefore spoke with somewhat less assurance than I had felt upon entering the school building. "Master Montgéron, Monsieur, a word with you, if I may."

"Yes? I really don't have time right now; noontide recess is almost over. The boys must be called in for their afternoon studies."

"Do you know what they've been doing, Monsieur?" I tried to recapture my earlier feeling of self-righteousness.

"No idea. No idea at all. What could they be doing that would do anyone harm?" He peered at me with shortsighted eyes. "Ah! It's young Sponde, I see. Is it Clément?"

"No, Monsieur, that's my older brother. I'm Jean. But Master, the boys are desecrating graves out back in the cemetery! Using the bones as game markers! It's unhealthy spiritually and likely unhealthy for their bodies as well. Who knows what those people died of? And who are they, anyway? The dead, I mean."

"Oh, that. Yes, they do play with those bones from time to time. Those graves were opened and desecrated at the same time the monastery was destroyed and the chapel burned. Just one of those things that happens in wartime. About three years ago, I think. Huguenots taking revenge for the Saint Bartholomew's Day massacres in Paris and elsewhere in France. After all, they slaughtered *sixty thousand* Calvinists in Paris alone and probably *forty thousand* elsewhere." He pounded his cane, emphasizing the number.

I reflected that the population of all of France was not all that great after the Hundred Years' War and the various bouts of the plague. The loss of one hundred thousand Frenchmen, even if we only considered the impact on the future population, was grievous indeed.

Maître Montgéron continued, "Our people murdered the monks, burned the chapel, and opened the graves. Any body that was not too far decayed already was thrown into the burning chapel to be incinerated with the rest."

"And you let the boys play with the bones of those monks whose bodies were reduced to skeletons?" I was deeply shocked that our side engaged in atrocities that matched the barbarity of crimes on the Catholic side.

"Yes... they're only Catholics, after all," Guillaume replied. "The boys should learn that we're all mortal."

"But, Sir, they're learning nothing from all this except to have contempt for the dead, and to coarsen their sensibilities. Surely, for the sake of their bodily health if not for their souls' sake, they should be forbidden to disturb dead bodies. Those graves should be filled in; those bones collected and laid to rest again. Letting the boys go on like this is... is like condoning the Jewish doctrine of an eye for an eye, a tooth for a tooth. But we're supposed to be Christians!"

I realized upon seeing his increasingly angry face that it was not for me, a mere adolescent, to be lecturing the rector of the school on Christian morals. "Forgive me, Monsieur, if I have spoken out of turn. But does the Queen know about all this?"

For the first time, Montgéron gave me his full attention. He knew that Henri, like me, was godchild to the king, and that our family was well connected at court. He hesitated for a moment, poking the floor with his cane. "I suppose you're right. What did you say your name was? We'd better make the chapel and the cemetery off limits until we can clean things up back there. Too dangerous for the youngsters. Might fall into one of those graves and it could cave in on them. I'll take care of it, thank you. What did you say your name was?"

I told him again, and then returned to my brother. "Henri, where did you get that skull and arm?"

"I'll show you, Jean." He led me back again to the cemetery, pointing out a grave near the outer limit. "You talked to Master Montgéron. What did he tell you? I know he doesn't care if we play out here!"

"He's going to have those bones put back in the graves and fill them in again. And the cemetery and church will be off limits. No more macabre games out here!"

"Aw, Jean—you're a mean old spoil sport!" Henri pouted up at me, his lower lip thrust out. But he obediently replaced the skull, the arm and hand alongside the rest of the skeleton in the grave he'd pointed out.

"Come on, Henri. You must wash before you go back to your studies. I brought you a surprise." I led the way back to the courtyard with its central fountain, and Henri washed his hands and face in the chilly water, under my supervision. After he had dried his hands on his cloak, I gave him the books. He was delighted with them, and forgave me, I think, for having interfered with his and his companions' not-so-innocent play.

I don't know what sort of impression was left on Henri by those ghoulish games. As for me, I returned to Lescar heavily burdened with the knowledge of the fragility of human life. Without my religion, I would even have said the *triviality* of our lives. Those monks probably had lived out their days in total dedication to Christ, in singing the Hours, and in doing charitable work. And what is their reward? To be massacred without mercy and burned, or to have their bones turned into playthings for wanton boys.

These atrocities are being committed daily in this War of Religion by Christians against Christians—each faction claiming that the other is heretical, thus justifying its own pursuit of the Devil's work. God forgive us all! I cried out in my heart.

My lessons while at Lescar were thus not limited to book learning. From there, once I had graduated in 1576, I traveled to

Toulouse on a scholarship from King Henri de Navarre and continued my studies there at the university in law and the humanities. I made friends easily, among the finest of them Pierre du Faur (better known by the Latin version of his name, Petrus Faber). I learned more from him than from most of my professors.

Perhaps not the most brilliant of my friends, if I am to judge scholarship, but one of the closest was Philippe Bodin. My memories of him are all the more precious because of the horror that nearly destroyed us both in the Battle of Coutras. But more of that later. I still weep when I think of him.

In Toulouse, I was one of the few Huguenot students at the University, and Philippe was Catholic. His famous brother, Jean Bodin, had recently published his *Heptaplomeres*, a dialogue among representatives of seven different religions, concluding in a proposal for a natural religion. Philippe was enthusiastic about his brother's revolutionary ideas and discussed them with me with great warmth. We would sit in one tavern or another near the classroom buildings, nursing a glass of wine, and talk for hours about problems of faith, our views of the essence of grace, its proper role, and whether a Mohammedan could be saved.

Our intense preoccupation with such abstract subjects may seem bizarre, but that was the spirit of the time and that is the eternal nature of young students, to become passionate over pure ideas. I never forgot Philippe Bodin in the years between Toulouse and Coutras: for me, he represents still the finest aspect of Catholicism at its most charitable and inclusive.

From Toulouse, I came to Basel in the summer of 1580, and remained there until shortly after my completion of the Great Work, my triumph on the night of October 22, 1583.

Théodore de Bèze

Other successes that year had nothing to do with alchemy. My two masters and friends Théodore Zwinger and Eusebius Bischoff published my translation of Aristotle's *Organon* from the original Greek into Latin with my annotations, and, later, my edition of Homer—a revision of the work I had completed as a schoolboy of twenty. This latter work came out in a luxury edition, beautifully printed, and dedicated with appropriate words of praise to Henri de Bourbon, King of Navarre.

Thanks to my father's letter of recommendation, I had been blessed with the patronage of Jean Calvin's powerful successor, now head of the Calvinist movement, Théodore de Bèze. My reworked Homer was prefaced with four poems lauding me as a scholar of Greek antiquity, one of which, to my great joy, was written by Monsieur de Bèze himself. But he must not have read my commentaries with close attention, for I had included a note expressing my amazement at those who cannot believe that one species, one substance, can be changed into another.

Then came the great reversal. The Reverend Sieur de Bèze happened to pass through Basel shortly after my Homer appeared.

One morning I was surprised and pleased to receive a note summoning me to an interview with the great man. I considered it quite natural that he would want to meet the son of an outstanding Calvinist such as my father, Iñigo de Sponde, to find out what sort of person his protégé might be. I was anticipating a pleasant session with Monsieur de Bèze, who would doubtless compliment me in person as he had done in his prefatory poem in my book.

I was shocked and amazed, therefore, to find him pacing the floor of his elegant rooms, his black doctoral robes flapping loosely about him, an expression like a thundercloud on his long, ascetic face. He turned abruptly as I was ushered into his presence, but he said not a word. He stood for a moment, towering over me at five feet nine, and then he deliberately swept around and sat behind a desk, gesturing that I should stand on a spot four feet in front of him. His scowl never varied. It was clear he wanted me to feel like a prisoner under interrogation—and I was intimidated.

At last, he spoke. "I have reread your edition of Homer, Monsieur de Sponde, with great attention this time, and I have leafed through your edition of Aristotle." He paused dramatically, then jabbed a long finger at my face. "You have been indulging in the fleshpots of sin! Wallowing in the filth of pagan idolatry! It would appear that you know those accursed authors of antiquity better than Sacred Scriptures! Do they not teach you in Béarn that the only book truly worthy of study is the Bible?" He picked up a copy of my Homer edition that lay next to his hand on the desk and dropped it again as if touching it defiled him.

"Furthermore, I have been inquiring into your activities. Your cronies, Zwinger, Bischoff, and the publisher Guarinius have vouched for you and for your piety. But I have other witnesses—your pastor among others—who tell me a different story. Let me hear it from your own lips. Have you faithfully attended our services?"

I was dumfounded. Why this sudden about-face in attitude? After all, Monsieur de Bèze *had* written a poem praising me, a poem included in the very edition of my Homer now lying on his desk. True, I'd been anything but regular in attendance at our Sunday preachings, as we often called our services. I'd probably gone three times during the three years I had been here. My priorities had been elsewhere: in my Greek studies and the publication of the results, and most of all, in the Great Work.

Facing this man who so much resembled an avenging angel, or perhaps a human version of the vengeful Old Testament Deity Himself, I was terrorized. I temporized. I stammered. "Y-yes, Monsieur... I mean, yes, I've gone to services. Maybe not *every* time...."

The Reverend Sieur de Bèze narrowed his eyes and sat silent, glaring at me through those slits. "You are all but lying to me, Jean de Sponde. I cannot believe an upright and noble man like your father Iñigo could produce such an ingrate of a son, who takes his and the king's money, then behaves in such a way. Duplicitous! Evasive! A vessel of bad faith! *I know* where you've been. Your friends, who lie and evade like you, also know where you've been."

He stood up abruptly, seeming to tower over me again, his jabbing finger only inches from my face, his voice rising to a thunderous pitch. "They have deceived me, and you have deceived me even more! But you will not deceive the Lord, when He comes in glory to pronounce the Final Judgment! If you ask me what this is all about, I will ask you only one question: Just where *do* you go to services since you've been here?"

Without waiting for an answer—which I could not have supplied, since my throat was too dry to speak—he turned and snatched up the handsome edition of Homer with the poem he had dedicated to me. He shook it in my face. "Your preoccupation with this compendium of pagan idolatry is revealed as an offense to God and to me, now that I know how thoroughly you have neglected your studies of the Holy Scriptures. Meanwhile, in reading your commentaries, I have also seen something much more dangerous. You condemn those who cannot believe one species can be changed into another. Only *Catholics* believe as you imply you do!" His utterance of "Catholics" dripped with scorn. "During the Eucharist! *Transubstantiation!*" The last word came out like a curse. "If you follow our faith, you *know* such a statement amounts to heresy. His tone changed to a hiss. But you seem to be working within our ranks to subvert our faith. Could that be so?"

I found a voice somewhere. "No, Sir! Not at all! Such a thought never entered my head."

His lip curled. I noticed his fury had not reddened his face but had whitened it. I shrank from him, seeing him once again as a deadly, vengeful spirit. When he spoke again, it was in a monotone. "Go. Leave me. Get out of my sight. I will expect you at Sunday services, and I *know* the congregation will be most interested in hearing your public confession."

Stricken, I stumbled out of the room. But I knew for a fact that one species—or substance, if you will—could be transformed into another, for I had done it myself in the alchemical laboratory. I wandered back to my room, bumping into people as I went, so sunk in shock and depression I hardly knew where or who I was. I assumed the disfavor of the head of the Calvinist Church would spell disaster for me in one way or another, but I could hardly foresee just how. After several days spent worrying at the problem, its importance began to fade for me.

I did not attend services that Sunday; I left town instead. I had received more bad news, this time from Béarn. It seemed my portion of the inheritance from my mother was in dispute: my brothers Clément and Salomon were claiming it for themselves. Instead of heading directly for Béarn to straighten out that problem, I first passed through Geneva where my brother Henri was studying. He and I were in constant correspondence. Henri was considering a career as a Calvinist pastor, and I, who had studied the Psalms of David and written psalms of my own, had encouraged him to dedicate himself to the service of God. Henri had considerable talent as a writer, and I also urged him to try writing poetry.

I arrived in Geneva on an icy day in mid-December. After searching in vain through the halls of Henri's school, I wound my way through the gray cobbled streets until I found the house where he rented a room. As I approached, he appeared around a corner. He stopped in his tracks, then came running towards me, arms wide. "Jean, Jean! I was hoping to see you!" He enveloped me in a bear hug.

"Henri! You've grown so much I hardly recognize you!" I held him at arm's length. He stood a foot taller than I remembered, and, just past his sixteenth birthday, he was beginning to resemble our father. "Did you have supper yet?"

"No, but I know a good tavern near here. Do you have any money?" Henri grinned at me, knowing I was chronically destitute.

"Just enough for a bite. After that I'll have to use credit."

We supped well on a thick vegetable and mutton stew, bread, and wine. As I feared, the cost of that plus the extra bit of drink money I gave the tavern keeper wiped out my small store of coins. I would have to beg my way across France after I left Geneva.

We sat up late that night talking. I told him about my experience with Théodore de Bèze, and he shook his head, making little clucking noises with his tongue. "Jean, it was a combination of things. First of all, you were wrong not to attend regular services at our temple—as we called our church to distinguish it from the Catholic house of worship. Beyond that, Monsieur de Bèze clearly disapproves of the Great Work; he might even think you're doing the Devil's work instead. To have skipped services to pursue studies in alchemy seemed to him a grievous sin. Besides, there's that note in your book about those who cannot believe one species can be changed into another. That certainly confirmed his thinking you'd been doing the Devil's work. You've studied the ancients instead of the Scriptures—a sin in itself—and then, instead of making a forthright confession of your fault, you capped it all off by hedging about your absence from services. That's five counts against you!"

I watched in admiration as Henri ticked off each of my sins on his fingers. He had our father's clear and logical mind, and he would be an important person one day—either in religion or in government, I was not sure which. "I think you're right on every count, Henri. I stand thoroughly indicted. But that man froze my blood. Is he always so long-faced and severe? Have you ever seen him laugh?"

"Yes, to your first question, and no, Jean, he has never laughed in my presence. His sermons are lengthy diatribes, full of threats of the Last Judgment; we are all terrible sinners in his eyes. I find them tedious and depressing—God forgive me for saying so. For me, the most trying aspect of our services is the public confession. You know all too well— obliged to stand in front of the entire congregation to reveal and analyze our sins, then accept correction. I get so nervous I lose control of my voice, even though I don't have much to confess—usually. But those who do must withstand that man thundering at them from the pulpit, glaring at them with those blazing eyes, and shaking his finger or his fist at them."

I could imagine how dreadful it must be for a poor sinner caught like a butterfly on a pin, held up for everyone to see and judge. "He thinks he's God. Perhaps he should consider the Final Judgment in his own case. I wonder how *he* will fare on that day when the last trumpet sounds, when he'll be brought before the Judgment Seat."

Henri shook his head at me in gentle disapproval. "Don't think vengeful thoughts. There's no health, no help in that. Judge not, lest you be judged, brother. We'd better get to bed; you promised to teach me something about poetic technique tomorrow."

The following day brought joy for us both. I taught Henri about poetic forms, rhyme, meter, and the rudiments of rhetorical figures. I wrote out verses from Homer, Virgil, and especially Horace as illustrations, and added some modern poets like the Italian

Ludovico Ariosto and the Spaniard Garcilaso de la Vega. Then I showed him what some of our own poets had done, people like Joachim du Bellay and Pierre de Ronsard.

We made a full day of it, and I bought him supplies, quills, inks and paper, leaving a promissory note behind with a reluctant shopkeeper. We ate that night at "our" tavern, where they extended me credit for the meal, perhaps suspecting I could never make good on it. Henri told me he paid those debts some time later with the king's money. King Henri de Navarre was funding his studies too.

I bid my brother a fond goodbye the next morning, promising to stay in touch and to visit as often as I could. Gloom settled upon me shortly afterwards. I had to go to the market and sell my horse in order to have a minimum amount of money to live on while I trudged across southern France. On the one hand, it gave me the means to fill my belly for a while, but on the other, it deprived me of an easier and faster way of traveling. I opted for eating—at least for the near future.

I found Huguenot farmers here and there, and even a few Catholics who were willing to let me sleep in the hayloft and break my fast with them. On the second day, the weather turned foul. It was late December, near Christmastide, and I had been lucky until now. I woke up shivering in a hayloft that morning to see a white world surrounding the farm that had sheltered me. As a watery sun climbed above the horizon, the snow changed to sleet, and then to a fine and misty rain. The Huguenot farmer came out to the barn, and seeing my head poking out as I surveyed the weather, he called me in for breakfast. Our feet crunched through a thin crust of ice during our trek to the kitchen door.

Three children, from two to four, huddled close to the fireplace, while a baby boy about a year old, sucked noisily at his mother's breast. I could see she was pregnant again. With the baby straddling her hip, she moved between the fireplace and the kitchen table, dishing up eggs scrambled in the skillet over the fire, shaving paper-thin slices of cured beef, and pulling loaves of whole grain bread out of the oven, which she asked her husband to slice. She must have been up since four or earlier to make enough bread for the day. I pitied her. She looked older than her husband, although they must have been about the same age. Constant childbearing and the demanding duties of the household were wearing her out too soon.

The farmer asked me to say the blessing over the meal, which I did, using the prayer I had been taught as a child. After enjoying their tasty food and companionship, I thanked them most warmly for their kindness and hospitality, and as I left, I pressed a coin into the farmer's palm. Since he began to protest, I interrupted. "If you don't want to accept this for yourselves, give it to someone less fortunate. Your pastor will find a use for it if you can't—after all, Christmas Eve is only two days away."

As I stepped outside, I realized the ice had become much thicker, and traveling that day on the roads would be hazardous. Nonetheless, I set off, skidding and sliding on the downward slopes—sometimes for yards at a time—and slipping backwards and struggling twice as hard to climb the upward inclines. I cut two saplings at the side of the road, lopped their branches, knocked the ice off them and sharpened the tips. I then used one in each hand to anchor me on those uphill and downhill slopes.

I had gone five miles with great difficulty, having suffered four or five falls, when I saw a white-haired man lying in a ditch off the side of the road, struggling to rise. He called to me in a weak voice, and I hurried to him.

"Thank you, my son!" he gasped when I reached him. "I was trying to get to my daughter's house. It's about a mile off the road, over there." He pointed with his chin and meanwhile tried to pull himself up, using me as a prop. "A neighbor came by my house early this morning and told me my girl just gave birth and is doing poorly."

Our combined efforts set him on his feet. He tried to take a step and gave a little cry of pain. He had badly twisted his ankle in falling and had skidded off the road.

"Show me which way to go, grandfather, and I'll help you get to your daughter's house."

"It's up and over that hill yonder, but I don't know how we'll make it—I seem to have hurt myself. And with all this ice..."

"If we don't, you'll freeze to death. Take one of my walking sticks. It'll give you support."

We struggled for two hours before coming in sight of the cabin. When we arrived at the door, the old man called out and was much relieved to hear his daughter's voice. She had lost her husband in an accident not long before, and now, after a difficult childbirth, was unable to care for herself.

While the father sat on the edge of her cot, comforting his daughter, wiping the baby's bottom and wrapping her more warmly, I built a fire—for the cabin was unheated when we arrived. I knocked ice off the axe, then off the wood outside, and cut firewood to last for a few more days, stacked it next to the fireplace, drew and heated water, then bandaged the father's ankle. I found dried beans and soaked a double handful in a pot full of water I placed on the hob. With the daughter's permission, I caught, killed, plucked and prepared one of their six hens, seasoned and boiled the beans. There was enough for our dinner and food to last the two of them for another day. The baby girl was weak but able to nurse.

When the meager meal was ready, the woman's father said the blessing, and both of them noticed I did not cross myself. "You're a Calvinist, aren't you?" the man asked, a look of concern on his face.

"Yes, so I am. But the Lord's command, that we love our neighbor as ourselves, applies to all Christians alike."

Our talk was a bit strained for a few minutes after that, but then they seemed to get used to the idea a heretic was sitting at their table. At the end of the meal, the daughter exclaimed, "You *are* a good man, anyhow!" I simply smiled in reply.

That night, I curled up next to the fireplace and slept as much as I could, waking with the baby's cries, the discomfort of the rough floor that made my bones ache, and with the cold when the fire burned down, a signal for me to rise and add more wood. Every time I moved, I was aware the old man was awake and watching me. His mistrust of Huguenots ran deep. Perhaps he feared I might succumb to a sudden savage impulse to avenge the Saint Bartholomew's Day Massacre by murdering them all in the bed.

The next morning had warmed enough to thaw the ice off the sunward sides of the slopes, and I saw the father could walk with the help of the cut sapling. As I prepared to leave, I wondered aloud. "You'll be fine for a day, perhaps, but after that, where will you find help and food?"

The old man nodded at me with a smug air. "There's a village not far from here. Father Huchet will help us, never fear."

I took about a third of the money I had left from the sale of my horse and laid it on the kitchen table. My motive was not entirely disinterested; I had a strong urge to demonstrate that Huguenots are not the villains Catholics believe us to be. They didn't notice what I had done, and I doubt they saw it before I was well away from the house. With it, they would be able to buy something to celebrate Christmas as well as goods to sustain their lives and the new life just arrived. I would soon have to rely on my ingenuity to find food, but I was young, able-bodied, and could manage. One family had done me a great favor the previous night, and, thanks be to God, I was able to repay it the very next day. I had played at being the Good Samaritan—and yet I was sincere.

I spent Christmas Eve buried for warmth in the hay of a lonely barn, with no farmhouse in sight. Driven by cold and discomfort, I was up at dawn and trudged on without finding food until late in the day when I came upon a village where the innkeeper's wife, "in the spirit of Christmas," fed me stale bread, a lump of cheese, and allowed me to sleep on the hearth, so long as I kept the fire from going out.

My first major stop, the following day, was Lyon, still recovering from a triple calamity. The city had been damaged extensively in the siege and occupation by our Huguenot mercenary general, the Baron des Adrets. A severe depression had struck the financial establishment in the city, and most of the distinguished bankers had moved away, even before the third calamity, the black plague, had struck.

As I walked the streets, I saw many empty, neglected buildings falling into disrepair. As I passed the once magnificent cathedral, I felt a pang of sorrow at seeing its stained-glass windows replaced with common glass, some of the cloister windows simply stuffed with rags. The façade of the thirteenth-century cathedral had borne the brunt of des Adrets' iconoclastic fury: its statuary had been shattered, and now it stood stark and denuded, pitted by cannon balls. No apparent effort had been made by a demoralized populace to repair the damage.

Our own temple had been destroyed in its turn, but upon discreet inquiry, I found that we held services in a small building near the Rhone Bridge. Since I had arrived on a Sunday morning, I sat through the hour-long sermon devoted to Saint Paul's first letter to the Corinthians, where he explains that every member of the community is of crucial importance to the health of the whole, just as every member of the body—the eye, the hand, the foot—is essential. I brooded. Just where did I fit in, I wondered? What indispensable body part did I correspond to? It seemed I was quite useless.

After the service I approached the pastor, a Monsieur Grégoire Toussaint, told him of my plight, and asked if I could work for a few days in exchange for food and lodging. He took me home with him and set me to cleaning his study and putting his books in order—for I had impressed him with my learning.

"You're too good a find to turn out with a spade into the garden. I never seem to have time to put my books away, and by now, I can't locate what I need for the references I want to make in my sermons."

For over a week, I worked in his library, devising a system for his books—ranging them alphabetically by subject—dusting them, straightening his piles of paper without unduly disturbing them, and making suggestions for keeping his sermons in order by subject with cross-references from the scriptural quotation or quotations used. Meanwhile, his quiet, mousy wife allowed me to sleep in a cot in the servants' quarters and served me at mealtimes while her husband regaled me with local gossip, politics, news of the war, speculations about Divine Providence and other such topics. They sent me on my way with a bundle of hard-boiled eggs, cheese, and a loaf of brown bread that would last me a week if I were careful.

Once on the road again, I followed the Rhône valley southward, skirting the mountain ranges on my right until they bent themselves, so their peaks were running east and west. I probably walked thirty miles every day, from dawn to dusk and sometimes well into dark. As I trudged along, I pondered the different manifestations of our faith in different people.

What I had seen of Théodore de Bèze had shaken and disillusioned me profoundly. I saw little evidence of Christian charity, kindness, or willingness to teach and gently lead the young—in this case myself—towards the right path. Instead, I had, so I believed, witnessed anger, suspicion and intolerance.

Anger is a sin, also for Huguenots, but perhaps his was *righteous* anger. Was righteous anger a sin? After all, Jesus was righteously angry when he overturned the tables of the money changers and drove them from the temple. Perhaps I should not make any generalizations about our faith from my own unfortunate experience. Nor could I make any generalizations about Monsieur de Bèze. I may have seen him on a bad day.

Besides, I had just seen the counter example: Monsieur Toussaint and his wife could not have been kinder or more charitable. I blessed them once again, as I had done at our parting, with a short prayer. I should have been left with a feeling of happiness at the divine balance I perceived, but instead I struggled with a vague feeling of depression. In my encounter with Monsieur de Bèze, it seemed that I was the sinner after all, for his actions had, as I now construed them, emulated those of Christ in the temple.

I stopped for a few days at Nîmes and again at Carcasonne, seeking out our people everywhere and finding, on the whole, a generous welcome. In Carcasonne, I worked as a gardener for the pastor to earn enough money to pay a cobbler to make me a new pair of shoes. Once on the road again, I found they rubbed and pinched my right foot across the instep, the left foot at the heel. The resulting blisters and pain slowed me, but I persisted in walking, wrapping my wounds with rags torn from the lining of my cloak. Eventually, I'd break those shoes in.

Armed gangs of brigands infested the roads from time to time. So far, I'd hidden before they saw me. Once, slouching along, my belly rumbling and empty, deep in worry where my next meal would come from, I didn't hear the approaching hoof beats until it was too late. I looked around in panic but saw only plowed fields to the left and right, and a few scraggly trees not big enough to hide me. I'd have to confront the riders.

They were seven, dressed in brown: dark brown breeches with black stockings and lighter brown jackets. Their hats were either dark brown or black. It was impossible to tell which side they were on. They would surely feel the same about me, also dressed in a combination of brown and black.

When the leader of the group saw me, he whipped his horse into a canter and bore down upon me, his six companions pounding at his heels. I stopped and stood at the side of the road, fearing the worst. He halted his horse just as he was about to run me over.

"Catholic or Huguenot?"

I gazed up at him, eyes wide with fear. I had a fifty-fifty chance of surviving this encounter. "Who are you, and why are you disturbing peaceful travelers on the public highway?" I asked him in a thin voice, trying to conceal the underlying quaver.

He shifted his reins to his left hand and drew his sword. "Catholic, by Christ!" He raised the sword as if to strike me down.

I raised my hand. "No, Huguenot. And how dare you take the name of Christ in your mouth at the moment you intend to kill a man in cold blood?" I was amazed to hear my own words, since I had never considered myself particularly courageous—or foolhardy.

He hesitated then lowered the sword halfway. "Can you prove it?"

"No. I have nothing on me to prove me Huguenot or Catholic. No cross, no crucifix, no medal, no beads, no missal, no Bible, and especially, no money. Search me and you'll see. You'll either have to take my word for it or kill me."

He motioned to his followers. Two dismounted and went through my pockets, feeling their way over my body. They found my handkerchief, my small knife, and an empty purse. When they had shown their master the negative results of their search, he questioned me again. "Where are you from?"

"Béarn. I'm returning there from Geneva." I chose to mention Geneva, the center of Calvinism, rather than Basel.

"Béarn. Yes. Mainly Huguenots there. What's your name?"

"Jean de Sponde. Son of Iñigo de Sponde, *Maître des Requêtes* for his Majesty, King Henri de Navarre."

He shook his head. "Your father's that important in Navarre, and you're out here wandering on foot on the highway, without a sou in your purse? I don't believe you."

I shrugged. "I'm a student. Students never have money. I sold my horse for money to buy food—and now that's gone too. But, unless you kill me, I shall be home before the week is out."

With a jerk of his head, the leader ordered his men to remount. For the first time, he gave me a ghost of a smile. "You have guts, my young friend. Here. This will buy you supper." He tossed me a coin as he sheathed the sword and maneuvered his horse around me. "Au revoir!"

"Au revoir et merci!" I called into the cloud of dust they left behind.

I reached Toulouse that night, and thanks to those highwaymen, I was able to eat a decent dinner, with enough left over for bread and ham the following morning, but I brooded over the source of that coin. Had a Catholic man been killed for it? A Catholic woman raped and widowed?

Four days later, I arrived in Tarbes, having begged a ride from a wagoner, and finally, before the week was out and about mid-day, I arrived at Pau in Béarn.

Chapter III

Anne

I rested in Pau for a day, sleeping and eating well, thanks to friends of my father's who took me in. Then, I set out for Mauléon-de-Soule, our home village. Despite the rest and food, I still felt tired and weak—all that walking on too little food had exhausted me. I was two miles from the village when I heard hoof beats behind me, closing fast. I was not as fearful here in Béarn as I had been farther from home, but I turned to see who was coming, and stepped off the side of the road. It was a woman, riding bareback and astride, her skirts tucked around her legs. I knew very few women who would—or could—ride like that.

When she drew nearer, I began to focus on her face. Her freckled nose and red hair looked familiar, though I could not place her. She slowed the horse to a walk and stopped beside me. "Well, don't you look gaunt and worn out! It's Jean de Sponde, isn't it? You've been gone for years! We used to play at *jeu de paume*, tennis, together—remember?" As I continued to stare at her with a puzzled expression on my face, she relented and told me her name. "I'm Anne Legrand, Jean! You *don't* remember, do you?"

I slapped my forehead. "Anne! Of course! Now I know you! You were about a foot shorter, round faced, much more freckled—a child, and now you're a woman! You insisted on joining all the boys' games, and you weren't such a bad player, either. Congratulations! You've certainly, uh, changed!" I blushed. I had wanted to say, "You've certainly grown up to be a beauty," but didn't dare. To cover my awkwardness, I quickly asked, "Is your father still a member of *Parlement*?"

"Yes, he is. My brother Georges—you and he used to get up to such mischief! —joined the Huguenot army to fight for King Henri and got himself shot with an arquebus ball about six months ago. He's home, but I don't think he'll ever heal properly."

"I'm truly sorry to hear that. But... perhaps you're too pessimistic. Those arquebus wounds take a long time. And speaking of the king and his army, is Henri here right now, or is he out campaigning?"

"He's here at the Château de Pau. I'm sure he'd like to see you—he keeps track of all the young people he's given scholarship money to, you know. But you must be anxious to get home to your father! There are only two of you Sponde children at home, now that Henri is off to Geneva to study."

"Yes, I'd better be getting along." I took a couple of steps towards Mauléon to illustrate my intention.

"Hold on, Jean. I can get you there faster than you can walk. Here. Grab my arm." She had turned on the horse, reaching down towards me.

"Will your horse carry both of us?"

"Of course! Otherwise I wouldn't invite you! Jump when I pull."

I nodded and took her arm. As I jumped, she pulled, and I was swung up and landed astride the horse right behind her.

"That's quite a trick! Where did you learn to do it? You're really strong!"

"My brothers taught me how. As for my strength, I never stopped playing those games, riding, hunting—all that. I'm the despair of my mother. If I could get away with wearing men's clothing, I would. Skirts make life so difficult! But never mind, just hold onto my waist, and we'll go!" She squeezed her horse's sides, putting him into a working trot.

We talked easily as we jogged along, as if we'd never been apart. She wondered why I was on foot, and I explained I'd been forced to sell my horse. I also regaled her with a couple of my adventures while on the road. We continued to catch up on mutual news all the way to the gate in the stone fence around our property, where I slipped off the horse.

"A thousand thanks for the ride, Anne. You came along just at the right moment."

"I'm so glad I did." Her smile revealed white, even teeth. "When shall I see you again?"

I was not surprised she was so forward, remembering her direct manner and competitive skills as a child. "Soon, I hope. As soon as I find another horse and rest up a bit, I'll be by."

"I'll be waiting, Jean," she told me quite seriously, without a trace of coquetry.

My welcome home was tumultuous. My father's second wife, my stepmother Salvata who had raised me, opened the front door, threw her arms around me, kissing me on both cheeks, complaining how thin I had become. "But I never realized what a handsome young man you are!"

Before I could take two more steps, the rest of the family gathered in the entrance hall. Her two youngest children, Jean-Jacques and Israël, half-brothers to me like Henri, danced around me until their turn came for hugs. Father, meanwhile, beamed at me from the sidelines, showing great forbearance until the youngsters made way for him to embrace me and clap me on the back.

"I'm sorry about the trouble with your inheritance. It's Clément, mainly. As eldest son, he thinks the lion's share of Catherine's property should be his by birthright. But her Will makes it clear she wanted it divided evenly between the three of you. Salomon, of course, appears to be willing to give his portion up to his brother—he always did appease Clément. But I don't think Clément should have any more than is due him. Catherine would never have approved."

"But how to proceed, Papa?"

He led me into his study, a room I knew well from childhood. Rectangular, with an ornately beamed and painted ceiling, it was warmed and illuminated by a large fireplace at the far end. At right angles to the fireplace stood my father's desk and carved oaken chair—both such a dark brown as to appear almost black. Behind him and on the opposite wall were bookcases built from floor to ceiling, laden with his books and papers—legal tomes and documents as well as books of poetry and literature in Latin, Italian, Spanish and French, Stephanus's dictionary and Valeriano's *Hieroglyphica*. There was also a copy of Calvin's *Institutes of the Christian Religion*, and a well-thumbed Bible, both a Vulgate version, and Erasmus's translation of the New Testament, heavily read and marked with strips of paper protruding from the top. A double window with round panes of thick glass allowed sufficient light to fall upon the desk during the day, and through their blurry prisms I could see the skeletons of leafless ivy branches that climbed the stone wall outside.

We spoke for over an hour, Papa recommending our course of action. I realized I was still a total novice in this world of legal wrangling—despite my law degree from Toulouse—for the situation required more politics than law. I merely agreed to his suggestions, for the alternative courses of action I knew were legal might not be acceptable to my brothers. We would need to take the matter to court, Papa told me, although he suggested I might speak to King Henri about it, which might shorten the process.

"Speak to the king, Papa?"

"Yes, why not? I let him know you were coming when I received your letter three weeks ago. He told me he wanted to see you when you arrived. It certainly took you long enough to get here!"

I told him about my visit to Geneva, and that his son Henri was getting along very well. Better than I was, I thought. And then, almost as an afterthought, I told him about Théodore de Bèze. It was like a confession. I couldn't keep it from him. It wasn't a process I had thought through or willed. It came tumbling out in the end— all of it. I described my concentrated efforts in the laboratory and my final triumph, my conviction I had witnessed the transformation of one substance into another through the power of science and the grace of God.

I admitted my delinquency at failing to attend services, even telling him about my reservations with the Calvinist way of worship: the lengthy scriptural readings, when we could read all that for ourselves, the sometimes inane sermons based on one man's often tortured or forced interpretation of those scriptures, the excruciating public confessions—although I was very far from considering the Catholic way as a possible alternative. I knew he would be furious at me—and he was.

"You did *what*? You skipped services to experiment mixing the Devil's brew? You might as well have been indulging in black magic! Jean, Jean, how could you betray your upbringing, your heritage in such a way? Who led you astray? When did all this begin?"

"It began here in Béarn, Papa. Maître Geoffroy de Sales and Maître Delaunay Pirard were both adepts of the Great Work. They set me on the path I continued to follow at Toulouse, and then at Basel. I'm sure King Henri knows all about this." My voice rose along with my enthusiasm. "It is *science*, Papa, leading to the *truth*. It may even save us all, eventually, somehow. If we can know the secrets of Nature, we can begin to understand the mind of God, Papa."

He ranted at me afterwards for what seemed hours. At last, he seemed to have had his say. "You must tell King Henri all about this incident with Monsieur de Bèze when you see him. His Majesty has told me he would see you within twenty-four hours of your arrival—no matter when that might be."

We walked out of his study together, but by no means united in spirit. Still, despite my dampened mood, the dinner was delightful, as I luxuriated in the attentions of my family once again. I slept that night as I had not slept in years. My body recognized and conformed itself to the lumps and hollows of my childhood cot, and I relaxed as if I were again embraced by my mother's arms.

The king's chateau, his birthplace, was modest compared to many I've seen since. It is a jumble of towers and steep tiled roofs over stone walls, with servants' houses huddled right up against the outer ramparts. It is built on a spur of land above the Gave de Pau—a mountain torrent—and has a splendid view of the Pyrenees away to the south. Once inside, a servant led me to comfortable rooms, dark-beamed with tile flooring, heated by large fireplaces, decorated with the horns of wild goats, the heads of wild boars, and with forests of antlers: mementos of years of successful hunts.

I was given no opportunity to explore, but was ushered through a series of rooms, still carrying with me a whiff of the icy air outside. My guide and I made an abrupt entrance into the great hall, where Henri de Navarre sat, his legs stretched out towards the fire as he spoke to a couple of advisors. I later found out the older one was Philippe Duplessis-Mornay, and the one who appeared to be about my own age was the Sieur de La Force, two of Henri's staunchest allies and constant companions.

The king glanced my way and motioned for me to sit—an unusual privilege in the presence of royalty. While he finished his conversation with his ministers, I had time to examine him at leisure. He was a short man, neither handsome nor ugly, with large though heavy-lidded blue eyes in a long, narrow face, framed by light brown hair and a beard. He was aptly nicknamed "long-nose," for it was prominent as well as long and slightly drooping, giving him a short upper lip. He gave me the impression, now that I was old enough to evaluate such things, of great potential energy, and yet he radiated calm. The two gentlemen to whom he had been speaking concluded their business, and with slight bows, they departed, passing me by with a nod on their way out.

Henri then turned to me. "Young Sponde! Jean! Come over here and warm yourself! It's beastly cold outside."

I approached Navarre, took his hand, and bowed over it. "Your Majesty wanted to see me?" I asked, still wondering why he should take the trouble.

He looked me over, his head tilted. "Yes, you've become a man, Jean," he said, "but certain quarters don't believe you're maturing as you should. You've stirred up some strong feelings, it seems. I'm always interested to hear what my young protégés are doing with the stipends I give them for their education, and they tell me you've been using yours to experiment with alchemy!"

I was taken aback at the accuracy of his news. "Yes, Your Majesty, I have been studying the Divine Science. In fact, I began studying it before I left Béarn. You have a number of adepts right here, Sire."

"Hmmm. Yes, I know. But your fervor for science has not, it seems, been matched by an equal devotion to our faith." He turned to a small table next to his chair and began to shuffle through the documents piled on it. "Yes. Here it is. A letter to me from Monsieur Théodore de Bèze. He says you lied to him, and then disobeyed him—not attending services the Sunday after he had reprimanded you. What's this all about?"

A medley of emotions nearly overwhelmed me: anger that Bèze had gone so far as to denounce me to the king, fear that His Majesty might withdraw his favor. I took a couple of deep breaths. "Sire, when he questioned me, I hedged to the point of prevarication, I admit, but I didn't *lie* to him. He asked me if I had attended services faithfully, and I answered that I had attended, though not every time. The truth is that I attended maybe three or four times in three years. Not a good record, I know. An abysmal record. I confess that Monsieur de Bèze terrified me. I hardly knew what I was saying."

I had paused to look for a reaction and received none. The king simply nodded, expressionless, then said, "Go on."

"As for going to Sunday service after that, I had left Basel by then—on my way back here to fight for my inheritance that my brother Clément is trying to steal from me. I admit that my departure might have been hastened by fear of standing up in front of the congregation and Monsieur de Bèze and confessing what a sinner I've been. That's about all, Your Majesty." I let out my breath in a sigh.

Henri smiled for the first time. "Most of that sounds to me more like schoolboy truancy than like mortal sin. Maybe you aren't as much a grown man as you look. But this wrangle with Bèze doesn't sum up your accomplishments over the last few years. Sit down, Jean, and tell me more about your work."

Again, I was flattered I was allowed to sit in the royal presence—and by royal invitation! As I was bending my knees to take a chair, a striking woman appeared in the room, regally dressed in a long green gown that revealed shapely curves. I straightened my knees again, trying to hide my admiration. The lady, seeing that the king was talking to someone, paused near a table at the far side of the room and picked up a book lying open there. She was tall, nearly as tall as I, with glossy brown hair that lay in natural waves down to her shoulders. Her dark eyes gave the two of us an appraising glance.

"Corisande!" the king called, "Come join us! Corisande, this is Jean de Sponde, son of one of my most valued councilors. I think you've met his father, Iñigo. Jean, Corisande is my nickname for this beauty—she's Philibert de Grammont's widow—he was the Comte de Guiche, you remember."

I rose and bowed to the lady. "So pleased to meet you, uh, Madam."

She smiled at my awkwardness. "My real name is Diane d'Andoins. Corisande, as you probably know already, is a name out of the romance *Amadis de Gaule*—Henri was mad about the work when he was younger—and it gives him pleasure to call me that."

I smiled back at her, taken with her husky voice that struck me as very sensual. Her use of the king's given name and his pet name for her told me they must be more than casual acquaintances. She was sizing me up, her glance keen and intelligent.

"Do go on with your conversation, gentlemen," she said, "I'll just sit over here and read until you're done."

The king nodded, then turned back to me, asking once again for an account of my activities other than the incident with the head of the Calvinist Church. I gave him a summary of my studies in Greek antiquity, the publication of my Latin translations of Aristotle. He knew of the Homer already, since I had dedicated the book to him, but I reminded the king of the prefatory poem in the Homer book written in my honor by Monsieur de Bèze. Navarre laughed as I imitated Bèze's subsequent angry rejection of my books and the inspiration behind them, which he had reduced to the swinish level of "wallowing in the filth of pagan idolatry."

I told him about my visit to my brother Henri in Geneva, and a quick account of my difficult trek home. He was disturbed and angered at my story of near-death on the road at the hands of a band of Huguenot brigands.

"Damn those marauders!" he cried, "They pretend to be zealots, but they're nothing more than murderers and thieves! They're turning the countryside against me. I can't afford to lose potential allies down here in the south. It's the only firm ground I have."

He looked at me now with a speculative expression. "Seems to me you've had enough schooling for now. I need someone who has studied law and the latest humanist learning who can also be a competent fighter. Have you had any military training, Jean?"

I shook my head, somewhat abashed. "No, Sire, none. I'm a fair hunter, though—a good shot. Perhaps I can learn the rest."

"Stay here overnight, Jean. Come out hunting with me in the morning. Five of us are going out at daybreak for deer—perhaps for boar. Whatever we run across. You'll be the sixth. I'll judge your talents then, and maybe recruit you for your king's service."

He nodded, dismissing me. "Robert!" he called to the valet hovering near the door, "Show Monsieur de Sponde to a room. He'll be dining here tonight and joining the hunting party in the morning. See that he has the proper equipment."

I rose and departed, and as I passed Corisande, our eyes met in a long look. She was not flirting with me, but rather, I felt, looking into my very soul. An extraordinary person—the king was lucky to have such a companion!

From the documents of Diane d'Andoins (Corisande):

Jean de Sponde is a strange young man—he and I locked glances as he left the room after his conversation with Henri this afternoon. I felt as though I could read his thoughts, and perhaps he could read mine as well. He either has a great future, or he will allow his private demons to destroy him. He seems unusually sensitive and intelligent.

I believe he readily understood my relationship to the King of Navarre—the king's mistress. Not that Henri remains faithful to me. He's incapable of that, at least physically. But he recognizes my ability to analyze our political situation, and even, upon occasion, to plan military strategy. I'm an excellent chess player. He depends upon me to clarify any situation—supply background, and all that. You might say I am Henri's intellectual mistress; someone he always returns to. Bedding me is almost beside the point.

Some people speculate that his unusual agility in bed-hopping may go back to his babyhood, when he was passed from one wet nurse to another, never having the time to become attached to any one. Jeanne d'Albret, his mother, was too busy to care for the boy.

Anyway, it was unthinkable for her to nurse her own child like a peasant woman. Jeanne and his father left him among commoners to grow up understanding just how rough life really is. Neither of them wanted him to become a limp young fop like his royal cousins in Paris.

In many ways, Henri's childhood among peasants stands him in good stead. He is tough and wiry, seems to have limitless stamina, and he is acquainted with all the occupations of the lower classes. He's the people's king. A good thing, for he has inherited a dreadful situation, marooned on this island of Calvinism, Béarn, between His Holiness's most Catholic realm of Spain and the Catholic Church of France—the Gallican Church, as we call it. It will take a miracle to save us from being crushed.

I know Henri has plans for this young man. He has mentioned Sponde to me as a worthy successor to his father. Henri also has hopes for the younger half-brother, another Henri, now studying in Geneva at his expense. I think Henri—*my* Henri—wants to use Jean de Sponde as an ambassador to Switzerland and Germany. Jean might do well in such a position; he knows enough languages, I'm told. My own Henri will certainly test his mettle in the next few days.

Jean resumes:
I stayed the night and several days thereafter at the Château de Pau. During the hunt on that first morning, I had no chance to shoot at a deer, but Navarre noticed I rode well and gracefully, fearlessly, too, as we leapt over fallen trees and stone fences in our pursuit of the game. We returned that day with only a single deer, shot by the Duc de Miossens.

Sometime that week, the king solved the problem of my inheritance by speaking with the judge who was to settle the matter, and my part of mother's legacy eventually came to me without further litigation. My attention was thenceforth concentrated upon increasing my warlike skills.

My days were occupied with pistol practice and in learning to fight with the sword. Blessed with good coordination, I grasped the rudiments of swordplay before long, but I would never become a true expert, since I had begun so late. As for my shooting, I was already a fine marksman and became still better. I did not attempt to learn the arquebus, since only foot soldiers used that. If I were to go into battle, it would be with sword and pistol, riding like a gentleman on horseback, where the arquebus is useless.

I chafed at all this mindless activity that kept me physically tired and prevented any reading or study. I worried that the king had misread my character and my talents and would try to force me to play a role I could not fill. But I was caught and forced to dance to Henri's tune. Meanwhile, I rationalized that all this was most likely a temporary phase, and my new skills might well stand me in good stead one day.

The king was an avid player of the *jeu de paume*, the game the English are calling "tennis" because we shout *"tenez!"* as we serve the ball. He insisted I play with him, and there too I could shine, since I had played with great gusto during my childhood, when one of my most formidable opponents had been Anne Legrand! Navarre was a fine player, the two of us evenly matched. Unlike most highly-placed people, he did not mind losing and was happiest when the match was fiercely fought, long and exhausting—win or lose.

It was hard to get away from the Château de Pau, but I managed to visit my parents' home that Sunday—to fetch things I needed, clothes mainly, and to catch up on the news. I also made a point of going with the family to the temple, hoping to get back into my father's good graces. That first Sunday was an ordeal, since I was obliged to make public confession, at last. It seems to me the Calvinist system is particularly harsh, for it concentrates only on one's misdeeds. No one ever hears about the compensating good works—so I would stand before the congregation as the blackest of sinners, with no redeeming qualities.

The time ritually set aside for confessions comes early in the service. There were two minor sinners before me, and then I stood, inwardly quaking, and began: "I confess to you, Almighty God, and to this congregation…" I proceeded to detail my infractions: my lack of fervor in attending services while in Basel, preferring to pursue my studies in Greek and my alchemical research, my disobedience to Monsieur de Bèze in not delaying my departure from that city until I had stood to confess to the congregation there—and all the rest. Then, still on my feet, my face hot, I gripped the back of the pew in front of me while the pastor reprimanded me, telling me what good works I must perform—extensive scriptural readings and meditation, secretarial service to my father—in order to compensate for my sins.

As I sat, thoroughly chastened, I saw Anne Legrand, her green eyes focused upon me, a few pews back. She looked especially beautiful, her face scrubbed and glowing, pink-cheeked and healthy. She wore a white lace kerchief on her head, patches of her glowing red hair showing through, a few escaped curls drooping over her forehead. She gave me a little smile of sympathy and a tiny nod before I turned my attention to the lector reading the scripture for the day.

After the service, I adroitly guided my family group in the direction of the Legrands, through the crowd lingering in front of the temple, making it a point to speak with Anne's parents and her younger brothers, all the while exchanging glances with her. Her older brother Georges was there, keeping himself in the background. Although it was clear he was reluctant to greet people, he welcomed me when I singled him out. He was as pale and weak as Anne was hearty, the left arm hanging useless, his body hunched and twisted towards that side.

"How's the wound healing?" I asked. "Anne told me about it. I'm terribly sorry."

"A little better, I think—I hope. The arquebus ball smashed the bones and tore the muscles that move the left arm, and it made a hole in my chest, too. I guess it'll be months before I have my strength back—maybe never. The doctors only made things worse."

We spoke a bit about the uselessness of doctors and the horrors of modern weapons. I told him my fears that I, too, would soon find myself in King Henri's army. Finally, I turned again to the rest of Anne's family, moved and depressed by my former fellow student's plight. When the others were engaged in conversations with my father and mother, I edged closer to Anne.

At last, I had a moment to admire her blue dress. Though modest, it did not lack for decoration. It had puffy sleeves and a shirred bodice, further adorned with an elaborate design in white silken cord all down the front. I complimented her aloud and then murmured, "Can you ride out this afternoon in the *Bois de Saint-Jean,* St. John's Wood, along the creek? I'll be riding that way and would like to talk to you."

She smiled and nodded. "I'll be there."

We parted, and I continued greeting other old acquaintances, feeling my way back into the community of my childhood. Most of the friends who were my contemporaries were married and gone, some to settle in neighboring towns, some, as Georges had done, to serve in King Henri's army. I felt a stranger, even though my family was gathered about me.

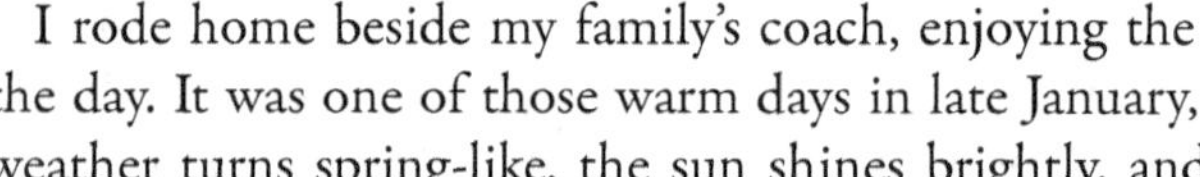

I rode home beside my family's coach, enjoying the beauty of the day. It was one of those warm days in late January, when the weather turns spring-like, the sun shines brightly, and the temperature rises well above freezing. When we arrived at the house, I had the groom take care of the carriage and the horses, and then I entertained the boys, Jean-Jacques and Israël, until Salvata called us inside to enjoy Sunday dinner, prepared by our cook Miriam under Salvata's supervision.

I peeped into the kitchen before sitting, just to revel in the orderly chaos that always reigns when family meals were prepared:

the tables covered with tops and peels of chopped vegetables and trimmings from meat, spilled flour, dirty bowls stacked and waiting to be taken out to the scullery for washing, ladles, spoons, pots and pans—the used ones sitting on the hearth, clean ones hanging on hooks from the ceiling beams along with bunches of dried herbs—discarded towels and aprons trailing off table corners.

The dinner featured pork roast flanked with boiled vegetables: greens, whole garlic, and onions. My father had killed a wild pig on Friday. We were served thick slices of pork, vegetables, and a ladle of gravy, and we mopped up the juices with chunks of Salvata's whole grain bread, freshly baked.

During the meal, my father seemed to be in a much better temper with me than he had before services. After the custard dessert, I began telling them the news from the Château de Pau. "The king has a new mistress."

Mother covered her mouth with a napkin; father frowner but leaned forward. "Well, who is she?"

The king's womanizing was common knowledge. "She's the widow of Philibert de Grammont, Comte de Guiche. You may remember that he was killed during the siege of La Fère three years ago. Her name is Diane D'Andoins, but the king calls her Corisande."

My brother Jean-Jacque's eyes sparkled. "What's she like? Is she pretty?"

I grinned at him and Israel, both eager for details. "She's a handsome woman and a Huguenot. Dark, wavy brown hair and brown eyes, a little taller than the king, with good features. Most of all, she's extremely intelligent and well informed. I wouldn't be surprised if she were his closest advisor."

"And what about Marguerite de Valois—or Margot as everyone calls her—that papist wife of his?" Salvata asked.

"I hear she's at the Château de Nérac where Navarre usually holds court. She came from Paris just as far as Nérac to remind him to remain loyal to the throne and to his brother-in-law, King

Henri III, who, I hear, might ally himself to our king. They tell me she's at Nérac against her will. She hates the provinces."

Father shook his head. "At Nérac? Why didn't she come here to be with her king, her husband, at the Château de Pau?"

"Because both she and our king are unfaithful to each other. That she came to Nérac at all is due to machinations of the Queen Mother, Catherine de Medici, who thinks Margot's charms can win our king over to her son's side. I learn more every day about the queen's serpentine plots, hatched in the Louvre or at Blois— wherever Henri III's court happens to be. I think Navarre stays at Pau to escape Margot, mainly."

We called a halt to gossip, and at two in the afternoon, when the day was at its warmest, I excused myself to ride out for some exercise. I galloped off at once to St. John's Wood. I had ridden along the creek for some ten minutes and was beginning to worry that Anne had not been able to free herself from her own family circle, but suddenly she was there, trotting her horse to join mine.

"I was waiting in ambush," she called, laughing. "I got here a good half-hour ago and waited in the little glade back there. I knew you'd pass by eventually."

We rode downstream for a mile or two, not able to do more than exchange an occasional phrase, since the trail was narrow, forcing us to ride single file. We finally reached the Gué d'Alès, Alès Ford, then led our horses about a hundred yards beyond that to a low waterfall with a dry ledge where we could sit and dangle our legs.

Anne seated herself on the flat rock and patted a spot next to her, inviting me to join her. We sat for a while looking at each other in silence, smiling, then glancing down shyly, each one waiting for the other to find a topic to begin our conversation. At last I hit upon something. I was sure of her answer, since I had seen her face that morning in church.

"I hope you don't think I'm a monster, after hearing my confession this morning," I began.

"No, of course not! Everybody sounds like a monster if they're not allowed to tell the whole story—why they did what they did. It seemed pretty clear to me you simply got carried away with your studies."

"True enough, but that's not all, Anne." At this point, I began to babble, caught in a theme I'd repeated so often to myself that it seemed almost like a litany. "I didn't go to services in Basel because I've become dissatisfied with the way we Calvinists have come to worship. Not that I like the Catholic way—speeding through Mass in Latin so fast the parishioners can't follow, with the priest's back to them—but I don't like our interminable preaching, either. There's got to be a better way. Very few preachers are talented enough to keep my interest for an hour, not to mention an hour and a half! But I'm sinning in thinking such a thing, I'm sure. I like our congregational singing and the Scripture readings. But..."

"For goodness sake, why talk about all that, Jean?" Anne cut off my flow of words with an impatient wave of her hand. "You're always so grim and serious! If you don't watch out, that crease between your brows will become permanent. Surely, you didn't invite me out here to discuss the comparative merits of Catholics and Huguenots! I've heard about that all my life, and I've had enough of it to last me two lifetimes. I want to talk about your studies, your work—what you want to do with your life. You've been at the Château de Pau for a week now, and you went there, I hear, just for a short talk with the king. What happened?"

"Oh!" I paused, realizing how boring and gloomy I must have sounded. "Navarre simply kept me overnight to go hunting with him next day, and then he asked me to stay. He'd heard all about my doings in Basel, straight from Théodore de Bèze himself, who denounced me to him in a letter. King Henri thought very little of it, didn't seem to take it seriously. He asked me more details about my studies and my life, so he got a balanced picture: my side and Bèze's. But he needs me for something, I'm not clear what, and he's having me learn swordplay and improving my marksmanship with a pistol. He has taken me out hunting with him just about every day, and for the moment, anyway, I'm his favorite partner at tennis. It's thanks to you, in part, that I'm a worthy opponent for him."

Anne gave a hoot of delighted laughter. "But what do you think he needs you for?"

"He says it's for my legal knowledge and my learning, but I have a suspicion it's to be sent to one of the foreign countries—and eventually to fight. He's looking for trusty, literate men to speak for him in Germany, Switzerland, England, and maybe even up north in Denmark and Sweden. He told me the royal house in Paris is spreading all sorts of rumors about how debauched his court is. They should talk! He needs to set the record straight."

"Oh, Jean, how exciting! You could continue your studies by traveling in all sorts of interesting places. But you've already been in Switzerland. Do you think they'll send you back there?"

I shook my head. "I've no idea, Anne." I noticed that she had begun to shiver. "Are you cold?"

"A little," she replied. "The breeze and the mist coming up off the waterfall is getting me a little damp and chilled. Maybe we should go back to shore."

Although I was dressed in a leather jerkin with leather knee breeches, I, too, felt the coolness, especially through my sleeves. I stood, caught her hand and lifted her to her feet. She boldly encircled my waist with her arm, and I reciprocated. In that awkward position, laughing, we made our way back to shore, not letting go of each other even though I had to wet my feet twice in order to maintain the embrace. We passed by the horses and gave them each a pat before we dropped our arms.

From where I stood, I could see a huge oak tree, and beyond it, a brightly lit area. We walked that way, pushing aside underbrush and getting caught in brambles. Beyond the ancient oak we found a small clearing, brightly lit by the sun. Circular and about twenty feet wide, it sloped slightly towards the creek. Moss and grass carpeted it, along with a few leafy plants that might have been flowers earlier in the season. Only a few low shrubs marred the perfection of the little sanctuary.

"Jean, this is perfect!" Anne threw herself at me, arms wide, knocking me off balance so we both went down in a heap, laughing. On a sudden impulse, I tried to kiss her mouth; she resisted me, and we play-wrestled for a few minutes, just as we had done when we were children. She was much stronger now, perhaps even a match for me, certainly harder to hold than the wild little tomboy I remembered. At last, she let me prevail, and I pinned both her arms to the moss, kissing her at last.

"Wait, Anne, while I spread my cloak." I unfastened the neck clasp and laid it on the mossy bank. She stood momentarily, brushing twigs and moss off her dress, then sat on the cloak, her knees drawn up. I joined her, and we kissed again, but then Anne pushed me away.

"You were telling me about the king. I want to hear more!" I obliged by describing a boar hunting expedition and the ferocity of those wild hogs that would recklessly attack man or horse when they were cornered or wounded. The wounds they could inflict with their long tusks could be terrible—even fatal. Then I described Navarre's tennis style. We talked for an hour more, when Anne stood, pulling me up with her. "We'd better go. Mustn't give anyone cause to wonder where I've been."

I nodded reluctantly, bent to pick up my cloak and shook it free of moss and small sticks. "When can I see you again?" I reached out to touch her cheek with my fingertips.

She took my hand in hers. "It all depends on you. When can you come back from court?"

"All I know is that Navarre intends to move north to his chateau at Nérac before long. I'll try to get back before then. Maybe a week from now. I'll send a message to let you know if and when."

"It had better be when, not if!"

Once back at the Château de Pau, I learned from the butler in charge of packing provisions and organizing the transition that the king was planning to move the court within ten days. The next day, after a game of tennis he had won, I requested another quick leave of absence. He was feeling generous, particularly so since I explained I would be seeing a beautiful young woman to say good-bye—temporarily.

I arrived at the temple in Mauléon on Sunday, after the service had begun. I entered quietly, and sat in a back pew, paid little attention to the ritual or the sermon, fixing my gaze and my attention instead on Anne's head and shoulders, seen from the back and occasionally, when she turned, from profile. As soon as the minister pronounced the benediction, I approached the Legrand family, conversed with them for a while and then quietly arranged another *rendezvous* with Anne in St. John's Wood.

We met in the hidden glade I had discovered a week before, wasting no time at the stream. I spread my cloak, and we sat, flanks pressed closely together. I put my arm around her and drew her even closer. After we had talked quietly for a few moments about the week's events, I kissed her, first on her cheek, then her brow, and then lingeringly on her mouth. This time, Anne did not resist me, but responded with equal warmth. We began kissing in earnest, our hands busy finding their way under layers of clothing, unbuttoning and stripping each other of those unwanted barriers. The sun lingered warm in the glade, and the wind could not penetrate the thick surrounding vegetation to disturb us. We grew more passionate as I practiced the rudimentary skills I had learned from encounters with tavern maids while at Toulouse University and later at Basel. Anne seemed to be meeting my every move halfway. By now, I was thoroughly aroused.

"Anne, my darling," I whispered into her ear, "I want us to… come together now. May I…?"

She fondled me with one hand, the other arm pulling me close, whispering back to me with a catch in her delivery almost like a sob, "We shouldn't be doing this so soon.... But I want you, Jean, I've always wanted you, since I was a little girl. This is the fulfillment of a dream. Yes, yes, come to me!"

When at last I lay beside her, satisfied, I covered us with the edges of my cloak, for the sun had left our little idyll and the day was beginning to wane. We talked quietly for a while about what we would do now. I told her I would have to follow the king to Nérac, but that I loved her and would come see her every chance I got.

"Write in those times when you can't come, Jean," she requested.

"Of course, I'll write. You, too." I knew that she had learned to read and write from her father, who believed that women should know at least that much book learning.

We were shivering despite our close embrace, so we rose reluctantly, brushing each other off, shaking our clothing and donning it, giving each other one last check in the waning light.

"We'd better get home, or our parents will be worried. I need to help with the evening meal, too," Anne told me.

We made our way back to the horses. Then, after a final kiss and hug, we mounted and followed our separate paths.

I thought long and hard that night about Anne. I had very little experience in such matters, but with a sinking feeling in my gut, I realized that she had not come to me as a virgin. In Béarn as in Spain, virginity was a young girl's most prized possession. I felt devastated that I had not been her first and only lover. How could she have allowed such a thing? I remembered the speed and ease of her assent to my approach. But, I rationalized, if she truly loved me and would remain faithful, I would be fulfilled whether or not she was a virgin.

Her beauty bursting with good health, her laughing and sunny personality, her frank openness and generosity—these were the things I prized most. Her very virtues, her frankness and generosity, must have been her downfall. I prayed for guidance and finally went to sleep convinced that I had received it: I would protect her by never mentioning my doubts, never questioning her. I would love, trust, and cherish Anne until—if ever—she proved unworthy of my devotion.

Chapter IV

Travel in the King's Service

A large bundle of clothing and other necessities tied behind my saddle, I returned to the Château de Pau early the next morning, still preoccupied with thoughts of Anne. Upon my arrival, I was immediately swept up in general preparations for leaving Pau.

Navarre's favorite castle was the Château de Nérac, some distance to the north, where he had spent time in his youth. News had arrived that his wife, Princess Margot, despairing of influencing her husband in any way useful to the court at the Louvre in Paris, had departed with her train of servants to a neighboring château. There, she was in contact with Catholic nobles who might help her cause. The king did not seem to worry about this development, instead feeling relieved, free at last to return to his preferred 'home.' In a remarkably short time, goaded constantly by Henri, we were packed and on the road.

Once at Nérac, our sovereign immediately settled down to his multiple occupations. Navarre—a knot of competing impulses—pursued each of his interests with concentrated energy. The repercussions of his incessant activity spread outward through the court in concentric circles like rings in the water of a still pond when a stone is dropped. The king was a large stone. If he was not hunting, he was playing tennis. If not that, he was making love to one woman after another—never remaining sexually faithful to any but paying constant tribute to the intellectual acumen of one—Corisande. Or, he was plotting strategy with his generals and councilors, striding back and forth in the great room, waving his arms, proposing a course of action in a voice that shook the walls.

He gave me the title of Councilor, something that struck me as ironic since I always felt I was the one most in need of counsel. I was kept busy running errands and writing urgent messages to his dictation, giving him occasional advice about some aspect of the law, not to mention joining the hunting expeditions and the games. I felt that I might be an inadequate legal advisor—after all, I had no practical experience, only book learning.

But no matter how occupied I was, my mind turned constantly back to Anne, her robust beauty, her shining red hair, her intensely green eyes, her frank laughter. I'd thought I was in love three times before—if one can count an early adolescent infatuation—but none of those women had evoked such strong emotions.

It was a serious undertaking to ride from Nérac to Mauléon, and the king rarely allowed me a brief holiday. Since I saw Anne so seldom—at best once a month—I began writing sonnets to her. At night, by the light of a guttering candle, I stole time from my sleep, which I knew would be fitful. I had been trained in poetic technique and as a schoolboy had written poetry in both Latin and Greek, as well as in both those languages dedicated to the King of Navarre in the Homer translation, along with others interspersed in the text. As I wrote these sonnets to my beloved, I sent each one to her with an accompanying letter, for I was wracked by fears that she would forget me or reject me in favor of another lover:

Ce tresor que j'ay pris avecques tant de peine
Je le veux avec peine encore conserver,
Tardif à reposer, prompt à me relever,
Et tant veiller qu'en fin on ne me le surprenne. (Sonnet VIII)
    This treasure that I've captured with such pains
I wish to conserve it still with equal pains,
Late to rest, prompt to rise,
And to keep such a vigil that no one can catch me by surprise.
    Since my eyes, the surest watchmen,
Cannot remain at their dwelling-place,
It could still happen, in my absence,
That another nearer seize and carry it off.
    I do not wish, though, to torment myself thus.
Thy faith alone reassures and calms my worry,
And it will change never, provided I do not change.
    On this point one must be watchful and fleet:
In winning a great prize one wins a word of praise,
But one wins a thousand in not losing it.

To this, Anne replied—stung, perhaps by my lover's doubt, "My most beloved Jean, don't fret so much about my fickleness. I've loved you since I was seven years old and you were fourteen. During all those years of your absence while you were studying in one university after another, I managed to fend off offers of marriage by three men well-liked by my family. After so many pains on my own part to keep wedlock at bay for your sake, it's not likely that I shall change. Get some sleep, my dear; close your eyes; rest. Your treasure-trove is locked away, to be opened only by your key."

I saw her again soon after that exchange. I rode back to Mauléon, returning home first to enjoy an evening of food and gossip with my family, but the next day I cantered off to the Legrand home to see Anne. We were forced by a late March snow to stay inside under the watchful eyes of her parents. Still, Anne found opportunities to draw me into hidden nooks for a quick embrace and a fervent kiss or two.

"I will marry you, my best beloved, as soon as I know what the king would have me do," I told her. "I fear he's on the verge of sending me abroad, just as I told you last January."

"But has he given you no hint as to what he'd have you do, and where? I don't know how you can live like that!"

"No, no hint as yet. You're right, Anne, the tension is beginning to tell on me."

"I can see you've lost weight, and you were too thin to start with."

"But at least I'm becoming much more expert in swordplay. Even if I blunder, I'll still be safe, because no one can hit such a slender target!" I laughed, hoping to lighten the mood.

I saw Anne again in May, after sending more sonnets along with many letters. The weather was fine and balmy, allowing us to ride out together, to find our magic glade, and to make the most passionate love. Our day together began to wane, and we started putting our clothing to rights again, preparing with great regret to leave our special place. Anne held me by the shoulders at arms' length and looked earnestly into my eyes.

"You wrote me that poem in which you spoke of another man carrying off your 'treasure'. But now, I feel it in my bones that the time is coming very soon when you'll be sent away on the king's business. I might not see you again for years. How can I be sure that you, my dearest and most precious jewel, will not be carried off by a foreign beauty? Will you remain faithful to me?"

I took her in my arms and pressed her head against my chest. "My dear, I will be true to you until death. I swear it. More assurance than that I cannot give you."

She looked up at me, her green eyes smiling. "I believe you. And when you return, we will wed."

Anne's feeling of foreboding was borne out three weeks later. Back at Nérac, Navarre took me to one side. "What do you know about Catholic politics, Jean?"

"Very little. I know more about the differences in the two faiths than I do about the power games the two factions are playing. All I know is that there's a large group of Catholics that would rather see us Huguenots dead than bother to convert us—Saint Bartholomew's Day back in 1572 is proof enough of that. And there have been other mass murders since then—but that has happened on both sides. I know that Queen Catherine de Medici would have the Gallican Church line up with the pope in Rome, and that King Philip II of Spain, to further his own schemes, is anxious to help the Catholic side here in France, but I really don't know many details."

"You're more or less correct about the general picture," Henri told me, "but we're up against the Holy League, *La Sainte Ligue.*"

"The Holy League? I've heard it spoken of but know nothing about it."

Henri explained. "The League is a political entity, mainly of ultramontanists, and dominated by the Guise family—growing like a cancer throughout France, but particularly in the north."

"I've heard a little about the Guises—too little."

"They founded the League in 1576, Jean, four years after the Saint Bartholomew massacre. They are Princes of Lorraine and have a claim to the throne of France from that quarter. They've always played a prominent role at the royal court in Paris. I suspect their hunger for power and their religious intolerance led to the massacre. Their hands drip blood with the slaughter of thousands of innocent Huguenots."

I nodded.

"The Guises' power and influence have increased tenfold because King Henri's brother, the Duc d'Alençon and heir to the throne, just died. The news came only a few days ago, and the talk is that since Henri III has no heir and is unlikely to father one, and since the Duc, last of the Valois dynasty, is dead, that leaves me, great nephew of François I. I would be King Henri IV."

At that, the King of Navarre gave a hoot of wry laughter and shook his head. "But there's many a slip... many a knife blade... between the succession and the throne. My position is unimaginably precarious... because I'm a Calvinist. The entire Catholic establishment, and most especially the Guises, would rather die than see me, a heretic, on the throne of France."

I was astonished. "But how can they stop you, if you're in the direct line of succession, Sire?"

"Power, Jean. As Princes of Lorraine, they control a large territory to the north and east of France. Also, their close relatives control most of Brittany, Normandy—including Rouen—a large area around Amiens and an equally large one around Dijon. They're just waiting to seize Paris as well.... Comparatively speaking, we are mere dwarves. Our forces are concentrated here in Béarn down in the southwest corner of the country—barely a fourth of the territory they control. Looked at in terms of landmass, the picture is frightening."

I leaned forward. "Do we have any chance at all, Sire?"

"Very little, Jean. The Guises have great popular support. Just twenty-six years ago, François de Guise defended Metz against the Germans and Charles V, the Holy Roman Emperor, who was trying to conquer and annex all of Western Europe under his rule. You remember that François de Guise recaptured Calais from the English, after they had successfully held the city for two hundred years."

"Yes, I do remember. France owes a great debt to the Guises."

Henri continued, again shaking his head. "Right now, my informants tell me they're attempting to make a pact with Philip II of Spain—our deadliest enemy—after years of fighting them. But the court won't sign until they think they have guarantees against a full-scale Spanish invasion and takeover. They'll be negotiating for some time yet, I'm sure. That gives us a little leeway."

"Leeway to do what, exactly?"

"Here's where you come in, Jean. Oh, by the way," the king interrupted himself, "did you know that I was at the court in Paris for two years, between the ages of eight and ten? My playmates were Henri de Valois, now Henri III, and Henri de Guise! That Henri—de Guise, I mean—has been my wife Margot's lover for many years. Did you know any of that?"

I was taken aback. "No indeed, Sire." I didn't know what to say. "I-I'm very sorry."

"No need. I got stuck at that court as a child because fighting broke out between the Huguenots and the Catholics for the first time, and mother was called back home. She thought I'd be safest in Paris, at court. My marriage to Margot when I was nineteen was purely a political calculation on her mother's part, meant to make peace between our two religious factions.

Sad to say, it was a calculation that failed most abjectly—the marriage took place only a week before the Saint Bartholomew's Day Massacre. But Margot and I, despite everything, have some respect for each other, even though there's no love between us. We live in a sort of armed truce. She can take any lover she pleases. It doesn't concern me—except politically from time to time."

I considered the misfortunes of royalty and merely nodded in reply.

"To come back to you, Jean. You wanted to know what we would be doing while the Guises are mobilizing a foreign army to crush us. We'll attempt to mobilize a foreign army of our own. I want you to go to Germany and Switzerland to represent me at various Lutheran courts in Strasbourg, the Black Forest, and in the Calvinist or Zwingliite towns of Switzerland, and to negotiate for German and Swiss troops to come to our aid. For an effort like mine, to crush the power of the League, doctrinal quibbles among us have been glossed over. My informants assure me it is likely they will help me. I'll give you precise instructions if you agree. What do you say, Jean?"

I had known for months that something like this was coming my way. "I'll go, of course, Sire."

"If you raise... let's say... ten thousand foot and half as many cavalry, I'll consider your mission a success. Then, you can take a holiday afterwards. Travel a little more. Learn something of foreign customs. Just send a complete report back to me before you go off on your own, with names of the princes who've promised aid, and precisely how much they've promised. I want you to relax and have fun in your life—financed by me. I'll supply you with cash."

I knelt and kissed his hand, thanking him for his largesse.

He waved me away with a smile. "Rise, Jean. I give because I like you. You'll be doing a great service for me, and I'd like to repay you—I can afford to do so. That's all there is to it!"

I was given two days to say goodbye to my family and to Anne.

This time, after I paid my respects to her family, Anne and I simply walked out of her house and down the road together. There was no time for a ride to St. John's Wood.

"I don't suppose you have any choice, Jean. If the king orders you to go, you must go."

"It's not quite as brutal as it sounds, Anne—there's a small chance for a person like me to say 'no' but if I did, I would either be out of the king's service at once, or reduced to a menial job of some sort. Henri is courteous enough to make it *sound* as though I have some freedom of choice."

"Then he is a despot, but maybe kinder than most."

"He wouldn't see it that way. He thinks his requests are always reasonable, and only a madman would see things any other way."

We crossed a stile over a stone fence and sat in the shelter of a haystack. I took Anne in my arms. "My dear, I'll miss you every minute. Traveling is no pleasure—roads are long and rough and inns unreliable and uncomfortable—so at least you are spared that."

"Humph! You know I could endure all that—probably better than you can."

I looked at her sturdy frame and nodded. "Yes, you probably could. But the world is not set up to take full advantage of the talents and strengths of women. Only Corisande, the king's mistress, seems to have found a way to use her wits to the fullest, for the good of our cause."

Anne nodded. "Fortunate woman. But I don't want to be anyone's mistress. A *wife* to someone sitting very close to me, now *that* role I could accept."

We kissed long and gently, and Anne stroked my face. "I'll remember you just as you are right now. Who knows when you'll be back?"

"Just as soon as my duties are finished. Count on it!"

She stood, reluctantly. "We've got to get back to the house. Mother will be thinking we're up to no good. Which we usually are." She laughed, shook out her skirts, and pulled me to my feet. We strolled back arm in arm, and after formal goodbyes, I mounted my horse. I turned to wave several times as I trotted away, each wave answered by Anne who stood by the gate, watching me go. This time I felt a deeper pang than ever upon leaving her. I probably would be gone for many months, and much could happen in the meantime. I only hoped that Béarn would be safe from enemy attack.

I traveled in style, with two noblemen, chief allies of the king, to escort me and add the weight of their rank and authority to what I had to say. I'm sure he would have chosen them to carry his message rather than me if they'd had my education and wider culture. Both were slightly younger than I was, one not by much.

Two servants led pack animals carrying our supplies and gifts for the German and Swiss princes. It seemed strange to have plenty of money to buy wholesome food—if such could be found on our route—and to pay for comfortable lodging at inns. We followed the same roads I had trudged on foot coming the other way, and we reached Lyon in less than half the time it had taken me.

Once in Lyon, I hastened to pay my respects to the pastor, Grégoire Toussaint and his wife, and to make them a handsome monetary present for the poor, in the name of the King of Navarre, since Henri had authorized me to make gifts of charity. The pastor was impressed and grateful, astonished to see that the scholarly pauper he had sheltered not long ago had so quickly assumed a position of responsibility with a king.

Instead of following the road I'd traveled last December that led eastward to Geneva, we went north, passing through Dijon on the way to Strasbourg. There my mission began. I was impressed with the beauty of the city, and especially of the massive cathedral, built of pink limestone, now much streaked and darkened by age, weather, and the smoke of wood fires from surrounding chimneys.

I left the two servants with the pack animals at a centrally located stable while my two attendants and I walked the narrow streets, amazingly clean, swept several times daily by the merchants. We examined their wares without buying, since there would be no way to carry an accumulation of goods with us. I fingered the thin white muslin on sale at the cloth merchant's booth and thought how lovely Anne would look in a blouse made of such stuff. It should be cut to lie low on the bosom like the one worn by the merchant's wife, who displayed abundant enticing cleavage as she stooped to gather up a bolt of brocade to show another customer.

At last, I approached the City Hall, known there as the *Rathaus*, and was lucky to find the man I was sent to contact, Fürst Wilhelm von Stade, presiding over the City Council. The three of us took seats in the area reserved for the audience, and I continued to adjust my German to the version I was listening to, a dialect I already had encountered in the merchants' shops. Fürst Wilhelm concluded the session after a debate on lowering the salt tax had been settled, and he insisted that I eat and drink with him before retiring to a comfortable, small chamber with high mullioned windows.

After he and I had settled ourselves in the conference chamber, he rang a bell and ordered dessert wine and sugar cakes to be brought in to "sweeten our discussion," as he put it. Wilhelm was an exceedingly corpulent man who barely fit between the arms of the ample chair placed opposite me at the small inlaid table. We just had risen from an impossibly copious meal of Alsatian sauerkraut replete with smoked pork chops and sausages of all types, and now he was devouring one sugar cake after another, pouring himself three glasses of sweet white wine to my one. I sipped my *Spätlese*, as I explained the situation in France and our desperate need for help from the other Huguenot princes of neighboring countries. I made it clear that Henri de Navarre would be in a position to reimburse those who could spare soldiers to come to his aid.

"I'm no warrior, myself," Wilhelm announced, biting into yet another sugar cake, while I nodded gravely to acknowledge that self-evident fact, "but I can understand clearly the seriousness of your situation." He paused to chew and swallow. "Give me some time—say about three days—to get my commanders together, and you can present your case to them. Then they'll need some time to confer and come to their own decision. Meanwhile, you can count on my support."

A week later my escorts and I met with Fürst Wilhelm's commanders. After we had agreed on the monetary terms, they promised the King of Navarre a battalion of crack infantrymen and a troop of cavalry ready to cross the border into France at his command.

This experience in Strasbourg became the pattern for later discussions, which we carried on with greater or less success. Sometimes we were delayed for weeks, sometimes refused outright for various reasons. Either the little kingdom had barely enough soldiers to protect itself, or, fearful of upsetting a precarious peace with a nearby Catholic neighbor, its ruler would simply shoo us away.

Sometimes we blundered into Catholic regions and had to make a hasty departure. The situation in Germany was utterly confused, although the westernmost provinces closest to Switzerland were generally favorable to our cause. This did not apply to Constance or St. Gallen, both steadfastly Catholic. It was at Constance where Jan Hus—a forerunner of Luther and Calvin—had been burned at the stake a century and a half before.

We worked our way slowly up the Rhine valley and as we went, the German dialects spoken by the people became less intelligible to me. Fortunately, my ear was trained, and I have a good memory for language. At the mouth of the Neckar River we turned eastward, traveling through beautiful countryside with prosperous farms and neatly harvested fields alternating with dark pine and hardwood forests, until we reached Heidelberg, part of the Palatinate, now officially Calvinist. By now it was mid-October, and the leafy trees, turning color with the season, stood out in brilliant yellow contrast against the dark pines. By that time, we had collected promises for nearly six thousand foot-soldiers and half as many cavalry.

My first view of the castle at Heidelberg was from the bridge across the Neckar. I had seen many châteaux, but none had impressed me as more beautiful or better situated. When we had at last climbed the steep mountain to the castle gates, we identified ourselves to the guard as peaceful visitors from France. They then raised the barrier to admit us and our mounts.

The castle was just as lordly inside as out, its large windows looking over the compact little city below. It was comfortably furnished, with tile or polished wooden floors covered with finely woven rugs. The rooms, large and lofty, displayed splendid tapestries or murals and ceiling paintings depicting mythological scenes of battle or victory celebrations. Oil paintings of the royal family lined the halls and the staircases.

Among the curiosities that fascinated us all were the enormous tile stoves. Art objects in themselves, covered with tiles decorated with brightly colored mythological scenes, their efficiency was truly impressive; they heated those cavernous spaces to a comfortable temperature, even though outside a chill wind blew from the north. And yet, as we approached those statuesque stoves that stood twice as tall as any man, we found that they never became so hot as to burn a person who came too close. In fact, some had benches attached to them so that one could sit with his back pressed against the stove.

Such grandeur and efficiency presented a sharp contrast to our own châteaux. Ours were generally low-ceilinged and dark with small windows, heavy black beams overhead, and the huge, drafty open fireplaces that heated the rooms inadequately, making a continuous mess with wood chips, bits of fallen bark, and ash—not to mention smoke blown back down the chimney, or simply not rising on certain heavy days, instead filling the rooms.

We were ushered into a comfortable sitting room where the Fürst received us warmly and served us glasses of fine Rhine wine. He heard my account of the alignment of forces on the Catholic side and on ours, and the plans of the Guises and their Holy League to sign a pact with Philip II of Spain. This news was always my trump card.

The Fürst broke in on my monologue. "Philip II is still a Hapsburg, and like his father, Charles V, seeks world dominion. At least, he didn't inherit the title, Holy Roman Emperor!" He slapped his thigh and then drained his glass, continuing after nodding to a servant for a refill. "I shudder to think that with this treaty you speak of, Philip might be able to consolidate all the territory from Gibraltar to Denmark under his rule."

I nodded. "Precisely, your Highness. I fear that the Guises and the King of France combined would be unable to halt Philip's progress if ever he invaded France in force."

He deliberated, and after a few more exchanges, promised two more battalions of soldiers and a squadron of cavalry to be ready to move at Henry of Navarre's signal.

Once the negotiations were over, we were invited to stay for dinner, for there was to be a large company at the Schloss, the château, that night. We readily consented, for it would further our cause to become known as widely as possible among the German aristocracy.

I found myself seated next to a somberly dressed man with a long, severe face.

"I hear you are a Huguenot, an emissary from the King of Navarre," he began.

"Yes, that is true. My name is Jean de Sponde, of Béarn."

"Gustav von Seidlitz, a disciple of Thomas Münzer."

"Ah, Thomas Münzer—I've heard the name. Was he an Anabaptist?"

Von Seidlitz turned to face me. "Yes, in the sense that he didn't believe in infant baptism at all. Dipping a baby in water does not constitute baptism, no matter what words may be said over the child!" He struck the table with his fist. "Münzer once was an associate of Martin Luther's, but he disagreed with Luther and set up a community of his own. His enemies beheaded him in Mülhausen, in 1525."

"But his influence lives on, I can see." I was curious, never having met an Anabaptist or anyone resembling one. "Tell me about your beliefs, then."

Von Seidlitz peered at me unsmilingly. "My community believes that there should be nothing added to Christian worship that was not sanctioned in the Holy Scriptures—the New Testament, I mean, not the Old Covenant, suprseded by Jesus Christ. John the Baptist went about baptizing in the name of the Lord, and of course he baptized Jesus. But all biblical instances are baptisms of adults. To be truly *baptized*, a man must give his informed consent. He must also understand what that sacrament means. An infant cannot do either."

"I see. What you say makes a good deal of sense, but what about all the babies who die in infancy? Should they not have a chance at heaven, too?"

"God will take care of His own." His reply didn't really answer my question. "Furthermore, we repudiate violence and believe that all property should be held in common. The Church should have nothing to do with the state. What is Caesar's is Caesar's; what is God's is God's."

The man glared at me, bristling with hostility. He launched into an attack upon Lutherans and Calvinists alike for their intemperance, then centered upon the doctrine that distinguishes Calvinism from other sects, the doctrine of predestination. Von Seidlitz attacked it from the angle of free will. "If man is truly to have free will—and he must, if he is to be punished for his evil choices during his life—then he cannot be predestined to be saved or damned. We know many will be damned to Hell. But if they are consigned to suffer eternally *before* they have sinned, then God is imperfect because He is unjust. That cannot be."

"But," I countered, "if God is omniscient—and He is—then he knows the future as well as the present and the past. If he knows the future, then he knows what choices we will make, even though he does nothing to determine those choices...."

We wrangled on for a good half-hour, until the last course was served, and I got away, using as an excuse that I had to consult with my assistant. I could see that von Seidlitz's passions were running high. Despite his professed pacifism, I could easily imagine him becoming enraged enough to kill a man over these doctrinal differences. After all, it was happening all around us.

Chapter V

Travel for My Own Enlightenment

Christmas came and went, and we heard that sometime in December, the Guises had signed the much-feared Treaty of Joinville with Philip II. Now, the requests we'd been making in Germany, and lately to Swiss courts, became even more urgent and convincing. We already had collected pledges for an army of twenty battalions of infantry and eight squadrons of horse—about eighteen hundred men all told. We had exhausted our supplies and had visited every Lutheran or Reformed court in the region.

After a fierce inner struggle, I sent my two companions, the servants and the pack animals home to Béarn along with my report to the king. He wanted me to travel for my own education, to broaden my horizons, but the thought that now, of my own free will, I would stay far away from Anne, pierced me with pangs of conscience.

After much soul-searching, I finally wrote her a long letter, explaining the situation. I was in a position to learn about a world I might never have another opportunity to see. Navarre had almost ordered me to take advantage of this bit of free time. I had no idea where my curiosity would lead me, so the only place where she could send replies to my letters would be to my brother in Geneva. I would pass his way upon my return journey. I hoped Anne would understand, and I assured her of my fidelity in letters and a poem playing upon the ideas of distance, travel, and yet fixation:

> *Ne vous estonnez point si mon esprit, qui passe*
> *De travail en travail par tant de mouvemens,*
> *Depuis qu'il est banni dans ces esloignemens,*
> *Tout agile qu'il est, ne change point de place.*

> Marvel not if my spirit, which passes
> From labor to labor through so many moves,
> Having been banished at such a distance,
> Agile as it is yet changes not its place.

> Whatever you see in it, whatever it may do,
> It is planted so firmly on such sure foundations
> That it would never wish to suffer changes,
> Unless it be that fire can change its place.

> These two contraries are in me alone combined,
> Feeble movement, harsh fixity:
> But would you have clearer knowledge
> That my hope moves and yet changes not at all?
> It revolves around its point of constancy
> As the Heavens revolve around their center.

I decided that I would cross the Alps into Italy to see Rome, visit the Vatican, and find out for myself what Luther and Calvin had revolted against. My own convictions had been founded upon mere hearsay evidence. I had been told all my life that the Catholic Church was corrupt, its priestly hierarchy wicked, and that it deviated too far from the simplicity of true Christianity preached by Christ in the Bible. But it seemed to me that our own version of Christianity was far from simple, and that wickedness is not a monopoly of practitioners of any version of our faith.

There were many abuses among Catholics, certainly in France's Gallican Church—for I had seen them. There were violent hatreds as well: the Saint Bartholomew's massacre of sixty thousand in Paris alone was too monstrous to be expunged by any attempt at revenge. Still, I doubted that Rome could be blamed for what the French crown along with the population of Paris had taken it upon themselves to commit. I was curious. The Eternal City drew me inexplicably, and I obeyed its call.

I spent a day in a chaotic Vatican City. January 1585 had just dawned, and the immense structure of St. Peter's Basilica was still under construction after all these years. Back in 1517, when our century was still young, Johann Tetzel began selling indulgences throughout this region to finance this building—indulgences— the subject of one of Luther's most telling theses against the Church, the one most cited by opponents of Catholicism.

I stood still, watching the activity from a safe vantage point. Oxen drawing wagons heavily loaded with beams and roof tiles plodded through deep mud toward the building site; other empty wains returned. Swarms of workmen bustled about at ground lev- el, others worked with hammer and chisel on scaffolding; and, at dizzying heights, daring men placed tile on the unfinished dome. Masses already were celebrated inside the echoing interior, and religious of all conceivable orders darted about, doing their best to prevent their robes of many styles and colors from becoming soiled by the mud as they hopped from cobbled side-streets to slip- pery wooden sidewalks and back again.

I visited the Sistine Chapel and lingered there for more than an hour until I was forced to leave by ushers who were closing it for a private Mass. The paintings so recently completed by Michelan- gelo, dead only twenty years, took my breath away. It gave a unique insight into the full glories of a Catholic imagination, and as I contemplated the depiction of God's creation—especially as He touches the hand of Adam to awaken him to ensouled existence—I felt tears of joy. How could such beauty, at the same time so deeply symbolic and instructive, be in any way wicked or contrary to God's will? I left that sacred place feeling I had learned much; what I'd seen had changed me for the better.

The day after, I explored the remains of the Roman Forum. Though pitifully neglected, those mute stones, those massive arches and vast ruined buildings shout out the majesty and power that once existed there. I stood inside the crumbling ruin of the Coliseum and like so many visitors before me and doubtless visitors to come, I could hear the echoes of roaring lions and martyr's screams, the rumble of the crowd. My reaction was opposite to that of the poet Joachim du Bellay. Those moldering ruins filled me with awe rather than depression; I felt the concentrated power of two millennia of human lives and struggles from the foundation of the city to the present, a power that rises from the very stones. The neglect, chaos and dirt of the modern city of Rome did nothing to detract from that power.

I sat ruminating on my impressions in a tavern while gnawing on a lump of hard cheese along with a piece of bread nearly as hard and drinking a glass of good red wine that the tavern-keeper called "chianti." I had presented myself that morning to the French ambassador and was invited to a dinner that same evening at our embassy. Most Frenchmen of importance in the city would be there.

Dressed in my best, I appeared at the embassy shortly after the early winter nightfall. With a start, I realized it was now the first anniversary of my icy trek across southern France, from Geneva to Béarn. So much had happened in the meantime: I had fallen in love, become an associate of the King of Navarre, had learned sword fighting and other military skills, had been sent on a mission to recruit foreign mercenary soldiers for the Huguenot cause, and was now traveling for my own edification and pleasure—in Rome.

A valet greeted me courteously in the embassy's antechamber, removed my cloak and took it to a small adjacent room. A butler conducted me into a warm and brightly lit chamber, where about fifty Frenchmen were milling around, chatting at ease. I noticed somberly dressed men I took to be Huguenots mingling freely with brightly robed clerics. To my astonishment, I saw that here on foreign soil, French solidarity had won out over confessional differences, at least for the moment.

I accepted a glass of excellent red wine from a servant bearing a silver tray. The mellow flavor spoke to me of the Bordeaux region. From another loaded tray, I took a small slice of bread and smoked meat to accompany it. I sipped and munched my way towards one of the somberly dressed persons I assumed to be of my religion and struck up a conversation. He told me he was from La Rochelle, employed in Rome as a secretary and scribe for one of our permanent representatives.

"I'm amazed that we Huguenots are represented here in Rome," I commented.

He nodded. "We're here to monitor political moves on the pope's part that affect various countries, including France—especially France. We must know what plots we need to counter—or at least to be aware of. A courier takes the news to Henri de Navarre; we don't trust it to any commercial post. Up to now, no obstacles have been placed in our way, but no one knows how long our free access will last."

I was impressed by the efficiency of my king's means of gathering news. "Ah, I see! This way, Navarre need not fear that he is receiving a garbled or erroneous report. He receives it as directly as if he were actually in Rome!"

I moved on, and as I made my way towards another co-religionist, I was accosted by a tall man in a luxurious black robe adorned with a purple-lined cape. A bishop. He looked to be about my age, very handsome, with a cleft chin, penetrating blue eyes, his dark hair cut short and combed forward like an ancient Roman's. He wore an air of authority and confidence that far outstripped anything I could muster. I learned only later that he was the Bishop d'Evreux, acting as the French ambassador to Rome, chosen by the king of France, Henri III.

He greeted me, smiling. "Good evening, Monsieur de Sponde!"

I was taken aback. "I... I fear I don't know your name, uh, Your Grace."

"Of course, you wouldn't remember. It's Jacques Davy du Perron. I was still a parish priest when I met you and was dressed in anonymous black. I dropped by Bischoff's Press in Basel two years ago in '83, the day your Homer came out. Everyone was drinking your health, so I merely joined the congratulatory crowd, shook your hand, and slipped out. I did buy your book, by the way, and I've found your notes most helpful."

"Why, thank you, Your Grace. Very kind of you." I was pleased that someone in such an exalted position had noticed my book, but uncertain just what tone to take.

He nodded, still smiling. "I was particularly struck by one of the commentaries in your book."

I stiffened, knowing exactly which one he was referring to. I pretended innocence. "Oh? What commentary is that?"

"You express amazement at those who cannot believe that one species can be transformed into another. Now what inspired you to write that note?" He leaned a mite closer to me, at the same time holding out his wineglass to be refilled by a passing valet.

I turned a little to do the same, as it gave me a moment longer to think. "To tell you the truth, Your Grace..."

"Oh, please! Just call me du Perron, or just Davy. I prefer that to Jacques. I find these interminable titles tedious!"

"Very well... ah, Father du Perron.... To tell you the truth, I was deep in my alchemical experiments at the moment..."

"You do alchemy? How fascinating! But do go on. Sorry for the interruption."

"I was deep in my experiments—and I had just transformed silver into gold. So, I *know* one species, one substance, can be transformed into another—even on our earthly plane. Of course, I believe that alchemy is a *Divine* Science, you understand…"

"Fascinating. Fascinating, Monsieur de Sponde. But I hear the dinner bell ringing. I don't believe we have fixed dinner places, so may I sit with you? I'd love to continue this conversation."

My feelings were mixed. On the one hand, I found the bishop an agreeable companion, and on the other, I considered him dangerous. But as one who often rushes into danger of that sort, I consented.

A sumptuous damask cloth covered the table, gleaming with settings of fine imported porcelain, Italian silverware, and crystal. Handsome silver candelabra on the table as well as chandeliers above our heads shed a mellow light on the proceedings. Du Perron led the way to the head of the table and seated me next to him. Once we were settled and had been served our hors d'oeuvres, I asked the bishop, "And what were you doing in Basel on that day in 1583?"

"Returning from visiting my parents. I was born in Val-de-Joux, you see, not far from there—in French-speaking Switzerland, though, as you can tell."

"Then you must have been able to follow developments in the Swiss Huguenot community from close at hand."

"True. I think this whole split in the Church is an utter tragedy. If only some reasonable concessions had been made to Martin Luther in the first place, none of this would have happened. Luther was an Augustinian monk, and a good one. He had studied his Saint Augustine well—and he saw quite clearly how the Church has deviated from the saint's teachings. I think we'd do well to re-examine those, and perhaps move back, even a little, in that direction—maybe we could entice some of you back into the fold. As things stand now, Augustine most likely would be denounced to the Inquisition and burned—at the very least excommunicated." Here he stopped and laughed, shaking his head at the same time.

I shook my head, too. "It would be harder than that to entice us Calvinists. Especially after Saint Bartholomew's and all the atrocities that have happened before and since. Doctrinally, too, Calvin is farther away than Luther."

"Yes, quite true." He looked at me earnestly. "But you, Monsieur de Sponde, have already broken with your brother Calvinists on the most important point of all."

"Which is?" I already knew.

"The Eucharist. *You* believe one species can be transformed into another. You *know* it. If mere human efforts can change silver into gold, then surely it takes no stretch of the imagination, no leap of faith, rather, to accept the doctrine that the bread and the wine offered at Holy Eucharist are transformed into the body and the blood of Christ. You could join us tomorrow, no, today, without violating your innermost convictions."

I scarcely knew how to reply. I took a deep breath. "Of course! We *all* believe that for God nothing is impossible. He can change bread and wine into the Body and the Blood any time... But" and here I hesitated again, "I was born into the Calvinist faith that denies not that God *could* change one species into another, but that he *does* so every time a priest offers the sacrament. For us, the Last Supper is a memorial, not a reenactment of Christ's ultimate sacrifice." I paused, blushing for having preached at a bishop. "I can't just abandon a lifetime of practice without thinking long and deeply about the matter."

He nodded, his smile returning. "Yes, yes, of course. I understand perfectly. Well, I'll be officiating at Mass at Santa Maria Maggiore tomorrow morning. The homily will be "The Body of Christ, the Church." I would be flattered if you would come hear me. At eleven o'clock—so you won't have to get up too early." He chuckled. "Besides, Santa Maria in itself is well worth the visit. It has splendid mosaics, fascinating allegorical works, and afterwards, be sure to visit the church of San Pietro in Vincoli—it's nearby—to see Michelangelo's statue of Moses. It was actually meant for Julius II's tomb but has recently been moved in there. You *must* see that before you leave Rome!"

"I won't promise to be there, but I'll give it serious thought."

Our conversation continued, on only slightly less dangerous subjects, such as alchemy, which he knew a little about, and the Guises and their Holy League.

"They frighten me," he said. "From time to time, I've been religious advisor at the court in Paris, and knew Charles IX rather well. Henri III has made me Bishop of Evreux and now ambassador to Rome. After I've finished my duties here, he wants me to fill the same post—of spiritual advisor, I mean—for him. I'm thinking about that. Don't see how I can refuse, really. But I hate to immerse myself in all that turmoil again—and I fear the Guises with their machinations and their willingness to sell out to Spain. They're a threat to everyone, including their more moderate coreligionists, like myself."

"You and my king Henri de Navarre think a good deal alike!"

"Not surprising. Your king has a good head on his shoulders. The Guises will force Henri III, who actually would like to ally himself with Navarre, to make a pact with them—just wait and see. They hold all the cards at the moment, and Henri III, to hold on to the throne, might have to dance to their tune."

I nodded. "You're more in touch than I am. He might, indeed."

By this time, we were picking at a dish of nuts that had been placed before us to conclude the meal, a delicious one that I had paid scant attention to, thanks to the intensity of my conversation with this engaging young bishop.

The next morning, I did attend Mass at Santa Maria Maggiore. I can't say what impelled me. There was a fair-sized crowd there, but Bishop du Perron spotted me as he processed down the aisle and nodded, smiling in apparent satisfaction. The Mass was extraordinarily beautiful in that setting, and I was moved in spite of myself.

I paid close attention to the homily, preached with great intensity in perfect Italian, which I could follow easily. As I had foreseen, he spoke of the Church as of a once unified whole, lamenting the divisions that were tearing it apart. He spoke of moderation, tolerance, and painstaking examination of new or seemingly radical ideas, reminding us that doctrines we construe as heretical may in fact be teachings that one or another of the great Fathers of the Church had put forward. We should be better scholars rather than firebrands eager to kill for ideas that we hold to be divinely inspired, whereas they might be merely human and limited, and in some cases downright wrong.

After Mass, I sat for a few minutes musing on his message, which seemed sensible and moderate. I rose slowly and walked around the church, examining its treasures, one after another. The mosaics, that, according to Bishop du Perron, date back to the time of Pope Sixtus III, the early fifth century, are a glorious blaze of gold and jewel-like color, particularly those around the high altar. I was fascinated by the depictions of various scenes in the life of the Virgin Mary and of the baby Jesus, and felt slightly guilty to be so impressed by their beauty—since we Calvinists nearly have suppressed the veneration of the Mother of God altogether.

After I left that church, I again followed the bishop's recommendation and strolled over to the nearby church of San Pietro in Vincoli, which houses Michelangelo's statue of Moses. I stood for many minutes looking at that statue, again awed by the power of Michelangelo's art. The horns on his head puzzled me, however, and reminded me of depictions I'd seen of the ancient Greeks' Great God Pan. What could have motivated this great sculptor to add horns to the head of Moses, for forty years the voice of God to the Israelites? As a Huguenot, I knew the first five books of the Old Testament well enough to know that there was no mention of horns on Moses' head in any passage. In every other way, though, the statue truly epitomized the authority of the Lawgiver, the Leader par excellence.

I left Rome after a week of further explorations, traveling onward to Assisi, to enjoy the delicate art of Giotto and Cimabue in the cathedral there. Then I visited Siena. The Palazzo Pubblico in Siena is a huge but graceful structure with delicate columns, an ornate porch and a tall, slim tower in red brick. I climbed the tower and was rewarded by a magnificent panoramic view of the city and the surrounding countryside. The still-unfinished cathedral of Siena, a vast building dating from the thirteenth century—those "Dark Ages"—amazed me with the beauty of its black-and-white marble architecture and its marble mosaic floors, depicting allegorical figures and scenes from the Old Testament. The whole effect was harmonious, though dizzying in its complexity.

Florence is another city where I could have spent months just going from church to church, palace to palace. Many great families were still constructing their monolithic buildings, each vying with the other in opulence. Here, I saw much more of Michelangelo's work, since this was his native city. The greatest of all his statues there was his David, his head turned to look in the distance with a frown of concentration, apparently taking the measure of his opponent, Goliath. That statue is touched by the hand of God just as surely as David was.

It occurred to me to wonder just what I was doing, wandering like that from place to place to view Catholic art. Who else was doing that? To be sure, there were pilgrims who came to Assisi, for instance, to worship in the city of Saint Francis, but that was different. I seemed to be the only one who felt the need to feast my eyes on the beautiful creations of long-dead artists, some well-known, others anonymous. They had spent their lives depicting the glory of God as each saw it in his own way. Except for effigies on tombs and, more recently, family portraits, there was little art devoted to the aggrandizement of the individual.

Who were we Calvinists, I wondered, to decry such an outpouring of genius, flowing without pause over fifteen centuries? How did we dare destroy works in which someone had invested his very soul? Were our churches not poverty-stricken with their whitewashed walls, plain windows, and bare crosses? The artists who had created the art works I saw were not idolaters. No, I was convinced they were using their God-given talents to glorify Him, and that their works were good in every way.

Oddly, the more I saw, the more I thought about Anne, how she would react, what she would say about this work of art or that. I wrote to her at least three times each week, describing what I had seen. Not only did my letters give me the illusion I was in direct contact with my beloved, they helped me focus on those works of art, what I found remarkable in the churches, paintings, and sculptures. I let my lyrical imagination run free, sure she would forgive my excesses.

I also continued to write poetry, sending her sonnets whenever I had perfected one. I was inspired by the doves that seemed to gather in the central squares of Italian cities, and wrote her:

Si j'avais comme vous, mignardes colombelles,
Des plumages si beaux sur mon corps attachés...
   If, like you, strutting doves, I had
Such handsome plumage attached to my body,
No force could keep my spirit captive
By the unbreakable iron of a hundred new chains:
   On the wings of the wind I would guide my flight.
I would fly to that dwelling where my treasures are hidden:
Thus, seeing my troubles falling away,
I would no longer feel this cruel absence...

By such means I tried to ensure the constancy of Anne's love, by assuring her of mine. Since I had no means of hearing from her before I reached Geneva, I could only hope that she remained true to me, as she had promised. On the one hand, I trusted her, but on the other I feared my bad luck. The perpetual uncertainty was in one way beneficial, since I thought about her and wrote her continuously. I paid a high price so the letters would go to France by boat along the Mediterranean shore, since the Alpine passes were blocked during the winter.

In early May I set out to return to France. The passes through the Alps were treacherous, still deep in snow, but I traveled those terrible roads in short stretches so as not to demand too much of my horse. I joined three other travelers, glad to have others with whom to share the rigors and dangers of the crossing. It took three weeks to cross over, thanks to periods of abysmal weather. After every new snowfall we would be delayed at an inn for days, waiting for the road to be hand-cleared enough for travelers to squeeze through the mountainous walls of ice and snow.

I spent nearly all my remaining funds on those inns, whose prices were exorbitant. They knew they could demand any amount of money and they would be paid, for we had no alternative. Accommodations were generally clean and fairly comfortable. The Swiss, I believe, are constitutionally incapable of fobbing off dirty, miserable sleeping places while charging a fortune for them. I wondered, though, what happened to those travelers who ran out of money.

Food was Spartan but palatable and wholesome enough, featuring much goat cheese or the waxy cheese made of cows' milk, honeycombed with holes, or its more flavorful cousin, gruyère. Generally, we also would be served cured beef that had been hung raw and slowly dried out in these high altitudes at low temperatures. This was presented in paper thin slices along with excellent butter and the dark bread that would stay fresh for a week. I could see that it would be just as difficult for the innkeepers to receive food supplies as it was for us to cross the mountains.

It was a great relief to come down from those heights and to ride, at long last, into Geneva, anticipating a visit with my brother Henri. But, although his landlord handed me two letters from my Anne, Henri was nowhere to be seen. He was visiting Basel, I was told. My disappointment in missing my brother was mitigated by my joy in reading Anne's letters. She assured me of her love, told of her longing to see me, and expressed delight at my descriptions and poems. I hurried on, anxious to see her and hold her close once again.

When I arrived in the now-familiar city of Lyon, I sought out my one-time benefactors, Pastor Grégoire Toussaint and his wife. They welcomed me into their home as a guest for two nights. The pastor and I sat up late talking together, and I told him about my compulsion to travel over much of Italy to see the creations by Christian artists of ages past, in architecture, painting, and sculpture. He did his best to understand me, I think, but kept shaking his head as I described, with mounting enthusiasm, one city with its artistic glories after another.

"Jean, you should have been a sculptor or a painter, I guess. But there's no room in our religion for any art other than portraiture—or perhaps landscape painting. That's what the Dutch and the Flemish have begun to turn to, that, and village tavern scenes and the like. Domestic scenes. Women sweeping hallways. I visited Picardy and the Low Countries a year or so ago and saw their paintings. Maybe you should go up there to study!"

"But I'm not a painter, Grégoire. It's more that I'm fascinated with the history of all that—century after century of praise of God. In various forms, either depictions of Jesus, Mary, or even God Himself, or depictions of other people who worshipped Him most effectively: the saints. You can't tell me that's all idolatry and sin! If it were, then all those artists would be damned. Nonsense!"

"I don't have an answer for you, Jean. Just be careful what path you're treading. You seem to be veering off the straight and narrow—as far as I'm concerned, you are. Watch that you don't get burned at the stake! Of course, I'm joking. But you're walking a dangerous path."

I passed by the cathedral the next day, and now that I knew so much more about various periods and styles of art, I mourned even more profoundly the loss of the statuary around the portals and in the niches of the façade. How onerous, exacting, and long is art in its perfection and beauty, and how easy, degraded, and quick is the act of destruction!

Our army under the Baron des Adrets' command, firing cannons at the façade, had destroyed in a day or two the art someone had labored for years—perhaps decades—to create. How to calculate the crime involved? Was it equivalent to murder? I suspected it was, for it meant killing the outward and visible expression of a soul.

I had heard that Navarre was at Nérac at the moment, preparing to leave for La Rochelle. I hurried to join him, fearing he would somehow punish me for my long absence, months longer than the time he actually had granted me. I entered the courtyard of the château and dismounted, handing the reins of my tired horse to a groom, removing my hat and slapping it against my leggings, raising a cloud of dust. But I did not stop to change out of my travel-stained clothing. Dusty as I was, I went in directly to see Henri. I mounted the steps and walked into the great hall, where the king stood next to a large table spread with a map, a group of men clustered close about him. As I entered, he interrupted himself and called to me.

"Sponde, by God, you're back! I'd begun to believe you'd gone over to the other side!"

"Not likely, Your Majesty, seeing that I raised all those soldiers to fight for our cause! But I admit that I took your permission to roam a bit too much to heart. I beg your pardon, Sire."

"Nonsense! It was a woman, I bet—maybe more than one!" Henri grinned broadly, imputing his own inclinations to me.

"No, Sire—I was educating myself in other ways. Very profitable for me, but not in any material way."

He turned back to the group around him, mostly composed of his old friends whom I knew already. "Well, come join the group, Jean," he called to me over his shoulder, "I'll play you a game of tennis later this afternoon. You're out of practice. I'm sure to win." He laughed in anticipation, and then turned back to the map, continuing to point out the positions of the Guises' forces. I peered over his shoulder and could see that the situation had become much worse in my absence.

Chapter VI

Battle

J immediately tried to get away to see my family and, most of all, Anne, but the king detained me.

"No, Jean, I need you. Partisans of the Prince de Condé around La Rochelle are claiming territory—lands that should fall under my jurisdiction. I want you to look at the documents. We've got to settle this matter—whether Condé is their sovereign or I am." And so it went.

I wrote a despairing note to Anne, explaining the situation, worked as hard as I could for a week, found a tentative solution, and asked again for a leave. But another similar problem had come up, for which I was being paid to find a solution as the king's councilor and *Maître des Requêtes*. Legal quibbles had piled up in my absence, and Henri demanded that I deal with them before he would let me go. He grew tired of my constant requests, and tried to distract me, I think, with intensified military training in my "leisure hours," until I was almost convinced that I could do him credit as a knight on horseback. I continued sending Anne notes and poems explaining the seemingly interminable delays.

June passed, then July came, and we received the news, daunting but expected, that Henri III de Valois had signed a Treaty at

Nemours, repealing all previous edicts that had given some degree of recognition to the Huguenots. He had ceded nine key towns—mainly in the north and east—to the Guises and their allies. Although he had been favorable to Navarre before, he now had done an about-face and had pledged to assist in our annihilation. We knew desperation had forced him to sign such a treaty; the princes of Lorraine, the Guises, held far more power than he did. The network of the League was far more efficient, their advisors better informed, and they had the backing of Philip II of Spain.

I knew opportunities return home would vanish completely in the wake of these events, so I asked and received the king's permission to visit them for three days. "Be back here five days from now, Jean," he ordered, "I still need your expertise as jurist. We must make plans."

The next day, I rode out, first to see Anne, and then my family. The weather was hot and sultry, tiring for me and the horse. Anne and her mother were helping the cook prepare dinner for their large family when I arrived, my face streaked with perspiration and dirt. I dismounted, and the Legrand family handyman and gardener hurried into the house to announce my presence.

Before I had finished tethering my horse, Anne ran out the door and grabbed me, embracing and kissing me fiercely, heedless of my condition. "Jean! I thought I'd never see you again!" Her voice was unsteady, breathless from emotion. She wiped her face on her apron, streaking it with tears mingled with the sweaty dirt I had transferred to her during that kiss. We stood, looking at each other, wordless for the moment. And then she slapped me. Hard.

"Anne! Why?"

She cut me off. "I've been dying to do that for months." She amazed me with the change in her expression, her voice, her stance. "I'm furious with you, Jean. All this talk about loving me, about marriage—and the first chance you get, you stay away for months. Months longer than you would have if you really cared at all."

"But Anne, I wrote to explain mysel—"

"Explain yourself? Excuse yourself, you mean. The first shock was receiving that letter telling me you were breaking your word that you'd be back as soon as your duty to the king was done. When I finally was able to put myself in your place and could see what an opportunity that was, I was able to forgive you for exploring Italy."

"But I thought of you constantly, wrote you nearly every day."

"Yes, your letters—and they came in batches, sometimes, after two or three weeks of nothing—made it clear why you wanted to stay for a while. I wrote you, but knowing you'd not get them till you were almost home took away.my enthusiasm for writing. And after you got back to France, all those excuses! Why on earth didn't you break away and come to see me? You—"

I interrupted, one hand still massaging my jaw. "But Anne, the king—"

She snapped. "The king be damned! If you had any guts, or if you loved me enough—which you obviously don't—you'd have found a way to get his permission to come back here!"

"You're right, Anne. I should have tried even harder. I did try—often. But Henri simply wouldn't let me go. Every time, he would find something that made my presence indispensable. But you know all that! I wrote about it—and sent you all those poems. I was never—would never be—unfaithful! I love you, Anne, believe me!" My voice rose in a desperate crescendo.

"Yes." She nodded, the tautness in her body relaxing, her anger waning. "I suppose you do, in your way. In writing, mainly. I certainly love *you* in spite of your behavior. At least, I believe you when you say you weren't unfaithful. Well, come on." She led the way to the fountain in the courtyard, where I washed my hands and splashed my face repeatedly, as much to cool my slapped cheek as to wash off the dirt and sweat until Anne's final inspection passed me.

"About Italy, what you saw there... your descriptions... your poems—all that was inexpressibly beautiful!"

"I felt guilty the whole time.... I wouldn't trade the experience for anything. Well, almost anything. But, Anne, I'm a different person because of what I saw and did." I dared to reach out and touch her face where mud had streaked it. "I've smeared you with dirt!" I lifted a corner of her apron, wet it in the fountain, and washed the mud off her face.

She sighed, then preceded me into the house, leading the way into the kitchen. The cook ignored the commotion to continue preparing the meal with her back to us, but I noticed a change for the better in her mother's attitude toward me. She embraced me warmly, kissing me on both cheeks, apparently oblivious of the tension between Anne and me.

"Jean, how good to see you! You're back at last after all those travels! Anne read your descriptions of the beautiful places you were seeing—you have such a gift for words! I so enjoyed your descriptions of those cathedrals! They must be spectacular, especially that one in Siena! I could almost see it. Now, Anne, Jean, the two of you, get out of the kitchen and go talk somewhere. Take him up to your rooms, Anne, dinner will be ready in just a minute."

We obeyed her without delay, climbing the stairs abreast. As soon as we had turned the corner into the hall, I stopped, uncertain of her reaction. "May I kiss you, my love?" She smiled for the first time and held out her arms. We embraced for a fervent, lingering kiss, both of us savoring the long-delayed moment to the fullest.

She gasped. "Goodness, Jean! You're like a drowning man! Or maybe I'm the one who's drowning. You've quite taken my breath away!"

She took my hand and guided me into her rooms, a tiny sitting room with chairs and a desk, and a bedroom beyond with curtained bed and armoire. She gestured to the armchair where I was to sit, then took the chair by the desk. "Look," she exclaimed, opening the desk drawer. It was filled to the brim with my letters and poems, the letters bound with a blue ribbon, the poems with wine red. "I've treasured everything you sent. Of course, I didn't read the poems to mama, but someday the world will read them and will gauge the depth and height of your love for me."

"I'm so glad you kept them, my best beloved—I would have been crushed if you had not! But what about *your* love for *me*?" I dared now to tease her, "How deep? How high?"

Her face became still. "Immeasurable, my love. I tried to express that in those two paltry letters. Never, never fear, my Jean. You were—you are—always in my heart."

I leaned over and kissed her again, lightly this time.

"I had another offer of marriage while you were gone, but The easiest way to avoid pressure was to tell Mother we had pledged ourselves to each other. After all, you're not such a bad catch. I made much of the fact that you're close adviser to the king."

"Were your parents reluctant?"

"I think they suspected we loved each other from the beginning, since you got back from Basel, I mean, but they hadn't formed an opinion about you. When I began reading your letters to Mother—the descriptive parts only, of course—she took a liking to you. In matters like that, Papa always follows Mother's lead."

We were called to dinner and joined the rest of the family around the large table. I was asked to say grace, and I recited the familiar prayer my family had always used, adding words of thanks that I could be united with them at that moment. Anne's brother Georges and I spoke at length about the troops I had raised for our king. He seemed slightly improved, although his posture was still lop-sided, and his left arm, now shrunken and bound against his chest in a sling, had become paralyzed. It was clear that Georges would be in pain for the rest of his life and would never fight again. We enjoyed the food and each other's company, and before I took my leave, I quietly arranged to meet Anne once more in St. John's wood on the following day in the early afternoon.

My parents were happy to see me, as were the two boys, Jean-Jacques and Israël. I was surprised to see how much those few months had changed them—they were maturing rapidly. They were eager to hear more about my travels, and I regaled them, as I had Anne's family, with horror tales about crossing the Alps in early May.

This time, summer flowers bloomed in our glade, mainly white and yellow daisies. The surrounding trees were still decked with leaves of a delicate green, for summer was less advanced in this sheltered nook than elsewhere. I made a garland of daisies, alternating white and yellow, for Anne's hair. After our lovemaking, she sat with her ankles crossed while I lay with my head in her lap. There were no more recriminations; it was as if a tempest had blown over and all was sunshine again.

We talked of our plans. I would have to return the next day to an uncertain future. I feared there might be battle instigated by the Holy League so could tell Anne nothing definite. As soon as I was certain just what my future duties for the king would be, I would ask his permission to marry her. I was sure he would not object. Knowing that I was now a man with family responsibilities might prevent him from sending me on extended trips in the future, although if I were called upon to fight for my king, anything could happen. In any case, I pledged to move heaven and earth to marry her before the next year was out.

Nérac was in chaos when I returned. The king was preparing to ride out and take the offensive. He began by capturing small towns near La Rochelle and sent a message to the Duc de Casimir to gather together the promised army contingents from the courts of Germany and Switzerland. The duke was to mobilize that army and cut across the mid-section of France. Navarre intended to join those forces and then carry the war northwards.

This time, I was not chosen to carry the message, instead retained as a knight in Navarre's cavalry. I was involved in a few minor battles, Although I did not personally engage an enemy, Henri did—always leading us, reckless; placing himself in great danger at times, and displaying amazing stamina and endurance.

But the Duc de Joyeuse, under orders from Henri III to prevent Navarre from joining the advancing Germans and Swiss, led his army south into Guyenne. We attempted to slip across its front to join our allies by traveling southeast but were forced to confront Joyeuse's greatly superior forces on 19 October 1587 at Coutras, a few miles northeast of Bordeaux.

We moved as fast as possible with such a mass of men and horses: four thousand foot-soldiers and twelve hundred cavalrymen, including me, and our army boasted three artillery pieces drawn ahead of us by teams of draft horses. We found ourselves in marshy country, where the Isle and the Dronne Rivers flow together before they cast their waters into the great Atlantic estuary of the Gironde to the south and west.

Our artillery was some fifteen hundred yards ahead of the main body of the army and was crossing the Isle River to the south while the rest of us were still making our way through the Dronne at the Gué-de-Sénac, Sénac Ford. I was riding close to the knot of men that always surrounded Navarre, when I noticed a flurry of activity. Someone—a scout, it appeared—had just ridden in from the northeast, shouting and pointing behind him, in the direction he'd come from. I maneuvered my horse as close as possible.

"Sire! Sire! The Duc de Joyeuse and his army are camped just north of here! They're at La Roche-Chalais! That's only two hours' ride from this very spot, Sire! They'll be on us by daylight! They outnumber us, Sire. They have two thousand horse and maybe fifty-five hundred foot-soldiers." He and his horse stood trembling and panting after their long run, sweat running off both of them.

The commanders reacted at once, shouting and waving their arms. Most advised that we flee southward across the Isle River in the direction of Bergerac. Henri sat silent amid the tumult, only half listening to what his officers were saying. When he began to speak, he dominated the rest with his energy and his decisiveness.

"If we run, we'll be strung out in the middle of a bog in total disorder, and Joyeuse can cut us down at will. We'll make a stand, and we'll make it here. Before it gets totally dark, we must scout this ground. You, Turenne, go tell those men hauling the cannons to turn around and get back on this side of the Isle River! Soissons, La Trémoille, Condé, come with me!"

I followed the king's party scouting the irregular triangle of land at the confluence of the two rivers. The triangle stretched roughly east and west, its apex pointing in the direction of the Atlantic, some miles distant. On the north side was a knoll that someone told us was called the Butte aux Loups, Wolves' Butte, overlooking the Dronne River. The knoll was cut off from the Dronne to the north by a deep little stream, the Pallar, and by a treacherous bog. South of the knoll, occupying the middle of the triangle, five hundred yards of open ground sloped slightly down from the knoll. South of that, hiding the bank of the Isle River, rose a thick forest.

By now, darkness had fallen. Henri gave orders for the soldiers to rest for a couple of hours as soon as they were completely across the Dronne and could group themselves on that dry, sloping stretch of ground between the knoll and the woods. In the distance, I could hear a commotion coming from the direction of the Isle, shouts and curses, screams and neighs of horses. The cannons had become mired in the mud, and the horses were unable to pull them back to the north shore. The struggle to get the cannon back across the river and hauled upon the knoll lasted most of the night, and it was full daylight before they were cleaned and in place, ready to fire down upon the enemy.

Meanwhile, Henri and his commanders drew up the plan of battle. With the cannon to the far left dominating the high ground, the five commanders—Soissons, Condé, Turenne, La Trémoille, and Henri himself—would group their cavalry in squadrons six deep with a front of about fifty, and between each squadron would stand a troop of arquebus soldiers. The remaining infantry would remain hidden in the woods to the extreme right.

We picketed our horses and, wrapping ourselves in our capes, lay upon our saddle blankets, our heads pillowed on our saddles, for a short and fitful rest. When the first streaks of dawn lightened the sky, we began to hear the opposing army approaching from the north. Since they had come straight down the south bank of the Dronne, they had not been forced to contend with river crossings and were no doubt in fresher condition than we were. They came on quite deliberately at a steady march, apparently confident their superior numbers would carry the day.

Despite the extreme difficulty we had suffered in rescuing and placing our artillery, all was ready long before the enemy arrayed itself for battle. We watched them deploying their cavalry and their infantry a hundred yards in front and below us. Henri murmured in surprise to see Joyeuse arrange his splendid cavalry of two thousand horse in a long line only two deep with the infantry on either end. "He thinks to envelop our horsemen with his superior numbers. But, by the grace of God, we'll break through his lines and attack his cavalry from the rear!"

We could see Joyeuse's cannon were deployed to the left of their army, across from the forest where our infantry was hidden. The guns were not pointed in that direction, instead at us, the cavalry. Having never faced cannon before, I was horrified at the prospect, but tried to keep my terror to myself. The commanders seemed to be almost blasé about cannon balls.

I was in Turenne's squadron. He positioned his horse front and center of us to speak. "If one of those hits you, you're dead, very dead. But there isn't much chance of being hit—they're too few. Just ignore them. Concentrate on the enemy cavalry. That's where the real danger lies."

Navarre shouted a command and our cannon began to fire down upon the mass of infantry on Joyeuse's right side. My own trepidation increased as I watched the havoc we were wreaking upon those helpless men, mown down several at a time. Seeing this, Joyeuse gave the command for a general advance, and we rode down the slope to meet his army, singing our Huguenot battle-hymn:

La voici l'heureuse journée
Que Dieu a faite à plein désir...
The happy day has come
That God has made at His pleasure...

I considered the words at best ironic, but it did help to release some of the tension to bellow at the top of our lungs. La Trémoille's scanty squadron on our immediate right took the first shock of the enemy advance with an exchange of pistol shots, then a clash of sabers.

The captain on the opposing side, Jean de Beaumanoir—sieur de Laverdin, as I was later told—cantered towards our lines, shouting encouragement over his shoulder. His men thundered close on his heels. They crashed into La Trémoille's lines, fighting with such enthusiasm that our people were overwhelmed. Some were cut down on the spot; some fled towards the west only to be cornered and killed. Many galloped to join our unit or Condé's on our left. But I had scant time to observe the overall fortunes of the battle. I had fired my two pistols—ineffectually, as far as I could see—and without having been hit by any of the shots from the other side. I now wielded my sword as best I could, thanking God for all those lessons over the past three years.

Luck or the Grace of God was with me, for my first fight ended abruptly when my opponent's horse stepped in a hole and my sword, aimed at my enemy's chest, pierced his throat instead. The impetus of the charge carried me past him, and I didn't see what happened to him. A tall knight with a long reach immediately attacked, a far better swordsman than I. It was all I could do to parry his blows, one of which gashed my thigh.

I felt little more than the initial pressure of the blade, for my mind was elsewhere, and my heart pumped so fast I feared it might burst. I could hardly catch my breath; my excitement and fear overwhelmed me. I made a thrust at my opponent, causing him to veer his horse from my path, right into the sword of the man next to me, who dispatched him from the side before my adversary was aware he was in danger from that quarter.

I glanced down at my leg and saw that blood had soaked my breeches and was dripping off the sole of my boot. That single glance almost cost me my life. I looked up to see a knight with blood-smeared face from a head wound bearing down upon me, thrusting straight at my heart. I twisted in the saddle and made a counter thrust that—as luck would have it, not my skill—pierced his chest. I jerked my sword out of his flesh, and he clapped his left hand over the wound, dropping his horse's reins. But meanwhile his sword had slipped between my leather jerkin and my chest when I twisted to the side, and as he fell from his horse, his death grip on his sword dragged me off balance. I caught his wrist to lessen the pressure on my chest, trying to prevent the side of the blade from cutting me further, but I couldn't prevent the fall from my own horse. Both horses plunged forward, riderless, while the Catholic soldier and I landed in a heap on the ground. By that time, he had let go the sword, which I pulled free of my clothing. My breast just above the left nipple stung from a superficial cut.

The horses and knights engaged in heavy hand-to-hand fighting had moved a few feet away northward, leaving us in relative quiet.

My enemy lay gasping at my side. I turned to him, and for the first time focused upon his bloody face. I knew him. With the tail of my shirt, I wiped the blood away, smoothing his sticky hair back from his brow.

I cried out. "Oh God in Heaven! It's Philippe Bodin! Philippe! Forgive me!" It was the young man I had known, liked and admired so much at Toulouse—the man who had advocated tolerance, and who had even discussed the possibility of a universal religion. I was overcome with grief and regret, tears flooding my eyes. I prayed aloud. "Dear God, please! Please don't let him die!"

Philippe opened his eyes and focused on me, too, for the first time. "Jean de Sponde. I knew your voice. Sorry to meet you again... under such circumstances...." His attempt at a grin ended in a grimace. "There's no priest here, Jean, so *you* be my priest... hear my confession."

"Of course, my friend. Anything."

He waited no longer but began a quick confession of the sins that seemed to bother him most—none of them mortal. When he had finished, I spoke the words I knew would matter most to him: *"Ego te absolvo, in nomine Patris, et Filii, et Spiritus Sancti, Amen."*

That was what he had wanted to hear. He squeezed my hand, nodding his thanks. "The priest will... administer the Last Rites... when they find me."

Tears were running down my face. "God forgive me." I groaned.

Philippe looked up at me for one last moment. "I forgive you, Jea-... J-..."

The light went out of his eyes. The color left his face, his head fell back, and a bubble of blood frothed out of his mouth, burst, and crept down the side of his cheek. I had been supporting his upper body, and its weight increased, dragging on my arms.

I crouched there, rocking him, while the battle screamed and crashed, though receding minute by minute. Turenne's horsemen were fleeing back northward towards La Roche-Chalais, and the sounds of further engagements became dimmer as the distance increased. At last, there were no more shots, the only sounds in my immediate vicinity a few muffled groans. We had routed a larger and better-equipped army. The Battle of Coutras would forever be celebrated as the first of Henri de Navarre's great triumphs. I was far removed from thoughts of glory, sunk in misery and guilt over having killed someone—not just anyone, but one of my best friends. At last, I felt a hand on my shoulder.

"Jean, is this the first time you've killed a man?" It was Henri's voice.

I looked up at my king, blinking away my tears. "No, Sire." I paused and cleared my throat, then continued in a less shaky voice, "I think I killed another horseman just before—though I didn't wait to watch him die. But this was Philippe Bodin, my friend. I've killed my friend, Your Majesty. May God pardon me." I bowed my head to hide fresh tears.

His hand still grasped my shoulder. "This is war, Jean. There's nothing pretty, nothing heroic in it—unless it be an act of mercy. If you hadn't killed your friend, he would have killed you, I don't doubt."

"True, Sire, because we didn't recognize each other. But how monstrous that two friends try to kill one another!"

"Yes, and brothers kill brothers, sons their fathers. If I can find a way to stop it, I shall." His face appeared severe, almost angry. "Come, Jean." He lifted me to my feet, and together we started in search of my horse.

My wounded leg had stiffened while I crouched there with Philippe, and I limped badly when I put weight upon it. New blood began to flow as I stretched the cut muscle tissue.

"Ah! I didn't see that you are wounded!" He stopped, supporting me with his arm. "When did that happen?"

"After I killed the first man, Sire. The second was about to kill me—a much better fighter. When I didn't parry one of his thrusts just right, he gashed my thigh. But one of our men stabbed him from the side. Then, I fought Philippe..."

"I see. Well, you certainly did your duty, and those lessons in swordplay stood you in good stead, just as I knew they would." He was busy tearing a long piece of cloth from the lining of his cloak, which he now tied snugly around my thigh. "This will keep the lips of the wound together, so it won't bleed so much. Remind me what your horse looks like."

I glanced around. "There he is, Sire." I pointed at him. "The bay with the white hind stockings."

"All right. Stay here, and I'll bring him to you."

We stood in a field of twisted bodies, both men and horses, blood everywhere. A few men still lived, though barely. Some called feebly for help; others merely groaned. All needed help, and I stood there, stunned.

Henri caught my frightened horse after two tries, the horse jerking and shying away from him. He stroked the quivering animal and led him back to me. "War is even harder on the animals—they have no way of knowing what it's all about." He handed me the reins. "They're more sensitive than we are to the noise and confusion. The blood smells worse to them than to us. By the way, a messenger just told me we killed the Duc de Joyeuse." He shook his head, no sign of joy on his face. "Terrible shame. There was a good man, a fine general—a life simply squandered. Fighting for the League! For Spain!" He turned aside and spat. Then, remembering me, he laid a hand on my shoulder. "Here. Let me help you into the saddle." He hoisted me, bearing much of my weight in his arms.

"Thank you, Sire! I'll never forget your kindness!"

He smiled up at me. "Go back to the medical tent near the Butte aux Loups and find one of our doctors. I'll look around here a bit more."

I left him searching for men who could be saved among those lying on the battlefield and rode slowly back through the tangled bodies of the dead, trying to prevent my horse from treading on them. Once clear of the battlefield, I thought first of my horse and rode him down to the Pallar, the stream near the knoll. I watered him, then returned to more level ground, slipped off his back, picketed him, and went in search of an orderly and a doctor. I found the orderly first. "Give my horse some hay when you get a chance. He's the bay."

I pointed him out, and the orderly nodded. "When I can."

Upon finding the doctor, I took my place in line. There were many more seriously injured men ahead of me, so I waited patiently for an hour or more until my turn came. I had plenty of time to worry about blood poisoning. More wounded men die from that than from the wounds themselves. Orderlies brought us food, and we ate where we stood or squatted. Meanwhile, teams of infantrymen retrieved the bodies of our dead, lining them up on the ground. Another large team had already begun to dig a long trench that would serve them as a common grave.

The doctor unwound the king's bandage, cut my breeches leg open, and without probing the deep gash, gave it a cursory examination. "Wound's clean," he said, "We'll just keep it tightly wrapped. Lucky it wasn't one of those arquebus wounds. They're nearly impossible to treat. If you don't get blood poison, it'll heal by itself." He wrapped a fresh bandage around it and let me go. I didn't bother to mention the shallow cut over my left breast.

By the end of the day, we all knew that our victory had been overwhelming. We had suffered badly, with four hundred ninety-six dead. But we counted over two thousand five hundred Catholic soldiers lying dead on the field, and that grisly number included their commander and my good friend Philippe. What a rush of souls were pressing through the gates of Heaven—or Hell—on that day!

Besides the dead, we had taken hundreds of men prisoner and had collected heaps of arms and equipment. Many beautiful horses wandered riderless, and we led them with us when our army retired from the battleground. Navarre had distinguished himself in the eyes of all his men by his valor during the battle, for he had fought at the head of his squadron "like a simple soldier," as one simple soldier put it. Magnanimous in victory, he set free all the prisoners. He saw no reason to humiliate men who had fought bravely for their cause.

The body of Joyeuse was brought to the Château de Coutras, where the royal party gathered later that day to view it. Henri's companions were standing around the corpse laughing and joking when the king entered. He called for silence. "This is a time for tears, not laughter—even for the victors."

I was wholly in agreement.

Chapter VII

Wedding amid Turmoil

Navarre's behavior after that battle was unfathomable. Instead of pressing his advantage and leading us to join the Duc de Casimir and the German and Swiss troops that my escort and I had labored so hard to levy, he took up the captured flags and simply went home. He rode back to the Château de Pau, where Corisande still stayed, and laid his trophies at her feet.

From the diary of Diane D'Andoins (Corisande):
Henri presented the flags he'd captured at Coutras to me and lay on his bed for a brief nap before riding to rejoin the army. He intended to lead them to join the German and Swiss soldiers led by the Duc de Casimir. I let him sleep for half an hour; then I gently woke him, offering a cup of hot tea—an exotic new drink—and a plate of sweetmeats.

"Henri, a messenger is waiting outside for you."

He roused himself with a groan. "Who from?"

"He's coming from Spain, Henri. With frightening news… that will change your plans. Here." I set the tray on the night table. "I brought you some of this new drink—tea. They say it calms the nerves and wakes you up at the same time. Sounds like a miracle to me, but the Chinamen drink it all the time."

Henri took the cup and sipped the brew, wrinkling his nose. "Give me wine, any time. This stuff needs sweetening. Is there any honey?"

"In the pitcher next to the plate of sweetmeats. Shall I bring the messenger in here?"

"Might as well."

I returned to the audience room. "The king will see you now. Follow me." The man looked exhausted, dusty, and hungry—also worried. When we entered the royal bedroom, he looked about him with an awe-stricken face. He probably had never seen such a luxurious bed in his life, not to mention the carpets, tapestries, and window hangings. I had redecorated that room. Earlier, its floor was bare, the bed was ancient and smelly with ragged curtains. There had been no window coverings at all, but plenty of trophy antlers and boars' heads on the walls.

Henri scowled. "Well?"

The messenger knelt before him, twisting his hat in his hands. "Sire, I have bad news, begging your pardon, Sire."

"I thought as much. It's all right. I always expect bad news. Tell me."

"Sire, Philip II of Spain has an army mobilized and waiting at Perpignan. If you resume your march to the east to join the army of Protestants from Switzerland and Germany, Philip will invade. He intends to take the Kingdom of Navarre while you are absent. And he can do it. There will be no defenders left here, once you're gone, Sire."

"Is that all?" Henri asked as if that were a mere detail.

"Yes, Sire." The man searched his sovereign's face in puzzlement.

"Well, then, take this." Henri gave the man several écus. "Go get something to eat and a place to sleep. I'll think what to do. Thank you." He waved the messenger away.

Once the man was gone, Henri turned to me. "Well? What do you advise, my Corisande?"

"Obviously, you can't continue with your plans. You're not strong enough by yourself to confront Spain, and even with those forces from the East, you'd be decimated. You won't like my recommendation, Henri."

"Probably not. But you're the expert chess player, not I. Let me have it." Henri flashed a momentary grin.

"I would send a messenger to the Duc de Casimir, telling him the situation, asking him to retire back to the Swiss border. That way, he can save those men and perhaps keep them in readiness. At the same time, send a message to your own army, telling them to disperse but to remain alert—all but the army of Béarn. They should return here to guard the province. Then, just sit here. Everyone will wonder why you're such a poor strategist, but no one will be provoked into attack—especially not the Spanish. If Philip once crosses into French territory, there will be hell to pay. Even the Guises, especially the Guises, will not be able to persuade him to withdraw. We simply cannot risk a Spanish invasion!"

Henri thought about that recommendation for a few hours before taking his decision. He then sent the messengers as I had suggested. The first grim news came to us some days later: the army from the East had foundered. I regret to say that the Duc de Casimir led them badly; they had lost their purpose, and they were harried by Henri de Guise who—every bit the chess player I am—shadowed and decimated them, and they soon broke up and rode for home. A day or two after that, we found out why. The messenger to the Duc de Casimir had been intercepted and killed by an agent of Philip II, the message he carried read. The agent then substituted himself for the messenger and brought the news to the Duc that Henri de Navarre was dead. The rumor spread like wildfire, and the army, in a few hours, became demoralized and confused.

The opportunity to carry the battle northward and to strike at least one more telling blow against the forces of the League was lost. However, by his inaction, my Henri had saved France. I doubt that anyone will ever know.

Jean resumes:

I was only dimly aware of the lost opportunity, the waste of months of my own time and effort to raise all those soldiers and cavalrymen from Switzerland and Germany—I was still in shock from the battle.

Ever present before my mind's eye was Philippe's blood-smeared face, his anxious, pleading eyes as he asked me to hear his confession. There was no way to relieve my guilt. If I could have had recourse to the confessional, I could have asked counsel from someone, received advice and relief—but public confession would have held me up to public shame and misunderstanding. I begged God for His forgiveness, but could not believe He heard me, nor imagine how He could pardon me.

Further prayers died on my lips. I could not pray, for as I mouthed the words, scenes from the battlefield interposed themselves. Again, I was seeing—and what was worse, smelling—the devastation of war, the heaps of the dead, men and horses now lying in mass graves between the rivers Isle and Dronne. The battle had brought back tenfold the black depression I felt when I was still in my teens, seeing the remains of those monks at Orthez lying in their desecrated graves. I could not shake the deadening sense that life was hollow, stale, flat, and unprofitable in every way. The color had been drained out of it, and it had become one uniform gray.

I had ridden home with the king's party. I returned first to the family home and took to my bed. Truth to tell, I was exhausted, having lost nearly two quarts of blood, but the wound was only my excuse, not the real reason I burrowed under my bedcovers.

Salvata, worried about my wounded leg, fretted even more about my state of mind. For her, the great victory was a cause for rejoicing. My dour attitude came as a surprise and remained a mystery, even though I tried to explain I was mourning the loss of a friend whose death I had caused. So many young, brilliant minds, so many men far better than I had been cut off in their prime. Philippe Bodin was one of them.

Mother stood over me. "One would think you were on the Catholic side." She was only half in earnest, frowning down at me as I lay there, inert, on the bed. "You're in mourning as if you'd lost the battle."

"We did lose. I mean the Christian community. Catholic or Huguenot, we are Christian—or at least, we pay lip service to being Christian. Three thousand Christian men lay dead after that morning's engagement. That's more than the population of Mauléon!"

She shook her head at me, then bathed and re-bandaged the wound that miraculously did not become infected and left me to myself.

I remained in seclusion for two days. On the third day, I lay on my side in the bed, its curtains drawn back, staring gloomily out the window as sheets of rain drifted like smoke across the ruins of our frost-killed garden. I felt rather than saw a warm presence in the room. With two light steps, the presence moved nearer and sat on the edge of the bed. Now it stooped to kiss me lightly on the cheek.

A cheery voice spoke. "My, you look bedraggled!"

"Anne!" I embraced her like a man clinging to a raft in a flood and pressed my head against her belly, inhaling her woman smell. I rolled so that my head lay on her lap and looked up into her green eyes. "We must get married, Anne, right away, while the king is distracted for a moment. I still don't know what my future holds, but I don't think I can face it without you."

She hugged me then, and we kissed, gently. She stroked my face, tracing my eyebrows with the tip of one finger. "I quite agree. We must. I want to be by your side to face whatever the future holds—for both of us. That must be our common fate, not something you have to face alone."

We published our bans, and before the month was out, we stood in the church vowing our eternal love and faithfulness, until death do us part. Both families seemed happy with our union; they wined and dined us generously, and even the king dropped in with his usual entourage to raise a glass in our honor.

Our wedding night was an unalloyed pleasure. At last we could make love in peace, at our leisure, with the blessing of the entire community. No longer must we endure the discomfort of lying together under the sky and the trees, on the bare earth, for no matter how beautiful our glade had been, it was still uncomfortable and inconvenient—and draughty! Now, in the warmth and comfort of a good bed, its curtains drawn around us, we could play lovers' games and dally as long as we liked, at last falling asleep entwined in each other's arms. Salvata laughed at us when we came downstairs, yawning, at ten the next morning.

For the moment, we did not try to set up housekeeping on our own but stayed in my parents' house. My mood was greatly lightened by Anne's forthright and optimistic presence, but at odd moments I found myself still slipping back into the same gray mood. None of the problems of France had been solved by our union. My melancholy merely awaited another moment to creep over my consciousness like a fog.

I was convinced that the king would soon have another errand for me that would disturb any domestic tranquility I managed to achieve. However, Navarre remained quietly at the Château de Pau for the next two months, so Anne and I were able to celebrate our first Christmas as man and wife. We went to the Christmas Eve service with our combined families, feasting after midnight, delighting in the *bûche de Noël,* the magnificent Christmas cake Anne had baked as a thanksgiving offering for our collective safety, and for our blessed union.

Elsewhere in France, quiet domesticity had no place. March came, and with it the news that the Prince de Condé, Navarre's powerful Huguenot ally with whom he had fought the battle of Coutras, had been poisoned. By this time, Henri had moved back to Nérac, and I spent much time on the road, traveling between my home in Mauléon and the court. I was at court when the news arrived. Rumor had it that the Princesse de Condé, Charlotte de La Trémoille, who had been married to the prince for only two years, had murdered him. In this time of divided loyalties, no one was surprised, although many were angry.

Navarre made immediate preparations to interview the Princesse de Condé, who, he had heard, had taken refuge in a small château at Saint Jean d'Angély, a small town southeast of La Rochelle. Three of his favorites were to accompany him: Duplessis-Mornay, Miossens, and my friend Max, now titled "Duc de Sully" following the recent death of his uncle. The king had taken to calling him simply "Sully," and the rest of us followed suit.

"Jean, come along, now that you're here. We may need a good sword arm."

I assumed that Navarre was being ironic but couldn't be sure—his expression remained impassive. "Of course, Sire, if you need me," I replied, already missing Anne.

We cantered northwest, sparing neither ourselves nor our horses. The roads were poor, rutted and muddy from recent rains, and Henri's herald ruthlessly forced slower traffic off the road to make way for our party. Peasants in oxcarts and nobles in carriages gawked at us cantering by them, capes flapping in the wind, clods of mud flying from our horses' hooves, swords rattling at our sides.

"Look, mama, it's King Henri!" a grubby little boy shouted, pointing at our leader as we swept past.

When the horses showed signs of exhaustion, Henri slowed to a trot and stopped at a hostelry in the nearest town, La Réole, where he requisitioned more horses. We quickly changed the tack and resumed cantering towards Saint Jean d'Angély. Since we had a late start, we were forced by darkness to stop at an inn—in Jonzac, if I remember correctly.

I was amazed at the king's stamina. He seemed as fresh and energetic as when we had started out, whereas the rest of us were stiff when we dismounted. My recently healed wound protested with stabs of pain, and I hobbled slowly into the inn. By the time I joined Henri and the others in the dining area, he had already ordered wine for us all. As I came through the door, he raised a glass and pledged our health: "May we live long and useful lives, my friends, and may our marriages be more fortunate than poor Condé's!"

He told me later, after having drunk several more glasses, that he had been notified of plots against his own life—but not from his wife Margot. "At least, wanton that she is, she's not plotting my death. Why should she? She has total freedom now. If she changed husbands, she might find herself in a much more restricted situation."

We reached Saint Jean d'Angély the next day. Before we approached the château, the king stopped at another inn and sought out the innkeeper.

"Tell Monsieur Montaubon that Henri de Navarre is here and will receive him. Do you have a private room where we can confer?"

The innkeeper nodded, bowing, now that he understood to whom he was speaking. "Yes, of course, Sire. Come right this way."

Unlike the child in the road along the way, the innkeeper had not recognized Henri as the king he was. He was not the only one. We adults set too much store by external trappings. Only those who knew him personally could pick him out of a crowd of commoners. He wore the same undistinguished clothing as the rest of us. "I save the fancy togs for state occasions," he told us. "I grew up in clothes like yours, and that's what I'm comfortable wearing."

Now, he glanced at all of us. "Yes, come along, all of you. Montaubon, my agent here, will enlighten us on Condé's death. You'd be better off knowing it straight out than guessing about it later from garbled reports."

We followed him and the innkeeper into a square, dark-paneled room in the inn's interior. The innkeeper quickly gave orders that a fire be lit in the chimney, and he brought a tray of bread, cheese, and three bottles of his best wine. The fire had barely caught, and we had just taken seats around the square table in the center of the room when there was a knock on the door. It was Montaubon, a tall, intensely dark man. He looked straight at the king, paying the rest of us no heed.

"King Henri, Your Majesty." He swept a deep bow, removing his hat.

"Yes, Montaubon! Good to see you! Let's have the report. No time to spare, man. Tell me and these other gentlemen everything you know about this miserable incident."

"Well, Sire..." He launched into a long, circumstantial account of the night Condé had died. The Prince and his wife Charlotte had retired to their rooms to be served dinner there, as was sometimes their habit. The normal procedures were followed, as far as anyone could discover. Their cook, who had been in the Condé family service for a decade or more, produced a simple meal: roast pork, boiled greens, and squash accompanied by bread and wine.

The king interrupted Montaubon's flow. "Condé showed no symptoms during that part of the meal?"

"No, Sire. But then a second bottle of wine appeared with the cheese. A fruit compote was planned for dessert. But, Sire, Condé didn't get that far. After he sipped the wine, he pushed the glass away and sat there for, maybe five minutes, staring at it as if thinking. Suddenly he stood, clutched his throat, and gasped, "I... can't breathe...." He took half a turn around, and collapsed on the floor, frothing at the mouth. The Princesse called for help immediately, but by the time the physician could get there it was too late—her husband was quite dead. The wine in the bottle was not poisoned, since Madame had also drunk a glass of it. Only the wine in the Prince's wineglass was contaminated. The conclusion was obvious. Since no one else had come into those chambers except for the serving girl who brought the tray, the assassin could only have been Charlotte de La Trémoille."

The king stood and began to pace back and forth, head bowed. He wheeled and faced Montaubon. "I hear that Charlotte has always been somewhat shaky in her allegiance to the Calvinist cause. Is my information correct?"

"So, we understand. Rumor has it she has continued to practice her Catholicism in secret and confesses from time to time—when she has the opportunity—to the Cardinal of Lorraine, no less!"

I heard it all, fascinated, for I knew that the cardinal in question was Louis de Guise, co-founder of the Holy League, fanatically opposed to our cause.

The king continued to question. "Has he been in the vicinity recently?"

"Yes, Sire, he and his entourage were at Rochefort only a week ago. The church there was celebrating some local saint, I believe. He was also collecting information about the strength of the Huguenots at La Rochelle. And the Princesse de Condé was seen to approach the cardinal after Mass."

This was apparently enough information for the king. Henri thanked Monsieur de Montaubon and paid him well. Then, without another word, he strode out of the inn, all of us following, and we rode immediately to the château. The Princesse de Condé had been warned of our approach and was waiting for us in the main audience room. She greeted us formally.

"Your Majesty, welcome to the Château Saint Jean d'Angély. Welcome, gentlemen. Sire, I see several of my late husband's friends among you. This is a sad time for me—as I am sure it is for you as well. Please, sit down; join me in a glass of wine."

Henri declined the offer none too politely. "Madame, thank you for your generous offer. However, I hesitate to accept a glass of wine from you, since I am informed your husband died, poisoned, after accepting a similar glass!"

"So, his physicians tell me, but I cannot believe it. There was no opportunity for anyone..."

The king interrupted. "Exactly, Madame. I am told that you are the person who had both opportunity and motive. I believe you know the Cardinal of Lorraine rather well?"

Charlotte's face stiffened with foreboding. "Yes, Sire, he is a friend of mine."

The king persisted. "And when did you see him last?"

"Two weeks ago, after a Mass in Rochefort, Sire. But..."

Henri nodded to two armed men who had mysteriously appeared at the door of the salon. "Arrest this woman for the murder of my friend and her husband, the Prince de Condé. Have her conducted to the prison and held there until I personally request her release."

Charlotte drew herself up with a dignity I could only admire. "Am I at least allowed to take some of my possessions, Sire?"

"Make a list when you arrive at the prison, and one of my valets will see to that." Henri was taking no chances that she might hide a weapon or send a secret message to an accomplice while she was ostensibly gathering her effects.

Thus it was that the sister of one of his finest officers, a man who had fought at Coutras as captain of the squadron to the right of Turenne's in which I fought, was imprisoned for murdering one of the greatest princes of our faith, who had also fought at Trémoille's side at Coutras.

I boggled at the savage complexity of the situation. Was the assassination motivated by politics or by faith? I hoped the former, for I could not bring myself to impute such evil to any truly Christian cause. Was Charlotte truly guilty? It was hard for me to imagine. She had not denied the charge, but neither had she confessed; only that she knew the Cardinal of Lorraine. I knew and liked a prelate, too—a certain Jacques Davy du Perron, Bishop d'Evreux. Did that make me a turncoat, or at the very least a suspect person who could be accused and imprisoned on the slightest whim?

We returned to Nérac with the king. The only good thing that had come out of this tragedy was the greater consolidation of power in the hands of Navarre.

In the rush of events that crowded upon us that year, I forgot about Charlotte de La Trémoille. I know she died, but I do not know how since every account differs. In any event, her fate was one more illustration of the horrors of our situation. I have begun to think that Navarre had taken an astute political step in imprisoning her in such a way, knowing that a trial would drag things out too much, and that, in order to appease Condé's loyalists, he would have to "do justice" swiftly. Prompt and decisive action was sure to impress his own followers as well. In his eyes, the advantages more than compensated for the destruction of the life of one woman. My own scruples, however, were not so easily laid to rest.

Within a fortnight, another incident confirmed something the king had told me during that hasty gallop to Saint Jean d'Angély. I had returned to court after spending three all-too-short days with my beloved Anne and my family. I had barely entered the courtyard of the Château de Nérac, dismounted, and was handing my horse's reins to a groom, when a dusty rider came cantering into the château precincts. The guard accosted him, and I heard him say, "I have an urgent message for the king!" He was waving a document with an impressive-looking seal. The guard lowered his pike and allowed the man to enter. I hurried to the audience room. As I entered, I called a greeting to Henri and his circle of nobles and told the king there was some sort of messenger following on my heels.

At that very moment, the man burst into the room. He advanced directly toward the king without pausing to ask permission or offering any salutation or mark of respect—not even the most perfunctory bow—holding the sealed document out towards our monarch. The man's demeanor struck me as wholly bizarre: not behaving the way a person should if he were eager to deliver a message. Instead, his face was stiff as if with fright, his gait jerky with tiny hesitations as if he were forcing himself forward to do something repugnant to him.

Somewhere within me an alarm bell rang. Who was this person? Who had sent him? No one had challenged him, and yet he had gained direct access to the king and was now bearing down upon our unarmed sovereign.

I stood to the man's left, twenty feet away. Taking long strides, then running, I tried to intercept him as he approached Navarre. From the corner of my eye, I saw Sully running from the opposite side. The messenger shifted the document to his left hand, his right feeling inside his doublet. He reached the king, who took the document. Now I was at the man's side. He pulled his hand from the doublet, and a long, curving knife gleamed like a razor in the light of the high windows. I flung my arms around his body to throw him off balance just as Max grabbed his knife arm.

The king, his attention more on the paper than on the messenger, opened the document and read aloud, "Death to heretics!" He took two swift, instinctive steps backward, raising his arms to ward off a stab. Sully and I held the would-be assassin fast. Max twisted the knife out of the man's hand, against little resistance.

"Guard!" Henri shouted, "Take this man prisoner—and see if you can find out who sent him. Who *did* send you?"

The man merely shook his head.

Those who had been in the audience room crowded around the king, all talking at once. The guard had trouble making his way through the crush. Some were thanking God for saving our king; others demanded the instant execution of the would-be assassin.

Henri shouted them down and then spoke quietly to them. "Peace, gentlemen, please! Thanks to Sully and Sponde, the man never touched me. Once again, I've been lucky." He paused to watch the guard do his work. "Lock him in our most secure cell. I'll come down presently and question him."

The guard tied the man's hands behind him and led him away. Then Henri turned to Max and me. "Thank you, Sully and Jean!" he exclaimed. "I owe the two of you my life. I must be more on my guard!

From the diary of Diane d'Andoins (Corisande):
The king made love to me last night, but only half-heartedly, for indeed, he was heartsick. Afterwards, we sat up in the moonlight, Henri's arm lying heavily on my shoulders.

"Corisande, I had terrible news today. Charlotte de La Trémoille is dead. Stabbed in her cell by a mystery assassin. I jailed her so I would appear decisive and stern to the Prince de Condé's followers—even though I suspected she was innocent. After all, what sane woman would poison her husband without hope of saving herself? The other reason was to save her life. I hoped to keep her quietly out of the way until there could be some break in this madness—until she could get a fair hearing."

"A break in this madness? You must be dreaming, Henri. Perhaps in a hundred years. But you were forced to imprison Charlotte, that's obvious. Condé's people are far more fanatical Calvinists than you are. Any number of times, they've been on the brink of disobeying you to follow the Prince's extremist policies. I've understood your mixed feelings about Condé's death, Henri, you know that. He had nearly as many loyal followers as you, and—although they claimed to be your allies—you could never tell whether they would support you or not. We've played that balancing game for years."

"All true. So, when the prince was poisoned, I knew I must act *as he* would have acted under similar circumstances. That's the only way I could hope to keep them at my side."

"Right. And now one of those bloody fanatics has murdered poor Charlotte. All she's guilty of, in all probability, is a continuing friendship with Louis de Guise, the Cardinal of Lorraine."

"For Condé's fanatics, just that much sealed a death warrant for her. And one of them carried out the sentence."

"Henri, I know you'll pay no attention, but you truly must be more careful. Yesterday's attempt on your life could repeat itself at any moment—and from any quarter—from your own people in Béarn who think you're acting too slowly, from Condé's people who fear you'll make peace with Henri III, or from the League, the most likely. You need my feminine wiles more than ever." I managed a grim grin in the moonlight.

He gave my shoulders a squeeze. "Yes, my clever Corisande, I'm well aware of all that. It's the fate of royalty in hard times. Assassination is in the air."

Jean Resumes:

A week had passed when we began hearing about increased turmoil in Paris. It seemed that my Henri's two former childhood playmates, Henri de Guise and the king, Henri III de Valois, had come into direct conflict.

But as our informants told us, Parisians had taken the real power away from both the king and the Guise family. Henri read a dispatch aloud to me.

In Paris, Catholic lawyers, royal officers, and clergy have organized themselves in "revolutionary committees of public safety" in all sixteen *quartiers* of the capital city. Known collectively as the *Seize*, they constitute a powerful political machine independent of the Guises, the municipal authorities, and especially the king.

"Henri, perhaps we can use that situation to our advantage." I held up a second dispatch. "You've read this one, of course, but this part is important." I singled out the short passage and read:

Certain Catholics have refused to abandon their king, and who stand behind Henri de Valois and even behind Henri de Navarre—recognizing him as the legitimate heir to the throne, preferring him to Henri de Guise. Such Catholics are called *"politiques"* by the Leaguers and are being persecuted as 'without religion.'

"Faint hopes, I know, Henri, but perhaps we can weave a plan around them. We could send— "

He interrupted my thoughts to read further from the first dispatch:

The League drew up a plan for the Duc Henri de Guise and his youngest brother, Charles, Duc de Mayenne, to enter Paris with several squadrons of cavalry. Henri III was outraged at this open bid for absolute power. He ordered the duke to stay away from Paris. He then strengthened the guard around the city and sent runners to the east, to summon the Swiss forces that were still mobilized, begging them to come to his aid, which they did. He quartered them in the Faubourg St.-Denis.

"Perhaps Henri de Valois can use those troops to our mutual advantage. What do you think, Henri?"

"Don't get your hopes up, Corisande. There is more:

Doubly alarmed by the popularity of Henri de Guise among the people, the king ordered the Swiss soldiers to station themselves at various strategic points within the city to assert his authority. But the people, whipped into a frenzy by sermons and speeches from prominent members of the Seize, became alarmed, fearing another massacre—of Leaguers this time. They mobilized and set up barricades by stretching chains across important streets. Meanwhile, despite the king's precautions, Henri de Guise entered the city by the Porte St.-Denis simply by pulling his hat down low and covering his nose and chin with his cape. As soon as he was inside Paris, the citizenry recognized him and crowds gathered around him, shouting, "Long live Guise, pillar of the Church—now that you are here, we shall all be saved."

My Henri shook his head. "That must gall the king. He's always been jealous of Guise's ability to attract popular support. He himself managed it for a while before he became king—he led some successful campaigns against us Huguenots. But lately, he's gained the reputation of weakness, vacillation, and temporizing."

I agreed. "There's more than a grain of truth there. And since Guise has achieved the status of national hero, his power is increased tenfold. After all, it is he, not the king, who is seen to have foiled our attempt to take over the southern half of France. Now the League can push their alliance with Philip II of Spain and can get popular backing for Spain's planned attack on England with that so-called 'Invincible Armada.' I hear its construction is nearly finished. It sounds like a wild scheme, but it may well succeed. It's clear to me that the Guises hope, by assisting Spain in attacking England, to bring down Queen Elizabeth and that way avenge her execution of Marie Stuart—herself a Guise, by the way."

Henri sighed. "Yes, the Guises have international ambitions. Spain... England... they may even try to annex the German provinces next. But here at home, they've lost no time in acting on their popular advantage, especially after Henri de Guise returned in triumph from expelling the German and Swiss armies. All Paris considers him a savior.

"Up north, the Duc de Mayenne has been doing what we've done in the south. He's taking one city, one province after another. He's already taken Picardy and captured and occupied Amiens on the coast. Despite the king's attempt to stop it, the Guises are ready to place the port at Amiens at the disposal of the Spanish Armada for assembly and supply. Mayenne tried to capture the largest and best port, Boulogne, but thank God, he was beaten off by stronger artillery fire from the city's defenders."

"Those coastal folks are too experienced. They've dealt with other swindlers from the sea, pretending to be friends, but coming ashore to rob and pillage. The Boulognese weren't about to open their port to Mayenne's friends, the Spanish."

My Henri cocked his head. True, but I fear that's the only bit of good news. He resumed reading:

The king, fearing for his own safety, had failed to use the four thousand Swiss guards at his disposal. He delayed and lost the initiative, realizing the capital was already in the hands of the League and the Guises in any case, and use of the guards might bring on another massacre. He abandoned the city, creeping out of the Louvre to his stables in the Tuileries, mounting his horse and retreating to Chartres. This left Henri de Guise and the Seize in charge of Paris. Any magistrate or official who has remained loyal to the king has been summarily dismissed. Some of his supporters are now locked up in the Bastille. Like the king, others have fled the city. The gates of the city are secured, and no one can leave or enter without express permission of the new revolutionary government.

The situation, already disastrous, became much worse within days. It was obvious to me that, with the King of France on the run, the Guises could now dictate terms. Indeed, Henri III de Valois—doubtless under pressure—soon reaffirmed the Treaty of Nemours and swore to fight heresy "without ever making peace or a treaty with the heretical Huguenots or any edict in their favor." His every move confirmed the general opinion of him as "weak, vacillating and temporizing."

He recognized the Cardinal de Bourbon, another Guise, as his rightful heir—not Henri de Navarre—and affirmed the legitimacy of the government of the Seize in Paris as well as the authority of the Duc de Guise in all military matters. The king was "persuaded" to convoke a meeting of the Estates-General for fall, to plan all-out war against the Huguenots. The latest message confirmed what we dreaded. Henri de Valois surrendered to all the Guise's demands and approved all their provisions by signing the Edict of Union in July 1588, in addition appointing the Duc de Guise commander-in-chief of his own royal army.

Jean resumes:

I was at court when the rush of bad news came in and now explained it all as best I could to Anne, as I lay with my head in her lap one day in late August. I'd been granted a couple of weeks to enjoy my life and had spent them in leisure activities at home. Anne and I traveled together to a commercial fair in Toulouse, where I insisted on buying her four yards of green watered silk for a new dress. The color was a perfect match for her eyes and would bring out the beauties of her red hair. We wandered among the booths, admiring goods of all types. I purchased a new knife of exquisite manufacture, its hilt inlaid with mother of pearl.

Back at Mauléon, we went hunting together—an activity she still enjoyed, her prowess demonstrated by the handsome buck we brought home. We played tennis, and she proved to be a powerful opponent, just as I remembered from my early adolescence. "You might even beat our king!" I exclaimed, panting and sweating after a particularly hard-fought match.

We rode out into St. Johns Wood one day and decided to visit the scene of our courtship, our idyllic glade. It was still just as lovely on this late summer afternoon, still covered in daisies and deep in moss where the shadows retained moisture despite the heat. I spread my cloak and we sat inhaling the cool, fragrant breath of the forest. Anne began to discuss the situation in France, drawing on the knowledge I had gleaned from court. "I have a terrible feeling we'll be involved in more war before long. Am I wrong?"

"If King Henri III tries to revolt against the tyranny of the Guises, or if he and they present a united front against us, we certainly will have war."

As I continued to lie with my head in her lap, Anne ran her finger over my eyebrows, smoothing them upward and outward away from my nose. "These brows are one of your most distinguishing features, my love, but they almost meet over your nose. They make you look far too intense."

"But I am intense. They probably reveal who I really am!" I laughed.

She returned to serious matters. "What will be the next step in this tragedy that's playing itself out in our country?"

"God only knows, Anne. The Estates-General is scheduled to meet in a little over a month. We'll see what comes of that.

Shortly after our tryst in the woods, I was able to tell Anne hopeful news. I had learned that a delegation of so-called "*politiques*," loyal Catholics but opposed to the League, had gone to see the King Henri III at Chartres. They were angered by the humiliation the Guises and the League had inflicted upon their king—even though the delegation might have been more loyal to the institution of the monarchy than to Henri III personally. They told him more Catholics were coming over to his side, because, as they put it, "It is a great pity when the valet dismisses his master." They dubbed themselves "royal Catholics."

I told Anne, "Even Navarre has proclaimed his loyalty to the rightful king of France, Henri III, offering to fight for him, to assure his throne against the usurper, the Duc de Guise. And he called on all good Frenchmen to do the same."

Chapter VIII

Assassinations and a Mission

ince the death of Condé, Henri de Navarre had enjoyed the support of the zealots who formerly had favored the Prince's uncompromising stand against all things Catholic. He convoked a meeting of Huguenot officials in La Rochelle. As Magistrate and Councilor, I attended and participated, along with our king's closest entourage. Our purpose was to spread the news of the League's latest moves and to counter those moves as best we could.

We first learned that the Estates-General—a parliament and advisory assembly made up of nobles, clergy, and upper bourgeoisie, normally led by the king of France—was now controlled by the League. They met at Blois. As might have been foreseen, the delegates, mainly League appointees, merely ratified the League's earlier demands and made them more rigid. Henri, Duc de Guise, and his brother Louis, Cardinal of Lorraine, were now confident they had won control, and Henri III would henceforth be a helpless puppet in their hands.

They deigned to pay him a visit in his retreat in Chartres, where he received them graciously and with generosity. Although the king appeared to accept his defeat with fortitude, he had many reasons to seethe underneath. Not only because of the Guises' treason, but because he could not forgive his ministers and his mother, Catherine de Medici, for their advice. Thanks to their counsel, he gradually had made so many small concessions to the Guises that now they were in full control.

During our debate over what steps to take to counter the spreading power of the League, I sided with the moderates. We proposed that we approach King Henri III, to try to make common cause with him against the Catholic extremists. Many voices were raised against any compromise.

I stood and spoke. "While it is true that we hold most of the southernmost provinces and the area around La Rochelle, at least half of France is in the hands of the Guises and their allies. It would make sense to combine forces with King Henri III. With his holdings and armies added to ours, we might win back the country."

A burly, sandy-haired man stood up in opposition. Dressed as a soldier wearing a breastplate, a polished cuirass buckled around his torso, he glared at me, his brown eyes flashing with anger. He thrust his undershot jaw still farther forward. "Who are you, anyway, Sponde, to propose such a weak-spined policy? Are you a secret member of the 'Royal Catholics'? I say we stick to our own people and fight to the death! Long live the Huguenot cause! Long live Coutras! Death to *all* Catholics!" A few scattered cries of approval broke the silence. I learned later that this zealot was Agrippa d'Aubigné, who conceived an enmity for me at that moment that never ceased.

Hours later, the council passed a resolution, sending it by courier to the temporary court at Chartres. It demanded that King Henri III grant us religious liberty. I had voted against it, believing that putting any such demand before the beleaguered king was pure foolishness.

Navarre began planning another military campaign to capture more towns in the vicinity of La Rochelle, to assure Huguenot dominance over the area. He set about assembling supplies and re-mobilizing his forces. During the next weeks, I supervised the couriers. Some came from field commanders, others informed Navarre of events in Paris, Blois, or Chartres. I made sure each incoming messenger was carefully vetted before allowing him access to the king. Henri kept his counsel about the content of the messages until early January 1589, when one morning he summoned me. I thought he would ask if I would be willing to accompany him on his winter campaign. Instead, he revealed the content of those dispatches.

The morning was chilly, and the audience chamber, its temperature near freezing, stood empty of the usual courtiers. I found Navarre alone in a small side room, cozy by comparison. A roaring fire drove out the worst chill. The walls and ceiling, beams and all, had been painted a yellowish cream, smudged by smoke. Musty tapestries hung ceiling to floor, depicting the naked goddess Diana interrupted at her bath, angrily transforming the hunter Acteon into a stag, his slavering dogs waiting in the background.

Henri beckoned me to his side. "It's too bad monarchs don't have divine foresight, Jean. Our demand for religious liberty arrived in Henri III's hands just as he received a message from the Estates-General, ordering him to annihilate us."

"The Fates are hostile to our cause, it would seem, Sire. Which side did he choose?" I thought I knew the answer already, fully aware that the King of France was virtually helpless, altogether at the mercy of the Guises.

"I believe our adamant demands, clashing with the ultimatum of the Estates-General, pushed him over the edge to commit terrible crimes. I knew him as a child. Only something that struck at his innermost soul would cause him to do the things he has done. I'm sure he also acted to avenge the humiliation he'd suffered at the hands of the Guises and their allies."

My breath caught in my throat. "Sire! Terrible crimes? What crimes?"

Henri raised a hand. "All in good time, Jean. Just over two weeks ago, three days before Christmas, the Estates-General still were parleying in Blois. The king conceived a desperate plan. To carry it out, he had to be in close contact with the power mongers, all lackeys of the Guises. He decided to move into the Château de La Noue."

"That's quite close to Blois, if I remember right."

"Correct. His plan involved a charade, a show of political force and resistance. He convoked his Council of Ministers for a meeting the next morning, then invited the Guise brothers, Henri and Louis, Cardinal of Lorraine, to attend."

"What did he hope to accomplish with a meeting of the Ministers?"

"Just the question the Guises asked themselves. I have further details from a clandestine messenger who was at the meeting."

"Go on."

"Duke Henri de Guise had been warned that the king hated him enough to have him killed, but, convinced of the king's weakness of will and character had replied, 'He would never dare!'"

"I begin to see where this is headed."

"You don't know the half of it, Jean. Several others close to him—the Papal Nuncio, his mother the Duchesse de Nemours, and his son—begged him not to go, but he ignored them and went to solve the mystery of the meeting of the Council of Ministers. And his brother, the Cardinal of Lorraine, came along, fully confident of the king's helplessness and their own strength."

"And they misjudged the king after all."

"To say the least. Meanwhile, the king had sent runners summoning the Quarante-cinq, the Forty-five, one of the few organizations still loyal to him and violently opposed to the League.

They're actually a squad of assassins. He posted them in his room, his antechamber, and on the stairs to his room."

"A rat trap."

Navarre gave a quick nod. "The king had instructed the Council not to begin the meeting until the Guises and the Archbishop of Lyon, a powerful Leaguer, had arrived. The meeting was called to order and discussion of the first item on the agenda had begun, when the Secretary of State, Revol, whispered to Henri de Guise that His Majesty wanted to see him in his room at once. Guise nodded and rose, relaxed and unsuspecting. The escort took him to the king's room and shut the door behind him. He froze in sudden terror as members of the Quarante-cinq confronted and saluted him mockingly, their knives drawn. He turned to run, but they seized and stabbed him to death. He slipped and fell in his own blood at the foot of the king's bed."

I shook my head, feeling slightly nauseated. "And the king watched this?"

Henri nodded and continued as if in a trance. "Cardinal Louis, too, had been summoned for an audience with the king. He was waiting in the next room when he heard the struggle and his brother's despairing cries for help, his screams of agony. He cried out, 'Henri! I'm coming!' He rushed to go to his brother's aid but was seized and overpowered. Members of the Quarente-cinq tied his arms behind him and dragged him off to a cell. He was left there trussed like a sacrificial animal. Next day he, too, became one: he was stabbed to death on Christmas Eve."

Navarre continued, his account as vivid as that of an eyewitness. I was transfixed. "Below in the Council chamber, the members could hear the screams and the noise of fighting from the upper floor. Henri III immediately sent a squad of the Quarente-cinq down to the chamber. They arrested the Archbishop of Lyon before he fully understood what was happening and could make his escape. The king then sent more members of the death squad to

Blois and Paris, to arrest the Duchesse de Nemours and Henri de Guise's son, along with a number of the leaders of the League, especially members of the Seize in Paris."

"But the king surely can't believe he can get away with such monstrous acts!"

"I fear it won't be for long, Jean. He saw that the grisly task was not finished with the assassinations and the arrests. He knew that the people—those that supported the League—would consider the two slain men as martyrs. To make sure no relics or symbols for martyrdom would be left, also to prevent the bodily resurrection of the duke and the cardinal, he had their bodies hacked to pieces and burned to ashes. These were scattered to the winds so no resurrection could be possible. His revenge thus extended to eternity. The king then piously attended Christmas Mass."

Stunned and heartsick, I paced for a while. "I suppose he thought since he was damned for killing one Guise, he might as well kill the other. But burning the brothers and scattering the ashes... then attending Mass—that is unspeakable."

"The reaction has been severe. Even his mother, Catherine, was horrified. He came to her as she lay on what would prove to be her deathbed, crowing, 'I've cut the heads off the Hydra!' and she is reported to have replied, 'My son, you never properly studied the myths of antiquity. The Hydra had nine heads, not two—and it grew two new heads for every one cut off. You've merely killed two men who left many friends.'"

I gave a bark of approval. "Ha! That woman, under other circumstances, in another country, might have made a wise ruler, though her devious schemes often misfired miserably. What was the reaction in Paris generally?"

"Just what you would expect. They appointed Charles de Guise, Duc de Mayenne, mayor of the city to replace La Chapelle-Marteau, imprisoned by the king. He also took command of the noble wing of the League. You remember he led forces against me just a few months before our victory at Coutras. That family is just like the Hydra! Heads everywhere! Anyway, the fury of the people knew no bounds. There have been screams of 'Murder! Fire! Blood! Vengeance!' For over a week, angry mobs have surged through the streets calling down the vengeance of God upon the tyrant, Henri III."

"Do you think his life is in immediate danger, Sire?"

"Of course. Just as mine is—only he is even more beleaguered than I. Assassination is everywhere right now—and it may well come to him, at any moment. With the recent loss of his mother, he must feel terribly alone."

"Ah." I remained silent for a moment. "I wonder if French politics will be any simpler in her absence. Her efforts to promote peace succeeded only in confusing the issues and causing more conflict. Was she responsible for the Saint Bartholomew massacre?"

"We'll never know how that really got started. It's not useful to try to trace that—and I was on the spot when it happened." He paused for a few moments, his gaze far away, remembering that terrible experience. When he spoke again, it was on a different subject. "As you know, I'll be starting a campaign to capture more towns around here. I want you with me, if you can spare the time from your domestic duties."

I would have loved to tell him I could not spare the time, but as a dutiful courtier, I assented. "Sire, I'll always be at your side if you need me."

He gave me three days, my usual leave time, during which I rushed back to Mauléon to lie in the arms of my beloved and bring my family up to date on the terrible events in Paris. As we sat around the dinner table on the first night, I gave them a detailed account of King Henri III's actions.

Salvata was horrified. "I will pray for him. He's sure to be damned if he gets no special grace from God!"

I nodded. "Yes, we need to pray for him. He and his entire family have been cursed, ever since the death of François I. Even before that, ever since the battle of Pavia where François received that head wound. He was never the same after that. Uneven, moody, prone to outbursts of unreasoning rage. And Henri, his second son, the least talented of his male heirs, married Catherine de Medici, who had inherited the pox from her father."

My father interrupted, "And we've seen what happened with her three sons—tainted from birth not only by Original Sin, but by the disease of their grandfather." He began to enumerate the Valois kings, Catherine's sons. "François II, so feeble he was barely able to survive his own coronation; Charles IX, also weak physically, a nervous wreck, totally dominated by his mother, and who—we'll never know for sure— may have ordered the Saint Bartholomew Massacre. And now Henri III. Henri dresses in women's clothing, surrounds himself with effeminate male hangers-on, and is incapable, it seems, of fathering an heir."

During this discussion of our poxy royalty, Anne sighed several times, glancing at me, making nervous little movements, quickly suppressed. She must need to draw me aside for a private talk. I excused myself from the table as soon as I thought it polite, and she rose at once, taking my arm and leading me upstairs to our rooms.

"Sit down, Jean, I have something urgent to tell you. In the midst of all this talk of murder and misbegotten royals, I have important news, although compared to what's happening in this country, it may seem trivial—but not to us."

I sat quickly, somehow full of foreboding. "Well, Anne, out with it! You've been anxious to tell me something ever since I got here!"

"Gently, my love. I am with child!"

This took my breath away. I had feared some sort of bad news, but these good tidings utterly surprised me. I gathered my wits enough to rise, grab her, and dance around the room. We paused, and I kissed her and held her close. "Our prayers are answered! A child of our own!" I tried to grasp the full implications of that statement as I led her to sit next to me on the side of the bed. "What joyful news! I'm delighted... but worried, too. What sort of world will our baby inherit?"

"You know better than I. A very uncertain world, my love, but it has always been so. Perhaps not quite as dangerous as now but always uncertain."

"How long have you known?"

"I suspected something by the middle of last month after skipping my monthly cycle. But recently there were other small changes. I was suspicious enough to consult your mother. She looked me over and pronounced the verdict. 'You're pregnant!' And my own mother agreed."

I wrapped my arms around Anne as we stood there, holding her and pressing my cheek into her wavy red hair. She spoke again. "Do you want a girl or a boy?"

"I really don't know, my love. A son and heir would be wonderful... but a girl would be safer with France in the turmoil she's in right now. The son and heir could come later. If we have a boy right away, we might lose him to the war."

She exhaled a great gust of air. "Well, at least we think alike on that score! Let's go back downstairs. Your mother knows about the baby, but your father doesn't. You should be the one to tell him."

We descended to share the glad news with my parents, now sitting in the salon.

I was more reluctant than ever to return to Nérac and Navarre. I wept as I parted from my Anne, and she wiped my tears on the hem of her apron. "Just be very, very careful, my love. There are now three of us to think of."

I trotted away, turned backwards in the saddle to see her standing there until the curve of the hill hid her from me.

I rode onward, torn by the pain of parting and by black foreboding. Filled with visions of death on the battlefield, I lived the battles yet to come, sure to be thrown into the struggle when Henri resumed his campaigning. I arrived at the Château already exhausted from having fought imaginary engagements. My intuition had not been wrong.

I found Navarre informally dressed, a warm robe over his shoulders, its fur collar drawn close against the evening chill. He was sitting at a small table with Corisande, playing chess—and losing, although I could tell she was trying to help him without becoming obvious.

He looked up and without preamble told me what he wanted me to do. "Go check your gear, Jean. We'll be heading out at six in the morning.

"Six, Sire? That's before daylight!"

"Yes, we'll be taking the town of Niort tomorrow. Clean your musket, oil it and your sword, and be sure your body armor's ready. I want you to have time for sleep, too—you'll need to be fresh in the morning."

"Yes, Sire." I hurried off to do my king's bidding, visiting the stables in addition to the other tasks Navarre had listed, to see that my horse was well bedded, fed, watered, his shoes still in place, his hooves in good condition. I checked my saddle, bridle and other tack, even though I take good care of them in the normal course of things. It would never do to have a girth give way in the midst of a sword fight. I slept at last, though fitfully. I worried what Anne would do if I were killed.

Henri became a whirlwind of energy. As good as his word, we captured Niort the next day, and within the week, Saint Maixent and Maillezais. The weather turned icy, and the steady blast from the snowy Pyrenees penetrated our clothing and armor. When we rode into camp the night after Maillezais surrendered, we were nearly frozen and many were ill, including our king. I noticed his spasmodic cough before we dismounted. Like the rest of us, he stamped his feet on the frozen ground, flapping his arms against his chest and sides to warm himself but was again taken with a paroxysm of coughing, and he began to spit blood. It was pleurisy, the same illness that had carried off his mother, Jeanne, and had already nearly killed him three times before.

I ran to his tent and yelled for his physician, then grabbed a blanket, quickly warming it over a campfire, taking care not to singe it. Folding the warmed surface inside, I ran to my sovereign and wrapped his body. He sighed in relief, but I could see from the hectic spots on his cheeks that he was a very sick man. His physician, Nicolas Dortoman, already at his side, assisted him back to the tent.

For the next three days, we remained in suspended animation, waiting for the crisis that would either kill or heal our Henri. Those of us close to the king huddled around campfires near his tent, watching the physician and his servants running back and forth. We felt desperate, for without him, the Calvinist enterprise would collapse. Twice, the winding-sheets were brought to wrap his dead body; twice we let out a collective groan and cries of lamentation, but twice he rallied. When the crisis came, the fever broke. Our king was saved. I noted the date as one to remember, January 10, 1589. If he had died, France would have been rudderless, and calamities undreamed of would have struck our realm, for Henri III de Valois was incapable of ruling without his mother, and the League would have lost our land to Spain.

When Navarre had regained his strength after surprisingly few days, we resumed the campaign. The remainder of January and February passed in a haze for me. I have a confused memory of brutal cold, long rides, hunger, mud and sleet, while we captured ever more towns: Loudun, Mirebeau, Vivonne, and l'Isle Bouchard. They all blur together in my mind as I try to recall each one.

Vivid, however, are the memories of the pain I felt in being separated from my Anne at a time when she would surely need me. I wrote her whenever there was a lull in campaigning, sending my letters with the king's messenger who shuttled between us and the Château de Pau. Corisande was there, and the king sent her regular reports of his progress. The messenger, for a small consideration, was happy to drop my letters off at Mauléon on his way.

Fortunately for Anne and me, there were few actual battles, since most of the towns surrendered to us after we surrounded them and cut off their supplies for a few days. Finally, on 4 March, Châtellerault fell to us, and Henri drew up a manifesto to the three estates of the realm. He asked Duplessis-Mornay and me to perfect the text he had already written. As I recall, it went in part something like this:

In the whole Estates-General at Blois not a single person dared pronounce the holy word "peace," in which the only salvation of this realm will be found. We have all done and suffered evil long enough. We have been mad, senseless and furious for four years. Is that not enough?

We billeted in Châtellerault, marking time to see what effect the proclamation, backed by the startling success of the military campaign, might have. After ten days, a carriage appeared in town, escorted by a cohort of King Henri III's cavalry. It was the Duchesse d'Angoulême, come to invite Navarre to negotiate. Our king, after settling conditions of the meeting, agreed to parley with Henri III.

The royal party met our cavalcade on the outskirts of Plessis-les-Tours, and together we all rode to the château. A crowd of the local citizens, hopeful that peace might finally be possible, had gathered to watch Henri III. There were shouts of "Long live the king." Some even shouted, "Long live the *kings*"!

Now was the time for intense negotiations. Navarre, on his side, pledged on his honor to preserve freedom of worship and liberty of conscience for all Catholics. For his part, Henri III revoked the edict of Blois, which, five months earlier, had disinherited Navarre from the legitimate succession.

In May, the two armies joined. Together, we made our way slowly towards Paris, subduing towns and villages along the way. We then took all the towns around Paris, forming a noose around the capital city. By late July, Henri III had taken the bridge of Saint-Cloud and had established himself in the town, while Navarre set up headquarters in Meudon. During all of this campaigning, I had remained close to my king, serving him in any way I could. But now that Anne's time was so close, I begged him to release me to be with her when she bore our child.

"Sire, this is our first child. It's very important to me. I can't express how important."

Henri interrupted me. "Of course, Sponde! I understand! You've been a great help to me in this entire campaign, but I can see you need a break. We all need one, but your case is truly urgent. I have a post without an occupant in La Rochelle right now. My Lieutenant General of the Sénéchaussée has resigned his position. It's not an easy job to fill, but I'm sure you can handle it. It requires collecting taxes, overseeing the police force in town, and keeping order generally. It brings in a generous monthly stipend, and a fine apartment in the center of the city goes with it. Would you like to take on the job?"

"It sounds like a godsend, Sire. I'll be able to keep my wife and child in decent style and continue serving you. Yes, Sire, I accept. I humbly thank you for your generosity."

Anne was already in labor when I arrived in Mauléon six days later. Salvata and the midwives were with her. My wife, my treasure, had been in labor for seven hours. Salvata came running out of the bedroom to embrace me.

"Jean! Thank God! She's not in trouble yet, but she's so tense! I think she's afraid, and her fear is constricting her. Come! Maybe seeing you will help!"

I followed her as she dashed back into the bedroom. Anne was seated in the special birthing chair, apparently between pangs. I knew nothing about the process of giving birth, so could only guess at what was happening. She was pale and shaking. Sweat stood out on her face, and her hair, a shade darker than it should be, lay in wet strands over her forehead. She caught sight of me, and her strained expression gave way to a glorious smile.

"Oh, Jean, I thought you wouldn't be here! I'm so glad!" She seized my hand and kissed it, pressing it to her wet cheek. I leaned over and kissed her on the mouth, then on her clammy brow. I could see her body relaxing. She heaved a great sigh. "This is the hardest thing I've done in my life, Jean, but now you're here, I think I'll be able to do it."

The midwives were tugging at me, wanting me to leave the room. "They want me out of here, Anne, but I'll be right outside, leaning against the wall beside the door. If you call my name, I'll come to you instantly."

She squeezed my hand. "You're my love. I'll be all right now."

And she was. The baby came within the hour. It was a healthy baby boy with a loud voice and an excellent appetite. And Anne, my buxom, healthy Anne, had abundant milk to offer our newborn. I was delighted to see his hair, red like hers, and eyes that seemed blue at first turned out to be gray, like mine. We decided to call him Jacques.

Two days after his birth came frightful news. The messenger on his way to the Château de Pau stopped by to chat with us. Thanks to having to deliver my frequent letters, he had come to know Anne and my family well,.

"I knew you were here, Monsieur de Sponde. Our king said to give you his greetings, and that he hopes the baby came all right."

"Just fine, Thomas. Come in, make yourself at home, and share a glass of wine with us. I'll show you the child. His name is Jacques."

"Ah! A boy! Excellent luck, Monsieur. But I'm bearing important news—and I don't know if you'll call it good or bad."

After I had served him his wine and Anne had shown him baby Jacques, we sat down together to hear his story.

"There was this young fellow, a monk it seems," he began. "The way I hear it, he was given a forged letter, supposedly from Achille de Harlay. You know Harlay, don't you? He's violently opposed to the League, and as far as anyone knows, he's in the Bastille. Anyway, the letter asked for an audience with King Henry III"

Salvata interrupted. "I'm sure one of the Seize must have forged the letter."

Thomas the messenger merely nodded. "The monk, whose name is Jacques Clément, if I remember right, got to Saint-Cloud where the king was staying, ate and drank with the servants that night. Then the next morning he presented himself and his letter at the king's bedroom."

I was incredulous. "And nobody suspected anything?"

"No—not even the servants thought it was queer when he took a huge knife out of his sleeve to cut the cheese the night before. Stupid, I think. Nobody like that Clément would get within yards of our Henri de Navarre. Anyway, the king's Procurer General escorted Clément to the royal apartment and left that monk alone with the king, since the young fellow had said his visit was confidential."

"That was the stupidest thing of all!"

"Absolutely right! As soon as that monk was alone with the king, he pulled out that knife and stabbed Henri just below the navel. The king screamed, and then the guards ran in and killed the monk. You know how those belly wounds are. It took hours for Henri to die, so that gave him plenty of time to tell his closest people that he accepted his cousin Henri de Navarre as his rightful successor. He also called in his noblemen and ordered them to be loyal to Henri IV, and they promised. Our Henri got there just as his childhood playmate was gasping his last, and only had time to embrace the King of France before the end."

I expected Navarre to recall me to Paris now that he was king at least in title, but no word came. I did hear that Paris was in no mood to capitulate to him, but was still under the sway of the Guises and the Seize, who already had declared the Cardinal de Bourbon King of France as "Charles X"—another Guise. Neither were Henri III's Catholic noblemen all that enamored of Navarre, the heretical monarch. He still had a long and arduous road to travel before he would be accepted as successor to the last Valois king.

We moved to La Rochelle as soon as Anne and the baby could travel comfortably. The apartment that went with my new position was ideal. We began with only a few sticks of furniture. I drew on my royal stipend and we bought more—a fine dining table and chairs, chests, a proper bed with velvet curtains for ourselves and a beautiful fruitwood crib for Jacques. I had brought a few tapestries and rugs, and we laid them and hung them to best advantage.

Meanwhile, I was learning my duties as Lieutenant General the hard way since my predecessor was not there to instruct me. Fortunately, his secretaries were, and I reasoned that they probably knew the job better than the former incumbent. It became apparent almost immediately that this would not be a pleasant task, especially not tax-collecting.

Nor was keeping the peace a simple matter. There were factions of Huguenots in the city, some of which were still loyal to their dead Prince de Condé and dubious of our king's morals and his true allegiance to the Calvinist faith. Others were loyally devoted to Navarre, and still others—more hidebound still—were scandalized at anyone who did not follow Calvin's *Institutes of the Christian Religion* to the letter. There were still many Catholics living in a state of siege but refusing to give up their ancestral properties. I pitied them trying to endure the flaring passions of the Huguenots around them. All of these were the people I was supposed to persuade to see eye to eye on financial matters and matters of justice! As I worked my way into it, I lulled myself with the thought that the job would become easier with greater familiarity,

We were kept informed of events around Paris by messengers who were constantly coming and going—just as they were coming and going to the Château de Pau, Corisande's chosen residence.

From the documents of Diane d'Andoins (Corisande):
Henri writes to me almost every other day. It pleases me that he thinks of me so often amid his constant battles and political scheming. I write him back at once—most times able to send a reply by the same messenger. It keeps me on my toes, since I am trying to advise him on strategy from a distance, on the strength of information that is sometimes three days old—which means that my advice will be six days out of date when it reaches him. It's almost an exercise in futility. I warn him not to take my advice too seriously in case the situation has outrun us, and I hope he heeds me. He's generally more levelheaded than I give him credit for, so I expect he is acting on his own best judgment.

The first bad news came when he told me he was forced to retreat from Paris already in August. After Henri III's assassination, a number of important noblemen did honor their word to the dying king to stay with Navarre, but the Keeper of the Seals and a host of petty noblemen deserted him, taking their men with them. The royal army fell rapidly from four hundred thousand to some eighteen thousand.

Henri was pressured to convert by the nobles—Catholic, of course—who did remain with him. François d'O reminded him that all kings of France must swear to uphold the Catholic faith, and if he intended to be crowned, he must do the same. Henri tells me he went pale with fury at that ultimatum, but he realized that the nobles had nearly eight hundred years of tradition behind them—since Charlemagne, in fact. All the kings of France have taken the oath that they would "preserve at all times true peace for the Church of God."

Also, the king must swear to be diligent to "expel all heretics from the land and also from the jurisdiction subject to the king." How can Henri expect to continue France's tradition and remain a Calvinist? Of course, the noblemen—both Catholic and Huguenot—are uneasy! He embodies the very heresy all legitimate French kings are supposed to expel.

Henri tells me he temporized, declaring that "he desired nothing more than to be instructed in the Catholic faith by a legitimate and free council—which he would convoke within six months," and that "he would maintain and preserve the Catholic, apostolic and Roman faith in its entirety, without altering anything." But that proclamation was considered a betrayal by some of the Huguenots, and La Trémoille, for example, left with many of his friends and allies.

His friends then advised him to withdraw south of the Loire, but fortunately, one of my letters reached him in time to prevent that. After all, who would believe him legitimate king of France if his decrees came from Limoges? I advised him to go north to Normandy to seek help from the English. At the same time, he sent other generals, each with a complement of soldiers, to Picardy and to Champagne, to confirm what Henri III had already done: to establish the seat of legitimate French government in Tours while Paris was still occupied.

My Henri took his little army north to Normandy. He was well received in Dieppe, sent messengers to England, and set about fortifying Dieppe and its eastern suburb Le Polet, across the River Béthune. All this because he knew that young Charles de Lorraine, Duc de Mayenne, would lead an army out of Paris to crush him. The messenger told Henri that Mayenne was boasting that he would either throw the king into the sea or bring him back to Paris in chains.

Confident as he was, Mayenne marched slowly, reaching Dieppe three weeks after Henri did. Mayenne had four thousand cavalry and twenty thousand infantry to Henri's thousand cavalry and four thousand foot-soldiers. But as at Coutras, Henri had chosen his position very well, forcing Mayenne to attack with only part of his strength.

Henri wrote me the following account: "Bloody and furious battle began at daybreak, all the more fearsome because we were outnumbered four to one. But, when their attack came upon the second trench, our troops there—Swiss troops originally recruited by Sponde—held firm, showing superhuman courage. God lifted the fog at just that moment, so our canons could begin firing from the hill where the château is located. They were decimating Mayenne and his cavalry, and he withdrew on 6 October."

Henri's appeal to the English had been answered handsomely. By the 19th of that month, his army, swelled by those new troops and by the forces of the Duc de Longueville and Jean d'Aumont, numbered fifteen thousand men. With these, he dashed south to try to take Paris before Mayenne could get back there. He attacked the city on the first of November, but came up against its fortifications, where he was stymied.

Meanwhile, Mayenne had returned and filtered his twenty thousand men into the city. Henri realized his gamble had failed, and he withdrew to Tours, where Henri III already had set up a government-in-exile, now taken over by my beloved king, Henri IV.

Chapter IX

See Paris and Die

Anne and I had christened our first-born son on 20 October, right after the king had won the unlikely victory over the Duc de Mayenne. I felt faintly traitorous as I sent a fervent prayer up to God, thanking Him for sparing me that battle. The accounts we received of it made it sound like a repeat of Coutras—although the opposing army did not suffer as many casualties. But, if I'd been there, my luck would not have held, of that I was certain.

My relatively quiet existence at La Rochelle was not to continue for long. I received a summons from King Henri on November 10. I was to ride to Tours to receive orders there. My misery at being forced to leave my little family was far worse than it had been the last time when I left Anne pregnant at Mauléon. I turned my duties as lieutenant general over to my secretaries, checked my horse for lameness or other possible problems, cleaned my tack, and set out—this time with tears on both sides. Anne had not wept earlier, but now that we had a child to think of, the possibility of losing me was more than she could bear. I embraced her, kissing her radiant hair and burying my face in the hollow between her neck

145

and her shoulder. I at last tore myself away, taking a last look at little Jacques. This time I believed that calamity would strike me, a conviction much stronger than the vague forebodings I had felt on parting from Anne before.

Tours is a bustling but small city on the banks of the Loire. It boasts charming houses, almost all with exterior staircases enclosed in towers—*tours*—leading from the ground floor to the upper stories, perhaps the source of the city's name. King Henri received me in a handsome château he had taken over from his predecessor. He invited me to eat with him and his nobles, and I was delighted to have arrived just in time for a royal dinner. We enjoyed a hearty soup of pork and chicken along with celery, carrots, and other vegetables; succulent slices of wild pig roasted whole with chestnut and apple stuffing, spinach, hot fresh white bread with a golden-brown crust, and copious quantities of excellent red wine from the region. Dessert was a tart full of cherries and apples with plenty of honey as sweetener.

I was feeling quite mellow after such a sumptuous meal, and when Henri drew me aside, my feelings of impending disaster had left me—I had let down my guard.

"I need you to get inside Paris, Jean. I must find out what's happening there. I think we've interrupted their supply lines to some extent, so they may be hungrier than they would like. I need to know that. A hungry population is more likely to come over to my side than a well fed one. Also, of course, I want you to find out just who are the Seize—the local leaders of the League—and how they've organized the city. Finally, I need you to contact the *politiques*."

"The *politiques*, Sire?"

"Yes, the Catholics who remained loyal to King Henri III. I must find out if they are willing to come to my aid in one way or another, either as additional spies from within, or as open and vocal opposition to the Guise government in Paris. Will you take this risk for me, Jean?"

My heart was in my shoes. "But Sire! My Béarnais accent will betray me at once!" My voice was tight, almost tremulous. "They'll throw me into the Bastille before I even set foot into the city!"

"Sponde, Sponde! Use your head! You speak Swiss German—that dialect they use on our eastern borders. You've spent time over there, and you know how they speak French! Pretend you're from Lorraine! Just use that accent and you'll get by. I need someone educated and intelligent for this job!"

The king's urgency and his reasoning convinced me. In any case, I could not have refused. I agreed to spy for him.

"Come back later tonight—say about ten. I'll give you detailed instructions then."

"Yes, Sire." I left his presence with dark foreboding.

I arrived on foot in Paris a week later, on 23 November. The sun was setting, highlighting in pink a huge windmill built upon a vast round tower, to the right of the road. The tower was so massive that it dwarfed the multi-story house the miller had built, using the tower as its rear wall. Just ahead of me, I could see the Porte Saint Jacques, the southernmost gate in the fortified walls of the city.

When I reached the gate, I accosted the guard and used my best imitation of a Strasbourg accent—the closest I had come to Lorraine, also presenting my bogus safe-conduct letter that identified me as Guy de Toule. The guides laughed at my speech until I drew myself up haughtily and told them that my family was very close to the Guises. They waved me through.

The rue Saint Jacques, a wide boulevard paved with cobblestones, had been swept earlier that day and was still relatively clean except for piles of horse manure. But on either side of the street crowded a bewildering jumble of tall and short houses with narrow alleyways running between the clusters of buildings—some of the alleys choked with debris, and all of them filthy and reeking, since the inhabitants appeared to dump their "night soil" out the windows.

I went towards the sound of church bells: a sacristan somewhere up ahead and on my right was ringing the Angelus. The idea had occurred to me to ask a priest or a caretaker at the church for directions, since such a person, I reasoned, would most likely take the time and the trouble to guide me.

The little church was not far away. I entered and had to remind myself to take holy water and cross myself, to genuflect towards the front of the church before seating myself in a dark corner on one of the pews. After all, I was supposed to be Catholic—a friend of the Guise family! I sat for a while, easing my tired feet, waiting for a beadle or a priest to appear, all the while breathing in the heavy scent of incense. I peered around the sanctuary at the crucifix above the high altar and the many idols, the crudely executed statues of saints and of the Virgin Mary. This was clearly a poor little church that likewise served the poor: the equivalent of a small country parish.

At last a priest did cross the sanctuary behind the altar rail, and my sudden movement as I rose from my seat caught his eye before he could duck back into the vestry. He was a short man with a shock of graying hair, his lean but square-jawed face clean-shaven.

"Father, could you help me, please? I'm new in the city—just came in the Porte Saint Jacques—and I have no idea how to find anything in such a confusion of streets. I'm looking for the Cochon Bleu Inn."

The inn would be my starting point, according to my king's instructions. I had done my best once again to imitate the accent of those Frenchmen who live along the Rhine, but I shivered inwardly at the priest's cold, dark-eyed scrutiny.

"You sound like an easterner, but you look like a southerner. And there's something a bit strange about that accent. Just where *do* you hail from?"

I lied. "I'm from Toule, Father, but my mother was from Toulouse. When I was little, I spoke like her, and my playmates and schoolmasters ridiculed me for it. There may still be some Toulouse in my speech. But never mind, Father, can you help me?"

He considered that for a moment, head on one side, then must have decided not to question my speech any further. "The Cochon Bleu. Hmmm." He paused, pursing his lips. "I think that's an inn off the Place Maubert. If it's the establishment I have in mind, you'd walk as far as the Île de la Cité. Don't cross the bridge. Turn right along the riverbank, and the first large open area you see on your right is the Place Maubert. There's a cross in the middle. Walk around the left side of the Place and take the second side street—can't miss it; it's right beside the cross. The inn should be about three doors down—if it's the one I have in mind."

I thanked him, and since he watched me still, I remembered to pause and genuflect in the direction of the tabernacle of the Host. As I was leaving the sanctuary, I passed beneath the statue of the Virgin. In case the priest was still observing me, I placed a coin in the collection box in front of the statue, knelt, lit a candle, and pushed it into an empty holder next to the flickering stubs of wax lit by previous worshippers. I bowed my head and found myself actually praying, "Blessed Mother, please keep me safe from harm for the sake of my dear Anne and my beautiful child. In the name of your son Jesus, Amen." When I rose, I glanced behind me to see the priest still standing there, staring after me. He gave me a chill. Was I that transparent?

I heaved a sigh of relief upon leaving the church and descending the steps to the street. Here, at least, I was an anonymous figure in the midst of a crowd. Most of them, I guessed, were hurrying home to their families—parents, wives, and children. Certainly, to a tasty dinner somewhere. I was hungry and tired, anxious to find the Place Maubert.

The priest's directions proved to be precise. The Cochon Bleu tavern had a placard on the door announcing rooms to rent upstairs. I entered and sat on a bench at one of the long tables with six other customers. When the tavern keeper saw my signal, he nodded in my direction. He was fully occupied bringing wine, bread, and roast pork to a noisy group of men seated around a smaller table in the opposite corner of the inn.

While he busied himself with them, I amused myself deciphering the half-literate carvings on the oak tables. The names of local "celebrities," who sought an easy route to immortality by recording their passage here, vied with obscenities carved by the angry disillusioned, the names of women surrounded by crudely carved hearts pierced by arrows, and verses of doggerel. The floor, covered with damp sawdust, had seen much wine spilled, had absorbed grease, and was scattered with gnawed bones. I'll not speak of the rest.

At last, the innkeeper came my way. He was visibly tired and disgusted with his customers and the world, and he gave me scant attention. "*Eh bien?* Well?"

I bridled at his gruff tone but voiced the phrase I had been instructed to say, the words that would identify me as an agent of Henri de Navarre. "Do you happen to have any wine from Toule? Only white wine will do."

"Wine from Toule? Are you out of your..." He stopped short in what had begun as an angry diatribe. "Ah... wine from Toule. White wine. If monsieur will follow me, I will show him what we have in our cellars."

This was the agreed-upon exchange. He had recognized me as someone sent from the legitimate successor to the throne of France. He jerked his chin toward the rear of the tavern, and I rose to follow him. At the back of the room he held open a door, and I'd barely passed through before he clapped it shut behind us. We were in a gloomy and narrow hallway, lit by a couple of candles guttering in holders hung on the plastered walls, once whitewashed and now yellowed by stains of moisture.

"You must be Guy de Toule. I have a room waiting for you upstairs. I'll send up some food and wine—you're probably hungry—and after this crowd is out of the tavern, I'll come up and give you what information I have. Come. I'll show you the room."

I obediently followed him to a narrow staircase at the end of the hall, then up into darkness. As we passed by, he snatched a candle from its holder to give feeble light to our upward progress. We climbed two floors. He apologetically explained that the first floor was rented out as a brothel.

"Keep your door barred, because drunken customers sometimes climb too far and might burst in on you in the middle of the night. I'll send a boy with your food and wine. He'll knock like this—" he rapped three times, paused, then added two quick raps. "Take a nap if you wish. I'll get your food as soon as I can, but it might be two hours before I'll be free to come talk to you."

"Thanks. I'll make myself at home."

He made a circuit of the room, lighting two candles in their holders: one on a ledge against the wall, the other in a niche above the washstand. After he had left the tiny room, I examined the bed. It had a decent straw mattress with a heavy quilt laid over it to minimize scratching, and a warm blanket.

The pillow was disreputable, saturated with stale sweat, its odor too powerful to tolerate. I would sleep in my undergarments and use my rolled-up clothing as a pillow. The other furnishings were limited to the washstand, a pitcher of water and a cracked clay basin. Under the stand, a chamber pot. I used it at once. Then, neglecting to bolt the door, I stripped off my jerkin, rolled it into a ball, and dropped on the bed. I was so exhausted from my journey that I hardly had time to toss the malodorous pillow on the floor before I was asleep, my cheek resting uncomfortably on a jerkin button. I didn't have the energy to change position.

I was awakened by a knock on the door: three knocks, a pause, then two more. I had barely sat up, bumping my head on the sloping ceiling, when a boy came in, bearing a tray of food: bread, red wine, and a generous slice of beef roast—or perhaps horsemeat—with a chunk of yesterday's bread soaked in a ladleful of brown gravy. The delicious aroma woke me completely, and I leaped to my feet, groping in my jacket pocket for a coin to give the servant who had brought this food worthy of the gods. He accepted the coin, bit down on it—an idle gesture since it was brass—then bid me good night and turned towards the door.

"What do I do with the empty dishes?"

"Leave them on the washstand, monsieur. If your door is unlocked tomorrow morning, I'll come for them."

"*Merci.*" I nodded, and he departed, closing the door behind him.

I had not realized how desperately hungry I was. I cut the bread into pieces and swabbed up the tasty gravy, savoring it for a few seconds before taking a double gulp of the red wine. It was table wine but smooth, neither biting nor musty. I finished the meal in short order, wishing for a glass of water to wash it all down, regretting the clear mountain waters of Mauléon. I left the candles burning and lay back, just for a moment, closing my eyes, thinking I would lock my door in a moment.

I awoke with a start. From my position, lying on my back with my head on my jacket, I could see that the candles had inexplicably burned down more than half way, and I felt a presence, a warmth, next to me on the bed. I sat up half-way, again bumping my head on the ceiling.

She was a delicate creature, scarcely more than a child. Her wispy, dark hair curled around a heart-shaped face with high cheekbones, eyes indigo pools reflecting the candle flames. One thin arm wound around my neck, its hand stroking my right ear, the other hand busily threading its way through the opening in my underdrawers. I was already aroused before I fought my way up through layers of fatigue to semi-consciousness. I propped my-self on one elbow, pulling her face toward mine. I gave her a pro-longed, open-mouthed kiss, hoping that my breath would not be so foul as to revolt her.

On the contrary, she groaned and pressed her body against mine, returning the kiss and thrusting her tongue into my mouth and far down towards my throat, engaging my own tongue. I recoiled, since I had never had the experience of such a kiss, at the same time finding the friction of its penetration irresistibly stimulating. By now, she had penetrated my underdrawers and was manipulating my penis. She had pulled her skirts up, naked to the waist.

I clutched her, rolling on my side, my teeth set, the temptation to enter her all but overwhelming. I doubt I would have resisted her, but I was unexpectedly rescued. Two things happened simul-taneously. With a sudden chill, I noticed she had released my neck with one arm and was now groping the pockets of my jerkin, and I heard a sharp rap on the door. Again, those three knocks, a pause, and then two more.

I leaped to my feet, pulling the jerkin from under the *gamine*. Carrying it looped over one arm, I stepped across to the door, stuff-ing my wilting penis back into my pants. I opened the door to the innkeeper, who took in the scene with cynically raised eyebrows.

He barked an order. "Marie Jeanne! Out! Now! This man is out of bounds. If I catch you back in here—or any of the others—I'll see to it, you're back on the streets!"

The willowy girl rose slowly, casually tugging her skirts down to cover her nakedness; then with a defiant toss of her head in the innkeeper's direction, she moved to the door, favoring me with a final, burningly seductive glance.

The innkeeper swiveled to face me. "You're from the provinces, of course. These women are experts in getting a man aroused before he knows what's happening. Then, when he's at the peak of ecstasy, they rob him—usually of something compromising so they can blackmail him, or at the very least all his money. A high price to pay for a few seconds of tomfoolery. I'm amazed at you. On the one hand, I'm surprised that our Henri would send someone so green, but on the other, I can see how shorthanded he must be. Must rely on novices like you." He paused for breath.

I tried to come to my defense. "I woke before she could rob me, thank God. But she'd already got me going while I was still unconscious. I fell asleep after that delicious roast."

He nodded. "Yes. Well, I knew you were hungry. A pig's foot would have tasted like ambrosia to you. Should've left the boy up here to guard you. Tell me, now, are you awake enough to memorize the instructions I'm supposed to give you?"

I was sitting with my head bowed, mentally begging my Anne to forgive me. How could I have let myself go so far? I had thought myself to be of sterling character. Was I an immoral weakling after all? I raised my head. "What? Yes, I'm awake. Just kicking myself for my foolishness. What's your name, by the way?"

"My name—real name—is no concern of yours, nor would it be of any use to you. I repeat. Are you in any condition to memorize the information I must give you now?'

I nodded. "After all this, I'm sure I am. Tell me. But if you need to give me complicated directions about streets, churches, and all that, maybe we'd better wait until you can trace it all on a piece of paper."

"I've got a map of the city. By somebody named Belleforest. It's quite clear—though it doesn't give the finer details. Good enough to get you around. I'll show you on the map tomorrow. But for now, listen."

I nodded again. "I'm here. All ears."

"Paris is divided into sixteen districts or *quartiers*."

"Yes, I know that."

"For every *quartier*, there's a Chief Leaguer."

"I see what you're getting at."

"Each *quartier* holds a meeting once a week in quiet times. But these aren't quiet times. The people are up in arms. After the assassinations of the Guise brothers, they know anything can happen. They rejoiced when King Henri III was murdered, but now they live in fear of 'the Heretic,' as they call him. They're ready to fight."

"I know that, too."

"Then it won't surprise you to hear there will be a general meeting of the Seize this Sunday. That's tomorrow. You need to be there."

"But how exposed will I be? Who will be there? Just the Seize? Or will there be a general gathering?"

"There will be a crowd of the 'faithful' there to hear the deliberations. You should be able to fit in without calling attention to yourself."

"What time?"

"After Vespers service. You'd better be there for the service, though. Be very pious. Tell a few people you're from Toule. That's in Lorraine, and everyone will assume you're one of the chosen."

"All right. So, tell me how to get there—where I'm supposed to be for this Vespers service."

"Easy. I assume you came in from the south, probably the Porte Saint Jacques. Am I right?"

"Quite right. I stopped for my first directions at a nameless little church very close to the gate. Frightening priest there. I think he suspected I was not what I was pretending to be."

"Never mind, you'll probably never see him again. Very well, if you came in that way, you probably came to the Place Maubert by way of the street that follows the River Seine eastward from the Petit Pont, the Little Bridge."

"I asked what the name of the bridge was. They called it the Petit Châtelet."

"Right. It has two names, but it's the same bridge. You go back there, only this time, you cross the bridge to the Île de la Cité. You'll be passing in front of Notre Dame de Paris. On your left, you'll see the spires of La Sainte Chapelle. Go across the next bridge and keep going north until you see the city walls and the gate, the Porte Saint Martin. On your right you'll see two churches. The taller one behind it is where the meeting will be held, in the refectory, after Vespers. Clear?"

I repeated his directions. It was a straight path northward after I had turned onto the first bridge across the Seine. "But Navarre told me my most important task would be to contact the *politiques*. Where and how am I to do that? He needs to know what support he can count on—if any."

"All in good time. Tomorrow's meeting will be more than enough of a challenge for you. Concentrate on that, and I'll give you the information you need about the *politiques* later. I'll leave you to get some sleep, now, but for God's sake, bolt your door this time before you go to sleep! If you can't even keep the girls out of your room, how can you hope to survive tomorrow's meeting with that bunch of wolves?"

I promised to bar the door and did so the minute he closed it behind him. I remember opening the dormer window a crack to let in some of the frosty night air, smelling of wood smoke. If I could stay warm enough, at least I could breathe fresher air for the remainder of the night.

The next day, I pored over the innkeeper's map of Paris, memorizing the route. Then, I wandered into the streets to see how accurate the map had been. I crossed the Seine to visit the huge public market called Les Halles to gauge how much food was making its way into the city. There was still a great deal: fresh vegetables from the country, varieties of meat and poultry, and more varieties of fish. But the carts were not heaped high, and shoppers were complaining that their favorite meat or fish was not available. The merchants shrugged, telling them that food was harder to get these days, now that so many suppliers had been cut off from Parisian markets by the Heretic's troops. "Be thankful we can supply you with basic necessities!" one of them told a disgruntled customer.

Les Halles was recognizable from a distance by the stench of rot, vegetable, meat and fish combined, but it attracted me nonetheless, since it offered so many more varieties of food than I had ever seen in one place, from wild mushrooms to calves' brains. I bought a freshly baked *baguette,* still warm from the oven, long and fragrant with a crisp, golden crust, a smoked herring along with a pat of butter and red wine from a booth selling it bottled or by the cup, and retired to a corner where I sat on the curb and ate my lunch.

I would need to tell my king there was no severe shortage of food in Paris—not yet. People were at the grumbling stage, but they were certainly not going hungry. If he were to besiege the city, it would take at least two weeks for the population to begin to feel any shortages.

Having satisfied my own hunger, I meandered down the rue Saint Eustache as far as the Porte Montmartre, then back eastward along the curve of the city walls. As I walked, I could see the arms of more huge windmills somewhere beyond those walls, turning majestically in the wind. They must be grinding the grain that supplied the city with its daily bread. Bakeries seemed to be producing plenty of bread, so far. I strolled past the Porte and the rue Saint-Denis, finally ending up at the Porte Saint Martin. From there, the church where the meeting would take place was clearly visible. I decided to go inside, just to be sure I could find my way later, after dark. The interior was badly lit by a few candles and the sooty stained-glass windows. Nonetheless, I could see finely wrought statues here—particularly one of the Blessed Virgin. She must be centuries old, I mused as I stood beneath her, contemplating the faded polychrome that enhanced rather than detracted from her beauty—the graceful sidewise twist of her body, the delicate features of her face as she looked in loving adoration at the Christ child in her arms. The other statue of great artistic value depicted Saint Martin, for whom the church was named. He was shown cutting his cloak in half with his sword to share it with a beggar, in whom he recognized Christ.

I returned to the Cochon Bleu in time for a meal, my anxiety mounting. My disguise as a citizen of Lorraine would soon be tested.

Vespers service was half over, and I had spent most of it observing the congregation from the darkest corner I could find. The priest had preceded the service with a homily frightening in its violence, calling down the wrath of God upon the heretic servant of Satan, Henri de Navarre, and all those who serve him. His strident calls to vigilance and battle readiness drew answering mutterings and growls from members of the congregation. A far cry from Jesus' message in the Beatitudes!

The priest announced the meeting of the Seize and the congregation in the refectory after the service. As soon as Vespers was over, he led the way, the entire assembly of nearly two hundred following. I detached myself from the shadow of the column near my seat and joined the mass of worshippers that followed the vanguard.

The Seize entered the refectory first and established themselves at the head table. I was impressed with their apparent social standing, mainly *noblesse de robe*—upper bourgeois: lawyers, clergy, and wealthy merchants. These were the leaders of the community. The rest of us were a motley group, although working class people were in the minority. Those who seemed to be filling more responsible though subordinate positions took all the chairs around the tables; the rest of us remained standing in the open area near the entrance door.

I paid close attention to the proceedings. The priest who had given the inflammatory address was the *chef* of this *quartier,* but the man who led the meeting was Charles de Guise, Duc de Mayenne himself, appointed mayor of Paris by the League. I memorized names as, one after another, the *chefs,* the leaders of the other fifteen *quartiers,* were called upon to report. There was Jean Boucher, Jacques de Suresnes, Robert Bottin, Eduard de Suffren—and on down the list, until he called on someone I knew. Father Georges Marquet. The priest, who had been sitting with his back to me, stood up. Clean-shaven, square jawed, with a thatch of gray hair, it was the priest from the church near the Porte Saint Jacques. Was it merely my insecurity, or did he single me out with his intense, hostile eyes?

As he was called, each man rose and reported on the munitions available in his *quartier* and on the number of able-bodied men who could be mobilized to defend it. The Duc de Mayenne also spoke to the assembly about the need to be vigilant, for everyone was aware that Henri IV would try soon again to take the city by armed force, by siege, or he would try to infiltrate it by stealth. He then asked each leader in turn what sort of provisions were laid by, and how long each man thought those provisions would last in case of siege.

A general discussion broke out among the Seize regarding those provisions. Some thought less food should be kept, some more. There were quarrels about what type of food should be stockpiled. Mayenne courteously asked the rest of us if we had any questions. Some men from among our group asked what was needed to qualify to join the militia of one of the *quartiers,* and they were told that one must at least own a sword and some sort of firearm with plenty of ammunition. The question was then raised, how much is "plenty" of ammunition?

The tenor of the questions and answers was aggressive and warlike; morale was certainly high. A more partisan crowd was unimaginable; their curses rained down upon Navarre, and upon Huguenots in general. The Cardinal de Bourbon—that elderly Guise—was often evoked as the true monarch of France.

I was repeating to myself the names of the Seize that I had just heard, mentally associating each name with the face and form that went with it, when the man next to me tapped me on the arm. "Who are you, monsieur? I don't remember seeing your face before."

I caught my breath in surprise at being accosted but answered him readily. "I'm Guy de Toule, at your service and the Duke's."

"From where?"

"Toule in Lorraine—as my name says." I was laying on my best eastern accent.

"Then you must know the Guises."

"Oh, yes, my family does. Personally, I've not had any direct dealings with them, but I'm a loyal partisan. I'm new in town and wanted to see how our faction is dealing with the present crisis."

"Ah yes, of course." He seemed to turn his attention back to the latest question from a member of the audience on the other side of the room, but he glanced at me from time to time.

The meeting broke up after more than an hour. I had already learned nearly everything I had been sent to find out and was anxious to set it all down on paper and send the information back to my king. I still needed to contact the *politiques,* and then I would leave this hostile city as soon as possible. It was clear that Paris was really governed by a coalition, though the Duc de Mayenne, as mayor, was its titular head. I was able to deduce the occupation of most of the leaders: there were eight clergy—five priests and three Franciscan monks, four magistrates, and the rest seemed to be merchants, since even their street clothes reflected wealth.

The mood of Parisians—if one could trust what this group was saying—was belligerent, fanatically devoted to saving the Catholic faith in France, and confident that they could do so. There was a slight shortage of food, but none of weapons or munitions, It seemed to me highly unlikely they would come over to the side of my king. Prospects for taking Paris easily looked dim.

I nodded to the man who had spoken to me, then set off southward on the rue Saint Martin. The night was overcast, and the street, though wide, was a medley of dark shadows, blackest near the houses on either side. I walked down the middle of the street. After all, there was no horse or ox-drawn traffic at this time of night.

I heard the sounds of footsteps behind me; but reasoned that it would be natural for any number of men from the meeting to be walking in the same direction I was. But as I went farther and a lone walker remained persistently behind me, I became convinced I was indeed being followed. I tiptoed over the cobblestones towards the left side of the street, then darted into the black hole that marked the entrance to one of the narrow streets intersecting Saint Martin. I shrank back against the corner house, waiting and listening.

The footfalls continued for three more paces and halted. I waited. There was no further sound nearby—only distant voices and the shrieks and snarls of a catfight down an alley. I waited. I remembered from looking at the map that these side streets ended in another wide avenue that led north and south. I could turn back south there and eventually come to the river. From there, I could work my way back to the bridge and thence to the Place Maubert. Gently, then, I eased away from the wall and crept farther into the blackness of the narrow street.

All went well until I had nearly reached the patch of paler darkness marking the location of the cross street running north and south. I had my eyes fixed upon that pale patch, and so stumbled over an iron bound wooden bucket directly in front of me that scooted over the cobblestones with a loud clatter. I froze again. Minutes passed, but I heard nothing. Perhaps I wasn't being followed after all. More cautiously still, I moved into the cross street and turned towards the Seine.

The street came to a T intersection after a few blocks, and I chose to return westward towards the rue Saint Martin. After weaving back and forth for a few minutes, I found myself on a pier with the noise of a flowing river, along with the smell of dirty water. Away from the tall buildings, I could see better—still dimly but enough to avoid collisions with the mooring posts set at intervals along the quay. I finally arrived at the bridge—the Pont Notre Dame, which I recognized—and crossed. It took me only ten more minutes to reach the inn.

The innkeeper was serving the last customers when I entered. He set down a plate before one of them, straightening and nodding at me as if to say he was relieved I had made it back in one piece. I nodded back. "Could I have a bottle of wine sent up to the room, monsieur?"

"Of course! I'll have the boy bring it right away." He turned back to the table he was serving, and I passed through the door at the back of the room and climbed the stairs.

Once in my room, I rummaged in the small packet of materials I had brought with me from Nérac: ink, a quill, and several sheets of paper. Using the wash stand as a desk, I set to work writing down the names of the Seize, the pattern of their organization as far as I had understood it, and the substance of the discussion I had witnessed.

The boy brought my wine, and while I was fishing out the proper change to pay him, he leaned over the document with open curiosity.

I shaded it with my hand. "Do you read?"

"Oh, no, monsieur, but I would like to learn!"

"Perhaps one of the priests or monks around here could teach you. There seems to be no shortage of them."

He shook his head. "But I don't want to be a priest or a monk."

"Perhaps you can learn to read and write without promising to join the clergy." I had by now found the appropriate brass coin.

He again shook his head. "They don't teach poor boys unless we give ourselves to the Church."

I made a sympathetic noise and handed him the coin, which he again bit down on. He left well satisfied, and I resumed my work. I finished my report around midnight, adding a note at the end telling the king that I would try to establish contact with the *politiques* as soon as I could. I determined to send the report on its way as early as possible the next day. For safekeeping, I folded the document and wedged it out of sight in a crack on the underside of the washstand, then put away all my writing materials.

I slept badly. I barred my door well and could hear any movement on the stairs, but it seemed to me that there was far more activity on the floor below than there should have been for a Sunday night. As soon as it was light outside, I rose and dressed, bleary-eyed, hiding the folded paper inside my jerkin. I clattered downstairs, to find no one up. I unbarred the door and went out on the street.

Workmen were already moving about, merchants opening their shops and putting out stands to display their wares. I walked along the rue Maubert away from the Seine, and a few houses down, asked a woman just leaving her house, "Do you know a cobbler by the name of Peyrou?" According to the instructions king had given me, such a person was supposed to have a workshop on this street.

"Ah, oui, monsieur!" She pointed to a house three doors down. "Go around to the back of that house, monsieur; Peyrou the cobbler has his workshop in the back."

I thanked her and followed her directions, arriving in the courtyard just as the sun began to illuminate it. I was too early for Monsieur Peyrou, so I sat on his workbench to wait. Half an hour passed, and I waited quite happily, warmed by the sun, feeling safe for the first time in hours. At last, a man in a leather apron opened the rear door of the house and stepped out on the stone step, stretching and yawning.

He looked at me, startled. "I'm so sorry, monsieur, have you been waiting long? I fear I overslept."

"No matter. You are Monsieur Peyrou, I presume?"

"Yes, yes, that's me. What can I do for you, monsieur?"

I repeated the words I had been told would identify me as Navarre's man: "My wife has a pair of blue satin slippers. Can you resole them with pigskin?"

He looked at me for a long moment as if he thought I had taken leave of my senses. Then the light dawned. "Oh! Oh, yes, but I would suggest kid leather."

Since these were the right code words, I stood and approached him. "I have here a document that must be taken to Henri IV. Can you manage that?"

He glanced around us, especially at a window not far above our heads. There was no one there. "Come." He spoke in a near-whisper. He drew me farther back in the courtyard, behind a grape arbor still covered with a curtain of withered leaves. "Give me the document." I handed it over, and he placed it in one of the pockets of the leather satchel that hung from his waist, dangling over his abdomen. I could see a collection of needles, awls, thread, small brass nails, brads, and copper rivets. "This will go out by runner today. Navarre will have it in less than a week."

I thanked him and paid him handsomely, more generously now that I understood the dangers of his situation. He escorted me back to the corner of the house, then loudly said, "Just bring those slippers in later today, monsieur, I'll do them in a day or two."

I promised to return soon and went out into the street. I realized how hungry I was and strode back to the Cochon Bleu through the rue Maubert, now becoming crowded with the morning's traffic. I was reaching for the inn's door handle when a heavy hand grasped my shoulder.

"You are Guy de Toule?" a harsh voice inquired.

I turned to see two burly men standing directly behind and slightly on either side of me. "Yes I am." I continued affecting my eastern accent. "Why?"

"You are under arrest, monsieur."

An icy shock quivered through my body. I broke out in a cold sweat, and found myself voiceless, choking out inarticulate sounds instead of the question, "Why?" But I knew why, and anything I might have said would either have been trivial or harmful, putting me or someone else in danger. They jerked my hands behind my back and tied them tightly enough to cut off the circulation. I realized I was shaking uncontrollably. I looked upwards and caught a fleeting glimpse of the innkeeper staring horrified out of the first-floor window. He withdrew at once.

Without a word, the men took me by both arms and marched me towards the river. I stumbled and nearly fell as we moved out into the Place Maubert, and when my captors jerked me back on my feet, I saw a dark shape shift position as it watched from the other side of the Place. It was the priest from the little church near the Porte Saint Jacques—Father Georges Marquet.

As the henchmen dragged me across the bridge, I choked out a few words. "Where are you taking me?"

"To your death."

Chapter X

Prison, Death, and Confession

The two men marched me past the Hôtel de Ville and from there past the church of Saint Jehan en Grève to the entrance of the rue Saint Antoine. This street became wide enough to accommodate four carriages abreast, but the gate at the end, the Porte Saint Antoine, was slightly offset and invisible. Instead, this wide and beautiful avenue ended with a looming fortress and prison. The Bastille. I winced at stabs of reflected light from water in the moat surrounding it.

The nearer we came, the more fearsome it appeared—a castle from the Dark Ages, massive and blackened with smoke and grime. As we crossed the drawbridge before entering that gloomy stone pile, one of my guards chuckled. "Take a look at the city in the sunlight. You'll not see that again." I was starkly reminded of Dante Alighieri's motto over the gate of the Inferno: "Abandon hope, all ye who enter here."

The guards marched, prodded, and dragged me through a courtyard, down a dark stair, where the air became colder and more fetid with every descending step. They thrust me along a damp and gloomy stone corridor, then hauled me down yet another stair, narrower than the last. The walls oozed slimy moisture, and we slipped on the stones underfoot.

I had the distinct impression that the air was not only malodorous but nearly suffocating. One of the guards produced a huge key from a ring at his belt and opened the rusty lock on a cell door. He gave me a shove, and I tripped—the cell was a step up from the corridor—but caught myself before I fell to my knees. The only light in the place came from a tiny window fourteen feet or more above me. They untied my hands, but clamped iron bands, connected by a short length of chain, around my ankles. Without another word, they gathered up the rope and walked out, slamming and bolting the door behind them.

I stood staring upwards, bewildered, in black despair at my sudden reversal of fortune. The shaft of light from that tiny opening fell on my face; my heart lay like a stone in my chest,

A hoarse voice jolted me out of my stupor. "Yes. I know how you feel. I was in your shoes only two weeks ago. By now, I feel right at home here." The voice gave a cackle of bitter laughter.

I peered into the darkest corner of the cell, the apparent source of the voice. "Who are you? Who's there?"

"I was Philippe Canaie, Seigneur de Fresnes."

I stared as a ragged and filthy figure limped out of a corner, dragging a set of chains identical to those I was now wearing. What he'd said froze my bones. I voiced my horrified bafflement. "Why do you say you *were* Philippe Canaie, Seigneur de Fresnes? Are you not still the same man? What have they done?"

"They put me to the question both physically and mentally. You know, young man, what 'the question' means, I suppose?"

I stared at Philippe Canaie, glimpsing open wounds through the rags that only partly covered his body, guessing at the extent of his bruises from what I could see of his filthy and encrusted skin in the half-light from the high window. "Yes, monsieur, 'the question' is torture. I've heard of your family, monsieur. You are Calvinist, I believe."

"Quite right on both counts. Torture and Calvinist. But before I tell you who I am, do introduce yourself."

I apologized. "Forgive me, Monsieur Canaie, I was forgetting my manners. I was going by the name of Guy de Toule when I was arrested." I hesitated to give him my true name, since he might be a spy, planted here to extract more information from me.

He continued. "Calvinist, too, no doubt."

I nodded.

"Too young, too inexperienced to cope with the situation here. I'm neither young nor inexperienced, but I was imprisoned just the same. I took too many risks. I was a lawyer at the Court of the *Parlement*, one of the foremost." He lowered his voice. "But I was an advocate for the rights of King Henri III, with obvious sympathies for his legitimate successor, Henri de Navarre. After the king's assassination and Navarre's attack on Paris, my voice became too strident for the usurpers to tolerate."

I remembered the fanaticism of the Leaguers at the meeting the night before. "Was there anyone out there still listening to voices like yours?"

"Oh, yes!" By now, he was almost whispering into my ear, a trembling hand gripping my wrist. "There are still many, mainly good Catholics, who remained loyal to the legitimate king of France, Henri III, however weak, benighted and sinful he may have been. My arrest was also meant to isolate and intimidate them—they're called *politiques*, you know—certainly to weaken their power and influence."

"But why would they torture you, Monsieur Canaie?"

"Come." He limped back into the dark corner whence he had emerged, as far from the door as one could get in that dungeon and patted the stone ledge next to him. I accepted the tacit invitation and sat. He continued in a whisper, and I wondered why he trusted me enough to confide in me. Probably he was half delirious from pain and privation.

"They wanted information about my brother Pierre. He's ten years younger than me, about thirty. No, thirty-one. He's in the royal army, an officer, and also an agent for the king. If I would betray his whereabouts, the League would be able to destroy an extensive spy network that has penetrated their organization, you see."

My voice rose, incredulous. If this man were truly who he said he was, he was indeed a hero. "And you've been able to resist them?"

"Yes and no. Fortunately, I don't know a thing about Pierre's spy operation. I could only tell them about his military rank and duties. That's public knowledge anyway, and they can't profit from that much information. So, you see, I did talk as much as I could."

"But they thought you were still withholding information?"

"They're convinced of it. They'll keep at it until they kill me, I suspect." He looked down and caressed the stone ledge where we sat. "This and the ledge against the wall at right angles to this one are our 'beds.' Now, tell me more about yourself and why you're here."

My captors already knew my movements from the moment I arrived in Paris, so I saw no harm in giving him an account of my two days in Paris. They seemed weeks ago already.

Canaie was especially interested in my account of the meeting of the League. "Ah! Father Georges Marquet, you say! He's one of their cleverest. You met him in the little church nearest the Porte Saint Jacques? That's interesting... that's not his church. I believe they must have posted him there to keep an eye on the comings and goings from that particular gate. It's the highroad from Provence, of course, and incoming people from Béarn would naturally pass through there. He obviously spotted you right away."

"Yes, I felt unmasked, before I began. And I even asked Father Marquet for directions to the Cochon Bleu Inn, in essence already informing him where to find the base of Henri de Navarre's spy network—one location, anyway. Then another of the Leaguers at the meeting, the one who wanted to know who I was, seemed to suspect that I was not who I claimed to be. I gave him my name, too. It was simple for them to put all that information together."

"Did you get a report off to King Henri de Navarre before your arrest?"

"I was just coming back from visiting the person whose name had been given me as messenger. I pray that he will not have been caught because of me."

"Yes. Let us pray." Philippe heaved a great sigh. "I must rest now, while I can. You'd better sleep, too, because they'll come to put you to the question at any time of the day or night."

I understood his need for quiet and retired to my own stone ledge where I lay down, hoping to find an area where the humps and hollows would match my anatomy well enough to allow me to rest without pain. Although it was still morning in the world outside, I felt exhausted from the waves of intense emotion that had swept over me. All I wanted was to sleep. Perhaps I would wake and find all this a mere nightmare.

They came for Philippe again during that night, bringing him back hours later, unconscious. They had left a crude pottery vessel full of water, and I used it to sponge the blood off his face, and I used my clean handkerchief to squeeze water into his mouth. I covered his upper body with my jerkin, afterwards lying down with my head in his direction so as to hear any movement or sound. Then I dropped off to sleep.

I supposed another day had passed before Philippe regained consciousness. He would not talk to me, but merely shook his head when I asked what they had done and if he was in pain. Then they came again. This time, they pulled him upright and started to the door with him. He was unable to walk, so both feet simply dragged behind him. The man on Philippe's left tossed over his shoulder to me, "We'll kill him now. His body goes into the Seine for the fishes."

The other man looked around at me with a grin. "And you'll be next. There's a reason why the fish in the Seine are so fat."

I took two hobbled steps towards them and the door, crying out "Philippe! Philippe!" but there was no response from anyone, least of all from the victim who, I hoped and prayed, was unconscious.

Time passed. Maybe weeks—I could not tell. My thoughts of Anne and Jacques tortured me night and day. How would they survive without me? I wept, remembering her embraces and the feel of Jacques' soft little hand on my cheek. I meditated upon death, a subject no stranger to me since my adolescence. A long poem began forming itself in my mind, this time not a sonnet, for the subject was so overwhelming I could not limit myself to such a compact form. I composed the first stanza in my mind:

Mes yeux, ne lancez plus vostre pointe esblouye
   Sur les brillans rayons de la flammeuse vie,
Sillez-vous, couvrez-vous de tenebres, mes yeux :
   Non pas pour estouffer vos vigueurs coustumieres,
Car je vous feray voir de plus vives lumieres,
Mais sortant de la nuit vous n'en verrez que mieux.
My eyes, cast no more your dazzled gaze
   On the brilliant rays of flaming life,
Seal yourselves, cover yourselves with darkness, my eyes:
   Not to snuff out your customary powers,
For I will make you see still more vivid lights,
But coming from the night you will see them all the better.

My only solace in that hellish situation was my faith and my prayers; my only other occupation, besides pacing my cell as I dragged my chains, was composing poems in my head. Small wonder, then, that each verse, each poem, centered upon the vanity of life and the eternity of death and on my belief in a hereafter—at that moment my only consolation.

I was "put to the question" once. They did not stretch me on the rack—something I feared more than death. The torture room where I was interrogated was lined with diabolical machines, including the rack. I knew that, once stretched on that device, I would be crippled for life, my joints dislocated, torn, and destroyed. But they merely beat me, first with the lash, then with fists around the face, head, and upper torso when I did not answer to suit them.

I revealed to my questioners that part of my mission already accomplished: The king sent me to find out who were the leaders of the Seize, how they were organized, what was the state of their supplies, and what were their main preoccupations. They had already beaten me thoroughly by the time they forced that much information out of me. I rationalized that, since the report had probably been transmitted to my king, there would be less harm done in telling them what I knew about the League and its organization. After all, I had been arrested after witnessing an entire meeting—and a high-level one at that—so they realized they had already learned everything I knew.

Nonetheless, they began to beat me again, this time to extract information about our means of sending messages. I feigned unconsciousness. They beat and kicked me for a few more minutes, but I remained limp and unresponsive, and they decided they were tired and would try again later. As it turned out, they never came back for me.

I learned afterward that poor Monsieur Peyrou, the cobbler who had passed my message—thus revealed as my means of sending messages—had been arrested, betrayed by the woman from whom I had asked directions. His wife, who had been a fervent partisan of the League all along, added enough information to make sure he was summarily executed. Such was life and death in Paris during the tyranny of the Seize.

My bruises and cuts had begun to heal, but I was suffering torments, especially during the night, from the cold. I had no more covering than the clothes I had worn into prison, and those had been torn during my arrest, then cut and torn further during the lashing and the beating I had undergone. There was no relief for me, scant food—or none—to help warm me as the weather became ever wintrier outside. It never became cold enough to freeze the water seeping through the walls that kept the stone floor perpetually wet, but it was too frigid for sleeping. I would nap for a few minutes, then awaken, stiff and shivering, and was forced to stamp around in my shackles, flapping my arms against my sides. Then I would lie down again to repeat the process.

I became so exhausted that I considered death a blessed state. Madonna-like images floated before my eyes. My beloved Anne held baby Jacques with her face bent toward him—but far from consoling me, such fantasies tore at my soul.

I had despaired of ever again seeing the light of day when the key grated once more in the rusty lock. I huddled in the darkest corner, just as poor Philippe had done, and waited for the executioner to enter. Instead, a black-robed figure appeared, held a brief conversation with the guard, and then turned towards the interior. He appeared as confused as I'd been by the shaft of light slanting down from far above, dazzling his eyes, but barely penetrating the thick darkness.

"Sponde? Jean de Sponde?" It was a gentle voice.

"Yes, I'm over here." There was no way I could hide from him in any case.

"Don't be afraid. I'm Father Cueilly of Saint-Germain-l'Auxerrois. I'm one of the Seize. You surely saw me that night at the meeting at Saint Martin des Champs. But I'm here to help you. The guards have given me half an hour—and I might be able to stretch that if we need the time. May I approach?"

"Yes, Father. At least, you're not here to torture me *physically*. I'm here on this stone ledge. How can you help me?" I was delighted to have human company, even though I feared that this man would try to pry what few secrets I had left out of me. He even admitted he was one of the Seize.

The priest began making his way to my side, now that his eyes were becoming used to the semi-darkness. He held up his skirts slightly to avoid contact with the filth and moisture on the stone floor. "Two people spoke to me on your behalf." His voice was low, as if he were telling me secrets he didn't want a third party to hear.

"Sit here, Father." I patted the stone next to me just as Philippe had done. I had nothing to lose in talking to this man—I would be forced to do so anyway. "Please tell me. How do you know my real name? Who knows I'm even alive?" I made no attempt to soften the bite of sarcastic skepticism in my tone.

Father Ceuilly sat next to me and, in a near-whisper, began to explain the situation. "My son, it was this way. Your casual request for directions from a woman in the rue Maubert led to the apprehension of the cobbler. The police deduced why you needed to contact him: he was a courier between spies inside Paris—like yourself—and Henri de Navarre."

"Wait, Father. What proof can you give me that you are not merely laying some sort of trap for me? I've been interrogated and thoroughly beaten once. I don't want to face that or worse torture because I trusted a 'friendly' priest."

"Let me give you the message I came to tell you, Jean. You can draw your own conclusions. Of course, I could give you your passwords—but you would merely think that they were beaten out of Monsieur Peyrou or the innkeeper."

I paused to think that over. "Well, go on then, Father."

"That unfortunate messenger, Monsieur Peyrou, had a list of code names, including yours, juxtaposed to the real names of the spies. His wife, who also betrayed him, searched his workroom and found a secret drawer containing that information and much more. Her industry in the service of the League will cost your king dearly—not to mention the cost in lives to those persons involved in clandestine work here in Paris. Your report to Henri de Navarre was not among the papers Madame Peyrou turned over to the League. It must have been sent before he was arrested."

"Thank God for that, at least—if you're telling me the truth. Now I see how you knew my real name. But how did all this information come to *you*? Are you so important that the police report their findings to you?"

"No, Jean, not more important than the other members of the Seize. But, you see, the Seize is a close-knit organization. It held another emergency meeting on the night after Peyrou was arrested, and the information was shared among all the members, including me. I just thank God I never used Peyrou as my own messenger!" I was baffled. "But why would you, a member of the Seize, consider using Peyrou? None of this makes any sense to me!"

Ceuilly barked out a short laugh. "Quite right. It's a tangled web, as you'll see. I play the role of Leaguer, and—God forgive me— preach fiery homilies against your king and now mine, and against all who work for him. Tomorrow I will preach a homily about you in which I will call you a *bouc puant*—a stinking he-goat. But despite all that, I try to save anyone I can. I am what the League calls a '*politique.*'"

"Dear God, I was sent to look for people like you," I blurted out, immediately aware that I had revealed one of my small secrets. I couldn't say more for a moment, and Cueilly remained silent, as if respecting my need to gather my wits. Finally, I asked, "And you said that two people are interested in me? Who are they? What do they want?"

"One of them was the Valet de Chambre and Royal Lector of King Henri III, a prelate by the name of Pontus de Tyard. The other is a bishop, a certain Jacques Davy du Perron, Bishop d'Evreux. The bishop pressed me urgently to save you."

I was thunderstruck that two such people should care if I lived or died. "Who is this Pontus de Tyard?" I had never heard of him.

Here, Father Cueilly lowered his voice to a point where I could hardly hear him. "Tyard was a fierce loyalist to His Majesty, King Henri III, as was I. He was a confidant of the king and knew that His Majesty had long been tempted to make common cause with Henri de Navarre. When I informed Pontus about your plight and who you are—a close associate of Navarre's—he, like the bishop, urged me to save you if I could."

"And how does Bishop du Perron know that I'm here? Why does he want to save me?" I, too, spoke in a barely audible voice.

"He is also a *politique*, a powerful one. He knows you have great influence on Navarre as well. You're surely aware he has followed your career with some interest, aren't you? He met you years ago, when you were a young scholar just publishing your translation of Homer with commentary."

I had begun to believe that Father Cueilly was not a spy; that he genuinely wanted to help me. I opened my true thoughts to him. "Yes, Du Perron told me he'd met me in Basel. I didn't re-member meeting him the first time—there was a crowd of people congratulating me, eating and drinking at a party given for me at the printer's establishment. He came by, dressed in black as you are now, and shook my hand. That's what he told me the second time we met in Rome at our embassy. He looked quite memorable that time—in full regalia."

"He told me you seemed to be a bit shaky in your Calvinist faith."

"Did he, now?" I fell silent, frowning, annoyed at the presump-tion Jacques Davy had shown in saying such a thing. But there was truth in his judgment.

Ceuilly broke the silence. "I'm sorry, Monsieur Sponde, I fear I have offended you."

"Not you, Father, the bishop. If I'm honest, though, I must admit he's right—in part at least. But, surely, all that's beside the point. How can you help me? It can't be easy to get a prisoner out of this circle of hell."

"For now, just tell me you'd be willing to go along with a charade we must play. I will tell the guards you've confessed to me and taken Holy Eucharist. I don't insist that you actually do either of those things, but if you're questioned, you must confirm that. With pressure from the Bishop d'Evreux and from me, as a member of the Seize, we should be able to get you out."

"But what will happen when I'm back with Henri de Navarre, and I let it be known that I did not, in fact, betray my faith?"

"I'll see to it that a rumor damaging to my integrity will be circulated—to the effect that I accepted a bribe from you. Something like that will be easily believed. I hate to ruin my reputation in such a way, perhaps for all time, but freeing you makes it worthwhile."

"Father," I said, turning to him with a sudden urge that I was unable to resist, "let me go half-way to meet you. I don't mean to convert to Catholicism, but it would heal my soul if I could confess to you—unofficially, I mean, if that's possible."

He was silent for a moment, and then said, "My son, it is my vocation to heal the sick and wounded in spirit. Tell me, and if I can relieve you—unofficially, of course—I will."

I buried my face in my hands both in shame and to help me concentrate. Then I told him about my doubts and struggles with my faith, my flaws of character, my cowardice, my fascination with and fear of death. And I even recited some of my poetry to him. At the end, he placed a hand on my shoulder.

"You have done well, my son. In trying and difficult circumstances, you have acted as a man of faith and of honor. For your sins, I do absolve you—and will do all I can to help you. Now, about the Eucharist?"

"I'm sorry, Father Cueilly. I simply cannot take that final step yet. Even my confession was more a personal impulse. I cannot give up the doctrine I was born into without much more thought. I hope you can understand."

He laid a hand on my shoulder and was about to speak when there was a loud knock on the door. A guard shouted, "Father Cueilly! It's been nearly an hour! Are you all right in there?"

My rescuer shouted back, "Quite all right. Just wait a moment: I'm almost finished here." Turning back to me, he murmured in my ear, "Have patience. It may be a few days, but you will be released. You may never see me again, my son. May God bless you."

"May He bless you and keep you from harm, Father Cueilly!"

The negotiations for my life took nearly a week, for I began marking the days off on the wall with a chip of stone, as I shivered and stamped about in the cell that grew colder with each passing day. At first light on the sixth day, my door crashed open against the wall and the guards came to where I was lying on the stone ledge. One of them had the key to my shackles in his hand.

"Your lucky day, Sponde," one of them told me. "Somebody pulled strings for you. Another few days and you'd have been food for the fishes."

Shocked at how feeble I'd become, barely able to climb the first set of stairs, I collapsed to my knees at the top, gasping for breath. I had not suffered like poor Philippe Canaie, but near-starvation, the severe beating, the cold, the emotional stress, and complete lack of exercise, had weakened me. The guards supported me, half lifting me as we crossed the courtyard. They escorted me across the drawbridge and to a waiting carriage. I was stinking and filthy, but the footmen showed no hesitation. They dismissed the guards and, taking me under my elbows, they lifted me into the open carriage door. Inside sat a handsome cleric with short black hair combed forward on his forehead like an ancient Roman senator, his intense blue eyes fixed upon me with an expression of concern and pity—Jacques Davy du Perron, Bishop d'Evreux. He immediately threw a warm cloak around my shoulders, embracing me in the process.

"Thank Heaven our intercession actually worked!" He seemed surprised at his own power.

"Your Grace, how can I ever thank you?"

"You're forgetting, Jean de Sponde, that I'm Jacques Davy. No titles between us, please!" He knocked on the ceiling with a staff, and the carriage rumbled away. "Besides, you must not thank me only. Several of us were involved in persuading the Seize to release you—as a good Catholic, of course." He smiled a bit at that.

I inclined my head, choosing not to comment. "Tell me... Father Davy. Who else?"

"Cueilly, Pontus and I worked through Charles de Guise, Duc de Mayenne. He's Mayor of Paris. He authorized the release and signed the documents. But..." He hesitated, shaking his head.

I leaned forward, tense. "There was some difficulty involved in getting me released, then?"

Du Perron nodded. "Not all the Seize were consulted, and not all would have agreed to grant you clemency. The Spanish ambassador, Bernardino de Mendoza, backs the most extreme members of the Seize. If it were up to them, you would be burned at the stake; simple hanging or beheading would be too mild."

"And our status right now is...?"

"Ambiguous. That's why I'm in a great hurry to leave Paris."

"Where are we going, then?"

"To Saint Cloud. The king has set up temporary quarters there; he's taken over the same château where Henri III was living before he was assassinated. He's close to Paris without incurring too much danger—he'll be leading the army on another campaign to the north before long."

We both fell silent while we passed through the city gate called the Porte Neuve. The guards paid more attention to the bishop's clothing than to his papers, which they merely glanced at. They waved us through, and we proceeded westward. As soon as I began to think we were out of danger, I began to question my companion.

"What's happened since I was arrested? What time of year is it? It's gloomy. Looks—and certainly feels—like the dead of winter. The trees are skeletons." I leaned forward in my seat, peering out the window, the luxurious cloak clutched tight around my chest. What had happened to my wife and baby after so long a time? Did they know that I still lived?

Du Perron answered my first question. "It's almost January, Jean. We'll soon be starting a new decade, the 1590s. It's hard to accept that so much time has passed and so much has happened."

I was too keyed up to ask what he meant.

From the documents of Jacques Davy du Perron, Bishop d'Evreux:
There I sat, facing Jean de Sponde, marveling that our efforts were so far successful. We'd been lucky, but the radical faction of the Seize could still send agents to pursue us. The Seize reflected the situation of Paris and of the entire country—internal divisions and strife everywhere.

Poor Sponde looked like a skeleton with smudged skin stretched over it. He certainly needed a good bath! I wouldn't have thought a little over a month could do so much to a man, but, as I remember him, Sponde was never robust. Always thin. Our success in getting him released was mainly due to my friend Cueilly. I suppose Pontus and I also had influence, especially with the Duc de Mayenne, even though he knew full well that we stood with King Henri III against the League, loyal despite the king's aberrations of all sorts—personal, moral, intellectual, and political.

I'd just come from Tours, where Navarre had set up his temporary government. The *Parlement de Paris* in exile was meeting there, and just about all the bureaucratic business of the realm—its legitimate business—was being carried on from that city. In effect, France had two governments. The one in Paris was run by the Spanish ambassador, Mendoza, a very clever politician. It was amazing how so many of the Seize let themselves be dominated by him, or, rather, by Philip II of Spain. What irony! They wanted to save France from rule by a heretic, so they turned our country over to a foreign power instead. Henri III was always aware that if you let those Spaniards in here, they'd find a foothold and never leave. Navarre would have his work cut out to dislodge them.

My thoughts and the journey itself were violently interrupted by an incident that nearly reversed our fortune. Another carriage overtook us and then, running close beside us, forced us off the road. There was much shouting and cursing, and our vehicle halted with a jolt, throwing me violently against the opposite seat, where Sponde was sitting. Fortunately, I only bruised my legs as I collided with the edge of the seat, otherwise catching myself with my arms. I opened the carriage door not blocked by the other coach and jumped out, skirting the rear of our coach. My driver protested loudly as two soldiers from the other carriage informed him they had come to arrest us. I approached them, drawing myself up, and with my most imperious air, bellowed at the two soldiers, "What is the meaning of this barbaric attack? Whose orders are you carrying out?"

"Orders of the Seize. There's an escapee from the Bastille in your coach." In his reply, the sergeant showed no signs of deference for my rank or station.

I snorted. "I beg your pardon. There's no escapee here. The man I am escorting was legitimately released; I have the papers to prove it."

The sergeant still showed no shred of respect. "We'd better see them, then, immediately." He thrust out his hand.

I tilted my head, eyelids at half mast, looking down my nose with a haughty air. "Tell me. Whom do you really serve? France? Or Bernardino de Mendoza of Spain? I happen to know that certain key members of the Seize are under his control. Do you count yourselves faithful Catholics? Do you serve God?" My voice rose to thunderous pitch as I now glared down from my greater height.

"Or those usurpers who would control and dominate our country?" I used the most provocative and inflammatory language I could think of on the spur of the moment, praying that my bluff would work. All the while, the wind was whipping my cape about me, and I turned so it flared out for greatest effect. Heaven was kind. My theatrics produced the desired result.

"Well… ah, Father… we hope to serve God *and* our country. The papers?"

I interrupted him. "Yes. Here are the papers, duly signed and sealed." I produced them from an inner pocket, again drawing myself up to full height and haughtiness. "I am a bishop of the Church of God, and you are to address me as 'Your Grace.' Is that understood? As bishop, I equal or outrank any member of the Seize!"

By now, the two men seemed thoroughly embarrassed. I sent up a quick prayer of thanks that I'd been able to cow them—so far. Now if only they would accept those papers without further quibble.

The sergeant, the corporal peering over his shoulder, thumbed the document. The corporal's blank stare told me he could not read. The sergeant could, although with difficulty. He scanned the first page, written in a scribe's fancy cursive, with many flourishes. When he saw the second page with its signatures—including that of the Duc de Mayenne—and its seals, he handed the document back.

"I'm sorry, Your Grace, there seems to have been some mistake. Perhaps my orders were superseded, and word didn't get to me on time…"

I nodded with haughty conviction. "That sounds most likely. Now, if you would permit us to get on our way, we have legitimate business in Saint Cloud." Then, as if an afterthought, "Who *did* send you to arrest us, by the way?"

"The order came from Father Georges Marquet to our post. It was marked 'urgent,' Your Grace."

Of course. Marquet would be violent in his opposition to Sponde's release under any circumstances—that priest would have made a first-rate hanging judge. He probably had heard that Sponde had been released and had rushed to get authorization from a small group of the Seize to arrest him and anyone aiding him. That, too, was like him. A fiery and hasty man.

The Sergeant was speaking. "Very well, Your Grace. A thousand pardons for the rude interruption." He turned towards their carriage and jerked his head towards it. The corporal took the hint and opened the door, holding it for his superior to enter. Meanwhile, I had also moved back around to the door of our coach.

"Well done, Your Grace," the driver growled almost under his breath from his high seat. We watched as the soldiers' coach turned and headed back toward Paris, and then I climbed into the carriage and closed the door. Sponde, pressing himself into the corner of the seat, no doubt holding his breath, gave a sigh of relief.

Color only now began to show in his cheeks. "I thought I was lost again, Father. You're remarkable. You handled the situation like... like a prince. And you *will be* a prince of the Church. With your presence, you'll be named a cardinal in no time. Fortunately for me, you truly look the part."

I waved away his compliments, but conversation became impossible as the driver shouted a command to the horses, and we lurched forward again. Both of us remained silent and thoughtful for a while. I thought of our new king. I'd been doing my best to get to know Navarre. First, I began talking to him about his former playmate, Henri III, and how it was with him towards the end. Without the pressure from the League, he would have made peace with Navarre months, maybe years, earlier.

I was with our present all-but-king, Henri IV, talking about his predecessor, when a messenger arrived, announcing that the State of Venice had recognized him as the legitimate king of France and that they would leave their ambassador, Giovanni Mecenigo, at

Navarre's court. Since Venice was widely known for its political cunning, they were sure to have an influence on other Catholic powers—maybe eventually on the Holy See. But not yet. Pope Sixtus V had excommunicated Navarre five years before, also excluding him from the French royal succession. That anathema would have to be reversed—a serious matter.

Henri would be forced to convert if he intended to rule this country. All kings of France, from time immemorial, have sworn to uphold and protect the Holy Catholic and Apostolic Church, and to expel all heretics from the land. Clearly, Henri must conform to that, and to do so, he would be obliged to cease being a heretic himself.

I hoped Sponde would hasten the process. It was clear Sponde's faith had been shaky for some time—at least ever since I'd known him. I sincerely believed he was Catholic in his heart. The situation was delicate, though. If I could lead him along the right path—gently, subtly—I would be doing distinguished service to God and our country, for Sponde could greatly influence our monarch.

But at that moment, my most urgent task was to tend to Sponde's physical needs—urgent ones—before in any way challenging his spirit.

Jean resumes:
After that frightening incident with the soldiers, I remained silent, thinking over our narrow escape. Bishop du Perron also remained quiet and withdrawn, his eyes at first taking on a far-away expression. Then he focused on my face, and, as we bounced and swayed along the road towards Saint Cloud, he sat for a while just looking at me with that half-smile of his before he continued to speak. He told me where he and the court had been and what Henri hoped to accomplish next.

"Henri plans on beginning a campaign to win back the north of France to our side. As you know, the Guises have dominated the entire northern half of the country during most of his reign. I know he'll want you with him."

"But… Father," I protested, again stumbling over his title, "I have a new baby, a wife who probably thinks I'm dead, and a position of some responsibility back in La Rochelle! I *must* go back there! It's unthinkable for me to do anything else!"

He nodded, the look of pity and concern returning. "Of course, Jean. Of course! We in the clergy—we celibates—tend to forget that most men have other worries and responsibilities beyond war and politics. Yes, certainly, your family must come first, and *then* the king."

"Will you back me if Henri seems reluctant to let me go?"

The bishop's lips twitched. "He won't refuse you. After all, he should understand—he's anything but celibate himself!"

We arrived at Saint Cloud at last, and the footmen assisted me from the coach. Davy took my arm, and together we walked into the château. As luck would have it, the first person we saw was the king himself, emerging from the main hall where he had just held an audience or perhaps a strategy session.

"Sponde! These good people did manage to get you out of that hell hole! Let me look at you!"

I cringed, knowing how grimy and disreputable I was beneath Davy's elegant cloak. "Sire, I'd rather you looked at me after a bath, some food, and some sleep!"

But he already tugged the cloak aside, no doubt getting a good whiff of accumulated grime. He looked me up and down, noting the scabs showing through the ragged remains of my shirt. "Beat you, did they?"

"Yes, Sire. But since I knew next to nothing, they learned nothing."

The king ignored my self-disparaging remark. "Thank you for that report. It *was* helpful—though costly."

"Yes, I know. I'm sorry for the losses, Sire."

"Not your fault, as I understand it. And, thanks to people like the bishop, here, I've been in touch with the *politiques*, and so learned anyway what you would have told me if you'd had a couple more days. You did well enough. Now, I'll order a hot bath for you, and have a good dinner sent up to your room. I'll want to talk to you about the future tomorrow when you're feeling better."

I would have asked his leave to return home to Anne and baby Jacques then and there but was not given the chance. Henri turned away after squeezing my shoulder, and I was left standing uncertainly with Davy, not knowing where to go next. The bishop motioned to one of the pages standing at the entrance to the audience hall. "Where is Monsieur Sponde's room?"

The page darted inside and came back quickly with the answer. "On the first floor, Your Grace. Third room on the left."

Davy again took my arm and together we made our way up the curving stair. I leaned more heavily on him than I would have wished, but he seemed not to mind. As we approached the third door on the left, four servants entered ahead of us, two carrying a tub, two carrying water. A cloud of steam rose from one of the water vessels.

"I'll leave you now, Jean. One word of advice. Don't eat too much of the good dinner they'll be sending up. After starving for so long, you could easily make yourself sick. I'll see you in the morning." He turned to go.

"Father! Your cloak!"

"Keep it, Jean, and think of me when you wear it. Good night, now." I watched him run down the stairs, holding up the skirt of his robe so as not to trip, his short cape flaring out behind him.

Chapter XI

Family, War

I awoke the next morning much refreshed, even though it had taken me an hour or two to get to sleep. Everything was so good, so comfortable, that it kept me awake. I smelled like a flower garden after my bath; my belly rumbled as it tried to cope with a small portion of the excellent dinner the servants had brought me; I lay like royalty between clean sheets, dark green velvet bed curtains drawn about me, warm and dry for the first time in weeks. I'd heeded Davy's advice and ate very little, but my stomach still rebelled at the unusual richness of the food.

Nevertheless, I rose feeling much stronger, surprised I had not heard the valets when they brought my breakfast of hot milk and honeyed breads. They had also laid out a handsome suit of clothes in shades of dark green with a tan waistcoat, brown silk stockings, and a new pair of shoes. I glanced at myself in the mirror before beginning to dress. The bath had taken some of the angry red out of the puckered flesh around the scabs on my back and ribs, but my bruises, now faded to yellow and green, were more visible than before against the pallor of my clean skin. That pale skin, stretched over nearly fleshless bones, gave me a cadaverous look.

I quickly shaved my cheeks and trimmed my beard as best I could with the utensils lying on the night table. The suit was comfortable and, from what I could see in the mirror, flattering, but the shoes seemed a bit narrow. I would stretch them soon enough. I just had sat down to breakfast when there came a knock on the door.

"Monsieur de Sponde, the king would like to speak to you as soon as you are ready."

I thanked the valet. "Where will I find His Majesty?"

"He'll be in the audience hall. At the foot of the stairs and through the double door, Monsieur."

I finished the last honeyed morsel, brushed the crumbs off my new suit, and went to obey the king's summons. I still had to grip the banister to maintain my balance and to keep my legs under me. It would take time before my strength would come back to normal. The guard at the foot of the stairs opened the double door for me, and I entered the tapestried hall, its tiled floor strewn with handsome rugs of Lyonese manufacture. Henri was seated at the head of a large table in a chair elaborate enough to be considered a throne.

"Sponde!" He looked me over, nodding with approval, but apparently noticed that I was still unsteady on my feet. "Sit here." He patted the chair next to his. "We need to make plans. I think the bishop told you I'm starting a campaign to retake the north from the Guises. When can you join me?"

"Sire, perhaps Bishop du Perron told you how desperately I want to see my wife and baby son. Also, I need to take care of that job you gave me. Heaven only knows what those secretaries have done in my absence—I left matters up to them, thinking I would be gone only two weeks or so."

"Yes, Du Perron did intercede on your behalf. Don't quite know why he should be so concerned about you, but he was persuasive. Very. I can tell you; Duplessis-Mornay and the other Calvinists are not happy to see that prelate hanging around me. They're sure he's up to no good.

"Well, this is what I propose. Go home to La Rochelle and embrace your wife, kiss your boy, and put your affairs in order. Stay there for a while, recover your strength, then join me in the north—let's say around the first of March. Does that suit?"

I was about to reply when he interrupted. "Oh, by the way, I wrote your wife a couple of times. Once to tell her that you were arrested in Paris but still alive—I have my spies, even in the Bastille, Jean!—and then yesterday, to tell her you were released, and are still in one piece. The messenger left taking messages south about noon yesterday."

I thanked my king most humbly. After all that, I could find no good reason to refuse his request that I rejoin him by the first of March of the New Year, 1590. That date seemed far in the future, in any case.

The carriage that brought me back to La Rochelle pitched and rumbled up the street toward my home. A week had passed since that conversation with the king, and I had gained strength, though not much weight. Henri insisted that I take a coach rather than ride a horse as I normally did, and although I had protested, I was grateful. I would not have been able to ride far, nor would I have been able to protect myself in case of attack on the road.

I leaned out the window as we neared the house and saw two women walking ahead of us, one of them carrying a bundle—a baby warmly wrapped—in her arms. It was Anne and our new maid! I called out as loudly as I could, but my voice was drowned out by the clatter of the wheels, and by the noises of other vehicles and the clopping of horses' hooves.

"Driver!" I yelled, "Catch up with those two women! The one with the red hair!" I pointed and gestured, and he grinned down at me.

"Yes, of course, Monsieur!" And, tapping the horses with his whip, he moved rapidly up until we overtook Anne with Jacques in her arms and Mélanie beside her.

I opened the carriage door and scrambled down. "Anne, my love! It's me! I'm back!"

She spun around, a look of utter surprise on her face. Then, quickly handing the baby to Mélanie, she lurched into my arms, nearly crushing me in her embrace. "Jean! Jean! You have no idea how awful it's been! We thought you were dead—that they'd killed you when we didn't hear anything for so long!" She was weeping now, so unlike my stalwart Anne. "I can feel your bones right through your clothes!" she sobbed. "What did they do to you?"

I never could resist a loved one's tears, and my own cheeks were wet. "They questioned me, my love, and beat me, but no actual torture. They starved me, of course. Now that I'm with you I'll heal and get fat in no time!" I chuckled, and she gave me an answering, tremulous, smile.

As soon as I had greeted Mélanie properly, I gave the driver, who had to carry out further orders from the king in any case, several écus and waved him on with my thanks. The carriage clattered away over the cobblestones. Turning back to my family, I asked Anne, "Where are you going? May I hold Jacques?"

She handed the baby to me, and I hefted him. He seemed much heavier than before I left. Perhaps that was merely an impression, since I was weak. But his face looked longer, more mature, his hands larger. "He's grown a lot in these past weeks, hasn't he? He's heavier!"

"Of course! As you must know, he's almost four months old by now. His movements have purpose and he'll start to crawl soon, I think."

"So soon?" I had no idea what the timetable for infant development might be.

"Yes. He's *our* child, so he's unique," Anne told me with a smile of pride. "We're on our way to the market, Jean," she continued, "to buy a few special things for supper that the cook didn't think of. To be more accurate, that *I* didn't think of. Now, you can help— we'll need more of everything now that you're home!"

Later, after a delightful dinner, with the baby sound asleep in Mélanie's care, we sat long before the fire, hand in hand, while I told her about Paris. She was horrified to hear of poor Canaie's fate and was moved that the trio of Catholic clergymen—Father Cueilly and the two prelates, Pontus de Tyard whom I still had not met, and Bishop du Perron—had worked so hard to free me. Her suspicions were aroused, however. "I wonder what their real motives are?"

"I wonder, too, my love. After all, I'm a relatively small fish, and a Calvinist to boot. If they were saving important Calvinists, they would have saved Philippe Canaie. It couldn't be just because Du Perron has taken a personal liking to me. It's something else. Something they think is important..."

After we retired, we made passionate love in the warmth and security of our own bed, in our own home. I don't believe I have ever lived a more blissful moment than on that night of relief, of fulfilled longings, of pure joy.

My domestic happiness continued throughout the stay in La Rochelle, but I cannot say the same for my duties as a municipal officer, Lieutenant General of the Sénéchaussée. Navarre's various edicts had been issued before my departure—imposing new taxes, restricting the city magistrates in their powers to pass new city ordinances, removing their authority to judge certain types of criminal cases and to carry out judicial sentences before they consulted with the king. I had explained to my secretaries that the taxes, however unpleasant, were necessary if Navarre was to continue fighting the League. As for city ordinances, the king worried that the Huguenot majority would persecute the Catholic minority in various insidious ways, and he wished to review their decisions before they became policy. The same motive lay behind his restrictions on criminal judgments and sentencing. After all, he counted on eventually being the king of *all* Frenchmen, not merely of Calvinist Frenchmen.

My secretaries had done nothing about enforcing the edicts in my absence, and now I discovered a host of violations and maneuvers to avoid observing them. I angered my secretaries first of all when I reprimanded them for their laxity in carrying out the king's commands. Natives of La Rochelle, they made me understand that they knew far more than I did about their fellow citizens' tolerance for such new rules and regulations.

As it turned out, there was no toleration at all. The magistrates informed me the king would have to send in his army to extract those cursed new taxes; they had always passed any and all legislation that had to do with municipal affairs and would continue to do so; and criminal cases affecting the city's welfare were their own business. Tempers flared, and I could see it would take more political talent than I could ever muster to regain a footing of civility, let alone cooperation. February dragged on interminably, with angry letters exchanged, angry words in council meetings. I was thoroughly miserable and wondered how much longer I could endure. I seemed to have alienated the entire city and found no one to go to for advice.

I took refuge, as I had done long in the past, in scholarship. I began translating Hesiod's *Works and Days* from Greek into Latin, and at last found a friend in the printer, a certain Jérôme Haultain, a learned man and a humanist. During those moments when I was not attending meetings of angry magistrates or drafting defensive letters, I would sit in Haultain's back room with my Hesiod and the makeshift Greek-Latin dictionary I had put together years earlier as a student, and translated, taking breaks to chat with the printer. It was clear that the project would not be finished soon, which consoled me, for it gave me an excuse to put aside my woes and escape into the fantastic world of Greek deities and heroes.

During that month, we received frequent reports of the king's progress in the north. He was successful beyond anyone's wildest expectations. He captured a series of important Norman towns as he moved northwestward from Paris: Le Mans, Laval, Alençon, Falaise, Lisieux, and Honfleur. One messenger quoted the king directly. "My deeds are miracles." I laughed, The naïve egotism was so blatant and so typical of Navarre. But two important cities, Rouen and Le Havre, both strongholds of the League, remained to be captured.

When my time of recuperation was over, my feelings were mixed. On the one hand, I dreaded leaving Anne and the baby so soon—and she was depressed at the thought that I would again place myself in danger, perhaps never coming back. On the other, I could hardly wait to be free of the office that had placed me in such an untenable position with the citizens and magistrates of La Rochelle.

Even the merchants had begun to slight us—overcharging and selling poor quality goods. We resorted to sending Mélanie's mother or her aunt, whom they didn't connect with us, to buy all our necessities. It was entertaining, in a sour sort of way, to compare the goods and their prices as they were quoted to them with what had been offered to Anne or to me.

When I rejoined the king and the army on the first of March 1590, as agreed, I found them quartered in Honfleur, a town at the mouth of the Seine. There were new people in Henri's immediate entourage: a certain Sieur de Morlas, with whom I had a number of conversations, and a minister of state, Rotan, who joined some of our talks. Oddly, he demonstrated to us that the myths of the ancient Greeks and Romans and the moral writings of such men as Seneca seemed to bolster the Catholic more than the Calvinist teaching. Rotan was himself Calvinist, but apparently wavering. I had mixed feelings about him. On the one hand, I felt he was betraying our cause, but on the other, I suspected he and I saw more eye to eye than I was willing to admit.

Meanwhile, rumors were everywhere. Philip II of Spain, alarmed by Henri's successes, was sending a vast army against us, coming by sea, from the south and the north. Finally, about a week after my arrival, we had definite news. Philip had raised five hundred arquebus soldiers and twelve hundred cavalry from Flanders to the northeast, but he had sent them under the command of Philip, Count of Egmont, to join the Duc de Mayenne's army in Paris. The combined forces were now marching against us, twelve thousand foot-soldiers to our eight thousand; five thousand horse against our three thousand.

Henri was undaunted, however. He gave us the order to march southeastward to meet them, and, after pausing near the town of Evreux for a couple of days, we continued to the southeast and met their army on 13 March on the Plain of Saint-André, near the Forest of Ivry. This time, we were not dug in, using natural obstacles to our advantage as at Coutras and Arques; we were meeting them out in the open.

Our commanders disposed us in defensive positions, but Henri regrouped our forces, telling us "the field of battle where we fight will also be our last retreat." He meant we were to fight to the last man; conquer or die. All very well for Henri, who was childless as yet and who did not love his wife. I thought of Anne and Jacques and grew cold.

Mayenne's army was drawn up in six groups of cavalry, infantry screening each group. We did the same but with one difference: the Maréchal de Biron's cavalry with two infantry units were held in reserve just behind the front lines. This time I was one of Biron's knights.

The pre-battle tension brought back Coutras more vividly than I could bear. Again, I could smell the odors of dead campfires, of massed horses and unwashed men, of fear. All unbidden, came vivid images of the aftermath of Coutras—twisted bodies of dead men and horses, thousands of them. Further back in my memory,

I saw the open and desecrated graves at Orthez, the rotting bodies of the Jacobin monks. Is that all there is? I wondered for the thousandth time. The fragility of life, the certainty of death and decay—these were realities. But what of the promise of eternal life? Right now, that promise seemed like the dream of a lost child trying to console itself in the dark.

The darkness of that morning faded into dawn gray, became pink and white, and then the engagement began with an exchange of artillery fire. As usual, our artillery did the most damage, and I shuddered as I watched those cannon balls, those volleys of shrapnel, strike horses and men alike, tearing them apart. Even at a distance, the scene was nauseating. All at once, so suddenly as to be unexpected, both front lines galloped towards each other and the battle was joined. It was hard for me to see who was gaining the advantage. Looking left, our captain Jean d'Aumont had put Mayenne's light horse to flight, but our Monpensier was struggling in an apparently equal battle with their Nemours, the line wavering back and forth, horses and riders falling in screaming heaps.

My king's delusion of invincibility served him well. I followed his progress thanks to his white plume, nodding ahead of his direct charge against the Duc de Mayenne, where he now crashed through the duke's lines. The Flemish general Egmont, however, just slightly to our left, was doing the same to the Maréchal de Biron's son and his light cavalry. My horse, Persée, a black gelding from the stable at La Rochelle, pranced and reared. He, at least, was anxious for battle. He made a great leap forward when Biron senior gave the command to charge Egmont's troops from their left flank.

He shouted, "Hold your fire until you're right upon them!" Henri had developed that technique for greater accuracy. We galloped in close, and for me, time seemed suspended. I noted each hoof beat, every breath my horse took, saw individual blades of grass as we flew by, while at the same time I felt benumbed. The distance was short but appeared to stretch into miles while pistol bullets from the enemy began to strike at random, here wounding an arm, there a horse's chest.

Then I heard, faintly above the other noises all around me, the command, "Fire!" I had my eye on a handsome blond man on a big bay warhorse, whom I shot point blank. I saw the look of astonishment on his face: I had hit him in the chest. My horse carried me past, and I had neither time nor inclination to look back. A knight armed with a lance bore down upon me. Persée was one of the lighter and more nimble horses, never trained in jousting—as far as I knew—but he seemed to understand the menace of that long, sharp pole bearing down on us. Just before I closed with the knight, Persée swerved to the left and then back again, and the lance missed its aim. I was able to strike the knight's right arm below the shoulder with my sword, effectively putting him out of the battle. He dropped the lance with a cry, grabbing his right arm with his left. His horse, on its own, cantered out of the mêlée, carrying its rider somewhere behind our lines.

I was attacked again abruptly by one of Egmont's men, a sword fighter this time. We fenced ineffectually for a while. My inability to overcome this man—my inferiority in swordsmanship—made me aware I'd not fully recovered from my imprisonment. I was weakening rapidly when I felt a blow on the head from behind, and, except for seeing the world swirl around me, I knew no more.

I began to hear before I could see. "This one's Sponde!" It was surely Duplessis-Mornay. "Get him out from under that horse!" I cried out as they dragged me forth. The stirrup digging into my abdomen tore my clothes and lacerated my flesh as they pulled me free. But other than that injury inflicted by my rescuers, I was merely bruised—especially the back of my head. My poor horse Persée had been killed in the fighting. I lamented him, for he'd saved my life in avoiding the lance-bearing knight.

We had routed Mayenne and his superior army, and my charge, led by the Maréchal de Biron, had been decisive. The king's trusty Calvinist captains—La Trémoille, Duplessis-Mornay, Rosny, and d'Aubigné, who still would not speak to me—had led the final charge and had been, as at Coutras, invincible. I noted that Henri's squadron commanders were nearly all Catholic officers who had come to him since Henri III's death—a sign he was winning in popularity against the Guises and the League. A major factor in the enemy cavalry's defeat was the lance. The outdated weapon had encumbered them and enabled us to outmaneuver many of them just as I had done. That decisive engagement became known as the Battle of Ivry.

From the documents of Jacques Davy du Perron, Bishop d'Evreux:
I returned to Paris with the Duc de Mayenne about three weeks ago and am now installed in the Episcopal Palace. Despite my past status as spiritual advisor to two Valois kings, it seems I can claim privileges from the head of the League merely on the strength of my rank as Bishop d'Evreux. I have a luxurious suite of rooms and the run of the place.

Of course, I can come and go within the city as I please, visit meetings of the Seize, attend any gathering. Among the members of the Seize, my status in the church hierarchy also commands respect and credence, even though some are whispering that I am a *politique*. But such rumors are generally not believed. The *politiques* have been described by their own leaders as atheists. Most of the faithful cannot accept the idea that a prelate can rise so high in the Church and be a partisan of "The Heretic destroyer of the Faith," as they style Henri IV.

Yet, despite his present heresy, I believe Henri to be our real, divinely sanctioned king by right of legitimate succession. My task is to convince him to convert either by my direct efforts or through those of certain people chosen as my proxies—especially Jean de Sponde. I do this for the greater glory of God and for the good of France, to help her return to peace and prosperity. If my country falls to Spain, I'm certain neither peace nor prosperity will be our lot. I am therefore passing to Henri's agents whatever useful information I can gather. My conscience is clear: I am not betraying my faith; I am saving my country.

History *does* repeat itself. I and many others expected that Henri, once he had won a decisive battle at Ivry and had driven Mayenne limping away defeated, would immediately lay siege to Paris, the next logical step. We were surprised that instead he went on holiday, capturing small towns with little or no strategic importance, bypassing Paris, a repetition of his behavior after the battle of Coutras. Then, too, he won a decisive victory, and simply went back to his mistress afterwards, leaving his allies scratching their heads.

In the respite the king has so graciously given them, the Seize has armed the city as never before, all fortifications in good repair. Henri finally attacked in force on May 12, and the city's defenders have repulsed him. Now, he has settled in for a long siege.

Soon after I arrived here, I went into the streets. I heard much wailing and lamenting; people gathered in small groups, mourning the death of the Cardinal de Bourbon. The League and the Seize had chosen him as the "legitimate" king of France and had given him the title "Charles X." No other candidate for the throne was acceptable to the League. In their Sunday sermons, the priests of this city had painted him as a benevolent father figure, a benefactor and a bringer of peace, something Parisians desperately longed for.

Meanwhile, I knew that Navarre had held the aged cardinal—in his eighties, I believe—in luxurious captivity for some time. I know that Charles de Guise, the Duc de Mayenne, could see himself as king, but he is engaged in a power struggle with the ambassador of Spain, Bernardino de Mendoza. Whereas Mayenne commands the noble wing of the League and most of its forces outside

Paris, Mendoza controls the Seize here in the city. He wields great influence, for Mayenne cannot hope to win battles against Henri de Navarre without the aid of Spanish reinforcements, probably under the command of the Duque de Parma, who, I hear, is a most able commander.

Mendoza, as ambassador of Spain, is pushing Felipe II's ambition to gain control of France by marrying the king's daughter, Isabel Clara Eugenia, to some carefully chosen French nobleman, and then have the Estates General meet in Paris to declare *her* queen of France. If such a thing should happen, my country would be reduced to a satellite of Spain. The League—especially the Seize—is blind and fanatical enough to allow such a thing to happen... but not Mayenne, I think. He can see more clearly. It is anyone's guess who will win the power struggle.

Besieged

From the documents of Jacques Davy du Perron, Bishop d'Evreux:

Navarre's forces occupy the towns around Paris that normally supply the city with food. Perhaps that is why he skirmished around so long before attacking the city; he was making sure the food supply was cut. I'm told that his men are spread thinly around the perimeter of Paris. Some gates are not blockaded completely, but we are beginning to feel the pinch just the same.

That "The Heretic" was unable to take the city has given the citizens' morale a boost and increased the mob's hatred. I've attended more fiery sermons against Henri, that "minion of the Devil," and seen more religious processions carrying the crucifix and holy statues than at any other time in my life. Not even in Rome does one find such religious fervor, such violent sentiment! The sermons draw large crowds, swollen now by manual laborers who cannot get outside the city to their usual work. One of them accosted me in the street.

"Your Grace, can you spare something for my family? I have no work, and no money to buy food." The man, threadbare but clean, was clearly not used to begging. He looked away in embarrassment after making his request, twisting his hands. A woman with two little girls clinging to her skirts stood nearby, perhaps his family.

I opened the bag of coins I was carrying and gave him enough *sous* to buy provisions for four people for a week—at least at the present prices. Who knows what will come next week?

"I'm sure your wife will spend this wisely. If the situation doesn't ease soon, come ask for me at the Episcopal Palace. My name is Du Perron, Bishop d'Evreux."

The man took the coins in his large, work-roughened hands, and tucked them behind his waistband. He was opening his mouth to speak when the woman came forward, making a little curtsey. "Thank you, Your Grace! I could tell you were a Bishop, Your Grace. You're such a fine gentleman and so handsome—I think Our Savior must have looked like you."

I was embarrassed. "No, madam, I suspect Our Savior looked more like your husband, here." I turned to him. "What is your trade?"

He blushed. "Well, I *am* a carpenter, Your Grace. I was working on the new houses in the Faubourg Saint Germain. But the gates are barricaded, and I can't get to my work…. I thank you for your charity, Your Grace. I'll find you again if I need to— heaven forbid!"

With that, the four of them turned away and soon were lost in the crowd. The little girls, who had peered at me from behind their mother's skirts during our brief conversation, still had their fists twisted in those skirts but were walking backward behind their mother, solemnly staring wide-eyed at me until the crowd closed around them. I worry that all the money I have will make little difference if this siege lasts much longer.

Two weeks have passed, and the carpenter has come back once, clearly reluctant but desperate. I contacted several burghers who were well off and convinced them to help support other manual laborers who were out of work along with their families. We might as well spread the wealth around. It's what Christ would have done, only he would have gone about it in a more radical way.

Lately, we've all had to limit ourselves to black bread, and meat is extremely scarce. What can be found is coming from the horses and donkeys that were in Paris when the siege began. It won't be long before they are all butchered and eaten. The poorer folk are already reduced to eating gruel made from bran.

Despite all that, our priests continue to harangue the people. I was at first taken aback, then amused to see Father Cueilly in the pulpit, preaching a violent sermon against Henri and all his allies. I could see that, for the moment, Father Cueilly believed what he was saying—after all, he deplores the suffering here as much as I do. He told us that this siege is like the siege of Jerusalem that we are martyrs for God and for the purity of His religion.

The power of his preaching has saved him from persecution by the Seize after his collusion in getting Jean de Sponde released from the Bastille. If they imprison or hang him, the people will see him as a martyr, and that very eloquent tongue of his would be stilled. He is far more useful to the League alive! Furthermore, they know that preachers like him are keeping the people in check. If the people think they are suffering for a noble cause, they will remain calm, and so far, they have been remarkably quiet.

Hunger is growing. Lately, I've eaten one meal each day, sometimes fasting entirely. What food I do get, I divide and share with the carpenter's family. It's little enough, but perhaps they will survive. Others are not so lucky. I've seen them snare cats in alleyways and butcher their pet dogs. I'm told they're even hunting the rats and mice in the cellars.

The city is darker than ever at night, and when I go out to a meeting, a servant lights my way with an oil lamp. Even that is a great luxury. By burning that oil, I deprive some poor soul of a few spoons of nourishment. The houses remain dark at night because of the lack of candles; the cheap ones made of tallow have been eaten. I notice by day there's not a blade of grass left along the streets or in the courtyards—all of it has been used for food. The people of Paris are dying from hunger.

Jean resumes:

"Sieur de Sponde!" The soldier saluted me as I trotted towards his position. I was making my rounds, inspecting the men who guarded the gates and the barricades. The soldiers knew me; my inspections were by now routine. I was approaching one of the gates without a guard when a man darted out from behind the barricade and slapped a roll of paper in my hand. "This is from the Bishop, Du Perron." He spoke so quickly I barely understood him. "He knows you're one of the regular inspectors of these walls, and asked that I deliver this report to you, personally."

I thanked the man, who scurried behind the barricade and through the gate before I could ask him how Du Perron was faring in that famine-plagued city—and how he knew I'd be at this spot at this time. Never mind. I read the report, a succinct account of the condition of the people of Paris. I recognized the bishop's rather brash style.

"Jean, I depend on you to convince the king that these people, the working classes, have suffered enough. He has to do something to help the women and the children in particular. They are starving to death in here. I buried three children in the last two days. Do your best, Jean. I know Henri doesn't want to harm the innocent. Jacques Davy."

I would shortly have concrete evidence that his words were true. I read Davy's words twice, then tucked the roll into my belt. As I continued my circuit of the city wall, I saw two children scuttling about in the underbrush near the Porte Montmartre. Both were ragged and dirty, and through their rags, I could see arms like sticks and clearly defined ribs. I stopped my horse and dismounted.

I called to them. "What are you looking for?"

The little girl came up to me first, dusted off her hands, then hid them in her skirt. "We're catching rats, monsieur. Some of the soldiers throw food scraps away near the gate, and the rats come. They're hungry too."

Du Perron's words were confirmed. "You're eating rats?"

"Yes, monsieur." It was the boy who spoke this time. He had a string on which two dead rats were tied by their tails. "My mother cooks them and they taste good. Well, maybe not *good*, but they're not bad. They keep us from starving. Mother says the heretics want us all to die of starvation."

I gave the two of them the section of sausage and the quarter loaf of bread I had brought for my lunch. "Take this to your mother, too. She can make it go a long way, I expect. Are there more children in your family?"

"Oh yes, monsieur. A little sister and a baby brother. We're all very hungry, monsieur."

"Well, be sure to give the bread and sausage to your mother!"

"We will, monsieur. Thank you!"

I swung back up into the saddle. As I looked back, I saw the boy wrap the bread and sausage in the tail of his shirt and tie the bundle to his body with his belt. They were following my instructions instead of eating the food immediately, even though they must have been faint with hunger.

I told Henri when I returned that evening, showing him the bishop's report.

He looked at me with some suspicion. "The bishop signs himself 'Jacques Davy' to you? Why?"

"Sire, I've known him for years, since my student days in Basel, actually. It was back when I published the Homer that I dedicated to you, Sire. He came to congratulate me on its publication. Then, I met him in Rome, and again when I was rescued from the Bastille. He has always insisted I call him Jacques Davy, Sire."

"Odd. I could've been more severe with this siege, but from what you and Davy tell me, I'm glad I wasn't. I hate to inflict starvation and suffering on women and children. I expect the people you saw are the poorest of the poor. The merchants and nobles are probably faring better, hoarding food that Davy doesn't know about. Still..." He sat and wrote the Parisians a letter, assuring them of his parental concern. He would allow three thousand women and children to leave the city.

We opened the Porte Saint Jacques, and out they came in a stream. They were too weak to do more than cling together and walk. I stood beside my horse and watched them as they straggled out. Quite a few women carried young children in their arms, who were unable to stand. One of these women passing near me staggered and nearly collapsed. I abandoned my horse and ran to catch her before she fell. With my arm around her, I guided her back to my horse's side. She was dirty and ragged, and exuded a sour smell as if she had been living in cellars. I eased her to the ground, to sit cross-legged with her child in her arms. She closed her eyes.

"Wait a moment, I have food here." I rummaged in my saddlebag and retrieved my lunch, bread and cheese this time, along with my flask of wine. I first gave her a swallow of the wine, then broke a morsel of cheese off the piece and held it to her lips. "Here's some cheese." The smell of cheese roused her more than my words or the wine. She seized it, eyed it, then ate it, rolling it upon her tongue, savoring it. I handed her the rest of the cheese and then held out my quarter loaf.

She took the food, and I gave her the flask as well. With surprising forbearance, she began to break off crumbs of cheese and then bread moistened with the wine to feed her child first. I watched over her while she and the child devoured the modest meal, then helped her to her feet again. Her little girl seemed to have regained enough strength to walk with her mother, holding tightly to her hand.

"Bless you, Monsieur. You have earned time off Purgatory for this."

I thanked her and watched them rejoin the crowd. Henri had set up a makeshift camp farther out in the country to feed them all. I felt proud of my monarch, behaving according to overarching Christian principles of charity.

His generals shook their heads over Henri's act of kindness, convinced that spies and agents of the Seize had left the city with those poor victims to carry messages to Orléans and other strongholds of the League.

Henri ignored them. "They're probably quite right, but the risk is worth it to save those children."

Meanwhile, Felipe II pursued his plans to annex France. He ordered the Duque de Parma to come to the aid of Mayenne, whose army had been outside Paris in Meaux. It was November by then, and the weather was beginning to turn bad. Henri decided to fight Parma before the roads became impassibly muddy, and we withdrew our blockading detachments and posted ourselves at Chelles, just north of the Marne River.

But the Spanish duke refused to join battle with us, fearing another defeat like Coutras or Ivry. Instead, he seized the town of Lagny, strategic for re-supplying Paris, and effectively lifted the siege. Henri had lost his bid for the city for the second time; his nobles began to go home to take care of their estates, and his army broke up. I, too, seized the opportunity to go home to La Rochelle.

Like the other nobles, I went to Henri to ask permission to leave, pledging at the same time my loyalty and service.

"Jean, I completely sympathize with your wish to go home to your beautiful wife." He sighed. "I've met someone myself, Jean. You remember that little trip I took to Cœuvres in Picardy?"

"Yes, Sire, that was after I joined the army at Honfleur, wasn't it?"

"I believe so. Anyway, she's the most beautiful woman I've ever laid eyes on."

I looked at my feet to hide my smile. Each new woman Henri saw was "the most beautiful." "Who is this paragon, Sire?" I struggled to keep the irony out of my voice.

"Her name is Gabrielle d'Estrées, temporarily residing at Chartres. I'll be laying siege to that city next."

"But, Sire, does Chartres have any strategic importance?" My question was more naïve than ironic.

"No, but while we are waiting for my nobles to take care of their business at home during this winter and on into the spring planting season, I might as well do something that gives me pleasure. I'll take Chartres *and* the lady."

"Sire." I bowed, wondering what would become of the brilliant Corisande—if she would continue to tolerate the king's infidelities, or if she would leave him at last.

"And Jean, while we're waging this amorous campaign, I want you to go to Tours to report on the activities of the *Parlement* of Paris in exile. I need your legal expertise there, too. Send me the reports, and I'll get your opinion on any touchy litigation that might affect me. Stay there for a few months, Sponde—only that way can you get a feel for the proceedings; whether they are favorable to our cause or not."

"What about my position in La Rochelle? What about my family?" I asked, alarmed.

"Turn the position back over to your secretaries. They're probably just as effective at the job as you were. They get nowhere with the magistrates and prominent citizens because they don't try to enforce my decrees; you get nowhere with those people because you *do,* and you antagonize them."

I blushed at his unflattering assessment of the situation. His brusque summary stung me, even though I had reported the circumstances to him. Obviously, others had done the same, not sparing me and my reputation in the least.

"As for your family," he continued, "bring them to Tours. Stay in the château. There's more than enough room. Ten families could stay there, and the place would still be empty. Just pack them up and take them."

I bowed again. "Thank you, Sire! This generous offer solves more problems than you can ever know!"

"Ah, Sponde, I think I *do* know."

I returned to La Rochelle in December, and celebrated Christmas with my family. After completing a book project with Jérôme Haultain there, Jacques Faye's *Harangues*, for which I wrote a preface, I began preparations to move my family to Tours.

By February 1591, I was comfortably installed with my little family in Tours. I attended parliamentary deliberations daily and wrote weekly accounts to Henri. But I had ample opportunity to make the acquaintance of certain parliamentarians, the President, Achille de Harlay and his brother-in-law, Jacques-Auguste de Thou. Both, as it turned out, were avid scholars of Greek and Roman antiquity.

We sat in taverns sipping the superb local wines. These accompanied leisurely conversations about the morality of the ancient Roman authors Cicero and Seneca. We recognized them as fathers of our modern ideas of justice, as applied under ideal circumstances in our legal system. De Harlay had been imprisoned in the Bastille for several months, released about the same time I was. He told me that the craftsman who had written the letter allowing the assassin, Jacques Clément, to gain entry to the bedchamber of Henri III, had forged his signature. Achille was both horrified and indignant that his name had been misused so mortally.

I had brought my manuscript of Hesiod's *Works and Days* with me and continued my translation, consulting Achille from time to time about the etymologies of Greek words. Jean-Auguste became a good friend and deferred to me in matters of Greek scholarship. This embarrassed me, for he was at least as competent as I was.

He had studied in Basel, as I had, but a few years earlier. He had also been a student of Théodore Zwinger, and we reminisced about the master's house, so light and beautifully arranged, with Hebrew, Greek, and Latin inscriptions lettered on the walls.

Jean-Auguste dabbled in alchemy, and I could be of assistance there, delighted to be back in the laboratory after so long an absence. We tried to repeat my success with the procedure outlined in *The Book of Abraham*, but neither of us had a copy of the book. Although I had thought my memory of the formula perfect, we never managed to duplicate the result I achieved back in Basel. Never again was I able to transform silver into gold, and I began to wonder if my first success had been a divine miracle after all.

In March, during King Henri IV's siege of Chartres, word came to us that Pope Gregory XIV had reaffirmed that Henri was excluded from the French royal succession. In this he confirmed Pope Sixtus V's excommunication and exclusion back in September 1585. I heard that Henri, preoccupied with besieging his beloved and her city, simply shrugged his shoulders and shook his head, saying only, "We'll see about that."

By April, we had the news that Chartres had fallen to Henri—and so had Gabrielle d'Estrées, according to Sully, who had come down to Tours for a quick visit. The king, he feared, would be occupied entirely with his love affair for the foreseeable future. He had better enjoy it—it had cost him quite enough!

My private big news was that Anne was pregnant, already three months along with our second child. I was delighted, attributing her condition to the burst of energy I'd felt back in January when Henri relieved me of the stress of joining the siege at Chartres.

The respite was brief, however. The king released me to return to my regular duties in July and taking my seven-months pregnant Anne and little Jacques, I returned reluctantly to our house in La Rochelle. Uprooting my family from their luxurious quarters in Tours proved to be more of a problem than I had anticipated. Jacques loved playing in the château grounds and the courtyard garden.

There were many horses in the stable, and he learned quickly how to behave around them. They tolerated him well, and I began giving him rides on one or another of them, leading the horse. His favorite was a tall dapple gray, one of Henri's carriage horses. The horse seemed to love Jacques, too, and lowered his head to allow the boy to stroke or pat his nose, while blowing his warm sweet breath in Jacques' face. The two became fast friends, and I hated to see them parted.

Anne, too, loved Tours. During the long days when I was gone to hear sessions of *Parlement* and afterwards to discuss legal questions or, more to my liking, authors of antiquity with de Harlay and de Thou, she would sit in a window doing needlework, visit young wives she had met at church, or take extended walks in the château's park and the nearby woods.

Often, she would leave Jacques in the care of Mélanie, and for the outings in the woods, she would pack a lunch and prolong the walk into a full afternoon's outing. She told me at night of the birds she'd observed, the fallow deer that had passed near her as she sat on a mossy log, or the fish she saw in a quiet side pool of the Loire River. Occasionally, she would take Jacques on those outings, too.

Her female friends became sources of information for me as well. Anne gained their confidence with her winning and frank personality. The ladies sometimes confided information their husbands had told them about political battles waged in the *Parlement de Paris*. The debates generally concerned the power of the Guises versus Spanish influence. Most of the parliamentarians feared a takeover by Felipe II and the loss of French sovereignty. Anne even heard the occasional suggestion that Navarre should accede to the throne—but such gossip was delivered in whispers.

It came as a shock to Anne and Jacques that we would have to return to the cold apartment in La Rochelle. That house was in the center of the city, with nothing but buildings and cobbled streets surrounding it. No park, no garden in the courtyard, no woods nearby—just the cold Atlantic with its winds and dark weather. The apartment might be filled with our own possessions, but it was also filled with harsh memories of cruel treatment and hostile neighbors.

"Is there any possible way to avoid going back there?" she asked me, her voice tight with foreboding.

"I'm just as sorry as you are, Anne," I answered her. "I hate that job, and I'm bad at it. I wasn't cut out to cajole people into doing things they refuse to do out of custom or principle. I end up tyrannizing them, and they hate me for it."

"Well, then, why don't you tell that to Henri? If he's your friend, he'll give you another job." Anne's fists were planted on her hips.

"Truth to tell, my dear, I don't know if Henri really is my friend. I'm a convenience for him, like most of us. Do kings truly have friends? I wonder."

"The least you can do is to test it out. Tell him you need to get out of that position, that you'd be far more productive in some other post."

"Anne, he already knows how poor a job I'm doing. He even quoted some independent reports on that score. And yet, he has ordered me back."

Her brows contracted. "If you don't stand up to him, you're not the man I thought I married, Jean."

I understood her anger. After suffering for months in cold and hostile La Rochelle, she had begun to make a true home in Tours. She hated the thought of losing her physical comforts and most of all, her friends. "I don't think this is the moment to confront him with such a request. I intend to obey his command no matter how painful to us it might be."

"You'd rather sacrifice your family than this shaky connection with the king, then." Anne's tone was icy, though her face had become flushed.

"I don't want to sacrifice either one! However shaky the connection, it's what keeps this family in bread and butter. I'd hoped it wouldn't come to a choice between service to my king and love of my family!"

Anne stalked away from me, and a decided chill between us lasted at least a week after we had arrived back in La Rochelle.

Our second baby was born two months after our arrival. This time, Anne had far less trouble. The midwives seemed more competent, and we were presented with a healthy baby boy, whom we named Jehan. He was christened on September 23, 1591.

From the documents of Jacques Davy du Perron, Bishop d'Evreux:
I have chosen to stay here in Paris, in the Episcopal palace, rather than join King Henri at the siege of Rouen. What would I do there? I'm not a warrior-priest like Archbishop Turpin in Charlemagne's army—at best I could give those going into battle plenary absolution, and then what? As for moving down to Tours, I don't think the moment is quite right. The king is not there, and my presence would be seen as a definite political statement, open to interpretations and speculations on all sides. It's more prudent to remain where I am until the king returns to Tours. Then, I believe, I could make a real difference.

The king is besieging Rouen. He tore himself out of his mistress's arms sometime in mid-November, to join his English and German allies. Rouen has been a stronghold of the Guises for many years and losing the city would be a great blow to the League.

Here in Paris, the population barely has begun to recover from Henri's siege, broken in August, last year. One deplorable result of the siege was the radicalization of the Seize. The most extreme fanatical elements both in religion and politics took over the leadership. I like good oratory as much as the next man, but oratory was sliding towards invective and worse. The wealthier and nobler elements in the Seize disappeared from Paris as soon as the gates were opened. Many already had smuggled themselves out so as not to have to endure the suffering and the starvation. This has left the leadership in the hands of the poorer lawyers and clergy. Since the Cardinal de Bourbon died, they've even considered establishing a Catholic republic! The moderate elements of the Paris *Parlement* have been in grave danger as a result, and I, too, was directly threatened.

About two months ago, I was asked to officiate at a Mass in the church of Sainte Geneviève. I gave a homily I considered a good balance between Christian forbearance and the prevailing political sentiments, telling the congregation that they must remember that Christ preached love and charity towards one's neighbor, not hatred and violence. Not only that, but they must give serious consideration to any peace proposals brought forward to end France's constant bloodletting, even if that might mean compromise. I could tell that half the congregation was with me, approving my moderate stance, but the other half was becoming increasingly enraged. Some even walked out during the homily.

About a week afterwards, at dusk, I was returning alone to my residence. As I passed through a narrow street between the rue Saint Martin and the rue Saint-Denis, a group of eight suddenly surrounded me. I recognized none of them since most of them muffled their faces in their cloaks.

Their leader came up behind me, wrapped one arm around my chest, and held a knife against my throat with the other hand. "Your Grace," he hissed into my ear, his sarcasm transforming the honorific into an insult, "we're on the watch for *politiques*, and your homily last week bordered on treason. We could execute you now as a traitor to the Church and to the League, but we'll be content *this time* with a warning. Don't preach another subversive homily, or there won't *be* a next time for you. Understood, Your Grace?"

I was terrified. If he slit my throat, I'd simply disappear into the Seine, turning up an anonymous, naked corpse somewhere downriver, and no one would ever know what had become of that bishop... what was his name? Du Perron? My voice must have betrayed my fear as I answered the man, "Yes, understood. But if you kill me, you'll kill a loyal pillar of the Church, no traitor. You'll be damned."

The man didn't release his hold but snickered at my all too obvious terror. "Yes, yes, to be sure, Your Grace. We believe your every word, Your Grace. This is a warning, a word to the wise. As you can see, we have the means to find and deal with you... *next time.*"

Those last words were delivered in a coarse whisper directly into my ear. I shuddered as he released me, but not before he drew the knife gently across my neck. The sting from the cut continued burning, compounded by the tickle of the blood that oozed its way under my collar as I hurried back to the palace. I shook for hours afterwards. I believe these were hirelings of a member of the Seize who has always frightened me for his fanaticism: a certain Father Georges Marquet. He would certainly have no superstitious awe of a bishop, nor would he be under any illusions about my invulnerability.

Another week passed, and the Spanish Ambassador, Mendoza, left the city. Although he represented one of the most fanatical Roman Catholic governments in Europe—not excluding the Vatican—he was more moderate than the Seize is now. I assumed he returned to Madrid for further instructions from Felipe II.

Left to itself without Mendoza's restraining influence, the Seize pronounced death sentences on three moderate ministers of the Paris *Parlement*. I raged when I discovered these included Barnabé Brisson, the First President elected as such by the League. I wept when the three ministers were brutally hanged.

Their loss—particularly that of Brisson—bitterly grieved those few of us remaining, trying to maintain some sanity in this city.

I did not witness the hanging itself but saw knots of people coming back from the execution, chanting slogans of "Death to traitors! Death to heretics!" As soon as I had crossed the threshold of the Episcopal Palace, I shouted for the secretary. Father Picard came hurrying down the hall. "Yes, Your Grace, what is it?"

"Do we have any priest going north out of this city? I need to get a message to the Duc de Mayenne right away!"

"Well, let me see... Yes, Father Mabillon. He could take a message to Meaux. He's leaving this afternoon, Your Grace."

"Excellent. Send him to my rooms in an hour. I'll have the message waiting."

The Duc de Mayenne received my detailed report, outlining the violence and insubordination of the supposed leaders of the League. Father Mabillon brought Mayenne's brief reply on his return:

"Thank you for the information, Your Grace. I'll see to this. Mayenne."

And he did, with violence. I confess to feeling a surge of savage joy as he entered Paris on November 18, seized and hanged the ringleaders of the incipient anarchy, imprisoned or expelled the other members of the group. Father Georges Marquet was sent on a tour of duty to Orléans, a move that would relieve us only temporarily.

Chapter XIII

Royal Missions

ean resumes:

While I was struggling to do my duty in La Rochelle during the next several months of 1592, official reports came regularly, keeping me abreast of the news. Henri continued besieging Rouen—unsuccessfully. Once again, the Duque de Parma entered France, luring Henri away from the siege in order to fight him. On February 5, Henri attacked Parma at Aumale and miscalculated—one of his rare mistakes. He was wounded and nearly captured, and Parma was able to drive the Maréchal de Biron and the rest of the besieging army away from Rouen.

My time in La Rochelle was not all business, not all unpleasant. Besides the solace of my family and the delight of watching my firstborn son, Jacques, grow in physical skills and mental and spiritual ability, I turned once more to Jérôme Haultain for friendship and discussion. Minister Rotan appeared in La Rochelle sometime during that year also and engaged me in long and earnest conversations about Calvinism as compared to Catholicism. It was clear he was about to convert and was trying to pump me for reasons to remain a faithful Calvinist. I fear that I was less help than I should have been. I didn't care for the man, and then, I was in no position to demonstrate the superiority of the reformed faith; I was too shaky myself. Bishop du Perron had been astute in his evaluation of the state of my soul.

Somehow, I lasted through that year in La Rochelle. I had decided that a year would be enough to prove that my family and I could survive in that city, in that position. But our situation did not improve. On the contrary, the citizens never ceased inventing ever more ways to make us miserable. Anne seemed continually depressed, and I knew Jacques was bullied at school. I determined to risk the king's anger rather than ruin all our lives. Early in January 1593, I sold my office in the Sénéchaussée to a reliable man and a solid Calvinist, a native of the city named Nicolas Benureau. Anne and I packed up—she with joy, I with trepidation—and moved all our goods back to Tours, where this time I bought a small apartment in the city center, not wanting to demand housing from King Henri after I had abandoned the post to which he had appointed me.

I contacted my friends Messieurs de Harlay and de Thou, who introduced me to Henri de la Tour d'Auvergne, Maréchal de Bouillon. After a number of conversations, he agreed to back me in a request to Henri IV that he grant me another post—otherwise, I would be forced to take my family and leave Tours at once, to go into retirement in some obscure corner. The Maréchal was a leader of the Huguenots and a devoted follower of Henri's, therefore a powerful voice in my favor.

It was at this time that I wrote a lengthy poem, "Stanzas of the Supper," which fully reflected my beliefs, and which struck the Huguenots as Catholic, the Catholics as Huguenot. To be truthful, the poem was halfway between. It begins this way:

Mon ame, esveille-toy de ta couche mortelle,
Ce jourd'huy ton Sauveur à son banquet t'appelle,

Où luy-mesme doit estre et ton vin et ton pain,
Ce père nourricier sera ta nourriture,
Pren son sang pour bruvage, et sa chair pour pasture,
Tu n'auras jamais soif, tu n'auras jamais faim.
 My soul, awaken from your mortal bed.
This day, your Savior calls you to his banquet,
Where he himself will be your wine and bread.
The nourishing Father your nourishment,
His blood for drink, his flesh for food.
You shall never thirst; never hunger.
My faith was becoming an ever more central preoccupation.

Navarre appeared in Tours that January, at a time of acute crisis in the government of that part of France held by the League. Their actions would determine the future of the whole of France.

Charles de Guise, Duc de Mayenne, had convoked the Estates-General in Paris. The deputies involved in that meeting represented each "estate": the nobility, the clergy, and the people. Such a convocation had for centuries been reserved exclusively to the legitimate King of France. The League, under the leadership of Charles's older brother, Henri de Guise, had committed the same breach of sacred tradition back in 1588, when they convoked the Estates-General at Blois, ignoring King Henri III's prerogative and authority. The insult had fueled Henri III's rage, ending in his assassination of Henri de Guise and his brother the cardinal.

Aware of that tragic recent history, the Duc de Mayenne had convoked the assembly under protest, bowing to pressure from Spain and from the radical conservative wing of the League.

The deputies had braved considerable hardship getting into Paris through the screen of towns and territories now pledged to Navarre, but by the end of January they had assembled—only one hundred twenty-eight of them, far fewer than usual. The Duc de

Mayenne, in his office as *Lieutenant-Général*, gave the opening speech on January 26, stating that the purpose of the meeting was to find a Catholic king for France. Next to him was an empty chair symbolizing the royal vacancy, and on the other side sat Cardinal Nicolas de Pellevé, representing the views, power and influence of the Vatican and of Spain.

Henri de Navarre, back in Tours, reacted immediately with two acts. In the first, he denounced the Estates-General, calling their illegitimate convocation an act of *lèse-majesté*. In the second act, he proposed negotiations, declaring that peace could come only through conferences between his own royal representatives and delegates from the Estates. Although Pellevé and other radical Leaguers violently opposed this idea, they were overruled, and a group of delegates were to meet with eight Catholic representatives of the king in Suresnes on April 29. The king's representatives included my friend Jacques-Auguste de Thou.

While all this was happening, Anne and I had settled in comfortably in our new apartment, which admitted plenty of light, appeared airy but remained warm, and was located within walking distance of the Loire and the woods where Anne and Jacques loved to roam. I went to court daily and sent the king my latest poetry including my "Stanzas of the Supper," but it took me almost a week to see Henri. He was extremely busy planning strategy regarding the meeting of the Estates-General, picking and interviewing his delegates to the meeting, and tending to other business having to do with the continuing battles between Huguenots and Catholics in other provinces. At last, thanks to the insistence of the Maréchal de Bouillon, Henri granted me an audience.

Henri was not one to mince words. "Sponde, I don't have much time to waste. You've dumped one post and are back to beg another, I suppose?" His tone was flat as he addressed me, and I could not tell if he were angry or merely disgusted, or both—he was certainly not cordial.

I decided to be just as direct as he. "Yes, Sire. That's the idea. I was unsuited to that position in the Sénéchaussée. I was not serving you well there, and I think you were aware of that, Sire."

"Yes. I was. Very well, stay here at court, Jean. I'll restore your stipend and I'll probably find some legal work for you in a day or two that would suit you better."

I bowed deeply. "Thank you, Sire. You are most generous." I was turning to move into the background when Henri spoke again.

"Your friend Jacques Davy du Perron, that Bishop d'Evreux, is here. He's brought someone I think you know, the Sieur de Morlas. They're anxious to talk to you."

I was surprised, but merely thanked the king again and made way for the other petitioners coming behind me. I looked over the crowd in that audience chamber to see if I could see the tall figure of Davy, but he was not there. I was walking down the hallway outside the chamber when someone laid a hand on my shoulder. Turning, I saw Bishop du Perron behind me, with Morlas at his elbow, a gray-haired and rather sharp-faced man whom I had met some time earlier in Honfleur. Morlas, like me, had for some time been questioning his Calvinism.

"Jean!" the bishop cried out, "Good to see you again! I think you already know my friend, the Sieur de Morlas."

"So, pleased to see you again, uh, Father Davy." I bowed, still uncomfortable with such an informal mode of address. "And how nice to see you, as well, Monsieur de Morlas!"

After the greetings were over, Davy asked, "Have you had lunch, Jean? We were on our way to the Lion d'Or over there. It's not fancy, but they have good wine and food that's better than average. After all, they're feeding the *Parlement*—and even the king from time to time. Come, be our guest! I have lots to tell you about Paris. Just came from there."

Curiosity and my liking for Davy drew me, and I accepted their invitation. Our "luncheon" lasted all afternoon. Davy began by telling me tales of the siege of Paris, and how he had acted as spy for Henri. His contacts had told him just where I would be and just when I would be riding the perimeter of the city. Thus, he was able send me the message that influenced Henri to release and feed three thousand women and children.

While Davy enthralled the two of us with his stories, I noticed three barmaids watching him and listening to his tales. They were not busy; the crowd that had come in for the midday meal had thinned out. From time to time they giggled and punched each other, whispering in each other's ears, clearly attracted by this youngish, handsome prelate. I was not surprised. His wavy black hair with its dashes of white above the ears, chiseled features, intense blue eyes and cleft chin would attract any woman. Oblivious of his unintended audience, Du Perron continued telling us about the rabid behavior of the Seize, the execution of Barnabé Brisson and two other members of *Parlement*, and Mayenne's revenge for the killings.

We were on the third bottle of the finest wine of La Touraine by the time we began discussing theology. The Sieur de Morlas, who had earlier kept silent, invited a change in the direction of our talk. "I suppose you're still a committed Calvinist, Sponde?" Seeing me hesitate, he turned to Du Perron. "Your Grace, I wonder if you could enlighten my friend Sponde, as you have me." Then turning to me, "You won't be able to refute these arguments, I'll wager a week of lunches at the Lion d'Or!" He sat back with a smug grin as the Bishop d'Evreux began his argument.

"Jean, you were brought up in the Reformed religion, I know, but perhaps you haven't given deep consideration to all of its doctrines."

"But I have, Father Davy. I've studied Calvin's *Institutions*. But let's hear what you have to say!" I was half drunk and eager for a theological argument. I had always prided myself on my knowledge of theology and my debating skills. Then, under the guise of inquiring into the complexities of Jean Calvin's theology, Davy proceeded to attack the doctrine of predestination in particular. His logic was impeccable, close-linked and persuasive. In the end, he asked me, "So, it's fair to say that Calvin believed only a few designated people would be saved?"

"Yes, I believe that's a fair statement."

"And God, because of his omniscience, knows from the beginning who those will be?"

"Yes, of course!"

"So, it's inescapable then that we are all *predestined* by that divine knowledge either to be saved or to be damned?"

My reply was delayed by the approach of the handsome young barmaid who seemed to be the leader of the trio. She curtsied. "Would the gentlemen care for more wine?" She addressed us all but had eyes only for Du Perron.

He looked inquiringly at the two of us, and since we both shook our heads, he told her, "No, it seems we've reached our capacity. Thank you for asking!" She left the table, apparently well pleased that she had at least been able to speak directly with the bishop.

Davy had paid her interruption scant attention. He repeated his question: "So we're all *predestined* to be saved or damned?"

"That's about it, Father," I replied.

"That's a very sad and gloomy doctrine, Jean. It leaves no role for free will."

"Logically, you're right. But Calvin would say that God, even though he knows what our free choices will be, does not force those choices. We freely damn or save ourselves by our choices."

"But God already has our spots picked out for us: either on a cloud up above, or in a roasting oven down below."

"Yes, that's how it seemed to Jean Calvin—and you know that he took much of his doctrine straight from Saint Augustine. And Jesus himself said in the Sermon on the Mount that very few will be saved." I took a big gulp of the white wine I was drinking at the moment.

"How do you react to all that, Jean? We Catholics believe that God intends for *all* of us to be saved, and that he allows us the free choice to save or damn ourselves. He invites us *all* to His table—and if only a few of us accept that invitation, it is by our own choice—free choice. There is no predestination, no picking favorites beforehand, leaving the poor sinner wondering if he is among the damned."

"I think that's much more humane," I agreed. "If God is merciful, and I would like to believe he is, then he would leave it up to us whether we want to take the path of salvation or of perdition, perhaps voluntarily limiting himself not to foresee and in that way predetermine our choice."

Du Perron stood up and stretched. "That's surely enough conversation for one day! Jean, you must be worn out with all this theological wrangling. By the way, I'll be officiating at Mass day after tomorrow. Would you come, please? I've invited the king. He said he'd be there."

I stood too, feeling dizzy from the discussion as much as from the wine. "Yes, I'll come, Father Davy. I still remember that fine homily you gave in Santa Maria Maggiore, years ago!"

He smiled and squeezed my arm. "I'll look forward to seeing you at Mass, Jean." As we walked out of the tavern, he continued speaking. His tone began neutrally enough but became more urgent by the end of the sentence. "You know, Jean, that if Henri is ever to become accepted as King of France, he'll *have* to convert."

"Yes, I know." I replied, "The oath all French kings take includes swearing that the monarch will defend the faith—meaning the Catholic faith, of course—and that he will rid the realm of heretics. Henri must know that too."

Du Perron stopped in his tracks and halted me, too, by grasping my left arm. He swung to face me, laying hold of the other arm as well. Then, looking me earnestly in the face, he told me, "You'd be doing us all a favor if you'd talk to him about that. You'd be doing

France a favor! He must make the obvious decision without delaying much longer. The longer he waits, the more blood will be shed. And, while you're at it," he added, as if as an afterthought, "you might as well think of your own salvation as well!" He gave me a little shake as I looked up into his earnest, pleading face, and then he released me.

I walked on, saying nothing, a bit stunned by Du Perron's intensity. At last, I replied. "I'll certainly talk to the king. I agree that he must act soon or risk the ruination of France. As for me... I have much thinking to do—about our entire afternoon together."

We parted shortly afterwards, and I walked home. Anne and Jacques had gone out, leaving Jehan in Mélanie's care. "They're somewhere out along the river, monsieur," she told me. "They'll be back before supper."

I decided to return to court to see if I could somehow set up a tête-à-tête with the king. He was still, or perhaps again, in the audience hall when I arrived. I entered and stood in the background for a while, awaiting a moment when I could approach him. He spotted me and, to my surprise, beckoned me over, giving me preference over several gentlemen who outranked me.

"Sponde, I need to talk to you privately. How about dinner tomorrow night? I have to go to that blasted Mass Du Perron is saying the next morning, but we should be able to finish our chat and enjoy a nice dinner well before midnight. What do you say?"

I was of course delighted at the opening this gave me, though apprehensive about the message he wanted to convey privately to me. Such a favor from the king meant that he would ask me to perform some difficult or dangerous task for him. "Of course, Sire, I'll be happy to come," I answered a bit hollowly through my thoroughly mixed feelings, "I was about to request a private meeting with you."

"Oh?" he raised his eyebrows at me. "Well, I'll find out why tomorrow at dinner. I'll see you then." And, with a wave of his hand, he dismissed me.

Around half-past nine the next night, dinner was served in the king's study, a room lined with books, the older ones bound in vellum, some brand new volumes in brown or red leather with shining gold leaf lettering on their spines. I would have enjoyed the opportunity to look them over. The servants brought in a dining table just big enough for the two of us, already covered with a white cloth, then two straight chairs, the place settings, and finally the food in tureens and casseroles, steaming and emitting enticing aromas.

They served a full-bodied red wine that glowed like a jewel in the lamplight, its perfume heady and redolent of grape blossoms. From around Avignon—something they had begun to call after the papal palace there— "château neuf du pape." Then came a pâté made with liver, finely chopped pork tenderloin, truffles, parsley and other herbs, surrounded by sautéed golden chanterelle mushrooms accompanied by plenty of crusty white bread. The main course, a thick slice of the tenderest venison, was garnished with fresh watercress, flanked by stewed carrots and small, mild turnips, and by delicate Italian pasta called "hummingbird's tongues," something that had become popular during the lifetime of the former Queen Mother, Catherine de Médicis. I used the plentiful crusty white bread for the pâté and then to mop up the complex sauce for the main course, made from the meat drippings and wine—I couldn't tell what else. Certainly, a dash of nutmeg.

In the midst of all these delights for the palate, Henri revealed his purpose for me. "I need you to act as messenger to my representatives in Suresnes, Jean. I've sent only Catholics to represent me, men who've recently come over to my side despite the fact I'm still Huguenot. I figured they would have better arguments against the Leaguers—after all, they had to rationalize their change of allegiance from the conservative wing of the Church to me. They're already up there, negotiating with the delegates from that illegitimate convocation of the Estates-General in Paris. A truce has been declared in the surrounding territories—in spite of opposition by the extreme Leaguers—and from what I hear, my chief representative, the Archbishop of Bourges, Renaud de Beaune, is making good headway with their man, Pierre d'Epinac, Archbishop of Lyon. If we can get Lyon on board, that's a huge gain."

"What is the message, Sire?" I asked, anxiety increasing in the pit of my stomach.

"I need to tell them that since no one can contest my right to the throne, my right of inheritance—even though they have used every trumped-up excuse to do so—my own course is obvious: *I will be king of all France and will brook no opposition.* Not from the pope, not from anyone."

"They already know that, Sire. That's hardly worth sending me up to Suresnes to tell them!"

"Right. I need to concede a point. Tell them that I intend to take instruction to convert to Catholicism in due course."

This, too, was not news. Henri had said as much before. I sat back formulating my next speech, since Henri had given me a perfect opening to introduce the topic of his *immediate* conversion. The servants came in at that moment, busying themselves with removing the dishes. The king and I were silent until they had left the room.

"Your majesty..." I began, only to be interrupted again by the servants bringing in a cherry pudding topped with whipped cream and two cups full of a new drink from the Indies, hot chocolate. We busied ourselves with the desserts for a few moments. I was astonished at the delicious flavor of the chocolate; I had never tasted anything remotely like it. "Your Majesty, this is an amazing drink... but that's not what I really wanted to say."

Henri laughed. "Yes, it does rather take your breath away! It's said to be a fine aphrodisiac—something I don't need just yet, and God willing I won't ever—and it's certainly nourishing. About the only good thing to come into France from Spain lately. Now, what was it you really wanted to say?"

"That you should convert right away, Sire. Don't wait. The longer you wait the longer this war will drag on." I had blurted out my thoughts without the slightest attempt at diplomacy. "Think of France, Sire. In order to be acknowledged King by all the people, you must go through the ceremony at the Cathedral of Rheims. And that *requires* you to be Catholic, Sire. When the oath and the ceremony of anointment were set up, there *was* only one Church. The only problems then were caused by tiny minority groups of heretics, perhaps by an invasion of Moors, or perhaps by one individual."

"Jean, Jean—I know all that. But even if I could find it in my conscience to change my faith now, what would I do about my Huguenot allies? They've stuck by me in thick and thin, sacrificing their lives with their families and their own lives on many occasions. A conversion would betray them all! I simply cannot do that, Jean."

"Sire, you'll *have* to do it. You must explain to them why it's necessary. Persuade them, show them there's no alternative—else we're at an impasse, and France will be divided forever. Destroyed."

Our conversation and dinner had stretched well beyond two hours, it seemed. "We'd better finish here if we want to attend that Mass in the morning, Jean. I want you to go up to Suresnes within the week. Can you do that?"

"I believe so. Anne will not be pleased to see me go back into danger."

"I understand. You've got two boys now. Congratulations on your second son, by the way, I never got around to saying that."

He gave me instructions about my route. "And, on the way back, pass through Orléans. I have a message for the bishop there. Terrible old Leaguer he is, but I want him to know directly from me that I'll be taking instruction in view of converting. Let him get that news out to his friends. Maybe some of them will come over to my side, and I'll have fewer to fight when the time comes. You should have no trouble on this trip, Jean; you'll be among friends most of the way. Just be careful in Orléans."

"That should be no problem. No one knows me there, Sire."

I accompanied Henri to Mass the next morning. As always, the Bishop d'Evreux was eloquent and persuasive in his homily, which was addressed to Henri. He appealed to the king's emotions, telling anecdotes about the sufferings of the French people who desperately needed peace and prosperity to return to the land, and for armies of foreign powers to be gone, no longer ravaging the countryside to sustain themselves. He quoted a woman widowed at the Battle of Ivry with whom he had spoken after a Mass where she had taken the Eucharist from his hands. She had said, "Henri would make a fine king for all of us. The first capable king since our beloved François I. If he were only a good Catholic like François, his great uncle!" Du Perron concluded, saying that he, like the people, longed for a true son of France to be their monarch, one who would put the country back to rights.

He joined us after the Mass, and the three of us launched into a discussion that soon enough turned to the differences in the two faiths. Henri was impressive in his knowledge of the finer points. "After all," he explained to us, "I was forced by my father to attend Mass when I was at the Valois court as a boy. And, after the Saint Bartholomew's Day massacre, I was forced to convert. Don't think I haven't had adequate instruction, already!"

By the time I left for Suresnes, Henri, the bishop, and I had met several times. Henri finally gave in and said to me, "Tell the delegates and representatives that I am resolved upon a reconversion, *'pour avoir cogneu et jugé estre bon de le faire'*—having recognized and judged it to be the good thing to do."

The ride to Suresnes took me three days. Henri had provided me with a good horse since I no longer had the stable of the Sénéchaussée to draw upon. The people in the fields and small village taverns where I stopped for a meal or refreshment seemed more optimistic and energetic the closer I got to my destination. They were taking full advantage of the truce. It was mid-May, and the growing season was underway; fields were green, sprouting with grain and vegetables. Roads were well-nigh impassible, though, deep with mud from the spring rains. I was thankful not to be traveling them with a carriage of some sort. I arrived spattered with mud on May 17, and had to wait an hour for the globs of mud to dry enough so I could dust them off before presenting myself at the Château de Suresnes, where the negotiations were taking place.

The corridors of the château were thick with people discussing, gesticulating. I made my way among them, hearing snatches of conversation as I passed. I heard someone addressing a certain Monsieur Villeroy as Monsieur le Secrétaire d'État—Henri's Secretary of State. I paused near him, then when I could interrupt without rudeness, I told him what Henri wanted his delegation to know: that he was resolved on converting—soon. Villeroy is Catholic, and he almost shouted for joy. "Merci! Merci, Monsieur de Sponde! This is fantastic news; our cause will be well served this day!"

When I asked him where I could find Renaud de Beaune, the Archbishop of Bourges, Villeroy told me that he was in conference at that very moment. He added that Epinac, the Archbishop of Lyon and the League's chief negotiator, was no longer contesting Henri IV's constitutional right to the throne, but only his religion.

"Come with me, Monsieur de Sponde. I want to announce this wonderful news to Beaune with you at my side. We're certain to win the day now." As we walked, he excitedly gave me more news. "By the way, were you aware that Philip II sent his Duque de Feria to try to sway the Estates-General to elect the Infanta as queen?"

"No. And?"

"And it was already too late when he arrived. They were already resolved upon meeting here with Navarre's representatives. They sent Feria packing, telling him that our salic law prohibits any woman from mounting the throne of France, and that our laws and customs also prevent us from calling forward as king any prince not of our nation."

We arrived in the negotiating room where a number of men were seated around a rectangular oak table, dark with age, on velvet-upholstered straight chairs. Villeroy was someone who commanded respect, and voices were hushed as we entered. "This gentleman is Monsieur Jean de Sponde, who is carrying a message from the king. He has an announcement to make." He turned to me.

I stepped forward, back straight, head high. With a ringing voice I made my announcement. "The rightful King of France, Henri IV, has sent me with the following message: he is now resolved upon converting to Catholicism, having recognized that such is the right course of action. He will take appropriate instruction as soon as might be."

Our representatives applauded, then turned back to their opponents. "Well, gentlemen, what further arguments can you possibly have now?"

Chapter XIV

Distant Light

Iwas anxious to get back to my family, and I missed Anne, knowing that she would be fretting constantly, wondering if I would return safely. I still had to carry that message to the Bishop of Orléans. I approached the city with some trepidation, since it was known for its extreme hatred of Huguenots. No one would welcome a messenger from "The Heretic."

I entered the city at noon, rationalizing my fear, telling myself that I was an anonymous traveler, just a man anxious for his midday meal. I had been riding since dawn, and my horse needed a break, too. I found a stable that looked clean and respectable, with a friendly hostler. I left the horse to his water, hay, and oats, and went to find a likely looking tavern, where I devoured a plate of andouilles—tripe sausages—with coarse bread and two glasses of passable red wine, then walked on through the streets.

Orléans is famous for being the city where Jeanne d'Arc led our knights in battle, successfully defeating the English in 1429. I stared about me at scenes similar to those she must have seen as a maiden warrior. There was a colorful outdoor market set up near the hulking ruin of the cathedral, which looked to have been impressive enough to cause visions in anyone, as I could tell from its shattered remains—although Jeanne d'Arc had needed no such supplementary inspiration.

We Huguenots had destroyed that great church about twenty-five years ago, and the city was still seething with fury over the atrocity. It would take a lot to win these people over to Henri's side. I walked around the ruin almost in mourning, seeking out what few carvings were left from our attack. It made me think of the cathedral at Lyon, although at least there we had been content with destroying the statuary on the façade, the stained glass windows, and the statues in the interior—we had not torn down the building. Finally, I stopped a passerby. "Where can I find the Bishop's residence, please?"

I was told to turn back west to the Hôtel Groslot. "If he isn't in the Hôtel, he'll probably be in the church on the west side."

I hurried to follow the man's directions and started across the open square in front of the Hôtel. I passed a pair of armed guards who apparently patrolled the perimeter of the square, paying little attention to them. I paused for a moment to look at the huge building I was approaching. It was here that Henri II's eldest son, King François II, named for his grandfather, had died holding the hand of his child bride, Marie Stuart, later to become Queen of the Scots. His brothers, who had succeeded him as kings of France, Charles IX and Henri III, had stayed here as well. It was a newish red brick structure, built early in the century, and to my taste not a handsome design. As I stood there, a hand was laid on my shoulder.

"Well, well! I hadn't thought ever to see you again, Monsieur Guy de Thou!"

The bitter sarcasm in the voice caused me to shudder. I jerked away to look at this man who was addressing me by the name I had used as a spy in Paris four years ago. It was a priest. Georges Marquet. I stared into his eyes like a rabbit at a snake. This was the man who had pointed me out to the guards before they had dragged me off to the Bastille. History repeated itself.

"Guards! Help!" he called out, his preaching voice carrying easily to those receding figures. I had pulled myself free of Marquet's grasp. He made no attempt to lay hands upon me again, but there was nowhere I could run—I was in the middle of a vast open plaza. The two guards sprinted up to us. "Take this man into custody. He's a Huguenot spy. I know him from Paris where we caught him red-handed."

"Right away, Father Marquet!" They saluted. Apparently, the good Father had already assumed some important office in the government here and was well known to the enforcers of the law.

"Wait! I have a message from King Henri IV for the bishop! I have documents... I protested, although I was already being jerked about, my hands tied behind me.

Father Marquet, watching the procedure with a faint smile, ordered the guards to search me. They patted my chest but did not feel the letter destined for the bishop that I had hidden in a pocket that Anne had sewn inside the lining of my doublet, next to my left breast. Wearing it against my body for nearly a week must have softened the paper, which made no crackling sound as they patted it. They did find the letter of safe-conduct in an outer pocket, informing the reader that I was a messenger for King Henri IV. They felt around my waist and over my back, running their hands down my legs and probing into my boots as far as my ankles, taking my belt-knife and small pouch of coins as they progressed.

Father Marquet was reading the safe-conduct. "*King* Henri *IV*!" he sneered, "I think the pope has other ideas about his kingship! You may be trying to pass yourself off as a messenger, but I know you as a spy."

"But, Father, I must see the bishop! I have a message..."

"Of course! Of course, you do. And a message for His Holiness, too, I'll wager. Well, you can tell it to Satan in Hell where you'll be going. I daresay he'll be more receptive!"

With my hands bound behind me, I hardly could produce the document Henri had given me for the Bishop of Orléans. I began to realize that it could be to my advantage not to show it—I might be able to use it somehow. If I were executed this time, when they stripped my body for disposal, the message would be found and taken to His Grace. My mission would be completed, even though my life would be forfeit. I ceased to resist, marching along in step with my unwanted escort.

Once again, without seeing any magistrate, unable to communicate with anyone, I found myself in a dungeon with chains upon my feet. At least now that June was coming on it would be warmer than the last time, I reflected, looking around the subterranean chamber into which I had been thrust. A wooden bench had been dragged out from the wall and was placed more or less in the center of the room, so the light from four small barred windows would fall upon it. The chamber was fairly large, probably intended to house five or more prisoners at need. Like the Bastille, there were mere stone shelves for beds, though here, piles of dirty straw were heaped upon them, doubtless alive with vermin. I sat on the bench, facing the windows, and buried my face in my hands.

I don't know how long I stayed in that one position, at first moaning in despair and rocking myself, then letting my mind wander—remembering, regretting, calculating, wondering, agonizing over Anne and the two boys. At last, at the end of my rope, I began to pray, asking God for his mercy and help in what I feared were to be my last hours. Focusing on something transcendent cleared my head and brought to mind those theological conversations I'd had with Du Perron. I was mulling them over when a key rattled in the door of my dungeon. I leaped to my feet, swung around to face the door, rigid and trembling. Perhaps now I was to be summarily executed?

A dark figure passed in front of the guard, in a black robe of a design I had never seen before. He spoke briefly with the guard, turning to me once the door had closed behind him with a clang. He paused, looking around, allowing his eyes to become accustomed to the gloom. "Never fear, Monsieur de Sponde," he said, calling me by my right name, "I'm not the executioner, nor even the priest come to hear your last confession. My name is Father Auguste Bouchard, and I belong to the Society of Jesus."

I let out a sigh of relief, reminded of a similar visit by Father Cueilly just before my release from the Sorbonne. Perhaps this visit augured well, also. At least I would have a live person to talk to. "What is the Society of Jesus?" I asked, never having heard of it before.

"Maybe you've heard the term 'Jesuit'?"

I shook my head.

"Some snide detractor named us that—and we adopted it. We call ourselves Jesuits now. We're a new order of men—well, new as clerical orders go, fifty-three years old. We're mainly missionaries and teachers." His voice was gentle, soothing. I looked closely at him. He had removed his broad-brimmed felt hat to reveal a tousled mop of iron gray hair, cut short, and a square jawed, clean-shaven face that glimmered pale in the gloom. As he approached me, I could see that he was about my height but burly, muscular rather than fat.

My trembling had subsided. "And what brings you to this cell, Father?"

"A certain priest, Father Georges Marquet, who acts as the League's advisor to the mayor, was bragging about catching a spy—the very one he had already ferreted out in Paris once, an agent for 'The Heretic.' He gave the name you had used as a spy, Guy de Thou, then named you by your correct name, Jean de Sponde. He laughed as he told me what a fool you are, Monsieur de Sponde, thinking you could deceive the authorities here with a safe-conduct from Tours and the claim that you were carrying a message for the bishop. I requested permission to check on you."

I shook my head in irritation as he spoke, then interrupted. "I may be a fool, but Father Marquet's minions didn't search me thoroughly enough. You see, I *am* carrying a message for the bishop! By the Grace of God, I still have the letter here, in King Henri's own hand. The seal is the impression of his ring—the seal of the Bourbons. I'm fortunate that Marquet was so cocksure."

The priest held out his hand. "May I see it?"

I pondered this for a moment. I had nothing to lose by showing him the letter, and perhaps everything to gain. He might even deliver the message for me, and by some means get me released. I reached inside my doublet, producing the letter from the inner pocket. "Here it is, Father."

He held it so that the light would strike it, peering at the handwriting on the front, then turning it over to examine the seal. "It looks quite authentic, all right. Would you trust me to deliver it for you to the bishop? I think he'll receive me."

I said aloud what I had just been thinking. "Father, I don't think I have anything to lose, although I'm taking a big leap of faith in giving up the letter. It leaves me defenseless, somehow."

He looked at me intensely, a crease appearing between his bushy gray eyebrows. "I assure you, by the living Savior in whom we both believe, that I'll do everything in my power to deliver the message and do whatever I can for you as well."

"Thank you, Father. If you can get the message to the bishop, at least that part of my task is done. I only hope I'll live to see my wife and boys again."

The priest took my arm. "Let's sit down for a moment. I'd like to find out more about you. I presume you're a Calvinist. Where from? You sound like someone from Béarn."

"Yes, Father, a Calvinist from Béarn."

"Huguenot by conviction or by birth—or both?"

"By birth, Father. My convictions are somewhere in between the faiths."

"What do you mean, my son?"

We launched into an intense conversation, in which I told him that unlike my fellow Calvinists, I had believed for years in the actual transformation of the bread and the wine into the Body and the Blood at Holy Eucharist. There were other aspects of Calvinism that I didn't approve of—the doctrine of predestination, for example. For his part, Father Auguste discussed the original reasons for Luther's dissatisfaction with the Church, and how the Church had since tried to remedy certain aspects that Luther had criticized.

"The Council of Trent dealt with many of the charges made by Luther and those reformers who followed after him: for instance, that we worship the Virgin Mary and the saints, and that our priests are half-illiterate, some of us not even understanding the Latin liturgy we say at Mass. How could such priests teach their congregation properly, not to mention their successors?"

"Yes, Father. Calvinists call you 'idolaters,' as you must know. And yes, we often sneer at the low level of learning in the Catholic Church. But there are other issues..."

"Yes, of course," he replied. "I just wanted to point out that the Council made it very clear that we do not worship the Virgin Mary, although we do venerate her and the saints. And yes, we do pray to her and to the saints as intercessors for us. I believe you also venerate the Virgin, do you not?"

"Yes, Father, especially at Christmastime. But we never pray to her, nor do we pray to the saints. We address our prayers directly to God, in the name of Jesus Christ."

"Yes. Well, there we must agree to differ—although you must know that we pray directly to God in Jesus' name as well. I just mentioned another charge: that our priests were (and still are) ignorant. We in the Society of Jesus have taken that very seriously.

Our founding saint, Ignatius of Loyola, believed he had wasted a good deal of time before he began seriously to educate himself.

When he set up the Society, he required all of us to begin by acquiring a thorough general education—including Latin and Greek, of course—studying every branch of learning. Then we specialize in philosophy, and after that, theology."

"What do you do with all that learning, Father?" Compared to most clergymen I knew, except for the ones who had become true humanists, such a regime as the one he was describing seemed unduly restrictive.

"We need all that instruction, my son, to teach. Many of us teach at the upper levels of study in the schools and universities. We're setting up schools in Paris and Clermont—all over France, Spain, and Europe in general. We're educating priests and confessors, and we also need that instruction to become adequate missionaries. We've gone to the Orient, you see, where we match our wits with representatives of some of the world's oldest civilizations. We'd better be well informed about our own civilization, our own faith, if we intend to convert others to our beliefs."

We discussed for about an hour, and then he took his leave. "I'll see to it that you receive enough good food to sustain you, Jean. And I'll be back to visit with you, if you wish."

"Thank you, Father Auguste. I'd be enormously grateful to you if you could see that I'm properly fed! And of course, I'd like to see you again, to continue our conversation. But tell me, Father—you have a rather odd name for a priest—is there a saint named Auguste? It sounds more like a Roman emperor's name. Or is it short for Augustine?"

"Ah! You're used to clerics who've taken a saint's name as their name in religion. I was christened Auguste Marie—so I'm Father Auguste. We of the Society of Jesus don't adopt names in religion."

"I see." I stood up and moved awkwardly with him towards the door, chains clanking. "I'm looking forward to another conversation, Father. It's frighteningly lonely in this place."

That night, I was brought a simple but edible dinner and a blanket. I decided to sleep on bare stone with the blanket wrapped around me rather than risk the filthy straw as a mattress. After all, I had plenty of practice sleeping on a stone ledge in the Bastille. Despite my precautions, I was unable to avoid the bedbugs that found me in the middle of the night.

Several days passed before Father Auguste reappeared. In the meantime, I kept my fears and longings at bay by thinking about our conversation. Auguste's next visit was at night. I had just finished my meal, consisting of stale dry bread and sausage—nonetheless edible and even tasty to me, hungry as I was—when I heard keys rattling at my lock. The door opened, and I saw the priest press a coin into the jailer's hand. The man saluted with a "Thank you, Father!" My newfound Jesuit friend was cultivating the jailer's goodwill.

"Hello, Jean!" Auguste swept off his hat and held up his hand in greeting. "Not too discouraged, I hope?"

"No, Father, but the waiting and suspense are tiring. Any news?"

"Yes, yes! I finally got in to see the bishop today. For the last three days, he's been taken up all day every day by meetings with Leaguers from Paris. And the day before that, he was in conference with his parish priests. Your imprisonment came at a busy time for him."

I was tapping my feet with impatience. "Well? Did you give him the letter?"

Auguste smiled reassuringly at me. "Oh, yes! He received the letter and read it right there in my presence. He asked me, 'Have you met this man Sponde who's mentioned here as messenger?' 'Yes, Your Grace,' I told him, 'He seems to be a good man, an honest man.' 'Huguenot or Catholic?' he asked then. 'Huguenot, Your Grace, but I think he's close to becoming Catholic.' 'Well, that's two of them, then. The letter from Henri de Navarre, here, says he's going to receive instruction—may already be receiving it—as the first step to conversion.'

"I asked him then, 'Do you believe what Henri writes?' and he answered me this, which I think is encouraging, 'I'd sooner believe what Henri de Navarre writes than anything Henri de Valois—Henri III—ever wrote. That Bourbon appears to be a man of his word, from all I've seen and read of him.' Then I asked him what he intended to do about you, Navarre's messenger."

"Yes? And?" I interrupted him in my impatience.

"And... what I recommend to you is patience—a quality you seem to lack! The bishop knows you're here in prison. It will take him a few days to decide what to do about that. You see, he has sent a messenger to Tours to check on you, and you'll have to wait until he gets back. Meanwhile, I intend to continue visiting you as often as I can, Jean. If his decision is too long in coming, I'll try to intervene again."

"Thank you, Father." I had no wish to irritate him.

"I brought you something to help you while away your time, Jean." He opened a case he was carrying and pulled out several sheets of paper, a quill and a stoppered ink pot. "If you want to write to your loved ones or to the king—anyone—here are your instruments! The guard will bring me anything you write and slip it under the door. I'll send it on, even if I'm unable to come see you myself. I've assured myself of his loyalty."

He closed and tied the case again, and I feared he was preparing to leave. I almost panicked, for I'd hoped to engage him again in a theological conversation of some sort, merely to prolong his visit. "To continue our talk of last time," I said hastily, "perhaps you can explain how it is that your church has come so far from the spirit of Jesus as revealed in the Scriptures?"

He looked a bit startled. "Far from the spirit of Jesus? What do you mean?"

"It's the accretion of all that ritual. The faithful, the 'flock', the common herd—like me—the people hardly are expected to participate in worship services, as I've seen them. They simply sit or stand or kneel, crossing themselves from time to time, hardly needing to pay attention. The priest up there with his back turned mouths the Latin words at top speed; the acolytes respond, and the only moment of real participation is the celebration of the Eucharist."

"That *is* the essence of the Mass, after all!"

"Yes, of course. But would you not agree that the rest of the Mass is important?"

"Of course, it is!" he snapped, a bit testily.

"Then shouldn't the faithful be able to follow it? Participate in it more fully, at least in spirit?" I sat down, patting the bench next to me. He smiled briefly, then took his place beside me.

"Most do—at least the minimally educated ones, but in a way it doesn't matter. If the priest performs the ritual as he should, it will be efficacious even if the worshipper doesn't fully understand or participate." He seemed somehow hesitant, as though he could see that the position he was defending didn't seem quite right, even though it might be common practice, considered orthodox.

"You see, Father, that's why we Calvinists go back to the Scriptures and to the practices of the early Church—as much as possible, given the little we know about it. Luther said it first. *Sola scriptura.* The Scriptures are the most important evidence we have, as Christians, for the very existence of Jesus. Without them, there would be no Christian tradition. They are clearly God-directed, God-willed, else Jesus' teachings would have been lost, or would have become so clouded with myth that they would have been indistinguishable from the myths of Greek and Roman antiquity."

"Granted," Auguste agreed readily, "but what are you getting at? You were criticizing the Church and our ritual, no? You *do* acknowledge the necessity of a church, do you not? Or do you believe that Christianity could subsist on the strength of the Scriptures alone?"

"Luther did say *sola scriptura.* But even he didn't believe that literally. After all, he established his own church."

"Exactly. Don't forget that Jesus himself 'ordained' Peter as the first head of the Church." Auguste watched me with a quizzical expression.

I decided to show off my knowledge of New Testament texts. "Yes. '*Tu es Petrus*, you are Peter, and upon this rock I will build my Church.'"

Auguste nodded. "That's not the only text relating to the Church, you know."

I chimed in, eager as a schoolboy. "Right. Jesus tells the Apostles that he must go to the Father, but that he will send the Holy Spirit to be with the Church, *eternally*." I paused, frowning. Suddenly the Reformed position no longer made sense to me. "But..." I hesitated and glanced at Auguste. He was smiling just a little, doubtless trying not to appear smug.

"But... what?"

"But Calvin—I'm not sure about Luther—accepts the writings of the Doctors of the Church and all the pronouncements of Church councils up to the year 500. That includes the Council of Nicea, of course..."

"And after that?" Auguste's eyebrows were raised, his lips still curved upward in that slight smile.

"After that... no, we don't accept the teachings of the Catholic Church."

"Think about that, my son. You accept Catholic teachings up through the year 500, and then, after a gap of a thousand years, in 1500, more or less, the true light suddenly dawns upon an Augustinian monk named Martin Luther. What was the Holy Spirit doing in the meanwhile, during those thousand years? That's a whole millennium of darkness. Did Jesus lie to the Apostles when he said that the Holy Spirit would guide the Church *eternally*? Don't forget, you have *Scriptural* authority for that."

"Ah..." I had no real argument; I already had seen that. But I thought I would try one last tack, feeble as it seemed to me.

"Perhaps God chose Luther, then Calvin, to bless with his special Grace. Perhaps he guided the Reformers to the Truth."

"If so, why would an all-good Deity refuse such grace and truth to all mankind? Why not enlighten everyone? The Turks? The Buddhists? Even us Catholics? It could only be a petty god who would pick favorites, and such an act would not embody perfect justice, goodness, mercy—all those attributes that Reformers, too, see in God."

Silenced for the moment by this Jesuit's logic, I could see he had more to say. "Go on, Father," I urged him.

He nodded. "Jesus spoke of one Church built so solidly that the very gates of Hell would not prevail against it. If it were to be invisible for a millennium or scattered as it is now, why, then, did he speak of building upon a rock? He did not say he would build upon the invisible air or upon many rocks, but only upon one.

Your Calvin warns against disunity. But who has broken Church unity? Everyman wants to be saved, and no one can achieve that alone. But," here he paused and shook his head mournfully, his face reflecting genuine sorrow, "for lack of a column of fire by night and a column of smoke by day, we have gone our separate ways in the desert. Just as the ancients made their own gods and then worshipped them, so we have done the same, making as many Christianities as there are people. But God wants us *all* to be saved, not one to be lost. Therefore, being One himself, he founded one Church, one Temple, one Arc, one Jerusalem. There, the members should have one belief in their hearts, one confession in their mouths."

I sat staring at him, amazed that he was exercising all this eloquence on me. "Yes," I agreed, "God is one, and so should we be. If only we knew the Truth, we could all agree. But..."

He continued, carried by his own rhetoric. "The assembly of Christians is not in a physical but in a spiritual place; it is a unity of faith and doctrine. Its rays are disseminated everywhere but its center is the same—like the sun. All the churches are thus united.

Should be thus united. But no. What do we see instead? Every principality has its own church that claims to be the only one. Surely God does not play with us. His one Church is before our eyes." He stopped, abruptly, fearing that perhaps he had gone on too long.

"I'll simply have to give this more thought, Father." I felt a strong movement towards Father Auguste's point of view. But I was still not happy with the idea of joining that congregation of passive worshippers, listening to an unintelligibly delivered Latin ritual. We were sitting side by side on the bench, Father Auguste sitting upright, looking at me with concern while I now leaned forward, staring at the floor, my elbows on my knees. I felt his arm slide across my shoulders. He pulled my body against his for a brief hug.

"Yes. Give it thought, my son. Give it your sincere thought, and God will shed his Grace on you, too." He stood up to go, calling the guard.

Days passed, and the excitement of those moments of hot debate faded into depression. I tried to keep my mind occupied with the task I had assumed: to give our conversations my sincerest thought. I recalled the writings of Luther, Zwingli, and Calvin. I could see their books before me, my hand turning the pages.

Of all the writings, Calvin's seemed to me the most consistent—a veritable fountain of complaints against the Roman Catholic Church. Mentally, I turned to the fourth book of his *Institution*, and began "reading" the passages expressing Calvin's irreconcilable hatred for the "tyranny of the papacy," where he equates the Pope with the Antichrist. The papacy and its dependent organization are not the true Church, he avers. But as I "read" on an on, I never found out what *is.* I begin to suspect that Calvin was establishing *his* dependent organization as the one true Church, himself the true pope, since he calls himself the Pastor of Geneva.

He recommends unity in the Church, the visible Church in which God uses men's ministry for teaching the people; the visible Church which should express the meaning of the Symbol in which

we profess belief; the visible Church in which is the communion of the Saints, the mother of the faithful, whose knowledge
is not merely useful but absolutely necessary. But he never says
forthrightly where this visible Church might be, and he denies
that it is the Catholic Church. But I suspect that Calvin was
wrong, for all the reasons Father Auguste had brought forward.
Pope or no pope, the Catholic Church was the One. Fallible or
not, it was the only church I knew of in the direct line of apostolic succession from Peter.

God does not play with us. His one Church is before our eyes.

I wrote letters, to Anne first of all, to let her know I was alive and
under the protection of a Jesuit priest, Father Auguste Bouchard.
I recommended that she consult with Jacques Davy du Perron,
Bishop d'Evreux, about him, and that she appeal to the bishop for
help in procuring my release. I wrote at length of my longing for
her, my love for my two dear little boys, Jacques and Jehan.

Secondly, I wrote to Davy. I assumed that he would wield greater
influence on the authorities in Orléans than King Henri would.
I outlined the two conversations I had had with Auguste, telling
him that I *almost* was persuaded to convert.

Finally, I wrote to the king. I told him the circumstances of my
capture, what I had experienced since then, and the fact that no
one seemed be able to get me released. I made it no secret that I
had also written to Davy, and that I was seriously considering converting, as I hoped he was doing at that very moment.

But my doubts and fears still plagued me. I thought of all my
friends, of my family—especially of my father, an unshakable
Calvinist, who would be so bitterly disillusioned in me. I felt
weak, buffeted by many winds, dashed about by waves of inner
conflict. At last I reflected that—although I might feel despair
about my life—language, that blessed gift of God, gave me a
means of redeeming it, of saving myself and perhaps of consoling

others. I turned to my greatest love, my poetry, and scribbled one draft after another, finally producing a sonnet:

Tout s'enfle contre mo, tout m'assaut, tout me tente,
Et le Monde, et la Chair, et l'Ange révolté,
Dont l'onde, dont l'effort, dont le charme inventé
Et m'abymes, Seigneur, et m'esbranle, et m'enchante.

All things billow against me, all assail me, all tempt me,
The World, the Flesh, and the Rebel Angel,
Whose wave, whose effort, whose invented charm
Sinks me, Lord, shakes me, enchants me.

What ship, what support, what sleeping ear,
Without peril, without falling, and without enchantment,
Will you give me? Your Temple, which your Holiness inhabits,
Your invincible hand, and your constant voice.

How now? My God, I feel the manifold struggle
Against your Temple, and your hand, and your voice
Of that Rebel Angel, that Flesh, and that World.

But Your Temple, your hand, your voice will be
The ship, the support, the ear, where that charm shall fade,
Where that effort shall die, where that wave shall break.

To express the anguish of the assault upon my soul, I chose one of the great clichés of prose or poetry: the world, the flesh, and the Devil. I chose to portray the world—life itself—by the classical metaphor of the ocean. In this world we all struggle in deep water that threatens to drown the lonely swimmer if there is no boat, no steady ship to bear him up. The ship, the *nave*, the Temple of God, is our only sure rock and anchor amid the flood. As for the flesh— in the broadest sense, our physical selves—only the firm grasp of God's hand, flesh to flesh, can support the sinner. To enable him to turn a deaf, "sleeping" ear to that charmer, the enchanter who is Satan, our ear must be attuned to the constant voice of God.

I borrowed the tripartite form of the first eight lines of the poem—the two quartets—from poets of the end of the last century, the ones who called themselves *Les grands rhétoriqueurs,* "Great Rhetoricians." Their sonnets can be split into three vertical columns. Thus, my first column could read: "All things billow against me, / The World,/ Whose wave/ Sinks me./ What ship/ Without peril/ Will you give me?/ Your Temple." The second column: "All assail me, / the Flesh,/ whose effort/ shakes me," and so on. But, to avoid monotony and utter stiffness, I end the second quatrain irregularly—completing the triple question "What ship, what support, what sleeping ear"—with "will you give me?" and spread the triple reply ("Your Temple, your invincible hand, your constant voice") over the last two lines.

But the battle breaks out only in the last six lines of the sonnet—the two tercets—where the first tercet evokes the combat between God and the forces of evil. The triple structure resumes in the tenth line of the poem, but now God's Temple, hand, and voice are opposed by the Devil, the flesh, and the World, attacking in reverse order. And those forces of perdition go down to defeat in that same reverse order, signifying their "wrong-headedness" and vain opposition to the power of God.

Conversion and Consequences

J was released on a windy day in early July. This time, I could walk out of the prison under my own power, thanks to the food Father Auguste's intervention had brought me. He entered my dungeon accompanying the guards to supervise my release, to watch as my shackles were removed, to see that I was treated humanely, and to accompany me out of the dungeon. As we trudged up the dusty gray stone stairs, Auguste told me that messages had finally come on the previous day from Du Perron and from the king as well, confirming that I truly was a royal messenger, not a spy, and that I should be released at once. The bishop had issued the order to free me.

We came out into blinding sunlight in the prison courtyard where the wind was blowing clouds of dust, pungent with the scent of dried horse manure and burnt-out torches. I half-expected to see Father Marquet or the Bishop d'Evreux there, either to turn me back or to waft me away. But there was no one I knew—the courtyard was nearly empty.

"What do I do now, Father?" I asked, looking about me in bewilderment.

"You're free to go back to Tours, Jean. Here." He handed me a small black leather pouch, coins clinking inside. "Where did you leave your horse? You had a horse when you came, surely?"

"Thank you, Father." I accepted the purse. "Yes, I had a horse—a good one from Navarre's stable—and left him in a stable on the rue de la Charpenterie. I expect he's been sold by now."

"I imagine so. There's enough in the purse to buy another. Compliments of the bishop."

"The bishop? Is he usually that charitable to wandering messengers?"

"It's true he wouldn't have thought of it if someone hadn't reminded him, Jean."

"And that someone would be a certain Jesuit priest named Auguste Bouchard, no?"

"Well.... yes." He hesitated, looking down and to the side as if reluctant to take the credit for a charity he wished to attribute to the bishop. He quickly changed the subject. "You have thought about our conversations, haven't you, my son?"

"Yes, Father. You've been most eloquent, quite persuasive. I'll be making my decision—soon. Whatever I decide, I want you to know that I'll never forget your compassion, your kindness and enormous help. Without you, I might be dead by now."

We said our farewells, embraced warmly, and I set off towards the stable, where I was greeted with asperity by the hostler.

"I waited two weeks for you to come get your horse. He was eating more than he was worth, so I sold him, finally. You didn't expect to find him here, did you?"

"Not really. But perhaps you have another good horse for sale?"

After looking over the available horses and haggling for half an hour, I bought a gray gelding named Mulot who seemed to be sound enough after I put him through his paces. He had good conformation: sturdy legs and a short back, a muscular neck, a face that would have been pretty except for the hump in his nose.

Kindly eyes, wise eyes. He carried me safely and rapidly back to Tours, to my family and my king.

As Mulot and I approached our little house, I caught a brief glimpse of Anne over the garden gate. She bent down, probably to pick a flower or a vegetable, vanishing from my sight before I could get a good look at her.

"Anne, my love, Anne, it's me! I'm back! I'm free!" I dismounted and tethered the horse, trying the gate only to find it locked.

From inside, I heard the clatter of a dropped garden tool, a wild cry with a tearful edge, "Jean! Jean!" and then quick footsteps hurrying to the gate. She flung it wide, and the two of us embraced, kissing more fervently than I can ever remember.

I held her at arm's length, recording every inch of her. Her face looked somehow softened, more rounded than I remembered, and her belly protruded just a bit more than was usual for her. "Anne! You're so beautiful! But... Anne, are you pregnant?"

"Yes, my love, I would have told you before you left—I was already certain because it was the third month, but you were so preoccupied, and then we were both so sure you'd be back within ten days at most! Yes, I think I'm due in November." Her words tumbled over themselves.

Wordless, I took her in my arms again, more gently this time. She spoke softly against my neck. "Jean, thank Heaven you're back! I was so afraid that God wouldn't let you escape prison alive twice. I'm so glad. Don't ever leave us again."

I assured her. "I never wanted to go in the first place." I murmured loving words in her ear, telling her how glad I was to be welcoming a new child into our home. I let her go at last, and without dropping my hands, she took a pace backwards and looked up into my face. "I got your letters and your poem—if I hadn't heard from you, I think I would have despaired. Your sonnet is truly magnificent, so dark and yet shining with light. How did you get out of prison?"

"I got out day before yesterday. It was thanks to the king's letter and to Du Perron's—but my real benefactor was a priest, Father Auguste Bouchard. Without him, my message to the Bishop of Orléans never would have been delivered. I would have starved or died of exposure, or they would simply have executed me as a spy on Father Marquet's say-so."

Anne wrapped her arm around my waist, and now began to walk towards the house, pulling me along with her. "Well, come in. I'll heat water for your bath—you need one badly—and I'll lay out clean clothes. You don't have to go to court today, do you? You'd better take a little time to rest—and I want you to tell me everything that's happened. Every detail. Thank God you're safe!"

At that point, Mélanie and the two boys burst through the door. "Papa! Papa!" They hurled themselves at me. Three-year-old Jehan embraced my legs, while Jacques, now nearly four, was tall enough to grab me around the hips. I lifted one, then the other to kiss them. Both promised to become handsome men, Jacques with Anne's red hair and my gray eyes, Jehan with my dark hair and his mother's green eyes.

"You're going to stay home with us now, aren't you, Papa?" Jacques asked, enunciating clearly in his high soprano.

"Yes, Jacques, yes, Jehan, I hope so. I'm sure the king will let me rest at home with you for a while after my ordeal."

"What's an 'ordeal,' Papa?" Jacques demanded.

I explained, and signaled to a beaming Mélanie, who had managed to welcome me home amidst the clamor of the two boys, that she should take them back in charge. I had to promise to spend time with them later that afternoon before they would consent to be escorted to their rooms.

In fact, I devoted the entire day to Anne and the boys. After tending to Mulot, I followed my wife into the garden and helped her cut fresh flowers from the border on one side of the boxwood labyrinth. She led me to the back of our garden, where Mélanie and

Lazare, the manservant, had planted a vegetable plot. It contained rows of lettuce, carrots, leeks, celery, peas, and beans. "I think we'll have peas and carrots for vegetables tonight and a fresh salad, too. We'll be eating leg of lamb as the main course."

"I can't wait." It would be my first proper meal in over a month. We sat together all afternoon, in the cool shade of a chestnut tree, then in the salon with the windows thrown wide to admit fresh air, and I told her everything I'd been through, including the details of my discussions with Father Auguste and my reflections afterwards. At last, I asked Anne her reaction to my latest struggles of conscience—for she was well informed of my spiritual difficulties and hesitations.

"I've given your problem a lot of thought, Jean. You know religion is not my central concern. I'd be perfectly content to remain a Calvinist by default until I die. Perhaps in my old age I might begin to take all that seriously... and I do have prejudices against Catholics. After all, they killed thousands of us in cold blood on Saint Bartholomew's Day."

I started to interrupt her, but she shook her head at me. "And the ritual of the Mass—it really strikes me as strange. Foreign. Puts me off, especially since I don't know Latin. But we've killed Catholics, too, maybe not in such spectacular numbers all at once, but tens, probably hundreds of thousands when you add up all the dead. You told me about the heaps of corpses after the Battle of Coutras.

"You see, my love, for me the issue of religion is not so important that I would die rather than convert. *You* are the important thing in my life. I would die without you. If you want to convert, Jean, I'll follow you." Anne smiled faintly, squeezed my hand, and quoted the Calvinist version of the book of Ruth. "'Whither thou goest I will go; and where thou lodgest I will lodge: thy people shall be my people, and thy God my God.'"

I took her in my arms. "I'm grateful to God that I have you, Anne, my dearest companion, my closest friend. I'm the luckiest man in the world. I pray you'll not live to regret your decision." We sat with our arms around each other until twilight.

At court, several representatives of northern towns embroiled Henri in negotiations, wanting to sell their allegiance to him for a fee. He was willing to buy them back. He explained to his ministers who protested, "Even the most exorbitant fee is cheaper than war!" It was an irrefutable argument.

When he at last had time to see me, I knelt before him humbly to thank him for saving my life.

"Stand up, Jean. No need to thank me." He yawned widely, barely bothering to cover his mouth. "Look: I'm out of patience with all this formality. I need to rest and eat something. Come back in an hour or so and join me at dinner, and you can tell me then what you learned. There may be something I don't already know."

I was reluctant to miss dining with my family so soon after my return but sent word that the king had detained me. Dinner was just as sumptuous as before, this time featuring a tender roast of pork surrounded by mild-tasting turnips and green beans. I began my report with the ordeal in Orléans, telling him in florid detail about Father Auguste Bouchard, representative of a "new" teaching order, the Jesuits. "If all Jesuits are as well informed, as talented in argument and rhetoric as he, the spread of Calvinism will be stopped in France."

Henri nodded. He knew of the Jesuits.

I insisted. "Without Father Bouchard's intervention, I would be dead. It was he who acted as your true messenger, Sire. He carried your letter to the bishop. I don't know if it made that much difference to a Leaguer like the bishop, but thanks to you and Du Perron, along with my Jesuit friend, I was released." I then gave him my first-hand account of the reaction of the ministers of the Estates General, telling him that they surely would accept him soon as their king. All that was missing was his actual conversion.

He laughed. "Yes, you've been out of touch for a month, Jean! They have accepted me—conditionally! Now, all I need to do is abjure, confess, take the Eucharist, the royal oath, and pacify the country. That's all. I still haven't resolved the problem of what to do about my staunch and true Huguenot allies. Those are the men who've been with me in this fight for a decade!"

"Yes, but Sire, most of your subjects are Catholic. If you ever hope to rule all of France, you *must* convert." I began to repeat the political and practical arguments.

His raised hand silenced me. "You know that I know all that— *ad nauseam*. What still holds me back is conviction. I need a clear conscience, a conviction that my conversion will save my immortal soul. I still remember the battles my parents had over that very issue. My mother was convinced I would be damned if I ever became Catholic and my father wavered back and forth between the two. Of the two of them, I preferred my mother—a steadfast and pious woman. Intelligent, too."

I hoped not to offend him. "Begging your pardon, Sire, but your mother could be all that and still wrong about the true Church."

Henri took no offense; instead, we talked theology for some time, and I exposed the ideas I had gleaned from Father Auguste and from my own reflections in prison. Some of those thoughts seemed to make an impression on my king.

In the next few days, I met repeatedly with Du Perron and the king. Under the bishop's influence and direction, Henri's resistance to conversion began to weaken. About a week later, he made his decision. He moved the court to Saint-Denis, just north of Paris, where he would abjure his Calvinist faith and take the oaths that would clear the way to confirmation of his status as King of France. Once again taking leave of my family, I followed, not wanting to miss seeing that important moment in all our lives.

French kings had been buried under the basilica of Saint-Denis from the tenth century onward, while coronations were usually celebrated in the cathedral of Rheims. Given the unrest and hostility in the north of France to Henri de Navarre, Protestant general and "heretic," he chose the more peaceful site of Saint-Denis for the unprecedented ceremony of his abjuration.

He settled into the town and employed me among many others to prepare the backdrop for the ceremony. Morlas, Du Perron, and I were chief organizers of the trappings for the royal procession, with Du Perron directing the proceedings. I contacted the churches and wealthy merchants both in Saint-Denis and in Paris itself, asking them to lend their tapestries to decorate the balconies and the streets along the route the king would take as he processed to the basilica for his abjuration. I also contacted all the florists for miles around, instructing them what flowers to bring, when and where, and I organized a team of people to see they were duly paid upon delivery. The flowers were to be strewn in Henri's path.

On 23 July, the king began to take instruction. What this consisted of was not, as would usually be the case, an introduction to the doctrines of the Catholic Church, with which he was thoroughly familiar. Instead it entailed a discussion of touchy issues such as the pope's authority in France, what reception Henri would give to the decrees of the Council of Trent, and just what form his abjuration would take. He rejected the first version, editing it himself, and on 24 July signed a revised document, acceptable to both parties.

The stage was set for the ceremony. After my announcement to the Estates-General back in May that the king would convert, there had been plenty of time for the news to be broadcast throughout France. Our preparations brought out the population of Saint-Denis, and the activity alerted neighboring Paris. So, on the actual day, thousands of spectators lined the streets awaiting the procession.

Last-minute lapses always occur on such occasions. A fifty-foot row of tapestries, hung by a single rope from balconies of the houses on the other side of the square in front of Saint-Denis Basilica, strained the rope beyond its breaking point, and the whole thing came down on the cobbles below. I ran across with a couple of men and a length of rope to splice the break and restore the tapestries to their places. We displaced the thick press of people standing under the balconies—some trampling the precious textiles—rescued the tapestries and moved those occupying the balconies as we struggled to get everything back into place.

Morlas had arranged seating for dignitaries, and for drummers and trumpeters to accompany the parade. We could already hear the drums and trumpets at the other end of town announcing that the procession had begun. As I paused, panting and sweating, on the balcony after draping the heavy hangings once again, I saw the Archbishop of Bourges come out of the basilica across the square opposite me. He took his seat at the top of the cathedral steps on an ornate throne of white damask, adorned with the coats of arms of France and Navarre. I finished hanging the last tapestry and clattered down the stairs, shoved my way back across the square through the mob and resumed my place at the corner of the basilica.

We waited in suspense, the incessant cheering becoming louder as the procession approached. *"Vive le roi!"* burst from thousands of throats. It was evident that the general populace had suffered more than enough from the war, and was eager to welcome the new king, even though his religious orthodoxy might be no more than skin deep. As the procession neared the square, the cries became a cadenced chant that deafened us all and drowned out any possible conversation. Only the drums and the trumpets could be heard above the shouting.

First came a large crowd of nobles and princes in their finest clothing, all marching on foot. At last the king came in sight. Henri cut a majestic figure, lean and fit, mounted on a beautiful white charger that pranced and curveted as flowers were strewn before its feet. The king, dressed in white satin with a black velvet cape draped over his shoulders and over the horse's haunches, nodded regally left and right, his black felt hat with its white plume emphasizing his every movement. The crowd became even more enthusiastic when they saw him. He was followed by the Swiss Guard in their red and gold striped uniforms, drums beating, their golden helmets flashing in the sun. Twelve trumpeters marched at the end of the procession.

When he was squarely in front of the basilica, Henri dismounted in one gracefully athletic movement, handing the charger's reins to a lackey in silken livery. My heart pounded and I held my breath as with slow and solemn movements he climbed the steps and stood before the archbishop. I could not believe he was finally taking this perilous leap.

"Who are you?" asked the archbishop.

"I am the king." Henri's voice sounded forced and strained.

"What do you ask?"

"I ask to be received into the communion of the catholic, apostolic and Roman Church." The king took a breath between the words "catholic" and "apostolic." He was obviously still struggling with himself.

"Do you truly desire it?"

"Yes, I wish and desire it." Henri cleared his throat after this statement, then he knelt and recited his profession of intent, "I protest and swear, in the presence of almighty God, to live and die in the catholic, apostolic and Roman religion, to protect and defend it against all comers at the risk of my life and blood, renouncing all heresies contrary to this catholic, apostolic and Roman Church."

I let out a great sigh of relief that he had made his way through that statement without seeming to hesitate at all. Henri produced a written and signed copy of his profession and handed it to the archbishop, and then, bending forward, he took the archbishop's hand and kissed his ring. I noticed that the hand that extended the document to the prelate shook badly. I should not have been surprised by Henri's undoubted emotion, but I was. I'd not realized his sensibilities were so strong; I'd seen him handle far more stressful situations without turning a hair. Perhaps he took his religion more seriously than his conversations with me and Du Perron would indicate.

The archbishop absolved and blessed him, after which Henri rose and, accompanied by the prelate, entered the basilica. The dignitaries entered next, and I followed them into the sanctuary, lit by thousands of candles. The sunlight streamed in multicolored shafts through the centuries-old stained-glass windows, making rainbow puddles on the worn paving, on the carpets laid for the celebrities, and on those dignitaries themselves. All the while, the people in the square kept crying *"Vive le roi!"* The sound rolled through the sanctuary and bounced off the rear wall, echoes colliding with the ever-renewed shouts. The king made his way to a special *prie-Dieu* under a canopy covered in velvet, embroidered with green *fleurs de lis*. Here, my king knelt and repeated his abjuration. Henri quickly wiped his forehead and face with a silk handkerchief. He was visibly perspiring. Was this another indication of the turmoil in his soul, or was he merely reacting to the heat of the day? Now the archbishop celebrated a solemn high Mass of thanksgiving. During the Mass, the king kissed the Gospels as they were brought to him; he beat his breast at the Elevation and received the kiss of peace.

Once the Mass was over, Henri returned through the streets the same way he had come—again bowing his head graciously left and right, accepting the plaudits of the crowd, making each spectator feel that the king saw and appreciated him or her. Obviously, he would be a successful monarch, if ever he were universally accepted. The very cobblestones rang with the shouts of *"Vive le roi!"* along with the clamor of the basilica's bells reverberating off the surrounding buildings.

I was busy for the rest of that day and part of the next dismantling the decorations that had served as such an effective backdrop for Henri's abjuration. In those few moments when I had time to think, I mulled over the king's reactions during the service, understanding his reluctance, so like my own, and feeling a strange surge of pity. I was preoccupied as I supervised the return of the tapestries to their owners, a procedure that was more complicated than it had appeared when we borrowed them.

When I finally returned to my lodgings, I found a brief note from Henri waiting for me along with a sealed letter: "Jean, thank you for helping to make the procession an impressive prelude to the ceremony yesterday. I will be staying on here for a week or two, but meanwhile, please return to Tours and deliver to *Parlement* the letter I enclose herewith and inform them of the mood of the people here and in Paris. You will receive further instructions from me in due course. Meanwhile, I will attempt to consolidate my strength and reunite my Protestant with my Catholic allies. Henri IV, Rex."

I was more than delighted to return to Tours and my family, and made a short trip of it, riding my trusty little gray horse, Mulot. As soon as I arrived in Tours, I delivered the king's letter to Achille de Harlay, who invited me to sit with *Parlement* the following day, when he, as First President, would read the king's letter. After opening ceremonies, he broke the seal and read, "Recognizing the catholic, apostolic and Roman Church to be the true Church of God, full of truth, unable to err, we have embraced it and have resolved to live and die in it." There was much discussion in *Parlement*, but the consensus was clear: the members felt a great relief that the matter of the king's religion had at last been settled. Many of them began making plans to return to their homes in Paris, for they were sure that the king would make his headquarters there once again.

Upon leaving the meeting room in the Château Royal, I strolled out into the rue Lavoisier, pleased at the immediate improvement in the king's relations with his subjects. I almost collided with two of Henri's close associates, Philippe Duplessis-Mornay and Antoine de la Faye, both Calvinists. Duplessis-Mornay laid a hand on my shoulder. He began more in sorrow than in anger, I thought, but his tone was brusque and quickly became icy.

"Sponde, you're partly responsible for this miserable situation. You and that blasted Bishop d'Evreux."

"I beg your pardon, Philippe—what miserable situation? Surely it's the opposite—for the good of the kingdom."

De la Faye stepped directly in front of me, blocking my path. "You know damned well, Jean de Sponde." Hostility increased as he spoke. "We know from any number of sources that you've been doing your best to persuade Henri to become Catholic—you and the 'Great Converter,' Du Perron. Well, now you have your wish. And now the king has betrayed all of us—those of us who are still faithful to our cause and our religion."

"Surely, you don't believe that Henri would betray his friends!" I was incredulous.

Antoine continued. "I was at Saint-Denis. Just before he started getting fancied up for that damned abjuration ceremony, he met with us—me and Sully and Henri d'Albret, and Max de Béthune and a couple of others were there, too—and he said goodbye to us. We were all weeping, including Henri. He swore never to allow anyone to trouble us because of our religion. But I'm willing to bet he won't keep his word. How *can* he? He'll have to bend to the will of the Catholic majority. Our cause is lost."

Duplessis-Mornay nodded. "I left Saint-Denis with most of Henri's *former* friends. I'm returning to my estate in Saumur, and I think I'll stay there indefinitely. Let the king's *new* friends fight for him now. I suppose he'll be joining the League next." He sneered. "And you, Jean? You're bound to make your fortune now. Just be sure to fall off the fence on the right side."

I left them after we had exchanged a few more words. I didn't try to defend myself, my position "on the fence," but I did try to reason with them, knowing all the while they could not help saying those vicious and biting things that hurt me so badly. I walked home in a dark mood; they'd made me as miserable as they were. Why could Christians not get together again as brothers? Would hostility never cease? Reason is a feeble defense against the passions. We deceive ourselves if we think reason ever rules. Even as we argue philosophy and theology—perhaps especially then— even as we mouth scholastic logic, the passions rule.

"Anne..." I had found her in her favorite corner, a window overlooking the garden.

She rose and hurried to me, knowing by small signs, by my tone, perhaps, that I was distressed. "What is it, my love?"

I told her about the encounter.

"Come, Jean, let's stroll in the garden." She took my arm and said no more until we were walking slowly between the little boxwood labyrinth and her long rectangular row of flowers, now a riot of reds, blues, and yellows with sprays of white baby's breath in between. "You chose a path of action, Jean. Since you're so close to becoming a Catholic yourself, you never thought much about the hurt your former Huguenot friends would feel if you succeeded in persuading Henri to convert."

I bowed my head and sighed. "You're right. I've been too wrapped up in my own spiritual struggle. But then, Henri didn't need much persuasion. He knew conversion would be necessary."

"But he feared it, too. You told me so yourself. He foresaw better than you did the reaction you've just had."

I told her about Henri's reluctance and obvious inner struggle during the ceremony of abjuration. "Yes, Anne, I believe he saw more clearly than I—and he also suffered because he'd just said goodbye to some of his best friends before starting that procession. He knew he probably wouldn't be able to keep his word to them. I pitied him then; I pity him even more now."

From the documents of Jacques Davy du Perron, Bishop d'Evreux:
Jean de Sponde has come to me for advice and consolation. He—and I—there should be no false modesty here—finally convinced the king that he must abjure his heresy and join the one true Church. I might have been able to manage his re-conversion on my own, but the task was made lighter and certainly much shorter because Sponde and I worked as a team, even though Jean might have been unaware of his tremendous influence. Henri took Sponde to be a good indication of what a large part of the Huguenot population was thinking—and there, he may have made a serious mistake. One of very few mistakes that man has made. But it was in our favor! Now, Henri must suffer the loss of his former friends, while I do my best to supply him with good new ones, including myself, of course.

As for Jean, he needs spiritual solace and consolation, inclined as he is to believe he has betrayed his master.

"Have I been a Judas to him, Father Davy?" he asked me a few days ago.

"In what sense, Jean?" I knew what he meant but wanted to see if *he* knew.

"I did my best to talk him into converting. I probably should have left his conscience up to him. He would have converted on his own without my constant urging. I feel I've betrayed him. He still has mostly enemies in the Church, and now he is suffering cruelly as his friends desert him. The only difference between me and Judas is that the 'kiss' I gave him was sincere. I meant only to do good."

"Jean, you know all the arguments; you used them yourself. The quicker he converted, the sooner the war would end, and the more lives would be saved. His Huguenot allies should understand that and accept it."

It sounded good, and it was true, up to a point. But I knew just as Jean did that a betrayal remains forever unforgiven by the betrayed.

From my point of view, of course, losing a few heretical allies was nothing when compared to the gains—for France as well as for God. And, no small matter, Henri had saved his immortal soul.

Jean's voice interrupted my reverie. "I think not, Father. They'll never understand, never accept."

Jean resumes:

I had been struggling in spiritual anguish for weeks. It was all very well for me to urge my king to convert, to applaud his decision when he finally took that step, and to pity him as he suffered the consequences. The encounter with De la Faye and Duplessis-Mornay brought home the gravity of those consequences. I would face similar and much more scathing attacks once I, too, converted to Catholicism. I didn't know if I had the moral courage to do that.

I would wake up bathed in sweat in the middle of the night from a nightmare about slanderous attacks upon me and even upon Anne and the boys. Worse, I feared the reaction of my own family—especially the bitter disappointment of my father. I spent the darkest hours of the night mentally composing letters to him. Should I take a flat, legalistic tone, or allow my poetic imagination to endow my words with fiery wings? No matter how I phrased it, I knew he would consider my decision a betrayal of his ideals, of my upbringing, my education—of all that he held most dear. Compared to the power of his reaction, Salvata's and my older brothers' would be trivial. But even theirs would be hard to bear.

When I did write the letter to my father, it seemed my pen was leaden, my mind and hand half-paralyzed. I threw away a dozen versions before I finally composed one that I considered marginally satisfactory. I begged him to try to understand, not to reject and renounce me, to forgive me enough to support me in the choice my conscience was forcing me to make. I would be overjoyed if he would come to my confirmation. I knew very well that he would never do that, but I believed I must invite him.

I waited for three weeks but received no word from him or from any other member of my family and so decided to go ahead with my conversion ceremonies. All this time, I continued to pray for strength and guidance. Anne did her best to show her support and her love, for she knew my inner struggle was consuming me. She did not complain when I failed to come to bed at all, or when I rose in the middle of the night, lit a candle in the next room, and spent hours scribbling.

At last, my prayers and vigils brought conviction that the time had come, and the hand of God was upon me. I had just dreamed a vivid dream that I took to be a true vision. In it, I was living the story in Genesis about Isaac, decrepit and blind, preparing himself for death. It seemed I was present as the old man laid his hand upon his younger son Jacob, mistaking him for his older brother, Esau, for Jacob had tied pieces of a goat's pelt to the backs of his hands and neck. In the dream, I saw Isaac giving Jacob the blessing due the elder son, and then I cringed at Esau's murderous fury when he discovered that the paternal blessing had been stolen. I followed Jacob on his journey of escape, when he slept with a stone for a pillow and had a vision of a ladder reaching to heaven, of angels upon the ladder, and God standing at the top of it. I woke filled with this vision and rose in the darkness to write down these words, to which I have often returned in moments of despair and adversity:

I will grasp this hand that weighs so heavily upon me…. It will never escape me until it has granted to me as well as to Israel its blessing, so I shall fear to meet Esau no more. Like Jacob, I only have, Lord, stones on which to rest my head, while the night of my misfortunes thickens around me. But by this Ladder of my faith, which reaches the heavens, Your Angels will come, and You stand at the head of it to assure me of my good fortune. And upon these stones of adversity I will build up Your House to praise you forever.

How true the words would become I had no idea at that moment. I only knew that I felt a great warmth of comfort; Isaac's hand—symbolically the hand of God—blessing me, his blessing protecting me against the fury of my enemies, "Esau," in my dream. I crept back into bed beside Anne, who embraced me, murmuring comfort, half asleep. I kissed her cheek, brushing back her hair, and fell asleep with her head on my shoulder.

The next day, I started to walk to the bishop's palace to ask Davy to hear my confession and to arrange for him to perform the rites of abjuration and confirmation. I had been sure that the confidence and reassurance the dream had brought me would stay with me, but as I walked, a great wave of fear came over me. Just what did I think I was doing? Why was all this necessary? I simply couldn't go through with it—the very idea was madness. I would return home and write my father that I'd had second thoughts, that I'd put behind me the temptation to betray our Calvinist faith. Nothing was irrevocable at this point, so why go on?

I came to a standstill in the middle of the street, people brushing by me on both sides. As I moved against a building to allow horses and carriages to pass unhindered, I realized I was sweating, my underarms soaking wet, and my breathing short and ragged, as if I'd been running. A tavern was close by, the very one where I had lunched with Du Perron and Morlas. I tried its door, finding it open even though it was still quite early. I sat at one of the tables and ordered cognac. My hands trembled so much that I dropped a coin as I paid the tavern keeper. He eyed me with cold disdain, taking me for a drunk trying to cure a bad hangover by drinking more. I sipped the drink slowly, hoping it would calm my agitation.

I tried to focus my scattered wits to analyze my situation. I already was a Catholic by conviction, if not in name, even though my scriptural thought patterns and associations were still—and probably always would be—strongly influenced by my Calvinist upbringing. I drew as much inspiration from the Old Testament as from the New, a truth demonstrated by the dream of the previous night. But no matter, I would always interpret those Old Testament passages in the light of the New. The life of Jesus and his resurrection were the all-important facts. I recalled my arguments with myself as I sat in my cell in Orléans—how and why I had become convinced that the Roman Church had to be the True Church. It was that Church which, itself guided by the Holy Ghost, had guided Christian souls throughout the centuries from Saint Augustine to our own time.

At last, I tipped my glass bottom up, swallowed the last drop of cognac, rose and left the tavern without a backward glance. My armpits had dried somewhat, which I took to be a good sign. I suspected I'd just been sorely tempted by an evil spirit and had not succumbed.

As I entered the antechamber of the bishop's palace, a young priest greeted me. I smiled at him. "Could you please let Bishop du Perron know that Monsieur de Sponde is here to make confession? I think he has been waiting quite a while for this."

The young fellow raised his eyebrows. "Yes, monsieur, I'll tell His Grace that you're here. De Sponde, you said, correct?"

"Yes, Father. It's de Sponde."

He disappeared through a door, and I stood waiting, pacing the floor. Du Perron came bustling through the same door after about a quarter of an hour. He was dressed simply, only narrow borders of purple showing on his simple black cassock.

"Forgive the delay, Jean! I was writing to the king. Come, my friend. I'm sure you know what the rules are, how you're supposed to confess on your knees in a dark cubicle. But we'll stretch a point."

He led me through his office, past his untidy worktable piled with documents. He'd clearly been writing, for several crumpled pages lay on the floor beneath the table where he had tossed them. We entered a small sitting room with brocade-upholstered chairs and matching drapes framing tall windows that overlooked a formal garden bright with yellow and white daisies, accented with blue asters. Allegorical paintings on the walls framed a small fireplace, black and empty now in August. I noted in passing the high relief grape carvings on the mantle. It struck me that I was absorbing small details of my surroundings just as I had when I rode into battle at Ivry.

"Sit down, Jean. Your choice: you can either look at nature or at art—whatever is less distracting."

"I'll face the garden, Father Davy." I began my confession as formally as I knew how, with "Bless me, Father, for I have sinned." From there, I recited my sins as I had analyzed and categorized them: uppermost, the sin of pride, and the suffering that had brought upon me and my loved ones. I told him of my doubts and hesitations—perhaps a lack of fortitude—and of the struggle I'd been through that very morning. In the end, he absolved and blessed me, and congratulated me on having made a "good confession." My penance was a set of ten Old Testament readings that I was to meditate upon in the light of the Gospel. Bishop Davy knew me well. My penance would be my pleasure.

We then set the times for the formal abjuration and confirmation, both of which would take place during a solemn high Mass two Sundays from that date.

"Normally, these things are done either at Christmas or Easter, but we won't wait that long, Jean. You'll need time to gather your friends and family, though. Will two weeks be enough?"

"I've already written my father and stepmother and have received no reply. I've written my brother Henri, too. I *think* he'll be here. I do hope so!"

When the day came, I had invited only two friends, Antoine de Thou and Achille de Harlay, along with my immediate family: Anne, who was very pregnant, Mélanie and the boys. My beloved brother Henri also had come, and I blessed him for it. He had spoken to me before the ceremony.

"You're absolutely sure you want to take this step, Jean?"

"Yes, Henri. I feel very nervous right now, but I've examined my conscience enough about this. You know my convictions about the Eucharist; my reasons for believing the Church of Rome is the true Church. Here I stand; I can do no other—to quote someone who came to the opposite conclusion!"

Henri embraced me. "Well, brother, follow your conscience as best you can; I know this step comes after long prayer and meditation. That's all we can do in this life."

"Thank you, Henri! Are you still pursuing your studies to become a Calvinist pastor?"

"Yes, I want somehow to devote myself to the religious life. I'm not certain at this point how that will work itself out—but yes, I study."

I squeezed his arm. "Good, Henri. You'll find your way. Now, I think it's time." I entered the church and moved to the front near the altar. The glow from the stained-glass windows reflected off my satin jerkin and breeches, for I was dressed in my finest clothing. Perhaps my outer appearance proclaimed confidence, but I felt just as frightened and shaky as on that morning before my general confession.

Davy officiated at the ceremony and the Mass, at which I took my first Eucharist as a Roman Catholic, receiving the Host from Du Perron's hands. I found it odd to see that he was more touched at this moment than I seemed to be. His eyes brimmed with tears as he whispered, "The body of Christ." Afterwards, I thanked Mélanie for coming, and asked her to take the boys home, since one of the priests in attendance said we were to be whisked away to a magnificent dinner, laid on by Father Davy.

He gave a beautiful toast to begin the dinner. I was, finally, overcome with emotion at his kindness and generosity, and wept—both in relief that the step had finally been taken, and with gratitude for his gracious guidance and friendship throughout.

Conversation around the table was lively, and a couple of the priests, Davy's assistants, congratulated me on having helped persuade the king to convert.

"It was mainly Bishop du Perron's doing, not mine." I realized my words were becoming slurred. I was drinking too much.

"Not according to His Grace, it wasn't!"

I'm told that the bishop personally escorted Anne and me home in his carriage sometime around midnight.

From the documents of Jacques Davy du Perron, Bishop d'Evreux:
My poor friend Jean enjoyed little peace after his conversion. The news spread with surprising rapidity, and vile attacks from Huguenot writers began immediately. Their major theme: Jean had converted to curry favor with the king, to further his career. One attack attempted to show that Jean was an unprincipled climber. It featured the rumor that after writing "The Stanzas on the Supper" celebrating the Eucharist, Jean presented the poem to Henri but saw that the king had a new mistress. He then, so the rumor goes, immediately wrote another poem, this one celebrating adultery. The attacks descended to a point where they portrayed poor Sponde as an amoral whore, willing to abandon any principles for profit.

Agrippa d'Aubigné, the most talented and scurrilous of his detractors, circulated a Latin poem, later published in his *Confession de Sancy,* in which he compared Sponde with the monk, Jacques Clément, who assassinated Henri III: "You [His Holiness] who have wished to canonize Clément might as well canonize Sponde. Both ambushed the lives of kings; the one took the king's life, the other his soul and his heart."

The poem was clever enough to enjoy great popularity, circulating widely among Huguenots. To me it seemed obvious that the violence of the attacks reflected the high esteem Jean de Sponde's co-religionists once held for him. They knew he was a man of value, high moral standing, impressive humanistic learning, and great eloquence. They had to vilify him to discourage others from following his example.

Jean did what he could to counter the slanders. With courage and, to my mind, some naiveté, he decided to respond to these unwarranted attacks with a treatise. He would explain himself. He showed a draft to me even before the king returned to Tours, and almost a year before it was published. The "Declaration of the Principal Reasons Which Induced the Sieur de Sponde, Councilor and Maître des Requêtes of the King in Navarre, to join the Catholic, Apostolic, and Roman Church" declared: "My union with the Church is a fully reasonable action, and for its defense I will never spare my pen, nor my tongue, nor my very blood, with God's help." Sponde went on to say his conversion resulted from his faith in God, not from his thoughts about men or from a desire to gain favor with the king. In his dedication, he spoke to the king in these terms: "I acknowledge that the miraculous work that God has brought about in you has overjoyed me. But that same God who is my witness knows, though all the world would condemn me, that I leaned my soul more upon Him than upon you."

Men of good will and faith will believe him, no matter what their religious persuasion. But most men are not graced with such insight.

Jean resumes:
The king returned to Tours about six weeks after his abjuration, and right after my own conversion. I stood with Achille de Harlay and Antoine de Thou in a group welcoming him back. He passed along a row of us on his way to the audience hall, all of us bowing in turn. He was all smiles and nods, stopping to embrace this or that person, shaking hands lingeringly with others, sometimes with both hands to add extra cordiality.

He worked his way down the line to where I stood. I could see that there would be no question of an embrace for me or even a handshake from my sovereign. As I bowed to him, I caught a glimpse of his face when he looked at me. His mouth was set in a bitter line and his eyes flashed as if in anger. He was blaming me for something. I had to wait and see what it would be. I sent word to Anne that I would be late that evening and stayed until the last courtier had left. Henri never once raised his eyes to mine or acknowledged my presence in that audience hall, where the crowd dwindled down to very few. At last, I was alone with him.

He stared at me now with a mask-like face, a tiny muscle twitching in his left cheek. "They tell me you are now a Catholic. Congratulations."

I shivered at his icy tone and I must have winced but answered as if I had noticed nothing. "Thank you, Sire."

"I suppose you believe that since you have followed me in converting, you deserve some special favor from me?" The question was hostile, spoken with bitter sarcasm.

"No, Sire. I have followed my conscience." I choked on my shock and hurt, knowing even as I spoke that I would never convince him of my sincerity.

"Of course! Of course!" His sarcastic tone cut me like a whip. "I remember what Théodore de Bèze wrote to me about you before I had the misfortune to make your acquaintance—that you are duplicitous, secretive, and an ingrate full of bad faith. I've read some of the revelations about you being published by your former friends. Perhaps they're being a bit unjust. But it seems clear, although I converted for reasons of state, not being able to unite my subjects and stop the bloodshed otherwise, that you converted out of self-interest. Is that not so?"

"No, Sire. I expect no favors." I felt my face burning, and I ached with injury and frustration.

"As for me, I've done the right thing, I'm sure...." Here Henri paused, looking inward for a moment. Clearly, he was not that sure. "But you were the one who pushed me... and pushed and pushed that I convert at once. And now, all my true friends have deserted me." He paused to breathe for a moment, and his next sentence came out like a cry of distress. "They've left me, Jean! Damn you to eternal flames! Now, I'll have to live with the likes of Du Perron, but I don't have to live with you fawning around me!" Henri walked the length of the room, then swung around to glare at me. His face, previously red, was set in the stiff mask I had seen when he first arrived. He spoke again, his words coming out like stones. "Those poems of yours, Sponde."

"Yes?" I racked my brains. None of the poems I had presented to him had been badly received—not that I could remember.

"You had the temerity to criticize me when I left Corisande. And there were other innuendos critical of my behavior with women. I was—am—angry."

"I'm sorry, Sire. I wish you had told me then. But is that all?"

He shook his head and a gleam of triumph came into his eyes. "I've seen your stanzas 'On the Death of B.D.F.'"

I suddenly felt cold. It was a poem I had written while still in shock after learning of a new friend's suspicious death. Belesbat du Fay was among the men I had met and liked during the brief time I was at the siege of Rouen. Afterwards, he was somehow mixed up in the murky beginnings of the king's affair with Gabrielle d'Estrées. Was du Fay one of Gabrielle's lovers? Or had the king seduced the man's wife? I was not sure. I only knew that du Fay had been murdered, and my private poem had hinted as much, and had very obscurely pointed a finger at Henri as the responsible party. I blurted out, "How could you have seen that? It was written for me alone!"

"Kings have their sources of information, Sponde, always remember that. In that poem, you all but accuse me of murdering that man du Fay. That's *lèse-majesté*. I could have you executed for that."

I was silent. I could think of nothing to say.

The king took two steps in my direction. "But I'm a merciful monarch; I won't do that. In return for your past service, I'll do no more than rid myself of you. Never contact me again, under any pretext. Get out of my sight, Jean. Go!"

Despite my fear, hurt, and confusion, my overwhelming sense of the injustice of his behavior, I understood. His conversion had been a step that he knew must be taken, and he had paid a terrible price. The friends of his youth had all turned against him, and he was in mourning. The poem on du Fay's death had fallen into his hands when he needed to strike out at someone to alleviate his feelings. While it was obscure enough that I could have explained it in a different, more innocent light, it was clear that Henri had heaped up my "misdeeds" in such a way that he would hear of no explanations. My poor sovereign: a pitiful, lonely, but highly dangerous man. I bowed low and then said, "Sire, I'm terribly sorry all this has worked out so badly for you—as well as for me. I'll go now. Adieu, my king."

I left the château weak and trembling. The calamity that I had feared would follow Bèze's condemnation of me over a decade ago had finally fallen upon me, and as I walked the short way to my home, I racked my brains wondering what to do now.

From the documents of Diane d'Andoins (Corisande):
Since Henri abandoned me after he met Gabrielle d'Estrées at Cœuvres in Picardy four years ago, I've been thinking. We had not been lovers for some time before that—but he had wanted to keep me available as a companion and advisor. I think he discovered, during his lengthy campaigns in Normandy and his siege of Paris, that he could do without my advice as easily as he had done without my body.

He came to see me in December of 1590 to tell me that our liaison was ended, but that I could live at his expense at the Château d'Amboise for as long as I liked, not too far from Tours and the court. We wished each other well, and I packed my belongings and moved them into this lovely but cold and lonely stone pile. I am not completely isolated here—I've cultivated a circle of friends, and I occasionally travel. My friends have kept me informed, bringing me news from the *Parlement* and Henri's court at Tours as well as from Paris. I hear all about the doings of the Seize and the Leaguers, there and elsewhere.

Recently, the big news was the account of Henri's abjuration at Saint-Denis. I didn't attend. I was told that the people were ecstatic finally to have some hope of getting the Spanish out of the country, and to have a Catholic king, even if he is shaky in his belief. In time, he may become more convinced of the rightness of his conversion, but I know him well. He is a practical man, not a spiritual one, and did what he did out of political expediency. But perhaps I'm selling him short. Henri has unexpected depths of feeling and intellect. I didn't live with him for years without finding that out.

The minor news concerns Jean de Sponde. I took a liking to that young man when I first saw him back at the Château de Pau in Béarn. His face gave me the immediate impression of depth—both in thought and sincerity. It is a thin ascetic face topped with a shock of straight hair, black when I first knew him, shot with silver now. Thick eyebrows form a solid bar over his eyes when he's worried or angry, or examining his conscience—unusual gray eyes the color of mercury, the irises bordered in black.

I always have known that Henri used him hard, without regard for Jean's private life and preferences, always demanding that he give his king something more: legal expertise and advice, a sword arm in battle, that Jean raise troops for Henri or spy for him at the risk of his life, that he run the Sénéchaussée at La Rochelle, that he be the king's messenger. I also knew from the start that Jean was in trouble with the Calvinist authorities even though he was a fountain of quotations from the Old Testament as well as the New. His faith, though strong, was not definable as Huguenot—not entirely.

It came as no shock when I heard that he had converted, about a month after Henri, for my informants had told me what a good friend to that Bishop, Du Perron, Jean had become. I began receiving reports of defamatory and cruel Huguenot attacks on Jean, and I don't think they will end soon. Then, I heard that Henri, blaming Jean for the painful consequences of his own conversion, had thrown Jean out.

I sent one of my valets with a message as soon as I heard that Jean was planning to leave Tours with his family, asking him to come here to Amboise to see me first. Jean and I have things in common, and I felt he needed moral support. He arrived about three days ago, riding a gray horse the color of his eyes, with black trappings. I met him in the courtyard—not the usual etiquette, but I never in my life stood on ceremony. He offered me his arm and I took it, guiding him up the staircase and into my favorite sitting room on the second floor of the château, a bright chamber with a balcony overlooking the Loire. He asked me, "Was it from this level that the twelve hundred were hanged?"

"No," I replied, "we're above that level—in many ways above that level."

He smiled, a bit thinly, I think. He was referring to a failed plot more than thirty years ago back in 1560, against Henri III's eldest brother, King François II. Those twelve hundred Huguenot conspirators were slaughtered, and their bodies hung from hooks on the façade below us. "We tend to forget to add those men to the total of the dead, to those who died in the Saint Bartholomew's Massacre, on the battlefield, on lonely roads...." Jean's brows were drawn together.

"Are you sorry you converted?" I asked bluntly, knowing that was what he was thinking about.

"No, Madame, despite my sorrow for the slaughter of my former co-religionists, I am not. After all, the Calvinists were equally ruthless, just not often in a position to wreck as much havoc." He raised those startling eyes to mine for a moment with a wry twist of his mouth.

I pressed him a bit more. "You truly have no regrets, even though the king has repudiated you, and your former friends revile you?"

He bowed his head at that and brushed back a lock of his straight hair that had fallen over his brow. "I was hurt and confused at first. Each new attack still hurts. I've written a treatise in self-defense—the jurist in me, I suppose—mainly for my family and my king. I know it won't make much impression on my new enemies, but it helped me understand my own feelings. I have understood, Madame, that we must bear crosses in this life. I spent much time avoiding the crosses I should have taken up, thinking the small troubles I had then, that I was willing to deal with, were real crosses. Now I know what one doesn't want to face, the deeply hurtful thing, *that's* the real cross. For me, that's Henri's rejection, D'Aubigné's satires, all that." He paused and looked up at me with a sheepish grin. "I'm sorry, Madame; I didn't mean to preach—or to confess! Tell me now, why did you ask me to come?"

"Call me Corisande, Jean. That incessant 'Madame' bothers me. I asked you to come for two reasons. First, to let you know I understand your feelings. I, too, have been repudiated by the king. In my case, it's because I'm a woman. You know all too well, I expect, from your own observations, that for Henri women—most of them—are useful for a quick toss in bed, or to provide an heir. He'll need to repudiate Margot and find another one of royal blood to perform the second task for him. As for the first, they are legion. I flattered myself that I was special, that he needed me for a different purpose, that he valued my advice and would keep me as a first-rate counselor, even though I was only a second-choice mistress. But he really prefers masculine company when it comes to advice, you know, and probably resented depending on me during those years. When he found good ministers who could advise him, he got rid of me."

Jean glanced at me sidewise, shaking his head. "That's ingratitude, uh... Corisande."

"Yes, but at least he gave me a stipend and magnificent housing—cold and uncomfortable and lonely as it is. You, he threw out without a penny, I hear."

"Not so. I still have a small income from those early offices—of Councilor and *Maître des requêtes*—that he awarded me in Béarn. That should sustain me and my family—on a very modest level, of course."

I felt relieved that Henri had not been downright cruel to Jean. Of course, he may simply have forgotten about that residual income from Béarn. I continued, "Well, Jean, the second reason why I asked you to come is this: I have letters and journals that I want to give you." I rose and went to the chest placed under the huge *gobelin* tapestry that covered the entire wall facing the windows. I already had packed an inlaid wooden case with the assorted documents I wanted Jean to have.

I returned to his side and moved my chair, so we were facing each other. "I want you to write your memoirs, Jean. You—like no other person—can shed light upon these times, upon the struggle between the faiths, upon all the complexities of the political situation, upon Henri's life and character. You have the sensitivity and the insight to do it well, without self-serving, without fanfare or exaggeration." I placed the case in his hands. "These documents will fill in gaps where your information might be sketchy or lacking. Promise me you'll write your memoirs, and you'll use my material."

He stared at the box for a moment. "I've already started a major project, Corisande. I'm refuting that treatise by Théodore de Bèze, attacking the Catholic Church. That'll take all my concentration. But perhaps, when I tire of theology, I'll write down a few memories."

We sat talking until the sunset turned the Loire the color of molten iron with flashes of gold, and then we continued conversing over a fine dinner I had arranged for the two of us. We relived the past decade with Henri, the wars, our lost friends, our triumphs and regrets. Jean told me he almost did not regret that his public career was irrevocably a thing of the past, for now he could devote himself to his scholarship and other writings. Anyone listening to us would have thought we were both aged friends who had come together after many years' separation. I felt old, but with a shock realized that Jean and I were nearly the same age: somewhere between thirty-five and forty.

Chapter XVI

More Consequences

From the documents of Jacques Davy du Perron, Bishop d'Evreux:

When I heard that Henri had repudiated Jean de Sponde, I was deeply angry. There was no rational explanation for it that I could grasp. I knew Henri well enough to realize I would never change his mind, but I determined to do what I could to reconcile the two.

He came to Mass every morning at seven, and I approached him as he entered the chapel.

"May I speak privately with you, Sire, after Mass?"

"Yes, of course, Your Grace. What about?"

"About Jean de Sponde, Sire."

He growled something in his throat, but nodded, somewhat ungraciously. "I suppose this was inevitable. You two are as thick as thieves. Oh, all right. I'll wait for you in the chapel antechamber."

I preached my homily on forbearance in the face of seeming faults in others, on the grounds that we are all sinners in the sight of God, and harsh judgments of our fellowmen merely add to our own burden of guilt. It was, I'm sure, obvious to the king that I was trying to prepare the way for the talk I shortly would have with him.

I found him waiting in the antechamber, arms folded on his chest, foot tapping. "A fine homily, Your Grace. But we are not all empowered, like you and our Heavenly Father, to forgive the misdeeds of others, nor are we saintly enough to wish to do so." His tone was sarcastic, as was his implication that I had somehow tried to place myself on a par with God.

Despite myself, I felt on the defensive. My king was a clever politician. "Sire," I began, "you've repudiated one of your most loyal and faithful servants, Jean de Sponde. He has come to me in his confusion, trying to work out the reasons why. He has risked his life for you repeatedly, Sire, and has always been loyal and obedient to any request. His service as magistrate and legal advisor—at great cost to his peace of mind, his family life, and even his health—that alone merits reward and gratitude. Your actions seem to me ungracious and ungenerous, to say the least! What has he done to receive such punishment?" My voice was rising and becoming louder; my outrage was showing too much. I feared that I was merely irritating the king, and so it was.

Henri snorted. "For one thing, the two of you ganged up on me and forced me to convert before I was really reconciled to the idea. I didn't have time to explain things to my *real* friends. They've all deserted me. And who are you, *Your Grace*, to question judgments I make about matters that don't concern you, and about which you are ignorant? Your domain is to advise me on ecclesiastical matters. You are overstepping your bounds when you meddle in my secular affairs!"

"I believe, as your spiritual advisor, Sire, I'm doing my duty to remind you of any moral problems with your behavior. I do this at the risk of my own position, I know. The reason you give for your rejection of Sponde is not adequate—not on *any* grounds, religious or secular. What aren't you telling me?"

"Damn you and the universe to eternal flames!" Henri shouted at me. "I have my reasons, and I'll tell them to you, but not here, where every crack harbors some cleric who'll run off and report my every word. You see, I *do* have some concern for Sponde as well as for my own welfare. Do you have someplace private?"

"Of course, Sire. Follow me." I led him back through the chapel and into the vesting room.

After looking carefully up and down the corridor and closing the door after us, the king told me *sotto voce*, "Sponde had irritated me before, preaching to me in some of his poems about my infidelities. It angered me more than I can say to have my sentimental life pried into and judged by a prig like him. But that alone was not enough to cause me to break off relations with him."

"Then what was? Surely not the fact that he urged you to convert! You should repudiate me, too, on those grounds."

"One of his poems was shown to me recently. It was stanzas in honor of a man who became a friend of his during the siege of Rouen, a Sieur Belesbat du Fay, killed at the siege of Quillebœf, not in battle, but by foul play. The man was the husband of one of my mistresses. Sponde commits *lèze majesté* in that poem, Your Grace. He accuses me of murdering the man."

"Openly, Sire?"

"No, but by clear implication, *I* believe. With all those counts against him I cannot tolerate that man around me any longer. Nothing you say can change my mind on the subject." And he stomped out of the vestry. He has not allowed me private access to him since that time, though I continue to function as advisor on protocol and other ceremonial matters.

It is February already. The celebrations of Christmas are over, and this New Year, 1594, is well under way. The king is prepared to move to Chartres, and I shall follow him there. Henri consulted with me as Bishop and Royal advisor to three kings, counting himself, about a location for his consecration and coronation. Custom would dictate that the ceremony should take place in the cathedral of Reims, but the Duc de Guise holds that city. The other sacred spot where kings have occasionally been crowned is Chartres. Henri intends to enter that city quietly in about a week and then spend another week preparing for the solemnity.

I lunched with poor Sponde at the Lion d'Or the other day. As he arrived the table, I congratulated him once again on the birth of his baby daughter. I had just christened her Catherine, after Jean's deceased mother. "How is the baby, Jean?"

"Beautiful, as you know, and a good child. I call her My Consolation. She even lets us sleep through the night... usually."

Once we were seated, I began with the question uppermost in my mind. "I know the king has repudiated you, Jean. Did he strip you of all income?"

Jean's lips quirked in a wry smile. "Not quite all. I do have enough money to stay in Tours until the end of May, perhaps, but then I must move southwest."

"Back to your family?"

"No, not the family. I'm not totally destitute, you see. Henri appointed me "Councilor" and "Maître des Requêtes" early on, back in Navarre. He either forgot about that income or left it to me to honor my father, Iñigo. They provide a pittance that will sustain me, Ann, and the children. But living with my parents and brothers—especially with my father—would be too uncomfortable. Daily recriminations about my conversion, you understand."

I frowned briefly. "Yes. I can well imagine. You say you'll move southwest. Where, then?"

"My father owns a property up in the Pyrenees, above Oloron-Sainte-Marie. It has a lodge, built of stone and pine—my favorite vacation refuge when I was a boy. I remember a huge fireplace tall enough for me to stand in it, with a spit for roasting a deer or a wild boar whole. The kitchen was always a center of activity, with a long trestle table for preparing meals and serving them to bands of hunters. The place has multiple bedrooms, each with its own fireplace for accommodating the hunting guests."

"That sounds like a good place for the boys. Would you be hunting, yourself? I know you're a fine horseman and deadly with a pistol."

He nodded with a twitch of his lips, not quite a smile. "Yes. I'll need to hunt to supply us with enough meat. My income won't suffice to buy it, so I'll have no choice. Plenty of game in those pinewoods, but hunting is dangerous—the terrain is rough."

"It sounds as though the place would appeal more to Henri than to you, Jean."

His eyes lost their focus, as if he were living a memory. "The lodge is built on a rocky outcrop above a rushing stream. It sparkles with the purest water, ice cold all year round—but I had to run down a steep incline and then trudge back up with a full, heavy bucket." He shook his head, now focused on me. "I have few illusions about the ease of living up there, but I can't face returning home."

"But you'll be cut off from the world up there. What will you do when you're not hunting, chopping wood or something physical like that?"

"I have resources, Father, a new project. Théodore de Bèze recently published a treatise attacking Catholicism, titled, *The Blemishes of the Church*, and written in seventy-five theses in imitation of Luther...." He paused and his lip curled. "only Bèze's ingenuity ran out before he reached Luther's grand total of ninety-five. I've begun refuting Bèze's work, thesis by thesis. The effort surely will occupy my mind while I bask in the serenity of those mountains. That will heal me. I'm already well started on my memoir, and when I get bored with that and Bèze, I've also begun to translate the works of Seneca, so, I'll have more than enough to keep me busy up there—those plays are innumerable."

I said goodbye to Sponde just before we set out for Chartres. I was sorry to leave him, but duty calls me to remain at the king's side just as I stood by his two predecessors. I could tell he was sorry to see me go, but I reminded him he has good friends in Tours, especially de Thou and de Harlay, and plenty of scholarly pursuits to keep him occupied. I also mentioned, in case he tires of his mountain retreat, that he should go to Bordeaux. That city has remained steadfastly Catholic throughout our Wars of Religion, and I have friends there, especially Florimond de Raymond, who took the succession of Michel de Montaigne as Councilor back in the 1570s, I believe. Raymond is a brilliant humanist and author; he should be a good companion for Sponde, since they have similar interests.

But I have little time to think of Sponde right now, fully employed in seeing that Chartres is decorated properly, and all is ready for the consecration and crowning of the king. I could use Jean's experience in decorating a city. He did a masterful job of adorning Saint-Denis for the abjuration.

We arrived in Chartres on the seventeenth of this month. Priests and laymen are scouring the city for tapestries and banners to hang from the balconies along the street up which the procession will climb to the cathedral. We need decorations for the interior of the church as well. Chartres Cathedral is one of my favorites for its location, the beauty of its windows, and the quaintness of its architecture. It was half burnt at one time; only one of its two towers saved. Oddly, the architect who restored it rebuilt the second tower in an entirely different and lighter style. The asymmetry appeals to me.

We discovered that not all the symbols of power the king must receive during the ceremony were still at Saint-Denis, where they normally are kept. In the fighting around Paris, the sword and staff had been stolen or destroyed, and the ermine cape damaged. Only the crown, the ring, and the scepter were intact in their place of safekeeping.

We had the most skilled blacksmith in Chartres forge a new sword for which the Archbishop and I contributed jewels for the hilt. We commissioned a skilled woodworker to reproduce the staff, which several of us remembered well enough from Henri III's coronation to sketch and describe it accurately. Also, we found an expert tailor who could duplicate the ermine cape. Gabrielle d'Estrées donated an ermine robe the king had given her three years earlier, which the tailor promptly transformed into a kingly cape. If we can find enough adornments for the street, all will be in readiness for the ceremony.

On Saturday morning, the king came as usual to Mass and heard a homily by René Benoist on the significance of the consecration and the unction. Benoist proclaimed that Henri was already *rex* by hereditary right, the title *dux* had been fairly won by his skill in combat, and now he would become *sacerdos*, like all the kings of France.

The highest officials in the land gathered at the cathedral and then, following the ancient ritual, two were designated to fetch the king. It already had been agreed they would be the Maréchal de Matignon, standing in for the High Constable, and myself—one for the secular kingdom, one for the Church. We found the king stretched out on a bed, clothed in a consecration robe, the one Henri III had worn before him, and who knows how many of his predecessors. The robe of stiff brocade, heavily interwoven with gold thread and covered with precious stones, obviously weighed many pounds. We assisted the king to his feet, descended the stairs and joined the groups outside.

The procession formed itself: archers first, then I joined the cathedral clerics and the choirboys. After us came the Swiss Guards, trumpeters, heralds, the Knights of the Holy Spirit, and the Scottish Guards. The king's immediate entourage included the Maréchal de Matignon who bore aloft the king's naked sword. Behind him came the four principal household officers: the Chancellor, Chamberlain, Grand Maître, and finally, the Grand Écuyer.

People packed the street, withholding their shouts, instead tossing flowers in his path for him to walk upon. As we approached the cathedral, the choir burst into song, intoning the ritual chants. We processed inside, passing over the sacred labyrinth inlaid into the floor near the entrance.

The ceremony began at once. The king knelt upon a lavishly upholstered *prie-dieu* and swore to keep the peace and dispense justice in the kingdom, and to "chase out of all lands under my jurisdiction all heretics denounced by the Church." The archbishop then approached with the holy ampulla, supposedly the one used at every coronation for the past thousand years. The symbolism of the holy ampulla could not be exaggerated, since the populace believed a dove had delivered it at the baptism of Clovis.

Henri unbuttoned the consecration robe, baring his chest and shoulders. He, alone among all of us in the procession, had walked bareheaded, almost like a penitent. His partial disrobing signified he was giving up his previous worldly estate to assume the royal religion. The prelate anointed Henri's chest and forehead with the sign of the Cross as he intoned, "I anoint you king with sanctified oil. In the name of the Father, and of the Son, and of the Holy Spirit, Amen." I wondered if only I saw that the king's face was wet with tears. The ceremony continued without interruption with the consecration of the sword, ring, scepter, and staff.

The Chancellor called upon each peer in turn, clergy and laymen alike, to bear witness to the solemn consecration. He then called upon the Comte de Soissons to place the crown upon Henri's head, the cape of ermine about his shoulders, the ring of office upon his finger. The king was given the scepter, the sword—belted around his waist—and the staff, placed next to him. As all of us knelt to pay homage, I could see he had regained control of his emotions.

During the solemn high Mass that followed, Henri took the Holy Eucharist in both kinds—the Host and the Chalice—demonstrating he was now a member of the clergy as well as head of our secular realm. He could now claim the traditional title of all French kings: *Rex christianissimus,* a title that for its antiquity and authority outweighed recent popes' designations of monarchs like Ferdinand and Isabella as "Catholic Kings," or like Henry VIII of England, "Defender of the Faith," whose title turned out to be a bitter mockery.

Once the Mass had ended, Henri strode through the cathedral door and into the sunshine, holding himself very straight, the scepter in his left hand, his ringed right hand wielding the staff. The crowd broke into screams of approbation and cries of "*Vive le roi*" as the heralds scattered largesse. The thunder of the bells of Chartres cathedral nearly deafened us all as we accompanied him back down the flower-strewn street towards his residence. France had a new Catholic monarch—but the League, Paris itself, and a large part of the countryside still did not recognize him, nor had the pope lifted his anathema.

Jean resumes:
Summer is wearing away up here in the mountains, and my two writing projects and the translation of Seneca are progressing nicely. It has been a cool season, with too much rain, leaving the steep slopes muddy and treacherous. Besides my writing, there are more than enough practical concerns to keep us all busy from dawn to dark. Keeping enough water on hand for our needs has been one of our most tedious tasks, and we've all shared in it. Mélanie and Lazare, the gardener and handyman who followed us from Tours, have been of enormous help, but I don't know how long I can continue paying two servants. I will probably let Lazare go before winter and do the heavy work myself. I can't see doing without Mélanie, who, I think, loves us all. She's been with us for years. She is certainly loyal, and is

wonderful with the children, who love her as much as they love us. My adored baby Catherine loves her, too, reaching out her chubby little arms and saying "Mé-, Mé-," short for Mélanie.

Our little vegetable garden—Anne brought seeds with us when we moved here in April—has not produced as well as I had hoped. We do have a good crop of onions, leeks, chard, some turnips and cabbage, and beans are coming on right now. Lazare and I scythe large areas of native grasses, let it dry, then haul it back for storage in the barn. Our two horses must have adequate hay for the winter. Poor Anne is not used to this incessant, backbreaking labor, nor am I. We are using only a small section of the lodge, just enough for our urgent needs—so Anne and Mélanie won't have to do so much cleaning.

So far, we've used the kitchen as both common room and dining area, and four bedrooms, but when cold weather comes, I think I'll eliminate one more room by moving the boys in together. Mélanie and Catherine are in one room now, and we will keep our room. That will save a bit more fuel. If we close off all the rest of those rooms—the reception hall, the upper floor and all that—the place might not be so hard to heat.

There was quite a bit of seasoned wood in the shed next to the kitchen, but it will burn too fast. I've been scouring the woods around us to find downed trees still in burnable condition, cutting them up and hauling in the wood. I remember from my childhood that a summer like this means that a cold winter will follow. I don't intend to gather wood in sub-freezing temperatures sometime along in January.

I must go down the mountain to Oloron-Sainte-Marie to lay in supplies for the winter: flour, salt, herbs, yeast, wine, dried beans, and peas. I need to buy powder and shot for my pistol, too. I'll make a list.

It would be good if we had a cow, but grazing is scant right now, and our stored hay will barely feed the horses. Again, I am hampered by my lack of funds. I will take Lazare with me to help me bargain and let him go after that. I'll send him to my father with my warmest recommendation. Surely, he will find a good position for him. At least we are not lacking for meat. I have brought down three deer and one boar since we moved in, and rabbits are easy to snare as they try to raid our garden.

We are totally isolated up here. Every two weeks a courier brings me a letter, often three or four, from Jacques Davy or from Achille or Antoine. Davy sent me a complete account of the king's anointing. He knows that, despite everything, I still want to follow the fortunes of my king.

A letter came early on from Corisande with an enclosure she said to include in my memoirs. It was her record of my visit to her at Amboise. She reminded me of my promise to write my memoirs, a promise I am already immersed in. I read those letters over and over until they are limp, falling apart at the creases. I'm dreading the winter for that reason, too—we'll be cut off from our last friends.

I had heard that the king had taken Paris before we left Tours but had no detailed account until a second letter from Davy followed me up here in April, brought by Monsieur Ducasse, a friend as well as a courier.

Davy wrote that Charles de Guise had appointed a new governor of Paris back in January, a certain Charles de Cossé, comte de Brissac, because he did not trust the preceding governor. From his point of view, however, the choice was a grave mistake. Brissac made almost immediate contact with the king, and plotted early in March, a few days after the coronation, to allow Henri entry into the city. The plotting went forward successfully despite surveillance by the Seize and the Spanish officials.

Mayenne himself may have suspected that something was afoot since he took his wife and children out of the city on March 6. The king wrote to Sully on the 17th, telling him he should come to

Paris on the 21st to help shout *"Vive le roi!"*—he was that certain of success. It seems unbelievable, but Davy reported that since no news of the king's plans had reached the Seize and their Spanish allies, three armed forces were able to enter Paris in the early hours of the morning on March 22—one through the Porte Neuve, one through the Porte Saint-Denis, and one by boats on the Seine. In each case, the entry was achieved thanks to allies on the inside who opened the gates and removed the chain across the river.

They met only slight resistance by twenty German soldiers, who were killed or thrown into the Seine, and Henri's forces came together at the Grand Châtelet. The king, dressed in full armor and escorted by archers and four hundred mounted knights, entered at six in the morning through the Porte Neuve. Brissac and the Provost met him and handed him the keys to the city. He rode past the Louvre and arrived at Notre Dame to hear Mass at eight, where a Te Deum was sung. When the bells of the cathedral rang out, the Leaguers and all Parisians knew that Henri was inside Paris.

At the same time, his agents were circulating throughout Paris, handing out leaflets assuring Parisians that his intentions were entirely peaceful. Some resistance began near the Sorbonne, but Guillaume du Vair and others quieted the Leaguers who were leading the movement. The king also sent messengers to the Duque de Feria, who was acting as the Spanish Ambassador at that moment, and to the army barracks where the foreign troops were housed to tell them that they would be spared if they withdrew from the city.

As the king rode back along the Seine to the Louvre, people flooded out of their houses and greeted him with cries of joy. He found that the Louvre had been kept in excellent order since Henri III's exile. He had lunch there, then again went out into the streets, enjoying the crowds who shouted *"Vive le roi!"*

Arriving at the Porte Saint-Denis around two in the afternoon, he watched the retreat of all the foreign troops—around three thousand—till then quartered in the city. There were Neapolitans and the Walloons, both groups vassals of Spain, and the Spanish troops. The Duque de Feria and his officers Tascis and Ibarra were among them, and the king shouted to them, "My compliments to your master (meaning Philip II, of course) but do not come back!" Henri was overjoyed at his peaceful occupation of the city.

He was magnanimous in victory. He informed the papal legate that he would be completely protected as a representative of His Holiness, and he sent a message to the Duchesse de Nemours and to the Duchesse de Montpensier, Mayenne's sister and mother, that he would visit them the next day. The Duchesse de Montpensier is widely believed to have incited Jacques Clément to assassinate Henri III.

He granted amnesty to all members of the League except for one hundred twenty of the most intransigent. These were outlawed. No one was executed, and no one imprisoned—something that angered the radical Huguenots who demanded that they be beheaded or thrown into the Bastille. Henri told them, "If you said the Lord's Prayer daily with a humble heart you would not speak in such a manner. I know that my victories are given to me by God's hand, and he forgives my trespasses as I forgive those who trespass against me."

Back at the Louvre, he received the homage of the members of the City Council, and confirmed them in their functions, even though some had been his deadly enemies. A delegation of the city's clergy also received an audience with the king. Davy ended his letter by telling me that the king, after the long day's amazing events were over, turned to his Chancellor, Cheverny, and asked, 'Cheverny, am I really here?' 'Sire, you can be sure of it,' the Chancellor replied. 'The more I think of it, the more amazed I am. It surely is an act of God—one of his greatest.'

We detained the courier, Monsieur Ducasse, loathe to let this representative of the wider world depart so soon. He was well informed about the fast-moving events in the rest of France, and we were eager to hear everything he knew. He sat at the trestle table, sipping wine, enjoying his status of news-bringer.

Anne, as curious as I am about political affairs, sat across from him. "Members of *Parlement* were still at Tours when we left, betraying their oath to meet only in Paris at the behest of the king. What became of them? What did the king do?"

Ducasse chuckled. "They simply went back to Paris and joined their fellows."

Anne planted her hands on her hips. "What? Didn't the king punish them for siding with the Leaguers?"

"No. Henri's clemency extended to them, too. He'd already issued a decree canceling all legislation enacted after 1588 that was 'in any way prejudicial to our king and royal law.'"

It was my turn to question Ducasse. "What about all those cities and lands to the north that were totally controlled by the League?"

"Some of those were also south of Paris, still. But the king's clemency won over nearly every city. The most important was Rouen, the main stronghold of the League in Normandy. Other Norman cities followed suit, until he now has most of Normandy under his control."

I burst out, "Thank God! No more bloody battles for the flower of France's remaining knights to sacrifice themselves!" I recalled my own experiences.

Ducasse nodded. "Henri is a clever tactician at home as well. He showed his orthodoxy to the Catholics of Paris by washing the feet of the poor on Maundy Thursday. He visited the sick; freed prisoners on Good Friday; and on Easter Sunday touched hundreds— I heard it was precisely six hundred sixty—sick people. Some of them really were cured. By the end of April, he'd won over the Sorbonne. They passed a decree recognizing him as the 'legitimate, most Christian king.'"

All this was joyful news, and I began to hope that Henri, now that he was convinced God's hand was at work in his life, could be more at peace within himself and more reconciled to the losses he had suffered because of his conversion.

My boys are in seventh heaven here in the mountains, just as I used to be. Jacques, now five, is a promising horseman, with a talent for balance and control. I have taken him on a couple of hunting expeditions, which delighted him. I was afraid he would be horrified at the bloodshed, but he has seen rabbits killed and dead deer brought into the house. He has watched me butcher them, too, so it seems that the act of killing them did not worry him unduly. On the other hand, the chase thrilled him.

I have taken both boys on many rambles through the woods, reciting the name of every plant, every tree, explaining if it was useful for human consumption or survival. I told them which animals lived in the forest and what were their habits—as far as I knew them. I took them to some of the favorite places I'd loved as a boy, especially a natural rocky amphitheater on a slope bordered by towering pines.

Within the sheltering rock walls, delicate ferns and wild columbines grow, and thick pads of emerald-green moss upholster the boulders. Nearby, a shallow cave holds dried leaves and pine needles from years past. I wondered, were I to dig deep enough, if I would find the wooden sword I'd left there nearly thirty years ago.

Although Anne was a bit apprehensive, I encouraged the boys to explore the forest and its mysteries alone. I reassured her. "It's better that they learn about the natural world firsthand and early. If they are not allowed out in it, they'll never develop an understanding and a love for God's creation."

I took one trip away from the mountains at the end of July, to Melun where I entrusted the manuscript of my treatise on my conversion to Catholicism to a printer there. On my way, I noticed that despite fighting and unrest here and there, the countryside generally seemed more peaceful than it had been in decades. I didn't stay long, for I had no money to spare, and as planned, I stopped on the return trip to shop for some of the goods we would need for the winter.

I'd scarcely had time to settle into the lodge once more when the news came. I sat on the veranda mid-morning on August 14. Cicadas buzzed in the foliage, birds warbled, and I was contentedly reading Seneca, when our trusty mail carrier, Monsieur Ducasse, came in sight. Although still far below us on the trail that wound up to our lodge, he was apparently in a hurry, urging his mule forward with taps of his whip. I waited while he disappeared behind a stand of pines at a bend in the road, then watched him reappear, still hurrying his mount. He saw me and began shouting from a distance. I could not at first understand his words, but then I made out: "Monsieur de Sponde! Monsieur de Sponde! Your stepmother Madame de Sponde needs you!" Then something about my father that I could not catch. I ran down the stone steps and met him several yards from our door. "What is it, Monsieur Ducasse?"

"I'm so sorry, Monsieur, but you see your father's... They've killed your father, Monsieur."

I was stunned. "What? Who killed my father? Who?"

"It's the cursed Catholics, Monsieur."

"Which Catholics?" I felt the ground receding from under my feet.

"A party of Leaguers. I'm so sorry to bring such terrible news, Monsieur. I have a letter here from Madame de Sponde." He began to rummage in his rucksack.

"Let's go inside. I need to know everything you can tell me."

He tethered the mule, and I led him up the steps, across the veranda and into the common room. Mélanie was punching down the dough for a batch of bread that would shortly go into the oven; the fireplace was lit, and the room too hot. I'd felt hot and then cold as I waited outside for Ducasse to tend to the mule and then as he followed me into the lodge. A loud buzz rang in my ears.

All the while, I repeated his words over and over in my head, "They've killed your father, Monsieur.... It's the cursed Catholics." I crossed the kitchen to the trestle table and grabbed its edge, dizzy, almost falling upon the bench, perspiration running down my face. I feared I might faint. "Mélanie, could you find something cool for Monsieur Ducasse to drink?" My voice sounded distant and weak.

Mélanie gave me a quick sidewise glance. "Of course, Monsieur de Sponde." She knew something was very wrong but did not acknowledge it. While she bustled around, I turned back to Ducasse.

"Tell me all you know."

"It happened just six days ago. A Leaguer named Du Laur led a group of partisans through Mauléon. It was mid-morning, and the *Parlement* was in session. They sacked the town and then raided Parlement. They took your father, Monsieur, and shot him."

I sat silently while Mélanie brought each of us a glass of white wine, another of water. As she approached again with a plate of bread and cheese, she overheard most of what Ducasse was saying.

Mélanie cried out, before I had had time to react. "Oh, my God, Monsieur de Sponde! May He have mercy on your father's soul! Poor Salvata!"

I sat there, in shock. My father dead, killed by Catholics. The bitterness of it was more than I could bear. I took a gulp of wine, choked on it, and my tears were a mixture of grief and purely physical anguish. Anne had come into the room, and Mélanie broke the news to her. Anne gasped and exclaimed, then came quickly to my side, sat down next to me on the bench and slipped her arm around me. I was still wheezing, but at last choked out, "Has my father been buried yet? How is my stepmother? My brothers— how are they?"

"All I know, Monsieur, is that your stepmother needs you. And yes, he was buried right away. It's August, and the weather is hotter down there in Mauléon. Here's Madame de Sponde's letter, Monsieur."

I broke the seal and began to read, holding the letter so Anne could see it. "My dearest Jean," it began, "I will break this terrible news to you without preamble. My most dearly beloved husband, your father, was murdered by a band of Leaguers two days ago. This letter will reach you too late to attend your father's funeral, for I am obliged to go ahead with that at once. Come back, my dear Jean. You must take care of the legal matters of inheritance and disposal of property. How I wish you and your father could have been reconciled before this unspeakable tragedy ended his life. At least he remained steadfast and true to the faith. Your loving stepmother, Salvata."

I turned to Ducasse. "What more do you know about the circumstances?"

He wiped his forehead and lips, then took a quick gulp of the wine, clearly sharing our shock and grief. "It's a terrible story, but I'll tell you what I know. Several outlaw groups, claiming to be partisans of the League, live by robbing and killing the innocent and the helpless. They've been attacking small towns in Béarn for the last month or so. One of those groups, led by a man named Du Laur, raided Mauléon on the eighth of this month. They rode through the town, breaking and entering, killing, collecting booty and food.

"They attacked the Parlement building and drove the members out into the courtyard. They had their sport with them, demanding that they abjure their faith on the spot. Some did, and they were beaten and robbed, but left alive. Your father Iñigo stood up to them, telling them he would never recant, and would be true to his faith until death. You know your father, Monsieur. He was always outspoken. If he'd been quiet, perhaps they wouldn't have noticed him.

"All the Parlement members were mistreated, but only two taken prisoner. When the horsemen left, they dragged Monsieur de Frexo and your father at the end of ropes. Monsieur de Frexo is only in his fifties. He managed to keep up the pace. But your poor father was an old man. Even so, he followed all the way to Saint-Palais, almost eight leagues from Mauléon! But then his strength failed him; he fell and couldn't rise again. Du Laur simply shot him in cold blood and left him lying in the dust of the town square."

Anne let out a little cry, and I groaned.

Ducasse continued, adding one last heartbreaking detail. "The people of Saint-Palais came out after the raiders had left and found your father lying face up with a hole in his temple, his white hair soaking in a pool of his own blood. That's how they described it. They bore him back to Mauléon in a wagon. They knew him, of course."

I blotted my tears and turned to embrace Anne, who pressed her face against my shoulder. She recovered enough to speak before I did. "Of course, Jean, you must go at once. Take Mulot. He's not the fastest horse, but he's the best one for distances. We have plenty of food here, so we'll be fine. We'll pack food for you. You're all right, aren't you, Jean? You were so white when I came in—I thought you were about to faint."

"I was. The wine helped, though." I turned to Ducasse. "If you can wait a few moments longer, I'll ride down the mountain with you."

Mauléon became a nightmare. Everyone treated me as a pariah—understandably enough. I had abandoned my former faith, and to my parents' friends and neighbors—who used to be mine—I was little better than the murderers who had just swept through the village. Often, I was reduced to saying, "Please. For Salvata's sake, for the memory of my father, would you be so kind...?" Usually my humility and gentleness would persuade them to produce the necessary documents, or witness a statement, but always with dark looks and great reluctance.

From my stepmother, I learned something about my father that I had heard but forgotten. Back in 1587, my father had been taken prisoner by the League in Niort. I was with Henri, fighting the small engagements that culminated in the Battle of Coutras. When I got home, my parents told me a bit about his ordeal, but not much. At the time, my mind had been on marriage and Anne, and I had not paid proper attention, didn't ask the right questions. While in his cell, he overheard a conversation by two officers in the League's army. They were standing under his window, commiserating. The army, commanded by General Jean de Beaumanoir, Sieur de Laverdin, was in total disarray for lack of provisions and fodder for its horses.

Iñigo noted what he had heard and bribed a guard to send his letter to Henri, who later routed that army. His victory was a signal accomplishment; I remembered what a fine general Beaumanoir had been at Coutras. Whether Salvata's idea was correct or not, I do not know. She believed that Du Laur singled out my father to take revenge for that piece of intelligence that had led to a defeat of one the League's armies.

My brothers Clément and Salomon arrived two days after I did. They also treated me with scorn and made my task as chief executor more difficult. Most of the property and the lion's share of the inheritance went to Clément, another large portion to Salomon, and a small sum to me. I was not sorry to see it go to my brothers; I would not have to endure accusations that I had somehow embezzled money or property that did not belong to me. My sister Marguérite, who did not come, also inherited very little, as did my father's children by his second marriage: my favorite half-brother Henri, Jean-Jacques, and Israël.

During that time in Mauléon, Henri was my consolation. He sat up with me in the evenings discussing matters of religion over several glasses of wine. He also showed me some of his poems. He is an intelligent writer, technically exact (and I flatter myself that I taught him that) but not talented as a poet.

I handed back the sheaf of poems. "Stick to prose, Henri. You'll make your mark there."

He took no offense. "I tried hard to emulate you, Jean, but I know my efforts are just versified prose. I'll follow your advice and turn my efforts elsewhere."

I was pleased at his calm acceptance. Above all, I didn't want to offend my little brother.

One of those evening talks took place as Henri and I were strolling in the garden. Just before we parted to go to bed, he draped an arm over my shoulder. "Jean, I admire you." He gave my shoulder a little squeeze. "You're a thoughtful man, and I know you didn't convert for frivolous reasons. You've also been completely honest and open about your thoughts and feelings. Surely the people around here should be able to appreciate your absolute integrity."

But they could not and did not.

The most emotionally draining encounters were with Salvata. Nothing I could say would reconcile her to my conversion to the Catholic faith. She repeated over and over that she could not understand me; that I had betrayed my father. Nonetheless, when I first arrived, she embraced me, weeping against my chest until she was exhausted. As the days passed and the legal matters completed, she became increasingly calm and self-possessed; she had resumed her daily activities, and I judged that I could return to my family without feeling I had abandoned her when she still needed support.

Once the estate was settled, I was more than happy to return to my mountain retreat, but the relative tranquility we enjoyed was cut short, this time not by human intervention but by weather. Only a month after I had returned in late September, it turned cold enough to freeze the water at night, fully a month before cold weather normally began. Then, in mid-October, we had a deep snow.

The boys were overjoyed and discovered they could slide down the trail to the creek on a short plank of planed wood. I showed them how to wax the underside so the wet snow would not penetrate and slow them down or stop them altogether. There were many spills and much laughter, and no consideration whatever of the dangers of their game. Fortunately, they didn't hit a tree or fall into the stream. That snow, which seemed so much fun to the whole family, was followed a week later by another, and another. The previous snows had no time to melt before a new one came, adding to the total depth.

Now, we spent most of our time in the common room, before the big fireplace. I spent an hour each day with my daughter Catherine, holding her on my knee, rocking her, and allowing her to pull my hair. I carved a doll for her of soft pinewood, and Mélanie sewed a little dress for it. Catherine seemed delighted but did little more than wave the doll in the air or chew on it. She understood much of what we said and was beginning to crawl. It would not be long before she would stand up. I fondly believed she would be a genius and was perfect in every way, though I was sorry she had inherited my dark hair rather than Anne's glossy red curls.

After Catherine was in bed, and despite the noise and confusion of activity around me, I hunched over the makeshift desk by the fireplace and worked at my treatise refuting Monsieur Bèze's seventy-five theses, *Blemishes of the Church*. I was making progress, having reached his proposition number thirty-seven. When that became monotonous or when I came to the end of my inspiration, I turned again to Seneca or to these memoirs, finding solace in remembering the times that now seemed so distant.

Though we kept the fire burning brightly, we were always cold wearing several layers of clothing even inside the lodge. Our three bedrooms were left unheated until nightfall, when Mélanie and I built a fire in each of their small fireplaces. She heated a large stone shaped like a round loaf of bread and passed it between all the sheets before we turned in for the night. It made a great difference in our comfort as we fell asleep. However, in the dead of the night, we would wake up shivering, and I would go through the rooms and build up all the fires. The boys began to sleep together, and

Mélanie took Catherine into her bed—and even so we shivered.

By mid-December, I realized we had miscalculated. If we were to have any hope of getting through the winter without starving, we would need to replenish our supplies of dried peas, beans, lentils, and flour. We had stored turnips, onions, leeks, and quite a few cabbages in a root cellar off the kitchen. At the rate we were using them, our fresh vegetables would probably last through the winter. Deer were becoming harder to find, though when I did kill one, the venison was guaranteed to last much longer than during the summer, since the carcass froze at once after I had butchered it. We still depended on Anne's prowess in snaring rabbits. But bread is the staff of life, and we needed flour.

I decided to go down the mountain, before the snow became even deeper. Choosing to ride Mulot once again, I tacked him up and swung into the saddle. I led the other horse, Brun, that I had bought in Tours to help us move into the mountains. The ride down the mountain was treacherous and took three times as long as it should have. Twice, when we came to particularly steep spots, Mulot slipped on hidden ice and fell to his knees. On one of those falls, he came perilously close to sliding off a precipice at the outer edge of the trail. My heart did not stop racing for a half hour after Mulot and I had nearly gone over the cliff, though he took the close call very much in stride.

Once we reached the village at the foot of the trail, I dismounted and entered the tavern for a hot drink and a bit of bread and cheese. The tavern keeper was suffering from a terrible cold and was sneezing and coughing dreadfully. When he brought my food, he sneezed again, excusing himself. "Worst cold I've had in years, Monsieur. Caught it from a fellow who passed through here five days ago, I think. He was complaining of headaches and fever." I commiserated with him, but gave the matter little thought, hungry as I was. I simply ate my bread and cheese and drank my hot mulled wine.

Now that we were off the mountain, I rode on through snow that dwindled in depth to a mere six inches. The road beneath the snowy covering was frozen in deep ruts, and Mulot and Brun had trouble finding secure footing. These were more dangerous conditions for them than the deep snow on the mountain.

We arrived at Saint-Palais—the scene of my father's murder—and I went about my shopping after pausing to pray for him in the square in front of the church where he had been shot. The area was covered with new snow and trampled by many footprints crossing in every direction. Despite that, my mind's eye recreated the scene as it must have looked on that terrible day—the dust, my father shot through the temple, collapsing on his back with his white hair fanned around his face, his red blood, vivid contrast with the white, soaking the ground. I tore myself away, trying to escape the violence of those images.

By nightfall, I had bought two hundred pounds of goods, a hundred-pound bag of flour from the mill, the dried peas, lentils, and beans in smaller bags, the powder and shot for my pistol. I left all that with the merchant I had dealt with last, instructing him to keep it safe until the following morning, when I would return for it, load it on Brun and start for home. When I asked for the best inn in town, I was directed to Le Cerf Volant. My two horses and I arrived just as it was becoming full dark; I stabled the two animals and made sure they were well watered and hayed, with a little grain to give them extra energy for the next day.

The interior of the inn was low ceilinged, smoky, and dark, but warm and filled with the delicious odors of roasting pork. It had been over a month since I had tasted pork, and I hadn't eaten all day. Anything would have seemed delicious to me. After arranging for a room, I sat near the fire and enjoyed a hearty meal that included a thick slice of fresh roast ham with beans and leeks on the side, accompanied by a mug of dark ale. The room contained two beds, but in this season the innkeeper assured me I would have a whole bed to myself. "Best room in the house, Monsieur," he assured me. "Chimney goes right up through there—keeps it warm all night. Rest well, Monsieur." I thanked him and rented a blanket, which cost me extra.

Toward morning I awoke with a headache, but went back to sleep, waking after dawn. The headache was still there, pushing from inside my skull against my eyeballs and brow ridges. I felt slightly better once I was moving around and had eaten a bite of bread and cheese downstairs. I paid the innkeeper, tacked the horses, and rode back to the merchant, where I recovered my supplies. Then began the long trek home.

By the time I arrived at the lodge, it was well after dark, and it was only thanks to the reflected light off the snow that the two horses and I had not gotten lost or fallen off the trail. All three of us were exhausted from struggling up that steep incline, sometimes through deep snowdrifts. I had dismounted halfway up, distributed the load between the two horses, and led them. I arrived chilled to the bone despite the heavy work of scrambling up the trail, knowing that I would be unable to use my hands to unfasten the ropes and the buckles on the tack—they were that stiff with cold.

"Anne! Jacques!" I called, when I had come close enough to the lodge to make myself heard.

Anne came out on the veranda at once. "Jean! Thank Heaven you're back! We've had another snowfall since you left, and it's beastly cold. Let us help you." As she turned to call his name, Jacques burst out the door.

"Papa! Papa!" He skipped down the steps, heedless of the ice, hugged me fiercely, followed closely by Mélanie, who praised God for my safe return. Jacques took Mulot's lead rope from my hand.

"Jacques, Mélanie, can you undo the knots on these bundles? I'll carry the supplies into the house." I clamped my frozen hands under my armpits, attempting to warm them as I waited.

The two went to work at once, and Anne joined them. Soon, all the bundles were lying on the steps, and Jacques took the horses back to the barn to settle them in their stalls and feed them. "Be sure to see that they drink water, Jacques. If they eat without drinking, they'll colic."

"Take some warm water from the house," Anne told him, "and see if they'll drink that before you give them their hay."

We carried the sacks of food up the stairs, and I then stationed myself as close to the fire as I dared. "Take your time and get warm, Jean," she said, "We'll eat afterwards."

I removed boots and gloves and hung my wet socks on the grate. It took half an hour to warm my hands and feet, my fingers and toes shooting excruciating pains up my arms and legs as they thawed out. I considered it a miracle I'd not suffered frostbite. It would have happened if there had been another mile to go. Anne served me a steamy mug of soup from a stockpot simmering on the hob. It was an essence distilled from rabbit and venison bones, flavored with salt and herbs—rosemary and thyme—along with onions and carrots. It tasted like nectar to me, strengthened me at once, and sped up the warming process on the inside while the hot mug thawed my hands.

Dinner was equally delicious, with venison stew and abundant crusty bread to mop up the juices. Nonetheless, I was beginning to feel unwell.

"Jean, we're nearly out of meat; only one haunch and a shoulder left. Do you suppose you could hunt tomorrow? Take Jacques with you. I hate to send you out so soon after this trip, but we mustn't run out of food!"

"Yes, I'll hunt; there's no way out of that! And you're right. It would be a good idea to take Jacques. He should start learning how to stalk a deer and maybe how to butcher an animal, too. He's very young, but he's clever. Too serious for his age, though." He was just past five.

That night, in addition to a recurrence of that fierce headache, I acquired a sore throat. By morning, I was hoarse as well, but felt better after a hot drink and a bite of bread slathered with boar fat, rendered and slightly browned in the skillet.

After breakfast, Jacques and I rode the horses through the woods, and when we came within a quarter mile of my goal, I dismounted, lifted him off Brun's back, and we proceeded on foot. Jacques struggled manfully in my wake through the snow, but I occasionally lifted him over a fallen log or carried him briefly in my arms when the drifts became too deep. Except for our breathing, we made as little noise as possible, never speaking. I admired my son's self-discipline. When he needed to communicate, he pulled my sleeve rather than calling to me, even in a whisper.

My goal was a spot where I had bagged deer before, a glade sheltered from the wind by crags on three sides. We climbed the rocky wall slowly, one step at a time, pausing so as not to make any regular sound, arriving at last where we could peer over the lip of the bowl-like formation. There were three deer sheltering there, about twenty paces away.

As I aimed for the buck, the pistol's click warned the deer and they looked around, every nerve tense, ready to bolt. But seeing nothing alarming, they were confused. Before they decided to run, I fired, hit the buck, and sent up a brief prayer of thanks to God. The two does plunged away through the snow. The buck tried to follow, collapsing after three leaps. He was still thrashing his feet as we approached.

"Papa! Here's the knife!" Jacques handed me the sharp hunting knife that I had allowed him to carry, and I quickly slit the buck's throat, watching as his steaming lifeblood poured out, crimson in the stark whiteness of the new snow. I noted how calmly Jacques observed the killing and the bleeding. I only hoped I was not hardening him unduly, and he would not consider all life—including human—as expendable for some practical end.

After the buck had bled thoroughly, we dragged him back to the horses. I rigged a sort of sled, cutting low branches of nearby fir trees, binding him on them, and sliding the entire burden across the snow, holding the trunks of the branches to which the buck's hind feet had been tied. We struggled through groves of low growing pines and firs, receiving repeated loads of snow on our backs and down our necks as we brushed through the branches. We finally arrived, and I heaved the deer across Brun's back, while Jacques did his best to help.

About this time, two wild pigs, a boar and a sow, came crashing out of the woods. Food was scarce in this early and severe winter, and they were attracted by the smell of blood. Fortunately, I had the habit of loading my pistol immediately after using it and was ready for them. I aimed at the boar and fired. I hit him in the neck, just forward of his left shoulder, and dropped him.

Jacques reached toward the knife. "May I cut his throat this time, Papa?"

I felt a stab of doubt at Jacques' eagerness to participate in the slaughter. "Not this time. Maybe next year, Jacques, when you're a bit older. He's not dead yet, and he might still slash you with those tusks, son." I strode over to the boar and dispatched him quickly. God had been kind to us today—two meat animals within minutes of each other. We bled the boar and loaded it, too—a heavy animal weighing over a hundred pounds—and made for home, Jacques riding behind the buck while I led both horses. Once there, I hung both carcasses in the shed outside, and despite my increasing physical discomfort, I gutted, skinned, and butchered them, teaching Jacques where the cuts should be made, allowing him to do some of the work under my supervision. By the time all that was finished, not only were we both chilled to the bone, I was truly sick.

That was the start of a long illness that has not left me yet.

Chapter XVII

Bordeaux

I grew rapidly worse. After running a fever for a day or two, my temperature rose alarmingly, my body drenched in sweat and shuddering with chills in alternating states of misery. The sore throat continued, compounded by general body aches, a blocked head and running nose and eyes.

Then the cough began. A week passed. About the time the cough started, I thought the fever was gone and my condition improving, but before that week was out, I could feel my chest becoming increasingly congested. My coughing only irritated the situation. The fever returned, and I felt faint, unable to combat this all-out attack, unable to breathe normally.

One after another, the rest of my little family fell ill. The children came down with it first, Jacques, then Jehan, and finally Catherine, but they all recovered in little over a week. Mélanie, who had nursed all the children with great care, fell ill during the second week, and she, too, recovered in ten days with only a cough to remind her of her recent distress. She was up and around, able to nurse the remaining sick child, Catherine, and me. Then Anne caught the disease. She could not possibly escape; we all lived too close together for that. I only marveled that she had resisted it so long. Anne's cold, like Mélanie's, lasted ten days, and Mélanie recruited Jacques to help nurse his mother and father.

Finally, the entire epidemic blew over—except for my own case, which got steadily worse. In the third week, I began to cough up great clots of mucous along with traces of blood. Mélanie and Anne helped me get up and move to the fireplace, where they wrapped me in warm blankets and gave me steady doses of hot liquid—mulled wine, hot broth from the stockpot, and plain hot water. I was not able to eat much but tried to swallow some of the food offered me, if for no other reason than to please Anne.

We were well into January, and my condition seemed to stabilize itself. I was terribly weak and thin, but coughing much less, and the congestion in my lungs had subsided to some extent. I still had a leaden feeling in my lower left chest. I became exhausted merely dragging myself out of bed and into the next room to the fireplace. The exertion always brought on a fit of coughing, after which I left a blotch of red in my handkerchief. One evening Anne hurried to me, as I was resting in the chair, and sat down next to me in front of the fire. "Jean, we must talk seriously, my dear."

"Yes... I agree. I've been racking my brains. We probably have three more months of winter, maybe more. We can't hold out that long up here unless I get well enough to hunt again. We'll need more meat soon. I can't imagine how I'll manage that—I can barely stand."

Anne took my hand, looking anxiously into my face, anticipating a negative reaction. "I know, Jean. We must leave here and go to Bordeaux. You told me that Du Perron had said he had a good friend there who would help us."

I'd been thinking along the same lines, although I could see no way to accomplish a move. "Yes, that's right. His friend's name is Florimond de Raymond, if I remember correctly. But leaving here... It's easier said than done, Anne."

Her rejoinder was eager; it was clear she'd been planning this move, hoping I would agree. "If this January is typical—and there are some indications it might be—there'll be a week of warm weather, and the snow will melt and pack down—I hope to the point where we can get a loaded wagon through it. Mélanie and I will load the wagon, hitch up the horses, and we'll get down off this mountain, Jean. It's our only chance."

I laid my other hand over hers. "Yes, our only chance: for our sanity, our health, and maybe our very lives. I'll try to get better quickly so I can help as much as possible."

"Don't fret over that, Jean. You need to save your strength. It's been warmer lately, have you noticed? We haven't needed so much wood to keep the place warm in the last two days. Maybe our January thaw is already beginning!" Anne leaped to her feet as if she were going to start packing at once.

I smiled up at her. "Let us pray to God that is so!"

"Oh, Jean, I've been praying all along."

Our prayers must have been effective, for the weather did warm up; the snow did melt during the day and was soon a mere ten inches deep on the road in the sunny spots, though everything froze again at night. Anne and Mélanie sorted through our belongings, deciding what would be indispensable. On the fifth morning after our conversation, Anne and I decided that we should not wait any longer; the weather was bound to turn cold and snowy again soon. We would start out the next day.

The two women used the horses to draw the wagon beside the veranda, then spent the day packing our goods. We left most of our belongings and all our furniture behind, although Anne carefully packed all my books and papers.

"You came up here to have the peace and leisure to study and write. Under no circumstances can we leave the fruits of your studies behind!"

I thanked her and embraced her in gratitude. I knew she was

leaving some possessions that had great sentimental value for her. "My dear, we'll close up the lodge and lock our things away as securely as possible. One day soon—next summer, perhaps—we'll come back and recover our belongings." There was no choice. I counted on the small inheritance from my father to enable us to furnish a very modest apartment in Bordeaux. The boys were excited by the activity, but a bit apprehensive about moving to an unknown city. I reassured them by telling them that "we have friends there," an exaggeration I hoped would turn out to be true.

The next day, the women again hitched the horses to the wagon. Jacques held Catherine, Jehan and I sat on the bench behind Anne, who would drive the team. I thanked God I had married such a strong and capable wife. Mélanie sat in the back with her hands on the brake pole. I told her, "If we start rolling too fast, pull the brake, release it, then pull it again and again in short jerks. Otherwise, we might go into a skid and out of control." She rolled her eyes at me, not in impatience but in fear. "Did you bring the shovels?" I asked Anne.

"Yes, my love, for the drifts in the shady spots." She clucked to the horses and we embarked on our perilous descent.

We had difficulty, as we knew we would. We came upon curves that had been in perpetual shadow, where the snow was still four feet deep. My sturdy Anne and Mélanie cleared a narrow passage through, and we progressed to the next curve. On one of them, the wagon skidded into the snowbank and embedded itself so deeply that the horses couldn't pull it out. I got down to lend a hand, but after five minutes I was coughing so badly I had to stop. I spat mucous and blood into the snow. By nightfall, we had slithered and slogged our way down the mountain. We stopped at the little tavern where I'd first come in contact with the disease that was devouring me. I noticed the landlord was not there; his son was serving two tables where four clients were about halfway through a meal.

I asked him, "Where's your father?"

He bowed his head sadly. "He was carried off by pleurisy over a month ago, Monsieur. Took a bad cold and couldn't shake it."

"I could see he was very sick when I passed by here last time. I'm so sorry."

The young man looked up at me. "Thank you, Monsieur. You look as if you've been ill yourself."

"Yes. The same sickness, I believe." I paused. "Is there anywhere in the village where we can spend the night and find a stable for the horses?"

He looked at me as I stood there trembling, pale and sweating, looked at the two exhausted women, their skirts heavy and wet with melted snow, and at the three children. "You came down off the mountain today? From the lodge?"

I nodded.

"You must have had some frightening moments"

I nodded again, then raised my eyebrows. "A room? Stable?"

"I was coming to that. My papa's room is empty now—Mother's been gone these three years past—and you're welcome to use that room. It's upstairs and large. There are two beds. You can stable the horses out back with my own horse. There's plenty of hay and a trough of water. I'll break the ice."

Anne pressed a couple of sous into his hands. "If you could tend to the horses, too, please? Maybe pull the wagon around behind where it will be out of sight, and then feed and water the horses?"

He gave her a mock salute. "Right away, Madame!"

We sat around a table as close to the fireplace as we could get, listening to the rumble of the wagon as the young fellow moved it to the rear of the tavern. I had done almost nothing to help all day but was about to pass out from exhaustion. So were the two women, for they had worked like ten men to get us safely this far. Catherine was asleep in Mélanie's arms; Jehan had curled up on the hearth and was also asleep. Only my staunch little Jacques was still awake, and hungry. "Will we get something to eat now, Papa?"

I ruffled his hair. "As soon as the tavern keeper comes back, Jacques. We'll gladly eat whatever he can offer us."

The dinner, abundant though mediocre, seemed downright delicious thanks to our famished state. Jehan woke up and ate as heartily as the rest of us. The scullery maid guided us upstairs as soon as we'd finished, and we divided ourselves between the two beds. Anne took the baby into the bed with us, and Mélanie took the two boys. The room was comfortable, heated by warm air rising from the large common room below, and each bed had curtains to keep us from becoming chilled when the fires downstairs died out. We stripped off our outer clothing and tumbled into bed. Washing up could wait until morning.

In Saint-Palais, we traded our wagon for a lighter and more elegant carriage that still had enough room for our belongings. When we arrived in Bordeaux five days later, we were tired, dirty, and hungry, but at least we did not present as bedraggled an appearance as we would have in that farm wagon.

We drove to the mayor's offices at once, and I asked the secretary about housing. He gave me a list of possibilities. I also asked him to recommend a good doctor.

"Ah! Try Monsieur Bréhier. He's a first-rate physician."

He told me where to find him, and we set off. First, though, we settled at an inn where we could leave Mélanie with the children while I visited the doctor and afterwards hunted for a home.

We found the physician in his home on the rue Saint Rémi, near the Garonne. He felt my forehead, looked into my eyes, then tapped my chest while pressing his ear against my body. He shook his head. "I'll bleed you," he told me, "but I don't expect much improvement from it. You have a long-standing case of pleurisy, which is next to impossible to shake. About all you can do is come in for a bleeding once a month and take plenty of chamomile tea. Other than that, you wait it out.

He produced a glazed clay basin, a strip of clean linen, and a small razor-sharp knife. After binding my upper arm with the cloth strip, he had me make a fist and then nicked the vein that was standing out in the hollow of my elbow. He loosened the cloth band. "You've already lost a lot of weight, I'll wager," he said, pinching the loose skin on my flaccid arm. "You may lose more." All this time, my blood was running into the basin in a thin stream. "Keep pumping your fist," he directed me. He extracted what looked to be about half a quart of the dark maroon blood, then bound another strip around the elbow and flexed my arm so that my hand touched my shoulder. "Keep your arm in that position for a while. Don't do anything strenuous or you'll start the bleeding again. You've bled quite enough already."

I felt light-headed, not to mention nauseous at the sight and smell of my own blood. I handed my coin purse to Anne. "Would you mind settling with the doctor? I don't think I can see straight."

She obliged, and Monsieur Bréhier took me under the elbow of my punctured arm while Anne took the other, and they assisted me to a waiting area in the hall.

"Sit here for a few minutes until Monsieur is feeling stronger," Bréhier directed. "Then, you should be able to go about your business as usual. There's a small tavern on the corner. Perhaps Monsieur would be well advised to eat and drink something. Especially drink."

We followed his advice, and after stumbling down his stairs and to the tavern, I did eat a bite of grilled sardine and a glass of wine. My strength began to come back to me then, and we began our hunt for an apartment. At each new address, I let Anne explore first: then, if she thought the place had possibilities, I would have a look. I was not strong enough to climb so many stairs. After several fruitless visits, Anne settled for the fourth place we looked at, probably for fear of unduly fatiguing me. The apartment's small, high-ceilinged rooms would be slightly cramped, but it was centrally located at the center of the rue Sainte Catherine and the street the physician lived on, the rue Saint Rémi. It was on the second floor, not too many stairs to climb.

We couldn't move in for two weeks. Though I kept our expenses at a minimum, my inheritance was nearly exhausted by the time we had the rooms freshly painted and sparsely furnished. I prayed that the cost of living here in Bordeaux would prove modest, so we could live on my income from the two largely honorary offices I held in Béarn.

As soon as the mundane problems of lodging were solved, I sent a letter to Monsieur Florimond de Raymond, informing him that I had moved to his city and would be most pleased to meet him. I included greetings from Bishop Jacques Davy du Perron. His response was immediate. He sent a note in return, saying he would call the next day. He was as good as his word. He arrived mid-morning and we received him in our newly arranged salon.

I welcomed him at the door and brought him up to our apartment, introducing him to Anne and the boys. He was very gracious. A tall man with dark blond hair mingled with gray, he seemed about ten years my senior. His deep-set hazel eyes peered out beneath heavy eyebrows; his nose was long and straight, and his mouth, with a prominent lower lip, gave the impression of pouting. I knew he'd been a Counselor at *Parlement* for twenty-five years at least, having taken the succession of Michel de Montaigne.

I apologized for the sparsity of furniture and for the bare walls, explaining my straightened circumstances. I was as forthright as possible about the king's break with me but did not insist that my conversion had been sincere—I did not want to protest too much. I did mention that my former fellow Huguenots had aimed scathing denunciations at me for changing my faith.

Monsieur Raymond leaned back in the chair. "Ah, yes. If it had not been for a letter from Bishop du Perron, who gave you his most heartfelt praise, I would have wondered about you. Where did you say you've been for the past few months?"

"In the Pyrenees, Monsieur. I moved my family to a lodge that belonged to my father, to find the peace and isolation to work on a refutation of Théodore de Bèze's attack on the Church. But once I was up there, I discovered I needed books I'd never thought of consulting before I left Tours, and I missed daily conversations with erudite men like Du Perron or Antoine de Thou. But I indeed found isolation in my mountain retreat. Far too much." I made a wry face.

Raymond raised his eyebrows at me. "No trips to the coast?"

"No, two trips. One in July to Melun to place a book manuscript, and a second in August, when the news of my father's death reached me. I had to return to Mauléon in Béarn to settle the estate. What's this about the coast?"

"Ah..." Raymond hesitated and shuffled his feet, embarrassed. "A slander has passed around. Supposedly, because you wanted to prove to your new Catholic friends that you were truly on their side, you are rumored to have joined a conspiracy to turn Bayonne over to the Spanish Crown. You were also supposedly involved in a plot to arm several ships to mount an attack on La Rochelle."

"That's absurd!" I cried out, half rising from my chair. "Who started such an abominable rumor?"

"I'm told it comes from Agrippa d'Aubigné, one of the leading Huguenots, who enjoys telling a good story, especially if it's at someone else's expense or if it increases his own glory." Raymond was watching me closely—I was unsure whether with sympathy or suspicion.

"D'Aubigné! He's hated me for years. Ever since I got up in a council meeting and recommended a compromise with King Henri III—when he was desperate to find allies to help him prevent the League from taking away his power. D'Aubigné called me a traitor then. Now that I've converted and 'deserted the faithful,' he's doubly anxious to make me out a traitor." I took a breath to contain my ire. "Ah, well, it's his nature to vilify with animosity, and my nature to bear it with patience. He attacks me as a Huguenot, with insults, and I'll defend myself as a Catholic, with modesty." I paused, then, curious, I asked, "Have there been any actual conspiracies to turn Bayonne over to the Spanish?"

Raymond nodded. "I've heard that there were several. As I understand it, they were plots by extreme Leaguers who would rather see Spain rule our country than a legitimate French king."

I shook my head "I see. Of course, my Calvinist detractors would want to link me to the most extreme and destructive elements in the Church, the better to discredit me."

Raymond nodded again. "So it would seem!"

The conversation continued, on less disturbing topics. Florimond de Raymond was an accomplished humanist and was intensely interested in my past publications and present projects. After another hour, he rose to go. "I would be very pleased if you could come to my home next Thursday. I'll be having a few guests there, and I'd like to introduce you to them. Also, I'd like you to see my collections—books, paintings, sculptures—things that would interest you, I think."

I thanked him warmly and accepted without hesitation.

Thursday dawned warm and sunny, and Monsieur de Raymond sent a carriage to fetch me. I was delighted for two reasons: I might have had difficulty finding his place, and I certainly would not have had the strength to walk there in my condition. I still had great difficulty breathing, and the slightest exertion brought violent paroxysms of coughing that amounted almost to convulsions, after which I would spit quantities of bloody mucous, and would be left gasping and drained of energy for at least half an hour. I learned not to do anything that would require strenuous effort.

The carriage clattered through a coach door and into a spacious courtyard. A valet helped me alight from the coach and guided me into the entrance hall of the house. I paused there to admire the decor. Alternating tapestries and oil paintings hung along the hall, depicting mythical scenes, some inspired by Ovid's *Metamorphoses*, from the Italian school. Two scenes of the Flood by Antonio Pollaiuolo stood out along with a painting entitled "Hercules' Choice at the Crossroads" portraying the hero choosing the right-hand path, steep, rocky, and thorny, turning his shoulder to the broad, well-traveled left-hand road. Other canvasses showed three of the hero's labors—all by the same painter. The tapestries, depicting the myth of Acteon, looked to have been woven in Lyon.

My host soon joined me and led me into the salon, where I glanced around briefly at the elegant furnishings, the bronze statues of Apollo and Diana—also Italian of the previous century. I was introduced to Raymond's friends, Malvin de Cessac, a fellow member of *Parlement* and a historian, Pierre de Brach, a well-known poet here in Bordeaux, and Honoré Laugier de Porchères, a young man about twenty-five years old, who likewise aspired to be a poet. Also there, I was pleased to see, were two Jesuit Fathers: Gaston Bonnat and Martin du Verdon. They knew Father Auguste Bouchard.

Conversation became lively immediately, and I found myself at its center, recounting my happy escape from prison at Tours, thanks to Father Auguste. I did not hide the fact that he, along with Du Perron, had played a key role in my conversion. After sampling some of Monsieur Raymond's choice white wines and nibbling sweet cakes from a tray a valet passed among us, we were invited to tour the garden.

There, truly, was a delight for the Muses! Raymond had collected beautiful ancient Roman statues of Hadrian and Jupiter, marble plinths also of Roman manufacture, still legibly inscribed with mottos. We strolled and debated for a few minutes, but I excused myself soon after and found a bench under a grape arbor, trying to hide my gasps for air.

Honoré and Father du Verdon sat with me and continued the conversation while I coughed into my handkerchief, blushed, excused myself, and finally recovered enough breath to join the talk once more. They courteously ignored my state and, when they were sure I was restored, asked what I was working on. I explained I was engaged fully in writing a *Reply to the Treatise on the Blemishes of the Church* by Théodore de Bèze. Father du Verdon knew Bèze's work and considered it deplorable.

I nodded. "Quite deplorable, but too intelligent to be ignored. I'm ideally placed to refute it, having been a Calvinist myself. I know how Monsieur de Bèze thinks." I turned to Honoré, who looked puzzled and explained, "Bèze's work is laid out in theses on the Lutheran model, but only seventy-five of them—thank God. I don't think my stamina would last for a full ninety-five!"

"And how far have you gone in your refutation, Monsieur de Sponde?" the Jesuit asked me.

"I'm up to the fifty-third thesis. The most important one is his thesis on the Eucharist. That's seventy-two. I'm anxious to chop my way through the thicket of his heresies to get at that one."

Father du Verdon smiled at me. "May God grant you enough time to finish your work."

I smiled back, realizing he knew I was sick unto death. I silently resolved to do everything in my power to complete my book. Besides, I did not want to neglect my memoirs.

The afternoon ended pleasantly, and I was cordially invited to attend Raymond's gathering on the following Thursday. It appeared these meetings occurred regularly, designed to keep culture and intellectual life active in Bordeaux. Honoré Laugier de Porchères accompanied me home and helped me climb the stairs. I invited him in for a moment and introduced him to Anne. After a moment's general conversation, he asked me, with great timidity, "Monsieur de Sponde, may I bring some of my poetry for you to read? I'm badly in need of a guide, preferably a guide with a brilliant background in ancient classical literature—such as yourself."

I was flattered, realizing with a shock that he took me for an "elder statesman" of literature. "Of course, Monsieur de Porchères! I'd be delighted to read your poetry! Anne, what day would be best?" I turned back to Porchères. "You see, unlike the great majority of men of our day, I respect my wife enough to ask her what is convenient for her." I spread my hands and laughed, "After all, I'm totally dependent on her good will and good offices!"

De Porchères laughed with me. "Please call me Honoré, Monsieur de Sponde. You as well, Madame de Sponde."

"Then you must call us Jean and Anne," I replied, and Anne seconded my request.

"How about calling on Saturday morning around ten?" Anne suggested. "Mélanie, baby Catherine and I will be out shopping, the boys will be in school, and the two of you can have a quiet session together."

Honoré soon became a favorite of the whole family. He loved to play with the boys, teach them games, and often helped them with their lessons. They called him "Uncle Honoré."

That first Thursday, after Honoré had gone, I regaled Anne with the delights of the afternoon, including telling her about the two Jesuit Fathers.

"I want to meet them, Jean," she told me. "If they're as pleasant and learned as you make them out to be, then I'll take instruction with one of them." She was most emphatic, ending her sentence with a determined lift of her chin.

For some time, I'd been wondering about Anne's state of mind. While we were still in Tours, the attacks upon me had remained uppermost in our thoughts, and I'd not thought it fair to urge her to convert to a faith that would bring her under the same vicious barrage. We had often discussed Catholicism, but in relation to me, not to her. Of course, I knew that, by temperament, she was not deeply interested in otherworldly concerns.

While we were in the mountains, she seemed eager to discuss each of Bèze's theological arguments with me, greatly pleased when her suggestions were incorporated into my refutation. At the time, I attributed her interest to our isolation, with no other form of entertainment available. Ann, however, assured me that she had been vitally interested in the whole process and had learned more about theology in those few months than in her entire life up to that point.

At Anne's urging, I invited the two priests to a dinner where Mélanie and Anne both outdid themselves in culinary artistry and grace of presentation. After dinner, we four sat talking in the salon, and Father Bonnat began to question Anne.

"I understand you wish to take instruction with one of us?"

"Yes, Father Bonnat. My husband converted to your faith a year ago, and I've reached a stage—of maturity, I suppose you could say—where I understand enough to want to join him."

"And you are willing to stand together with your husband in the face of all the vilification and hardships your conversion will bring?" Bonnat's tone was skeptical, as if he didn't believe a woman capable of choosing the thornier path. I wondered if he were baiting Anne.

It did irritate her that he seemed to doubt her seriousness. She began, a bit sharply. "I've stood by him, sharing his hardships and his heartaches up to now. I'm asking for instruction not merely because I'm Jean's wife and love him, but because I believe he's right. In a way, I've been participating in his refutation of Théodore de Bèze—I've not merely read every word Jean has written but have in some sense *lived* every word. I understand enough Catholic theology by now that I think your task should not be too onerous."

Anne folded her arms across her chest as she finished her statement. I felt a surge of pride in my wife's forceful delivery of her convictions that made her feelings unmistakably clear.

Father Bonnat smiled at her vehemence. "Very well, Madame. We'll arrange some instructional sessions and see what gaps we still need to fill. You have courage, Madame de Sponde, and I congratulate you—and am delighted you've chosen to join our Church!"

Anne abjured her Calvinist faith and was confirmed a Catholic within a month, after ten sessions with Father Bonnat. "She's almost as good a theologian as I am." He smiled at the exaggerated appreciation of her knowledge. As I witnessed the ceremony and took Holy Eucharist with her at my side for the first time, I felt a great weight lift off my shoulders, heaved a sigh of relief and happiness, and sent up a heartfelt prayer of thanksgiving. I was no longer some sort of religious hermit in my own family; Anne was with me not just physically but in spirit as well.

Since her confirmation, I've spent most of my waking hours scribbling and making progress on this account of my life. It's mainly for family use, but also for Corisande and Du Perron—and I am making good headway on my refutation of Bèze.

The refutation makes no direct allusion to Théodore de Bèze, not personally. His work fairly represents the so-called 'reformed' theology, and I battle against that: I would never attack any man *ad hominem;* to do so would be to betray the true spirit of the Church on whose behalf I write.

Meanwhile, my life has not been restricted entirely to writing. I've come to love and trust the members of my new circle, and I think they feel the same way about me. My generous friend Florimond de Raymond has allowed me to use his library, which has been a great boon to me. I've found everything I need there: Saints Augustine, Bonaventure, Thomas Aquinas, all the classical authors, and much more besides.

Our group meets at the homes of the three older men—Cessac, Brach, and Florimond. Honoré Laugier de Porchères, unmarried, has no quarters suitable to receive us; my own place is too small, and our two Jesuit friends can't accommodate a group either. So, we four depend on the hospitality of the others. We never lack for subjects of conversation, often reading our latest treatises to each other.

But I am fast becoming weaker. Honoré now escorts me *down* the stairs to Florimond's carriage on Thursdays. I lay my arm across his shoulders, and he takes me around the waist. That way, even if my legs fail me, I will not fall. I have lost enough weight by now that he can almost carry me up to the apartment. But the slightest effort on my part brings on prolonged coughing. There is more blood in my handkerchief now. Reluctant as I am to admit it, I try to face reality; I have more work ahead of me than time.

My latest poem, an addition to my *Stanzas of Death,* meditates upon the vanity of life. It reflects my depressed state of mind, my fear that my best efforts will also be blown away by the stormy winds of this world:

Voulez-vous voir ce traite qui si roide s'eslance
Dedans l'air qu'il poursuit au partir de la main ?
Il monte, il monte, il pend : mais hélas ! tout soudain
Il retombe, il retombe, et perd sa violence.

Do you see that arrow that, so violent, hurls itself
Into the air it pursues on leaving the hand?
It climbs, it climbs, it stoops: but alas! All at once
It falls; it falls and loses its violence.

It is the course of our lives; that insolence
That these Terrestrial Monsters nurse at their breasts,
Which now kisses the proudest summits of the mountains,
That now bruises itself on the rocks of these valleys.

Truly, such is our lives. When you have climbed

To that point of altitude, to that final point
Which cannot be forced, you must descend.
  The arrow is feathered, the air it flies pursuing
Is the battlefield of the storm: Ah! Begin to learn
That life is mere Feathers and the world the Wind.

If I cannot finish my treatise, my *Reply* to Bèze, I will have worked for the past many months in vain; this life will fall into oblivion, scattered like feathers in the wind, leaving no trace. If only I had more time—though not my will, but God's be done. And now I must hasten, for I sense that night approaches; I will soon be leaving my earthly habitation. When I die, it will be as a brave Christian champion, honorably, my weapon—my pen—in my hands.

Chapter XVIII

Final Words

I am Jean's half-brother Henri. My brother's memoir stops here. He soon became too weak to write any more. Before I add my own coda to these writings, I will insert here my sister-in-law Anne's letter to me in which she tells me in detail about my dear brother's death:

Letter from Anne de Sponde to Henri de Sponde, March 22, 1595:
My Dear Henri:

We have never communicated before in writing—only *viva voce* and with great cordiality on those all-too-rare occasions when we saw each other in the flesh. I am sure you will hear about Jean's death from other sources—from Florimond de Raymond and perhaps from Father Bonnat. But I owe you more and can give you more than either of them possibly could. I know that Jean would urge me to tell you all I can, since you were always his favorite brother who understood him best. I owe it to myself, too, to write all this down to help me remember those painful and yet transcendent last moments. He died on the evening of March 18, 1595.

He became pathetically weak in the last few days before the end. In the morning, he would stay in bed where I would give him breakfast. I had to help him eat and drink, for he soon became exhausted only lifting a spoon or a fork to his mouth. After breakfast, he would doze for a while; then just before midday he would waken, and I would read to him, or simply talk to him, telling him about the morning's activities. Once the midday meal was over, Mélanie and I would lift and carry him from the bed to his favorite chair in front of the fireplace.

He dictated a few letters to me and tried to continue his work on the refutation of Bèze, though his attention would begin to wander, and he would fall asleep. In carrying him, we had to be careful not to jar him or move too suddenly or he would fall into a fit of coughing from which he would not recover for hours.

During those last days, he accepted his rapid decline with great patience, telling me, if I showed signs that I had been weeping, that it was God's will. We prayed together, too. I don't believe Jean ever prayed that he be cured, although I most humbly begged the Blessed Virgin to heal him, if such were possible. But I tried to imitate Jean's resignation to the Divine Will in accepting his imminent death as a cross I must bear.

I am thirty-four and still feel young. Jean was only thirty-eight, although his hair, gone white over the past few months, made him look much older. It is hard to accept death at such an age. You, Henri, are still younger than I am, and normally neither of us would give death a second thought, although it is now all too plain to me that it can pounce unexpectedly upon us at any moment from infancy through hoary old age.

The day came all too quickly when Jean could no longer sit in his chair by the fire, nor could he swallow solid food. His coughing was dreadful to see and hear, raw and racking, with horrible gasping for breath in between. And he was coughing up bright red blood—his lifeblood. The skin of his face became transparent and bluish pale after those violent spells, and he lay as if in a faint.

I dithered over the decision to call Father Bonnat for the Last Rites. You have no idea how it tears your heart to admit that your best beloved husband is on the point of death. An abyss of uncertainty and reluctance wars with the pull of desperation and urgency. I hesitated, at the same time fearing I had waited too long, and at last sent Mélanie running out to the Jesuits' residence. Meanwhile, I sat at Jean's side, bathing his forehead, for his fever was high.

His eyes fluttered open—such incomparable eyes, so intense. In the devastation of his wasted body they retained the clarity of their gray and black, the whites pure as snow. Perhaps angels have eyes like his. Our son Jacques' eyes are only a pale echo of his father's. He smiled at me very gently and took my hand; he had been aware of everything. He whispered, "I'll be going soon. I hope Father Bonnat is not delayed."

I squeezed his hand, unable to answer for a few moments. "Mélanie should be back right away. If not, I'll go after Father du Verdon." Jean merely nodded almost imperceptibly.

When Mélanie returned, she was accompanied by Florimond de Raymond and Honoré Laugier de Porchères. Both men, like the two Jesuit Fathers, had become close friends. Their warmth and sympathy finally broke down my Stoic mask; I began to sob and couldn't stop myself. It was Jean who signed that I should come near, and he took my hand once more.

He spoke in a near-whisper, "My darling wife, please do not grieve so bitterly. Death is only natural, you know. I only regret that I'll not be able to see my children grow up, and that I was unable to support all of you as I would have liked during these last months. It does worry me that I'm leaving you next to nothing to live on. I wrote Henri some weeks ago, asking him to continue my stipend after I'm gone. Surely, he'll do that much." Here he closed his eyes, gasping, exhausted from such a long speech, and I was about to signal to Father Bonnat that he begin the sacrament of Extreme Unction. But Jean collected himself with a visible effort and continued. He'd never let go of my hand.

"As for me, I count myself most fortunate. God is indeed gracious, who has lifted me out of my error, and is now drawing me to Himself. Blessed be He."

Jean turned his head slightly and looked at the priest, nodding to him that the time had come. As Father Bonnat prepared to begin the rite, Jean again closed his eyes. He was failing fast. The priest began to speak, but Jean shook his head. He tried to say something, but his voice had failed him, so he signed that Father Bonnat should speak louder. Then he showed, also by signs and a smile, that he was now content; he could hear the Latin words.

He kissed the cross, joined his hands on his breast, and gave a deep sigh. There were a few more struggling breaths, each one more labored than the last. And then, Henri, his entire body shuddered, his hands jerked spasmodically, and he finally relaxed. I never had seen a person die before. The most certain revelation of the existence of the soul comes the moment after death. Only seconds after Jean took his last breath, nothing was left upon that bed but *remains*—a waxen, haggard ruin that didn't even resemble my beloved husband.

Father Bonnat distracted and consoled me by taking my hands in his, kneeling and praying with me. I hardly remember what he said, but I hid my face against his chest, his gentle presence a healing power by itself.

Florimond saw to it that Jean had a proper funeral. He was buried yesterday in the Cathedral of Saint-André, in a beautiful ceremony attended by a large crowd of the people who had come to know and love him during his short stay in Bordeaux. Most of the foremost citizens of the city were present.

I have Jean's refutation of Bèze here in my possession and his memoir, as far as it goes. I know there were other books, and that they are at the printer's. As a mere woman, I am not allowed to meddle in the serious masculine domain of erudition, so I have not been able to get any information from the printer on the two occasions I visited him. Please, Henri, try to rescue Jean's books that are already in his possession. Heaven knows what will become of them if you cannot retrieve the manuscripts and see that they are properly published in his name.

Since Jean's death, we have lacked for nothing. Monsieur de Raymond is supporting us and taking care of our every want. His kindness cannot last forever, and so, my dear Henri, I beg you to come to Bordeaux to speak with him and see what our true financial situation is. He will know if the king has cut off our last means of support. If he has done so, you can surely help us make some sort of plans for the future.

Forgive me for ending my letter on such a crass note, but I know that Jean would want me to carry on, to hold our family together at all costs, to educate the children and bring them up in the Catholic faith as he would have done.

Your loving sister-in-law Anne.

Henri de Sponde resumes:

Fortunately for Anne and the children, the small stipend did continue, and Anne received a letter from the king expressing his sorrow over Jean's passing. In the letter—all too brief, I think—he assured her that if the stipend from Béarn proved inadequate, she should let him know, and he would supplement it. Anne was too proud and angry to do that, however, so I helped Jean's family as much as I could, given that I have never disposed of much wealth. Monsieur Florimond de Raymond has been wonderfully generous and saw to it that the boys received the best possible education.

When I went through my brother's papers, I found that, in his *Reply* to Bèze, he got as far as thesis seventy-two, the one he considered the most important, the one on the Eucharist. Tragically, he never completed his refutation of that crucial section. Florimond told me he had been working night and day, almost without a break, unheeding of his friends' pleas that he not overtax himself so. The pleurisy that had plagued him for months carried him off in the end; his lungs no longer had the capacity to sustain him, and as Anne told me, he was terribly weakened by coughing up great quantities of blood.

Ultimately, though, it was the book that killed him. His good friend Honoré Laugier de Porchères expresses it best:

O Book, which issues imperfect from such a perfect soul:
Born posthumously, and your creator,
Before he saw you done, saw his life undone.

Cruel issue of such a gentle father,
Parricide, murderer, viper's spawn,
Mutilated child, and how are you born?
You arrive by rupturing your father's side.

As Anne had already informed me, my brother left other unfinished manuscripts—including this memoir, to which I am at long last adding this postscript. Florimond de Raymond shepherded my brother's *Reply to the Treatise on the Blemishes of the Church* through to publication, incomplete as it was. Despite Anne's efforts, I was unable to find and preserve his other works in manuscript. He had left two or three things with the publisher Simon Millanges in Bordeaux, all of which disappeared. I suspect they were later published under someone else's name. His manuscript of translations of Seneca's plays also went missing. Fortunately, his most important writings, his poems and his religious works, have seen the light.

After Jean's death, the worst slander against him was published by Agrippa d'Aubigné, in which my brother was painted as an adulterer, Anne as an adulteress. D'Aubigné alleged that Florimond poisoned Jean because he was thinking of re-converting, and that he died miserable, hopeless, and inconsolable—in short, damned. Florimond vigorously defended his friend, although I think permanent damage has been done to my brother's reputation by the mere publication of such libel. Posterity will forever believe "where there's smoke there's fire."

Nevertheless, those who knew him admire him still for the depth of his humanistic learning, his alchemical knowledge, his status as former jurist in King Henri IV's service, his theological penetration, his eloquence, his mind's acuity. He was also excessively modest, for most of his acquaintances—except his truly intimate friends like Florimond and Honoré Laugier de Porchères—know nothing of his poetry, one of the brightest jewels in his crown.

As for me, Jean's influence upon me was profound. I studied his *Reply* to Bèze; I meditated upon the conversations we'd had, and I converted to Catholicism on October 11, 1595, seven months after my brother's death, when I was twenty-seven. Du Perron (at that time an Archbishop and later elevated to Cardinal) sponsored and advised me—for love of my brother, I know. I took holy orders, first becoming a canon in the Saint-André Cathedral in Bordeaux, in due course becoming Bishop of Pamiers, in 1626. Following the examples set for me by my sponsor and my brother, I fought vigorously against the spread of Calvinism until I merited the title so scornfully given to Du Perron—I, too, became a "Great Converter."

As the duties in my diocese became ever more onerous, I began looking for an aide. Jean's son Jehan had taken holy orders some time before, and I took him as my auxiliary. He became Bishop of Mégare *in partibus,* and Abbot of the Abbey of Corbigny, a post that I resigned in his favor.

As for King Henri IV, his path was thorny; nonetheless, his star was rising ever higher. He barraged Rome with letters trying to persuade His Holiness, Clement VIII, to lift the excommunication of 1585. Nothing seemed to move the pope until our friend Du Perron and another ambassador, Arnaud d'Ossat, went to Rome in July 1595 to negotiate.

By September, an agreement had been reached. The pope consented to absolve Henri if he would recognize the insufficiency of the Saint-Denis abjuration, publish the decrees of the Council of Trent in France, re-establish the Catholic Church in all of France including Béarn, and appoint only Catholic officials to high office. A magnificent ceremony was celebrated in Saint Peter's, and Henri was legitimized in such a way that even the most rabid Leaguer could not object.

I often have wondered if Henri ever regretted the injustice he did my brother. The letter sent to Anne was too stiff and too brief to amount to a real apology. Nevertheless, I suspect that my own appointment to high office as well as Jehan's might have had a good deal to do with the king's influence, a quiet way of saying to his old friend, "I'm sorry."

Now he, too, is dead these fifteen years. Henri was assassinated in May of 1610 by a so-called madman named Ravaillac. Personally, I believe a conspiracy killed him, funded by agents from Spain. The ghost of Philip II, ineffectually raging for a dozen years against that "insignificant provincial monarch" who had foiled his ambitions to dominate Europe, took its revenge at last.

About the Author

Florence Byham Weinberg, born in Alamogordo, NM, lived on a ranch as well as a farm and traveled with her military family. After earning a PhD, she taught for 36 years in three universities. She published four scholarly books. Since retiring, she has written nine historical novels and one philosophical fantasy/thriller. She lives in San Antonio, loves cats, dogs, horses, and conversations with great-souled friends.

www.ingramcontent.com/pod-product-compliance
Lightning Source LLC
Chambersburg PA
CBHW051309300726
48976CB00002B/329